TO THE VICTOR
GO THE SPOILS

Wolf-Twin snapped his fingers impatiently at the young telepath. 'Tell me.'

'The wagons, sir. I don't think we should send them away yet. Lan Haarper has casualties and he's taken prisoners.'

How many wounded men did Haarper have? Wolf-Twin wondered.

'About half his regiment,' the Teep said before the question was asked. 'And there's thousands of prisoners.'

'Thousands,' Wolf-Twin said hollowly.

'Yes sir. A lot more than this Brigade.'

'It's a complete disaster!'

Death's Grey Land

Mike Shupp

Book Four of
The Destiny Makers

First published in Great Britain in 1991
by HEADLINE BOOK PUBLISHING PLC

A HEADLINE FEATURE paperback

10 9 8 7 6 5 4 3 2 1

This edition published by arrangement with
Ballantine Books,
a Division of Random House, Inc.

ISBN 0 7472 3584 8

Printed and bound in Great Britain by
Collins Manufacturing, Glasgow

HEADLINE BOOK PUBLISHING PLC
Headline House
79 Great Titchfield Street
London W1P 7FN

For

Mark and Lisa Bondourant
Thanks for the MREs, Mark—
I ate them.

The First Compact

To end eternal war, it is agreed by the telepaths and normal men that never again shall telepaths establish a separate state and exercise their dominion over men.

This Compact shall be preserved by the thoughts and actions of both human races and witnessed by the tiMantha lu Duois.

The penalty for violation, in thought or action, shall be death.

—circa Anno Domini 30,000

The Second Compact

To end the Second Eternal War, the Great Compact is reaffirmed by the Teeps and the Normals. It is also agreed by the Teeps and the Normals that never again shall Teeps employ their abilities in their service of national states and thus exercise their dominion over men.

This Compact shall be preserved by the thoughts and actions of both human races and witnessed by the spirit of the tiMantha lu Duois.

The penalty for violation, in thought or action, shall be death.

—41,000 to 43,000 on the Long Count
(chronologies vary)

Hemmendur's Solution

"We have observed that neither Compact prohibits the employment of the Teeps, in whole or in part, in any role whatsoever, by a single all-encompassing world state. I suggest to you that such a state must ultimately arise. By its nature, it will be everlasting and unopposable.

"I suggest as well that given that inevitability, we attempt ourselves to give birth to that state and shape its growth. If our intentions are worthy, our actions honorable, and our ambitions steadfast, we shall be successful, for we shall gain strong allies.

"Not the least of these will be the Teeps, who are entitled to a role in human affairs, and for whom I propose a most sacred responsibility—which is to ensure that men exercise no dominion over men . . ."

—Jablin Cherrid Hemmendur
47,350 L.C.–47,727 L.C.
(Algheran City Years 313–690)

Prologue

*S*he was falling through mist, toppling sightless, leaf-blown by unfelt winds, pendulum swinging, swirling around . . . down.

Then she was upon the ground, erect, unmoving, weightless. When she raised an arm, her body followed till she was perched on the toes of one foot, suspended until she willed that her arm descend. She could hear no sounds, not even the heart within her chest or the gasping breaths she experimented with. Her nose detected no scents, but the cool mist left the feel of water upon her face and hands.

The gray thinned about her and she could distinguish outlined shapes—fingers and a thin wrist when she raised a hand, knees and a bare foot when she knelt. The lighting was diffuse, only a shadow beneath her suggesting it came from above. As it improved, she saw freckles on her limbs.

Gravity returned with her vision, as if the mist had obstructed both.

Clothing. She wore trousers of stiff blue material and a white blouse. Unfamiliar short brown boots were on her feet, and her

1

head was bare. Her long black hair swung free. A wide belt
with many pouches rested above her hips.

She was weaponless.

She had a name. Kylene. Waterfall Kylene r'Sihuc.

No! Kylene Waterfall chi'Edgart.

She was—She did not remember what she was. It was unimportant.

She was the original Kylene. The real Kylene. Something
inside her insisted on that.

Telepath. Time traveler.

The words flowed through her mind without significance,
echoed by distant memories which faded as they failed to carry
her to this moment. Kylene looked about, then stepped forward, curious, not yet apprehensive.

The mists moved with her, it seemed, so she was unable to see
farther than a few man-heights. Eventually she accepted that.

She was on flooring, a yielding substance unlike raw land or
wood or heat-tamped pavement. A pattern showed as she progressed: great squares, alternately black and a gray which might
be white in true light, with edges the length of a dozen men.
Some squares held tall pillars of colored stone, carved into
symmetrical cones and hemispheres at their tops. The pillars
were cool, mist-dampened, too heavy to be moved. There was
never more than one pillar to a square, and Kylene saw none
appear or disappear, though suspicion made her linger.

A desire for movement grew within her at last, and she
continued along a row of pillars, without expectation, without
haste. One tall pillar had fallen, crushing a man's body. A
medium-tall man, dark-haired and heavyset, with nondescript
features, wearing a uniform. She noticed the details and recognized them without interest. She did not stop.

The mists lifted above her head and she was on plowed
ground, with humus-laden black soil underfoot. The furrows
were knee-deep and rock-hard, the unglazed earth damp to the
touch but unyielding.

She was a visitor, she realized. She could see but change
nothing.

What use was this?

"What use is this?" Her voice vanished without echo into the mists. Twice. A third time. Then she was falling through gray mists, toppling sightless, leaf-blown . . .

Without warning, she was in a city. The buildings were of squared blocks, cliff-tall, without windows or doors that she could see. Metaled cylinders rested before them or hung silently in the air.

Motion came abruptly to this scene. The gleaming cylinders skimmed over purple-tinted avenues; gnatlike objects in the sky swelled to droning cruciform behemoths far above, which then dwindled in the distance behind her. A humming filled the air, barely noticeable at first, but insistent once she had heard it. She saw no people, but small bridges for pedestrians rose over the ceaseless traffic and allowed her to walk through the metropolis.

None of it was familiar but she accepted it uncritically.

A city of Tayem's world, she told herself. A world far in the past.

She was looking for Tayem. She remembered that much of her purpose. Tayem. She remembered the name alone.

Night did not fall.

The city buildings became small at length, shorter and narrower, with more space between them. Hedges appeared along the roadsides, to shield low-lying houses from her view.

Countryside, she thought. And again, What use is this?

Ground collapsed beneath her, then formed anew before she could react. She was again upon soft dirt, and night covered the one Earth.

Faces passed before her, their ages and sexes indistinct, sightless despite their staring eyes, without thoughts visible behind their scarred foreheads. They receded. She saw an endless line of gray forms, stepping silently in prisoner ranks, stretching beyond the horizon. Then they were gone.

She heard waters lapping in the middle distance; then the sound died. A bird chirped behind her, but could not be seen.

A wordless rhythmical whispering began, the sound swelling as she moved toward it till it became a steady, pounding, head-filling *boom-boom-boom.*

A machine took form before her, ebony and silver, twice the height of a man. A log-thick lever, supported by pistons at both ends, seesawed to mark time for the beat, but she could not explain how the sound was produced. When she was very close, she heard squeaking from the mechanism, as if it had been running without attendance for long years.

She passed it by and did not look back.

Beyond was a barren flower bed and then a house-size block of concrete, seemingly dropped from a great height to fall into the earth at an angle. A squat cylinder of dark material jutted from one wall, and a tube protruded from a slot in the cylinder. Burnished metal, hand-wide, it pointed downward to the ground. She did not walk beneath it but approached closely enough to see it was blunt-ended. A sensation of great age clung to the structure, and fragmentary views of titanic battles rose to the surface of her thoughts. She sensed threats.

Imagination, perhaps. The visions faded as she withdrew, but she did not test her skepticism by approaching the next ruins she encountered, nor those that followed. She turned at right angles to the line they made and crossed a gravel roadbed into waist-high grass.

A night breeze came upon her, wafting the aroma of clover into her face. Insects chittered here and there, and once she trod through a clearing where cattle stood. The great concrete blocks were no longer visible, but a full moon had risen to mark their position. Stars sprinkled the sky; she recognized no constellations.

Imperceptibly, the Earth turned, bringing the lesser darkness that presaged dawn. Gray silhouettes solidified into stunted trees and weather-beaten farm buildings. Kylene passed through a bare courtyard, ignoring the ramshackle cottage with its open door, but continued down a small earthen path to a stone-walled barn.

She found no doorway, but the southern side of the building

was open. A man was visible, sitting on a roll of brown hay. Stocky, gray-haired, bull-necked, he held in the crook of his arm a tiny, white, curly-haired animal of a kind Kylene had never seen before, with pink skin below its fur. His hand was in its mouth, as if the man were inspecting the animal's teeth, but periodically he dipped his fingers in a bowl of white liquid. A woman waited behind him, dressed in homespun cloth, with the lines of age upon her face and touches of gray in her hair. Her face was placid.

Kylene watched from the entrance, waiting to be noticed. At last the man rose from his stool, to place the tiny animal in the woman's arms. She smiled gravely, but Kylene saw amusement in her eyes. Without cause she remembered the matron for an instant as a young woman.

The woman petted the animal, then placed it in a wooden pen in one corner. It bleated plaintively as she moved toward her husband.

"Kylene Waterfall," the man said evenly. "So your journey has brought you this far. We bid you welcome." This close, Kylene could see the scar of an old brand in the center of his forehead. The woman had the same mark.

A burr shaded the man's voice; Kylene knew the language she heard was not her native tongue. "Have a seat, little lamb-child." He waved a work-callused hand, and she noticed another hay roll.

The floor was dusty and echoed under her feet. Golden motes danced in slanted bars of sunlight. The hay yielded to her body softly, but strands pricked her hands as she touched it.

The man stared at her as she waited.

"Looking for help, I suppose. You'd think now and then somebody'd drop by our farm just to pay us a visit—but no-oo. Well. Do you remember your purpose now?"

She did, suddenly, and flushed with chagrin. "I want Tayem."

Put so nakedly, it seemed a childish request. Her own voice betrayed her—petulant and shrill. She made fists of her hands and stared at her lap.

"You want Tayem," he repeated. "How original you are, child. Now, I suppose, you're going to tell me it's a very complicated matter."

"It is," she agreed, still staring downward.

Then she was angry. "You know it is! You're supposed to know!"

He snorted. "I'm a broken-down old sword swinger, and that's about all, child. It's never been me that claimed to know everything. You think I'd be here if I were that smart?"

"Cimer," the woman chided. "Don't make fun."

He turned. "Well, Nicki, you know how it is. This girl comes here looking for—whatever it is—and I can give her advice. But will she take it? You know the answer. If she already agrees with it, she'll take my advice, and if she doesn't, she won't. It's a charade; you know it and I know it and Kylene here knows it. So why don't we drop it?"

"This is a charade, too," Kylene snapped, sweeping her arm about. "This old-farm-couple nonsense. If you're sick of charades, why did you do this? Never mind, you don't want to help and I'm going!"

"Stay seated, dear," the woman said calmly, and Kylene found, to her surprise, that she had not stood as she thought she had. She was no closer to the barn door.

In fact, despite herself, she was no longer angry.

"We-ee-ell." The man looked at her once more and rubbed a finger behind his left ear. "We have our reasons. I guess there's some point to charades. Sometimes.

"So. You were going to tell me there are two of you? Two Kylenes, both in love with the same man. So you're rivals with each other."

"Yes," she said and swallowed. "It is complicated. You know how . . . when I—when I killed Kalm . . . the man I—killed—it changed things. So then there were two of me. And—and—and—so we're rivals, but she doesn't know about me. And he doesn't, and—" She swallowed again. "I wish I had killed her, too!"

"That would be wrong," the man said flatly, and she shook her head sickly in agreement.

"I know, but I keep thinking it anyhow. I didn't realize it would be this hard. This complicated, rather."

"Yes, you did," the man told her. "You went off and created your rival, knowing what you were doing, intending to leave your Tim Harper to her—you were full of self-sacrifice then and proud of your motives and you knew what you did was honorable. Also, you were pretty sure he wouldn't have anything to do with you when he found you were no longer a virgin, weren't you?"

She flushed guiltily.

"Maybe you're right, maybe you're wrong," he went on. "I don't know the man. I see what you think, but you didn't put it to the test, did you?"

"No."

"Well. There wasn't anything wrong with your motives, other than that."

"Thank you," she said softly.

"But then you changed your mind! You got to thinking, didn't you? And you decided you had this all-powerful machine for traveling in time, and maybe you could just change one or two more things, and you'd get your man after all! But you haven't decided what the one or two things are, so you came and dumped your problem on me! Why did you do that?"

She tried to smile. "Women get to be fickle. Tayem says so."

"But you didn't go to Tim. You came to me, and I have to tell you, child, I can't solve your problem. And even if I could, it wouldn't solve your real problem." He held a hand up to stop her protest. "Two women in love with one man? Happens all the time. And what happens is that one of them gets him and one doesn't, and they learn to live with it, and often enough the loser decides she is the luckier one. Or they figure out how to share him—I see you never thought of that. You blasted stubborn selfish Teeps! But that wouldn't work, because *your man doesn't want either of you!*"

His voice dropped to normal volume. "If you can't find a fix for that, don't you see that the other problem is just make-believe?"

"No," she said. Tayem would love her, she knew. Just as soon as some complications, like his hopes for Onnul Nyjuc, his lost love, were removed.

In the background, the woman sighed.

"So look at your situation, Kylene," the man urged. "You've got this powerful machine—you both do—and you want to accomplish something with your life. And that's where you'd be if you had your man in your pocket. So find something to do, something good. Glory be, child! Most people find one life too short to do what they want in it, and you have two, and both of you are still young!

"Do different things. I see you've half thought to outdo your rival by being more like her than she is, and that can't work, you can't expect your man to make his choice by flipping a coin over you. Do what seems proper to you and don't mind if it makes you different from the other Kylene. Being the way she is hasn't won him; she can't see it yet, but you can. You don't have to keep your buggy in her ruts."

She thought about that, not seeing a flaw in the argument, but not convinced that being a *different* Kylene was superior to being the *original* Kylene, and not sure it was possible to be a different Kylene.

"And you might talk to your Tim," the man suggested. "He knows more about this time-travel business than you do, so he knows more than I. He might have something surprising to say. Or you might talk to your—hmm—little sister. I expect that if she understood, she would want to solve your problem, too."

She mumbled something. Those ideas were new to her.

"So. I told you, little lamb, I'm just an old soldier, and I and Nicki don't know all the answers, and can't solve your problems, but you've got a cudful of things to chew on for a while, and maybe you can find your own solutions. And if you want to come back, you're always welcome."

That was dismissal. She stood slowly.

"Will you go with our blessing?"

"I will." Kylene knelt, accepting the touch of work-gnarled hands upon her head. "Thank you, Lord Cimon and Lady Nicole."

Kylene awoke. She was upon her back, fully clothed, on a thin pallet resting on solid rock. A face hovered above, indistinct, oval.

"Lord," she whispered. Then awareness flowed back to her, memories of the true world—of Tim Harper, Alghera, Chelmmys, the Final War, the Project, and other realities—which disrupted the vivid dream images.

Dismay followed. She was still trapped in her personal quagmire. Cimon's final words had given her hope, but awake, she saw he had pointed her to no escape path. She shook with disappointment, her eyes closed, wishing she could embrace the hard pad beneath her and vanish from existence.

At the same time, she could not avoid noticing that her skin was clammy. Pent-up human odors filled her nose, and smoke from burning torches stung her eyes. She wanted very much to take a long, hot bath.

"A true sending!" The face's lips moved in time with the words. "You have met Lord Cimon and our Lady!" Below the head was a black tunic, with golden collar emblems of spindle and sword—a priest. He brought with him the giddying odor of theomantic elixirs.

She had no desire to speak, no ability. She shook her head feverishly, then thrust herself up from her pallet despite the resulting dizziness. On her feet, she looked about her, noticing other persons sleeping on the sanctuary floor.

She was in Fohima Alghera, at the heart of the Temple. A rhythmical droning was faintly audible. *Lord Cimon, guard us.*

Lady Nicole, guide us. Even through rock walls, the chant could be understood.

It was not her faith, but this world knew no other, and the priest's mind showed her what reactions were typical. Slack-jawed, Kylene pretended to lose the present, listening as if to familiar words, acting as if preoccupied by memories or contemplation. It was surprisingly easy.

A misstep shook the grown woman back into being. Re-awakened from the drug-induced stupor, she yawned, managing with effort to keep her eyes open.

An altar niche gaped before her in the gloom, the suggestion of faces carved from native granite and given life by shifting beams of colored light. Flame licked the edges of the brazier beneath. A thread of smoke corkscrewed upward to an unseen vent. Before she left, Kylene knelt, bathing her face in the vapor, inhaling as she was expected to do. Then, weaving as she stood, she dropped a pinch of incense onto the coals and went to the altar for a silent prayer. Perhaps the stern gaze of a sharp-chinned warrior watched her from the alcove, perhaps granite lips opened to speak. Kylene stared back, blurrily concentrating, resentful and seeing no resemblance to her vision.

"Your dream—" A hand clutched at her elbow. Kylene pivoted to shake the grasp, then brought her eyes back to the sculptures. But the God Manifest of Algheran theology was no longer there.

"A private matter," she said huskily. "It would mean nothing to you."

"Do you not wish an interpretation? It would be best not to . . . to be hasty. Especially now." Concern showed in the small man's eyes. Concern, and bone-weary exhaustion.

But no fear—no deep-down paralyzing fear, despite every excuse. His religion had given him more than it had her, she realized bitterly.

But she had experienced the vision denied him, and he faced great peril. For an instant, she hesitated. Then she pulled herself back from confession.

"It was just a dream. I'm sorry. It was a mistake. I didn't

see Cimon. I was hunting a man. I didn't learn anything. I have to go.''

She could give him only pity. It was not her world, not her war, and her reason for being there was her own business.

Cimon had chosen to give her no message for the priest. The certainty penetrated her light-headedness as thoroughly as a fall into cold water.

Kylene turned abruptly before she could be questioned further and took one of the white smocks from a hook on the back wall. After pulling it over her head, she left the chamber for the exit passages. Neither she nor the priest said another word.

Dream or truth? she asked herself while crawling through the darkness. Exertion and time had dispelled much of the effect of the drugs by then. A dream, certainly. Sober now, she could remember that people saw what they wished to see, and that time disproved most visions. She did not believe in Cimon and Nicole. The Algheran gods could give her nothing.

''Platitudes,'' she grumbled as she pulled herself by her elbows around a sharp turn. ''Ideas already in my mind. This foolish thing. Embarrassing, and just because . . .''

You had more confidence when you entered, a matter-of-fact man's voice said in her head. *Is it so hard to accept the reality of grace?*

''Yes,'' Kylene admitted. She sucked in her belly to slither over a concrete hump, then dragged her legs across. Would this passage never end? ''I know you don't exist. I was looking for help. I was willing to try anything, so I did what the stupid Algherans do. Like a child.''

Does it matter? the voice asked pleasantly.

Kylene coughed on dust. ''I am not a child now.''

We are all children. The burr was very plain.

Kylene rubbed her forehead with a grimy arm. ''Life was easier when I was a child. There were no evils then, no mixed motives, no complications, no people at cross-purposes. Was that grace or ignorance?''

*No, Kylene. Life seemed easier because you have forgotten
much of it. But it isn't children who need grace.*

"And adults can't accept it, Lord Cimon or whatever you
are. We have to fight. If any of us deserve your blessing, give
it when this war is over."

You need it now, the woman's voice told her. The tone was
ambiguous, forcing multiple interpretations at her, and she
sensed the man chuckling as she came to that understanding.
Then the voices lapsed into silence, and Kylene said nothing to
bring them back.

The passage was straight for several body lengths, giving
Kylene opportunity for thought even as she crawled more rapidly. The brand on Cimon's forehead in her dream . . . a
Cimon who was still a man and not God . . . the man had
known her name before Kylene spoke. Like—

No! Impossible. For Cimon and Nicole to be—

No! That was fantasy! In the history recorded by the Plates—
the parts that were not obvious myths—Cimon and Nicole had
sparked the wars against the telepathic rulers of the Second
Era. They were enemies of the Teeps. Their example had
guided normal men to victory. To imagine otherwise was—

A dream. So she knew her vision had been a dream.

Perhaps she heard a snort. Perhaps someone continued to
watch her through the skies and the Temple walls. But after
that, the silent voice was gone. Kylene stopped moving, hearing nothing now but the beating of her own heart. Her vision
did not matter, she told herself. Whether Cimon and Nicole
had truly lived and now ruled the heavens and men was not
important.

She pulled herself through darkness, toward the faint glow
that might simply be strain on her eyes or the end of the exit
passage.

Again toward a goal.

Fohima Alghera was still garbed in night when she emerged.
Most of the city was dark, but a double row of torches lit the
path leading up the hill and the entrance to the great cube-

shaped Temple. A beggar crouched at the side of the exit hole; a chain ran from his ankle shackles to a nearby post, to keep him from intruding on entering worshipers. Kylene pressed metal coins into the slack fingers, trying not to see the empty eyes, then surrendered her Pilgrim's smock to the woman at the head of the admittance line.

The line was huge. All the thousand people of Midpassage could have been added to it and it would seem no longer.

And there were longer lines, moving no more quickly, in the outskirts of the city, where people crowded into elevators descending through airlocks into huge underground bunkers, populating a city beneath the city.

F'a Alghera held fifty thousand permanent residents, she had been told, and countless visitors from settlements or other nations. No greater concentration of people was recorded anywhere in history. Could people who lived in such confinement or the greater compress of the shelters still be human?

Sick-stomached despite her resolve, she stumbled down the wide staircase, an anonymous figure, without speaking to anyone in the long line. Other people were faceless as she in the darkness; she met none of their eyes and felt no need to accept responsibility for them.

Not that she could have offered reassurance to them any more than to the worried hermeneuts within the Temple. She could have said no more than "Leave the city" or "Get to the shelters," and the sky-spanning images of the Warder had already said that.

Leave the city. As she turned, Kylene patted her belt with seeming nervousness, comforted by the tingling in the thick buckle as she faced toward her concealed time machine. The vehicle had not been disturbed.

Leave the city—she could do that with clear conscience.

She had seen enough of it—the city Tim Harper chose to serve—and wished to see no more.

And soon it would be gone. She was very near the Present. The inexplicable matter-shredding weapons of this world had already been tested in desolate lands. They would soon fall in

anger, leaving the hammer scars of gods upon the Earth to
mark where the cities of men had once stood.

At that moment, light blossomed from one quarter of the
horizon, a roseate glow which withered even as her eyes focused on it. Kylene waited, fingers on her belt, but no sound
was borne to her. A flare, she guessed, relaxing. A signal of
some sort from the dockyards where the troops assembled for
evacuation. Nothing had happened yet.

The deadline of the Alliance's ultimatum was sunrise.

The war that would destroy Fohima Alghera would begin
then.

The true Present, she reflected sourly. The very end of time,
in a world that had escaped the war which had yoked the
Algheran Realm into the harness of Chelmmysian empire. The
long peace here had been very close to the goal of the Algheran
time travelers.

And so very different.

So evil. Could worlds be said to have souls? Was this one
about to be punished for the evils it had permitted? For following the path other Algherans had set it upon? If it deserved
punishment, what would be their ultimate fate?

Another flare brightened the sky. Pavement was under her
feet as the afterimage faded, not the pebbled concrete of the
Temple steps but the sandstone texture of earth made to boil
before glazing. On her left the millipede line of humanity
shuffled along the front of the Temple. A child's voice made
complaint at intervals, rising above the susurration of footsteps, but Kylene was struck by the patience and restraint of
most worshipers. People were more resilient in this world than
in the one she had known, she admitted. Tayem had commented on that.

She shook her head and turned away, taking a dirt path to her
right. Crickets contested her passage, then retreated to dispu-
tatious assemblies as she continued down the hillside. Rain had
fallen recently; the ground was slippery and flamepod bushes
had pepper-scented the air.

Tayem had made her study maps of the city, so she knew

that at the foot of the hill was the avenue that in the true world bordered the Institute for the Study of Land Reclamation Issues. Here the Institute ground was parkland, almost an extension of the landscaping of the Temple Mount. There had been plenty of space to land the great time machine.

The street was without traffic, and as Kylene approached she had the sidewalks to herself. The streetlights here had not been ignited, and stars could be seen through tree branches.

The Crown, the Boat, the Running Man . . . Kylene picked out the constellations children had known in her world—did any bear the same names here?—but could go no further, then felt chagrin because she was unable to tell time from the position of the heavens. It was a countryman's skill; her life had revolved around villages which she had thought metropolises; she had deliberately ignored such forms of peasant lore.

She was free of snobbery now, she knew. Someday she would master the skill. But at this moment, she must settle for knowing the night was young.

Time to leave. Kylene exhaled softly and crossed the street.

This period of history was called the Fifth Era, Kylene knew. She had grown to adolescence in what she had been told was the interregnum between the First and Second Eras. Ninety thousand years had passed between her birth and this moment.

All knowledge of the First Era was lost, unless one counted the stories told by Tim Harper—the adopted Algheran who claimed to come from that time. He claimed that billions of short-lived men and women had lived then in huge continent-spanning nations. But he had also insisted that only one human race lived in that age. Even Kylene, who loved him, knew such memories were not to be trusted.

Tayem was a genetic freak, with forty-six instead of the fifty-two chromosomes of real human beings. He was a monster, despite his almost human appearance. Pasty-complexioned, feverish, irritable, and oversize, it was hardly surprising that he expected to die of old age well before reaching a century. Any telepath could predict that such a man might unconsciously distort the truth, hiding his abnormality from himself behind a belief that he was typical of his Era. Some of the Teeps in the Project suspected that Tayem had been lied to as a youth, to protect him from the harsh truths. It seemed likely, though Kylene had found that otherwise Tayem's mind was quite as sharp as any genuine human's was.

Nonetheless, even by Tayem's account, two races of men shared the Earth during most of human history: a handful of telepaths and a much greater number of Normal men.

During the Second Era, the telepaths—"the Skyborne"—had reached for world domination and achieved it, controlling the world from their mountain fortress, Kh'taal Minzaer. It was a world ruled more by ice than men; glaciers covered much of the northern hemisphere. People were few and poor.

No one now could guess how long the telepaths' empire lasted. According to history, the war that destroyed it lasted for twelve thousand years.

After that, Normals ruled, in smaller, short-lived states, often dominated behind the scenes by telepaths, which were constantly at war. Another Ice Age came and civilization fell apart.

A dark age of unguessable length followed. Finally, a group of telepaths built another state for themselves, which did not try to dominate its neighbors. The Normals organized against it anyhow, and after three or four thousand years destroyed it. Then, without additional purpose, the Fourth Era world fell apart, through warfare or the impact of still another Ice Age. They left to their descendants the Plates.

Throughout the world, indestructible records were left. Enormous ingenuity had been spent on preserving historical summaries and technical documents which would facilitate the birth of another advanced civilization. Even now, almost nine hundred years after their discovery, science and engineering seldom went beyond the knowledge in the Plates.

Except for time travel.

In the Fifth Era, the nation of Alghera had vied with the empire of Chelmmys for domination of the world—and lost. But a handful of soldiers and scientists had escaped from the capital, via time travel, to continue the struggle. Their efforts had changed history, but only in part.

In this remade world, their country and perhaps humanity itself faced total destruction.

The park was unlit, despite the warmth of the evening, and Kylene realized with a start that it was deserted—and that those responsible for city services knew it would be deserted. Evacuation, she thought, remembering the warning the Warder had given the night before. People were leaving the city, or hiding in caves underground. Suddenly, she felt alone and vulnerable, despite the time that was left to her.

She penetrated the bushes, finding a path which led up a small hill. At the top, she turned to get her bearings, then went on to her right. Here she saw a small fountain, recessed at ground level within a rock wall. She oriented herself again, remembering the number of paces to the time machine.

"Did you find out what you wanted?" A boy's voice.

Unwanted company. Kylene stood still. Not till the youngster approached did she realize the query was for her.

"You were at the Temple. I saw you coming down the hill. Did you get told what you wanted?"

The distraction was unwelcome. "No," she said.

"You had a dream, didn't you?" The boy was indistinct in the darkness, even his height hard to gauge. Kylene estimated he might be ten years old. He was short, that was clear, and thin, with short hair. "You came out of the Temple. Didn't Cimon give you a dream?"

"Yes." Kylene hesitated. "I'm not sure it meant anything."

"And they didn't tell—or you didn't take what they told you, is that it? My sister could tell you, I bet. You want to

come see my sister?'' The boy bobbed on his toes, either to
compensate for his shortness or to ensure that he kept Kylene's
attention. ''You tell her your dream, she'll know what it
means.''

''Perhaps,'' Kylene said reluctantly. As she viewed more of
the boy she saw clothing unkempt and poorly fitting and a
gaunt body. An outsider in this culture, then, as she was, his
poverty showing he was not only Septless but unprotected by
an Association. No true prophetess, then, but fraud of a sort—
the boy's mind showed her no threat.

She put a hand on her side, estimating the weight of her
coins, wishing he would leave her but aware she had time to
spare and unwilling to be rude. How long would such coins
have value? ''I don't have much money.''

The boy looked away from her. His lips moved silently.
Then: ''We'd be grateful for what we can have.''

The boy brushed past her. ''Cross here. Give me a minute,
first.'' The words were only muttered. Kylene barely understood them before the youngster was running. His steps clat-
tered.

Across the street, the boy dashed into bushes, concealing
himself, with his dark clothing, at the base of the shrubbery.
Grotesquely, his head reappeared almost at once, seeming to
float just over the ground as he looked up and down the street.
Such caution! Kylene watched agog, tempted to run the other
way.

Come now. The boy beckoned impatiently, his lips making
exaggerated slow motions, and Kylene read his gestures without telepathy.

No one is watching. We're safe.

Safe from what? Only fear of authority showed in his mind.
Or was it fear of adults?

Children! Kylene felt exasperation, but she had promised.
Fuming, she crossed the street at a deliberate pace, pointedly
facing erect the bushes where the boy had camouflaged himself. ''Now what?''

"Follow me." The boy scrambled to his feet without embarrassment. "They won't go after us here."

They? Kylene probed again, finding no sensible concern in his mind, but a hatred of anonymous men in black uniforms, irrationally coupled to a fear of doctors and medicine. Those were soldiers, perhaps, or Sept Housetroops—the boy had no understanding of their motives.

She followed, rubbing her jacket unconsciously, wondering.

"Up there." They had traveled only a short distance, moving in narrow passages between buildings rather than the streets, to reach a grassy quadrangle with buildings on each side. The park was still visible when she turned to look. Meanwhile, the boy pointed unnecessarily, his face turned away from the harsh arc lights that flooded the square.

Kylene flinched, feeling a chill along her back. What she had been brought to was a low-lying building of black-tinted brick, all corners rounded so straight lines were revealed only in the stairs leading to the second-story entrance. A brown pavement, pebble-surfaced under cobweb patterns of fallen leaves, surrounded the structure.

She had seen this building before, in others' minds.

Nyjuc House—the home of the senior Teep Sept. The images she had seen had showed the building decorated with banners to proclaim its prosperity and full of people.

To the east now, where the Sept's levcraft had once been parked, the pavement was broken. Dirt and ragged greenery outlined fractured slabs of concrete. Leaves and scraps of paper nested in the weeds. Other debris, wind-scattered, chance-gathered, had lodged along the sides of the building. Risers were missing at intervals in the curved staircase that led to the second-floor entrance. Above her head, windows gaped blackly, vacant of glass or bloodshot-streaked with cracks. Unfastened shutters dangled beneath them.

A sea breeze pushed at leaves, which fluttered sluggishly. Odors of decay hid the ocean scent. Kylene, listening for human sounds, heard only her own heartbeat.

"C'mon." The boy tugged at Kylene's sleeve. "She'll

be—'' His voice changed suddenly, becoming businesslike.
"Start thinking of your question." Pride glowed in his eyes as
he looked at the building. He muttered, more to himself than to
a listener. "Tried to keep us away from a home. We showed
'em. This is all ours. We showed 'em!"

"Here." The boy halted in the vestibule, holding out a
hand. "Wait." He whispered the words, then moved his head,
his eyes closed, self-consciously displaying his concentration.

Kylene looked back at the steps, replaying a captured memory, feeling as if for herself . . .

*The feel of polished wood whipping through her thighs and
the dizzying whirl of the world as she slid down the railing.
Just before the end, there was a bend where she lifted her right
leg and pushed with both hands, and twisted in the air to land
on her back in heaps of snow and laughter. She pushed snow
back in place, then, and got back in line to . . .*

For a moment, half-confused, she wondered if she was still
able to do that. An adult now, it seemed a pointless, dangerous
entertainment; she sympathized at last with the spoilsport mon-
itors who had conspired against her childhood joys.

But it was not her memory she recalled, not her childhood.

Had this little boy ever thought to play on the Nyjuc House
stairway?

"Okay." The boy relaxed, comforted with the belief that his
hearing had failed to detect motion within the building. Half
smiling, he pushed open the right-side door and pointed the
dark opening to Kylene. "That way."

That way. Kylene's memories told her it was the passage to
the married quarters. Without need for lighting she automatically took two paces leftward at the second windowpane and
moved diagonally across the corridor near its end. In the original world, this pattern sidestepped loose boards, not dangerous, but loud enough in their creaking to disclose the presence
of a child sneaking outside in defiance of authority.

Dirt skittered beneath her feet. Once this corridor had been
swept each day by the younger children, inspected each day. A

plaque, ostentatiously metal-plated, had hung from the interior wall, commemorating the founders of the Nyjuc Sept. Here— Kylene patted at the wall, finding only wood paneling and peeling veneer. The boy had not followed; Kylene, pushed upon by others' memories, was grateful to be alone.

Slowly she brought her emotions under control. This was not Nyjuc House. No one she knew had ever loved this dilapidated building.

Her mind opened up, probing, finding only the boy. A Normal boy, with nothing in his mind to show that he might ever possess telepathy. Despite reason, Kylene saw him as a trespasser. Why was he living here, in a building that should have housed Teeps? She probed deeper, finding no explanation.

"You're here." The boy's steps sounded twice, closing on her. Kylene waited passively as the youngster patted at pockets, smoothing down fabric to conceal things taken from elsewhere in the building.

"Yes." Kylene watched as the boy pushed at walls, seeking the pushplate that would activate the lights. Finally she heard a click. A triangle of yellow light appeared to one side, released from a raised doorway. Kylene saw without real surprise that it was the entrance to the Sept Master's chambers.

"Tried to keep us out. We showed 'em." The words carried only emotion, without reason or memory. Kylene followed him into the light.

"Sis." The boy pushed at a sleeping form. "Sis."

He grinned at Kylene, feigning authority. "Just a moment."

"Sure." It took effort for Kylene to speak. The air in this bedroom reeked of staleness, of decaying food, and of unwashed human bodies. There was no furniture, and the sleeping woman lay half on top and half underneath a mixed pile of blankets and sheets. Scorched spots on the walls and a charred floor showed where fires had burned. Paper and clothing were strewn over the floor. Infants' toys lay in a corner.

An animal den. She was grateful that curtains hid more from her.

"Aren't you worried about being here alone? If there is a war?" Kylene asked, striving for self-control.

"What war?" The boy pinched the woman's ear and wiggled it disinterestedly.

"Between Alghera and the Alliance. The one that might start tomorrow." Kylene waved an arm at the rooms behind the curtains. "The one everyone else is hiding from."

"Onnul hasn't told me—" The boy stopped abruptly, flushing guiltily. "It's just a story. They're using it as an excuse."

An excuse for what, Kylene wondered, but she had no chance to ask. "Eeee . . . Eeee-ahl-l-l-l." The woman moved, her legs thrusting under the garish blanket that covered her corpulent body. The blanket heaved upward, then fell down; perhaps her back had arched. Her head pivoted, surrounded by stringy blond-brown hair which seemed stuck to the floorboards beneath her.

"Customer, Onnul. Wake up." The boy knelt, shaking his sister's shoulder as he smiled insincerely at Kylene. "Just a minute now. Think about your questions."

As if in counterpoint to the words, something touched at Kylene's mind. Another mind, incurious, without self-awareness, sluggish. She thought of food, of eating, the sensation sharp within her mouth, then warmed with unfocused yearning, somehow sexual in tone. Warmth, comfortable resting places, the feel of a breast moving on her chest . . .

Instinctively, Kylene raised her shield, shutting the woman out of her mind. A Teep, a mindless Teep. The boy's sister was a victim of the plagues. A victim of the changed history other Algherans had created.

The woman moved listlessly, her eyes open but empty. She sucked on a finger, then moved it into a nostril. "Uuhth?" It was only a sound, without meaning. The boy patted her arm, still smiling predatorily, seeming to point her toward Kylene.

Kylene wanted to vomit. Instead, she swallowed, stepping backward, towards the doorway. "I can't," she gasped. "I'm sorry. I can't do this."

He turned, wide-eyed. "You promised! You said— What's the matter?"

Contagion. But the risk of that was small, Kylene knew. The plagues had occurred almost two centuries ago. Millions had died then, millions more had been affected, but antidotes had been found. The carriers of the disease had been treated. The dying had been saved. The disease had been eliminated.

It was only the effects of the disease which could not be cured. It was only the survivors who could not be eliminated.

"I'm sorry," Kylene repeated. "She's not a fortune seer, boy. She's just ill. Take her to—"

To the killers. No! The boy's thoughts slammed at Kylene almost as strongly as a Teep's would. He sniffed. "You promised. And then you didn't even give her a chance."

Kylene opened, then closed her mouth. It was not she who had harmed the woman, not even the Algheran time travelers. It was only an accident. A mistake everyone felt sorry for.

But she could explain none of that to a distraught boy.

And there were more pressing problems. "Get away from here," she snapped. "This city is going to be bombed tomorrow. Get out of here. Take her to one of the underground shelters."

"We aren't leaving. Even if—" The boy breathed huffily. "They won't take her away from me."

Kylene stared at him. "You'll be killed here. Your sister—"

"It won't—" The boy stopped, then started over. "Onnul's really good. She sees the future and she's helped a lot of people. You'll see! Just let me get her awake and—"

"No." Kylene wanted to gag. She wanted a bath. She wanted the feel of the woman's mind out of her memories. She wanted to run away.

"We have to eat," the boy said. "Give her a chance. Please?"

Money, Kylene saw suddenly. "Here." She clawed at herself, spilling coins from her clothes onto the floor as she backed out of the room. The boy sprang after them, scrambling on his knees for the metal. Released, his sister fell back on the bed-

ding, a flabby arm lying on the floor and pointing in Kylene's
direction.

At the bottom of the outside steps she began running.

Understanding cured nothing, she told herself, standing before the park which once held the Institute. She understood
what she had seen in this world. She knew how it had come
about.

For several years after their exile, the Algheran time travelers attempted to intervene clandestinely in the war that had
destroyed their nation. Even in hindsight, they had not appreciated the Alliance's superiority of manpower and matériel; it
came as a shock to them that history was not easily altered.

Becoming desperate, their planners decided to change history on a greater scale: the time travelers would prevent the
premature death of Mlart tra'Nornst. It was hoped that Mlart,
a great general of the fourth century, would continue the conquests that had swollen the Realm during his rule; eventually a
stronger Alghera would confront the Alliance and war would
be averted.

Disaster resulted instead. In the rebuilt world, science and
technology developed independently of the Plates. Among the
new inventions was genetic manipulation. A disease released
in war spread throughout the world.

The initial symptoms were those of the colds which had been
common in the First Era, and forgotten since. And like colds,
the disease was easily passed by contact. Unlike colds, the
disease progressed: it slew.

And there was no way to stop it.

Kylene sighed, stepping onto the grass. She had her breath
back by then. The panic which had made her flee Nyjuc House
had gone, and she could admit to shame for her flight.

But for a Teep, such fear was not unnatural. The plague
virus lodged in the brains of its victims. It killed one Normal
in five who contacted the disease; among telepaths, three in
five, and almost all the survivors were brain-damaged. The
world had had a million functioning telepaths; now fewer than

fifty thousand remained and those numbers were diminishing.

A world with fewer Teeps became more violent. Weaponry evolved to match human desires, culminating in thermonuclear missiles.

The Fifth Era might die and leave no survivors.

She pushed through a barrier of shrubs, then stepped again on the street that bordered the park. The morning fog was beginning to dissipate. A pink glow on the eastern horizon was already raising an edge of the light blue sky, and within a day of the tenth the final conflict would emerge. But at this moment, she had the sky and city to herself, for she saw no one else. Her boot soles crunched upon pavement as she walked toward the time machine.

Back, she told herself, and felt her heart lift.

Back to Tayem.

Part One:

Bearings
Kingdom of Loprit,
47,328 L.C.

Chapter 1

*A*t *dusk, the Midpassage innkeeper stood in his darkened* kitchen, staring through the doorway at empty tables. Above the tavern floor, only silences and shadows remained in his vacant rooms. There were no voices behind him.

The night was moonless. Outside, dark clouds hid the stars from view. A storm had come during the afternoon. Now mud was streaked on the pavement of the great Fourth Era road, fallen leaves stuck in layers to wet sidewalks, and dampness had accentuated the odor of his spice-impregnated wall coverings, turning scent into something cloying.

Before the war with Alghera, at ten-day intervals, a horse-drawn coach brought travelers to the inn and people to meet them. It had been a regular event, expected, prepared for, with cook and servers and bedmakers ready to give service. Then.

No coach had come during the last tenth of a year.

Before the war, foundry workers and farm laborers had come each night for beer and conversation, gentry had come to dine, men and women had sought each other out. There had been weddings, feasts, celebrations for children.

Before the war. His mouth moved soundlessly.

Woodenly, he walked past his bar and threaded through empty tables until he came to his outside door. The wide black road, from horizon to horizon, was empty of vehicles and people. The winding lanes that climbed the hills were empty. The windows of the workers' barracks across the street were dark and empty.

He sniffed and fastened the door's latches and pulled switches that turned off the last of his lights. A clay-tinged breeze pushed past him. Water chopped at riverbanks in the background. As he watched, the few remaining lighted windows of the houses on the hillside winked off; shutters were drawn. Only silhouettes were left before him and in the inn.

Shadows and emptiness in Midpassage. Waiting.

For the men. All the Midpassage men with the distant army, who would spend this night on water-soaked ground, waiting, with only canvas to keep away their Algheran enemies.

If only they were here again—if only everything could be made right again—if only Midpassage had people again—

He gasped, then tears ran down his face.

As he cried, far to the south, thunderbolts were striking.

Lightning had awakened him, Selvon Lerilton ha'Hujsuon thought, reflexively pulling blankets over his shoulders. Lightning, with a storm of cold rain to follow the previous day's rain, and muddy ground again beneath his blankets. Noise and discomfort and thousands of Algheran soldiers around him, all as real as the coarse linen uniform he slept in and the bulky haversack beneath his head despite the five centuries and more that would pass before his birth.

For a moment, he longed for his familiar Station cubicle. Warmth, his own bed, his own shower, his own storage cabinets, nearby friends and acquaintances, the support of his Septlings . . . He had a place there, a status; he was an Agent; he had respect from others, even admiration. It was easy to forget that he was also an exile there, surrounded by other exiles, all of them refugees from a Present three thousand years away.

The Station was underground, protected from discovery and the elements. In the two years he had been with the time-changing Project he had never been forced to face the outside weather.

In Lerlt's experience summer turned quickly into winter, and snow fell at this time of year, swiftly, cleanly, honestly. Rain belonged to spring and summer and should be warm. Posing as a native for most of a year had not changed his perspective. There was something unnatural about the truncated season these people fitted between summer and winter, something fraudulent and offensive in the cold, unexpected rain, something inhuman about the people who had adapted to this climate.

"Good for next year's crops," they'll be telling each other in the morning. *"Must be good for the crops. Hope it's good for the crops."* They like this weather.

Even the officers; they're no better than peasants, either.

And this, the famed Dicovys Division of the Swordtroop of the Algheran Realm—hah! Lerlt had met his share of Dicovys. Snobs, who traced their ancestry back to the nomads who established Alghera and who treated the members of the much younger Hujsuon Sept as commoners. Pedants, far removed from ordinary life. They probably needed instruction manuals to shit. Cimon take all the Dicovys!

Here—now—their Housetroops were only uniformed farm-boys.

Hicks. So we have to play at being hicks.

He growled. *When in Chelmmys, dance Chelmmysian-style.*

It had to be that way. There must be no hint of tampering with history to betray the Project to future generations. That Lerlt could understand. For other reasons, beyond his comprehension, it was necessary for the time travelers to blend with their environment. History could be changed only grudgingly, it seemed, bit by little bit.

But someday in a proper world, when the Project had succeeded and its exiles returned to their homeland, there would be no Chelmmys, no Alliance of Mankind to meddle in Algheran affairs, no war against Algheran independence. Alghera would be free and unrivaled.

Keep old Mlart tra'Nornst alive, he reminded himself. *That's all we need to do. Just keep one bullet from hitting him. Guard the bugger through the fighting at F'a Loprit this winter, so he isn't killed this time, and history will get better for us.*

Mlart the Great. The general whose victories had preserved Alghera from dissolution, the social reformer who had brought the old Septs to heel and built the modern Realm, the leader who had made Alghera powerful and large . . . until his untimely death.

History would be changed, Lerlt and his companions had vowed. Mlart would be kept alive. He would consolidate his conquests this time. There would be no civil war after his death, no stagnant period of rule of autocrats, no more truncation of the enfeebled Realm.

When the slave armies of the Chelmmysian Alliance reached forth to this continent, they would find a large, strong state capable of withstanding their demands. Alghera would smash the armies of its enemies in battle, as it had in the age of Mlart. It would foil the Chelmmysian dream of world empire, tear apart their Teep-serving Alliance, and punish those who had violated the Great Compacts.

Only time travelers could reach and punish *all* the guilty.

In the end, Alghera might rule the world instead of Chelmmys. An undercurrent of Lerlt's thought was that the time travelers who would make Alghera powerful would be powerful themselves. Women, wealth, luxuries, political influence—*Anything we want, we'll get. Anything we want to do to people, we'll do it. And no one will stop us because it'll all be our secret.*

In a world polluted by telepaths, he could have both power and secrecy. The knowledge inspired daydreams. Were they to be only fantasies or anticipations of additional facts?

Lerlt smiled wispily and opened his eyes. Drawstrings dangled over his head from a system of grommets and lacing that made two sheets of canvas into a single structure. When properly fastened, the primitive device kept rain outside the tent almost as well as stick-tight fabrics did. Now it was open, to air out the mildew-prone tent. Groggily, pent between sloping canvas and a slumbering tentmate, the time traveler contemplated its complexities.

Suddenly the night was painfully bright. Hammers smashed his ears. Air swept past him, hot as a desert sun. The earth rocked. Spilled against the side of the tent, Lerlt bounced face downward. Weight was flung against him. His face and arms were stung by weighted barbs. He tumbled against unseen obstructions, and felt himself bound. He was blinded. Fluid filled his mouth. Heart racing, he coughed his mouth dry, then gasped for breath.

Debris rained upon him, then stopped. Panicking, he fought against his bonds until his hands and face were free, until he felt air moving again through his throat. Then he paused, panting hurriedly, trying to understand—

Flames had pushed away the darkness. Running figures were on all sides. A corner of the black sky turned to boiling white clouds and purple glare. Men were shouting words made meaningless by his ringing ears. Gunfire crackled nearby.

A battle, he realized suddenly. The Lopritians had attacked. No account of history he had heard had mentioned this.

"Hals," he called, reaching across the canvas for his companion. "Hals! We have to get out of here!"

His hand felt dirt, pebbles, torn cloth. "Hals? Hals! Where are you? Don't leave me, Hals!" He squirmed desperately—then prodded something soft and yielding. Flesh. Already cooling.

Overhead, sharp-lined starbursts formed and vanished. Dust spurted on all sides. For an instant, a thousand glitters carpeted the ground around him and Lerlt saw as if by daylight.

One side of Halishar ha'Minursil's face smiled babyishly at the heavens, in innocent sleep. Above the Agent's lips, on the other side, there was space—a dark cavity. Tangled silver mesh covered gray-white fluid splashed with red. Brains. Blood.

Lerlt screamed.

A tall man, red-haired, dressed in the drab brown and gray of the Lopritian militia with officer's insignia on his sleeves, stood on the edge of a riverbank. His long hands were extended, the palms downward, as if he sought to hold back an animal at the gate of a pen. "Shrapnel, concussion, incendiary," Timothy Harper muttered as shells burst behind him. "Shrapnel, shrapnel—A little more grape, Captain Bragg—incendiary, shrapnel, solid . . ."

The words were to himself, keeping other thoughts at bay, as he waited. He held his anxiety inside him, and when purple-tinged flares threw his shadow out and illuminated his face, he grinned at the waiting men below the bank and turned his head so they could see him watching them.

Under his feet the earth shuddered minutely; rivulets of dirt flowed down the bank to dust the men's legs and muddy boots. Harper looked down at his orderly and smiled as the small man struggled to hold on to the reins of his horse. The mare was frightened. Harper saw equal terror on the pinched face of his orderly, but the man had his eyes open and his face to the front; he nodded to show concern and pretended it was for the horse.

Wind gusts pushed at his back; a flare lit up the opposite hillside so every bush could be counted. Light glinted from eight hundred rifles.

"Up—and at 'em!" Harper screamed suddenly, standing on tiptoe and pulling his hands backward as if to yank soldiers over the riverbank. "Go to it, Loprits! Kill Algherans! Go! Go! Go!"

As men scrambled past him, he did not think of History.

In his dream, he stood in darkness, his cold palms pressing against tall windows, while lightning flashed beyond a solitary hilltop and peals of thunder set the glass ashiver. Waiting.

A hand from outside that world rocked his shoulder. "Sir."

It was a hand that had awakened him on more mornings, more insistently, than his long-dead wife ever had, and he understood its purpose even inside the dream. He opened his eyes on darkness, then closed them again while he recognized his waking. No water-streaked windows, no dark landscapes mercilessly revealed by white flares . . . only darkness, his own breathing, an exposed knee and calf which had escaped from the imprisoning blanket, fingers tingling in air above his head, a sweaty forearm which had been his pillow . . .

As he moved, ancient leather creaked. "What is it, Grahan?"

"Cannons," Grahan Hemmendur said, and Jablin Cherrid ris Clendannan, lying on the couch in the command wagon for the Lopritian Strength-through-Loyalty Brigade, heard a long-off booming that was no longer thunder.

Mlart.

"Put the lights on." He pushed covers away, then rose from the couch. Beneath his feet, the cold floor of the great wagon creaked. Dust and grit scratched at his soles. Outside, visible through a small window, red and yellow flame pushed back black night and gray cloud, a watch fire flickering in a wind. An open barrel held rainwater. Blanket-shrouded bodies lay haphazard and featureless as fallen trees.

Beyond silhouetted tables and chairs, metal scratched against metal in Grahan's hands; tinder flared. Cherrid blinked against the dazzle, remembering the looming darknesses of his dream, then, as his orderly moved along the walls lighting the coal gas lamps, listened to the distant guns. In his nostrils were the scents of unbathed men, an acrid reek of anger and frustration, stagnant air, traces of spilled broth. Irrationally, he felt a flash of hatred for the too familiar surroundings. He put a hand out, touching folded cloth—blue breeches, a slippery-surfaced tunic, lace shirt facings—and metal insignia.

Done with the lights, Grahan waited for him to speak. He hesitated, feigning thought to mask his return to wakefulness.

Mlart tra'Nornst. Never defeated Mlart tra'Nornst.

"I will want Gertynne and young Wolf-Twin," he said finally, "and my staff as soon as you can get them here. Also, the cavalry officer on duty." Then, more graciously, "Your ears are still better than mine, Grahan."

As ever, it was giving orders which had finally brought him fully alert. *Poor Grahan.* "Who else is awake out there?" he asked, and began to put himself into clothing. "Was there any warning of this?"

"The sentries. No warning. It just started." Grahan turned toward the Ironwearer, still handsome as Cherrid remembered him being, still strong and vital in appearance, permeated but not yet stained on the surface by the indelible age they shared. "Do you want a breakfast?"

"Corn and barley again?" He winced inwardly, then nodded imperceptibly at Grahan's head shake. "Maybe later. I think I still remember what they taste like."

"Possibly. Do you want ris Daimgewln and his people?"

He gave that brief consideration. "No, not yet anyhow. His regiment will do what mine does, and there is no point in using two staffs to write one set of orders." He had more confidence in his own staff, he meant, and Grahan understood the point without comment.

"Shall I wake up the Hand?"

"Let him sleep." Cherrid hesitated, fazed by that tiny bit of insurrection but aware that Loprit and Lord Terrault ris Andervyll himself would be better served if the Hand of the Queen remained asleep or in dalliance with his Northfaring doxies. *Best to make a joke of it.* "Three heads on the pillow there, Grahan. You bring back the wrong one while we're busy and you will distract a promising young Ironwearer from his duty."

"Wolf-Twin can behave himself with the ladies," Grahan said.

"Who was thinking of Wolf-Twin?" Cherrid growled, and Grahan chuckled comfortably with him. *Poor Grahan,* he thought again, patting lace down upon his chest, his eyes already moving toward the map table. "How is it outside?"

"Nippy. The rain hasn't come back but it's still damp."

Which made the cannons closer than the sound suggested. Somewhat closer, but still six or seven thousand man-heights away. A half-day's march—in either direction. *Morning then before we see action. The middle of morning.*

Mlart. What avalanche was the Algheran commander releasing?

"A bad night for young soldiers," Cherrid said steadily. He turned his collar down and reached for a heavy, lace-embroidered blue jacket. He fastened all its buttons when it was on and was grateful for its warmth.

"A bad night for dumb soldiers."

He smiled, remembering being both, though from a great distance. "Remember when we started centuries ago? Lying near the fire before a fight, talking, during nights like this—"

"Because you could never get to sleep."

"I used to stay up and try to figure what the generals were thinking," he admitted.

"You talked about getting rich, Cherrid."

He chuckled. "We were going to found kingdoms. Remember? How did we ever get here?"

"By a boat, Cherrid. You were too seasick to ever think of going back."

Which was not his full recollection, but it rated another chuckle. "Go get the youngsters. Let ris Andervyll sleep."

When he was alone in the wagon, surrounded by sputtering lamps, he rubbed sleep from his eyes, then yawned and stretched muscles left sore by his short rest.

Cherrid was of average height and slim. His sandy hair was beginning to show streaks of gray and his forehead was creased, but his body was still fit for campaigning, though he rode more than he marched these days. His eyebrows were prominent, with bristling, unruly hairs; they gave his face a stern expression even when he slept. He had thin lips and a Roman nose.

Since the death of his wife, late in the last century, no one had called him handsome.

He leaned over the map table. His tunic crinkled as he moved, and clung clammily to his back, but nonwoven fabrics had been fashionable among the aristocracy for two decades; Cherrid no longer realized how uncomfortable his clothing was.

His fingers touched molded clay. Loprit, Alghera, Innings, the Necklace Lakes, the Torn Coast—all the familiar topography of his adopted land was before him in miniature.

Only the two hundred thousand soldiers of Alghera and Loprit could not be seen. Cherrid stared uselessly at the map, not for the first time, seeking some unfamiliar feature of terrain with strategic value.

As ever, he found nothing. He straightened slowly, and allowed himself to remember for a moment the daydream wars young soldiers had fought in peacetime nights. Grahan's kingdoms had featured desolate borders, walls, mountain-defended strongholds, wise and well-loved lawgivers. Cherrid's imagined lands had given him long lines of doughty warriors, good harvests, and at least one battle leader of undisputed genius. In the daydreams, the genius had been his.

Centuries ago. *We called ourselves warriors then.*

And we fought with swords and spears. He and Grahan had been only fighting men, he understood now, not true soldiers, with little more skill than the bandits they had fought. Organization, not armies, had conquered the world. What won battles in this age was not the cannons and other exotic weapons described in old historical records but the ability to pass orders down the ranks to single soldiers and know they would be obeyed. Drill and regular meals had made modern soldiers more terrible than any heroes of the ancient past; and now the greatest deeds of generals were counting rations and reckoning march distances.

Cherrid ris Clendannan was a general: commander of the elite Queen's Own Puissant Guards Regiment, strategic planner for the Strength-through-Loyalty Brigade. And his onetime friend was now his servant. They shared companionship still, but the years had whittled even at that. As the distant guns boomed, he thought of the chasms time dug between lives.

Behind him, the door sounded as it closed; the floorboards creaked. Cherrid stared at the sculpted world-within-a-world that filled the map table and touched the green depression that corresponded to the brigade's location. "Good morning, Rahm," he said without turning. "It sounds like our young friend is about to make us earn our pay."

Team Leader Rahmmend Wolf-Twin of Her Majesty's Artful-or-Industrious Requisitionary Corps, the brigade's quartermaster, yawned loudly and inarticulately in the doorway. "Ironwearer Ian Haarper? Ah-hh!"

Rivers gurgled in his deep voice. Moon-faced, heavyset, he seemed to waddle across the floor, his pudgy arms quivering as he rubbed his eyes with both hands. On the collar of his tan uniform, the tiny crossed swords of an Ironwearer gleamed. Close to the older man, the squat man smelled of cinnamon; cosmetic ointment glistened on his mahogany-colored skin. "Timmial can be your friend for tonight, Ironwearer."

Cherrid smiled but could not laugh. His hand waved over the map. "I need somebody to report what is happening, Rahm. And quickly. Do you mind if I send your Teep?"

"Dieytl Ian Callares?" The younger man hesitated, his thick lips moving in and out. "It's a bad idea, Lord Clendannan. You know the Hand is very insistent that we not violate the Compacts, especially against the Algherans. Besides, Dieytl doesn't know enough to understand a battle."

Who of us does? Cherrid wondered. *Even Mlart—*

Battles should not be fought at night. Armies should not lurch blindly into confrontations. Detachments should not act without orders. What madness or disaster had impelled young Timmithial Ian Haarper to begin fighting? What blunder? What enemy trap? "Then I have to go see for myself," he said, and before Wolf-Twin could object, "I cannot wait on secondhand reports."

"What is he doing?" The man who entered now was middle-aged, handsome in a sleek fashion, tailored as well as any dandy from F'a Loprit, but a competent soldier despite his dealings in politics. Gertynne ris Vandeign was the executive officer of the Strength-through-Loyalty Brigade; his signature would complete any order Cherrid saw fit to give.

There was no question of who ris Vandeign meant by "he." Gertynne's older brother Merryn was nominally in command of the force that had contacted the Algherans since most of the men came from the village on the ris Vandeign estate, but the real leader of the Steadfast-to-Victory regiment had always been the hired professional, Ironwearer Ian Haarper.

"I do not know," Cherrid said gruffly. "It sounds like a battle."

"At night? Why on the one Earth?"

"I do not know, Gertynne. Don't ask me. Look at the map! You can make up guesses right now as good as mine. Ask a Teep!"

Ris Vandeign frowned. "I thought . . . anyone else pulled into this yet?"

Cherrid nodded. "Just the militia, from the sound."

"Hmmm. There's no report from him?"

"No report," Cherrid said. "No warning, no request for permission to fight. I have no idea what the boy has run into, Gertynne. Rahm, go out and find that cavalry officer; tell him to get himself in here immediately. And tell Grahan to saddle a horse for me. And kick up some of those supernumerary officers the Hand brought along—we can get some use from the youngsters as messenger boys."

"Yes, sir." The wagon shook as the young man left. Cherrid scowled impatiently at the door, feeling half-envious of anyone with a definite task.

Mlart. What was the Algheran general doing right now?

He turned back to ris Vandeign. "Is your brother out there?"

"No, thank the Lady," Gertynne said, bending over the table. "Lan Haarper told Merryn to stay out of the rain and be comfortable; there was nothing ahead but a dull stretch of marching. So he's in my tent. Nicole's cloak!"

Cherrid murmured inconsequential sounds.

"The map doesn't show everything," ris Vandeign complained.

It showed enough. "Here we are," Cherrid said. He stabbed the map with a finger. "Here is your brother's regiment—" Another stab. "Here is ris Cornoval's two divisions—" A hand wave over the southern portion of the map. "—or where they were. Now they're battered to pieces and falling back to these towns. Most of them, anyhow—there is probably a soldier hiding in every hayrick between Six Rafts River and Barlynnt's Tower."

"Too many men are in the army. Not much haying done this year."

"Whatever," Cherrid said flatly. "Somewhere between them and us—" His hand dropped, slapping at the map. "—here are three divisions of the Algheran Swordtroop, Gertynne, a full corps under Voridon Mlaratin tra'Nornst himself, with one big victory behind him and looking for another. Not to mention any reinforcements he might be pulling from the Torn Coast area."

"Well." The second noble frowned, looking for solace. "We still have almost equal numbers, if we can join all our units. If we could come together at Port Junction—" He brought his hands together at an angle, quickly, so fingertips slammed against fingertips. "Mlart wouldn't expect it."

The shelling had lasted too long for Cherrid to believe that. "We will never get together," he said. "Not with tra'Nornst in the middle. Your gods and mine, working together, could not manage that miracle now."

"No way to bully our way through?"

"Not now," Cherrid said. "If he is not there himself, this ruckus the boy got into is bound to wake Mlart up. Southern Corps is scattered, Gertynne. Any competent general could hold the pieces in check with one division. This is Mlart; he will do that and throw everything else at us. Hard. When we are dead, he can finish mopping up the south."

Ris Vandeign *tck*ed and winced but did not argue.

"There will not be a soldier to stop him, Gertynne," Cherrid continued. "If we are not careful . . . we could lose the Shield Valley and half the kingdom in an afternoon."

"Retreat, then. Sacrifice ris Cornoval." Those were not questions.

Cherrid sighed heavily. "Retreat to Midpassage, certainly. And maybe back to Northfaring. Or further."

"What will we eat? We don't have supply caches behind us."

Do we have caches before us now? Cherrid wondered. But this was too large a problem to solve in one conversation. "We will be a little hungry," he admitted. "We will have to march a little faster. If we—well!" He nodded sadly, already summing up the campaign. "If we had been here two or three days ago, it could have made all the difference in the world. But—"

He snapped his fingers. Mlart had been too fast. No, Mlart had done what a general should do. "We were too slow."

"Was it the delay in leaving Midpassage?" Gertynne grimaced, showing strain, and Cherrid remembered that the town belonged to his family.

"No," he said, telling a partial truth. "Lan Haarper had to train the militia before we left. We could not move sooner."

"He took too long," Gertynne said.

Midpassage should have had a trained militia force years ago, Cherrid reflected, and that failure was not lan Haarper's. "We marched slowly and that is my fault as much as anyone's," he said. "Also, in my judgment, ris Cornoval fell back too quickly. He should have stayed in place, blocking those passes."

"Haylon had supply problems. He mentioned them in every letter to the Hand." Gertynne had handled the correspondence between the two Lopritian forces. "The Algherans didn't, and he was on their side of the mountains."

Now he still has problems, Cherrid thought sourly, *and the Algherans still do not and they are on our side of the mountains*. He hesitated, on the verge of repeating an elderly anecdote which would probably seem pointless to the younger man. "He was too cautious. Ris Cornoval is never comfortable in an advanced position. He always wants reinforcements and more supplies.''

"So he was the wrong man for this command?'' ris Vandeign asked, following unvoiced thoughts as well as a Teep, his face twisted into something masklike and savage. "I didn't appoint him, you know.''

"I know.'' Cherrid hesitated, remembering the long enmity between the ris Vandeign family and the ruling ris Andervylls, disturbed by what he had just seen. "We should concentrate on the Algherans, Gertynne. You are going to have my staff to boss for a watch; set a good example for them.''

Horse hooves *click*ed lightly on the surface of the road, barely audible above the jingle of harness and creak of leather. Beside the roadbed, distant campfires sparkled like fallen stars. At the edge of the pavement, a horse whinnied softly; her sleepy rider steered her from the verge. Tree limbs arched overhead and blackness waited before the riders, like the gullet of some monstrous giant.

Along the giant's tongue, Cherrid rose with two dozen men.

The distant cannon were infrequent now, the booming noise rising over a subdued stormlike roar. Ominously, though individual musket shots could be heard, the steady crash of volley firing was missing. Glumly, he thought about the implications of that, hoping that wind and forest sounds covered the noise he listened for.

"Nothing reported by our scouts,'' a florid-faced cavalry officer approached to say, his voice artificially steady and cheerful. "The road is free for the next thousand manheights.''

Cherrid raised his eyebrows, though the gesture was useless in the dark. "Do you remember the Necklace Lake campaign, Major? Three years ago?''

"No, sir. Wasn't lucky enough that time. My wife's first boy escorted slavers, he came—''

"Luck'' was not the word Cherrid would have chosen. "The aborigines staged very effective ambushes in circumstances like these. They had sense enough to let the scouts ride past them and to hit small groups with fifty or sixty men.''

"Oh." The cavalry officer looked about uneasily. "Would you like it, sir, if I put some men off to the side of the road?''

Someone who knew his job properly would have done that already, Cherrid thought, *even if the effort is probably wasted.* "Watchfulness is always a good idea, Major.''

"Yes, sir, I'll—'' the officer began, stopping when he noticed the Ironwearer was not looking at him. "I'll do that.''

"Certainly.'' Cherrid tugged at his reins, slowing his horse so he dropped back toward the officers he had brought with him.

"We have the road,'' one of the young men said, and Cherrid heard him. "We can move men from north to south Loprit and back faster than the Algherans can in their country. If we invade—''

"The road is no asset now,'' he growled.

"Sir?'' The man's head rose sharply.

"Mlart is *here*,'' someone else explained when Cherrid did not answer. "Inside Loprit. He can travel up and down the road as fast as we can, so there's no advantage that we get from it.''

Which was half-correct, and the old Ironwearer let the boy's remark stand. The fuller truth was that Loprit had made itself vulnerable by developing along the course of the great Fourth Era road. In Cherrid's homeland on the Mother Continent, nations had been compact, with villages and cities close enough to defend each other. Loprit, using a comparison made by young Ian Haarper, was a string rather than a hard-to-untangle knot, with three quarters of the kingdom's people and most of its wealth found in the cities threaded by the ancient road. On maps, the kingdom claimed wide territories to the east and west. In reality, those lands were barely inhabited, poorly defended, and ineffectually governed—tempting prizes for aggression. Without the Great Road, or with the network of smaller roads that crisscrossed the Mother Continent, Loprit would have been a tiny but prosperous nation; as it was, it had become large, wealthy, and fragile.

More cogently, the existence of the road removed strategy from the direction of war. Any battle that Cherrid could foresee would be a straight slugfest, with victory going to the larger force. With Osrild ris Mockstyn's three corps pinned to the defense of the capital in the north and Haylon ris Cornoval's men strewn like so much chaff in the south, the larger force would be the three Algheran Swordtroop divisions of Mlart tra'Nornst. Battle would destroy the Strength-through-Loyalty Brigade; only one of Cimon's miracles could prevent that.

Cherrid was four centuries old, his religious faith set long before the discovery of the Plates. He did not believe in Cimon and Nicole, nor in miracles.

The road sloped upward minutely, the ground more so, till it was even with the surface of the pavement. He smelled dung underfoot, heard his horse's hooves trod something yielding, and guessed that the group passed over an animal trail. He pictured nervous cavalrymen spooking impatient deer and smiled for a moment, privately.

Ahead, banks of earth rose above them. An abandoned wagon rested in the clearing on Cherrid's right, tipping precariously toward the pavement. Empty boxes. One of Ian Haarper's rest sites, he judged; rain had covered up the inevitable odors of urine and dung. *No stragglers yet. Surprising for this kind of weather. I wonder how he keeps them marching so steadily.*

Inwardly, he growled. He had heard no complaint about Ian Haarper's march discipline, and had never thought it worthwhile to investigate. The young Ironwearer had been proud of his men, and their training had seemed adequate. Cherrid had settled for those facts.

He should have found time to watch the militia, he realized now, and tested them at drill with his own orders. He knew very little about their capabilities. This was Ian Haarper's first major command; in training his men, the boy had showed aptitude, but Cherrid had never expected him to operate independently. Now he could only hope the youngster had done nothing rash.

There was a stir ahead finally, signs of confusion, brief commotion. When it cleared two men were riding back. One was the major, and he gestured uncertainly at the other. "Sir, we've met a messenger from Ian Haarper."

Behind him there were bonfires. A cooking area, Tim Harper had first thought, seeing the large tent nearby. Or an infirmary. Men from a North Valley company had reached the tent and slashed the ropes that held it up; they were shooting at the shapes that still moved and screamed under the canvas. Nearby, his soldiers yanked at dead men's pockets before obeying orders from their sergeants; a lieutenant impatiently kicked at them. A dying man stared stupidly at the wreckage that had been his arm and patted timidly at the blood that gushed from it.

Another step forward, another tightening of the noose around the Algheran neck.

Beside him, two platoons of Midpassage troops pushed through the woods, men covering each other as they advanced from tree to tree and firing constantly at the shrinking line of Algheran infantry. Harper could hear shouted words of command from one of the Swordtroop officers, even watch as the man raised his arm to order a volley.

A soldier kneeling by his horse fired; the Algheran officer fell back onto his side and did not move again. Harper nodded, then bent to slap the soldier's shoulder. "Good kill," he shouted, and the man smiled appreciatively.

Harper nodded again, then brushed his red-brown hair back with a broad hand, feeling sweat across his forehead. His fingers touched an old scar.

From another war. Another nation. He knew loneliness.

Ahead of Cherrid, men tugged at cables. Pulleys fastened to tree trunks multiplied their effort; a cannon trembled for a moment on the edge of a depression, then twisted into position;

a pair of thickset men wedged a log behind its wheels. Beside them other men unscrewed the base of the second big gun, swabbed it out with water-soaked pads, pushed in a shell and fist-sized powder sacks, and screwed in a fingerlike firing nipple atop the bronze casing. An officer, responding to signals Cherrid did not see, used a bar to turn a small wheel at the side of the gun. Within minutes, both guns were ready to fire again.

Cherrid touched his ear, tamping down beeswax. Even with that protection there was quite a lot of noise, he found, more than he had imagined entering the clearing. Heavy smoke made his eyes water. For a moment, he thought of the horses they had left at the back end of the clearing beside the artillery mounts. Artillery men deafened their animals permanently, he had heard. It did not seem so cruel now, particularly when he remembered most cavalry mounts were destroyed after a season of campaigning.

Overhead, the night skies were still dark and as they moved forward Cherrid felt surprise at how efficiently the artillery men worked. His second surprise was the realization that there were lights here—red-yellow lanterns on poles beside the two guns and the wagons that served them. For an instant, seeing flame close to powder, he was near to terror, but the attitude of the men reassured him. *Artillery match,* he reasoned, and a glimpse at one of the lanterns confirmed the guess—inside a sealed glass jar, something like gray rope smoldered.

Another new trick, he thought with pleasure. He'd used the big guns at night before this, pointed to sites where artillery crews should be placed and specified targets for them in daylight, but by chance he had never watched them at work. *So that is how they can do this.* Until now he would have thought it impossible to aim cannon during the night. Was this another of Ian Haarper's innovations?

No matter. At the end of the campaign, all the artillery units of the brigade would use the technique. When the war was over, it would be widespread in both armies, and in half a century commonplace throughout the world. Cherrid, remembering the year-to-year sameness of his youth, still marveled at

the way ideas were suddenly like water, arising from anonymous springs and flowing outward, undammable, in all directions. He had contributed nothing of his own, but it was still
satisfying to witness the change, to know that men of the
present day were more than passive recipients of Fourth Era
largess.

An officer with a lantern approached, ending Cherrid's
musings. His cavalry escort bunched before him, then moved
aside uncertainly. The Ironwearer grimaced wryly, suspect-
ing he displayed the same combat-jitter awkwardness, then
made gestures at the artillery officer. Where was his commander?

Forward, the man signaled, not noticing or ignoring Cherrid's rank. At the front of the clearing.

The big Ironwearer, Cherrid's gestures asked. The flame-
topped man—where was he?

Forward of forward. The man mimed ignorance when asked
for more information. His eyes turned back to the waiting gun
crews.

Cherrid waved dismissal. Feeling like an interloper, he led
his group forward on foot. After a moment, detailed by the
artillery officer, one of the gunners joined them and led them
up the road cut.

A hundred man-heights distant, the gunner brought them to
the artillery captain, a lean man perched above the road with
his arm fastened about a sapling while he stared outward at a
blackened hillside. The gunner scrabbled upward toward him.
Cherrid's eyes followed the captain's gaze.

Across a small valley, insect figures gesticulated. Minute
drops of red blinked along the edges of an oblong shape and
from its interior, like sparks about a burning hide; tufts of flame
and smoke showed the damage done by the guns. Below that
was a narrow gleaming band—a stream swollen by the autumn
rains into a river. Killguide Rill, maps called it; Cherrid wondered for an instant what long-forgotten incident that commem-
orated. High above the water and the battle site was the great

road, bridging from one hill to the next like a plank over sawhorses.

Foolishly, the men with Cherrid knelt by the roadside banks or half concealed themselves behind trees, though they were beyond musket range of the fighting. He smiled briefly, amused, knowing they would view his exposure as courage rather than common sense, then stepped toward the artillery officer.

Thunder rang out, wind struck downward. For an instant, the trees and pavement of the road gleamed redly. Over Cherrid's head, a shell flew. Splinters of the wood block which had held it within the gun barrel rained down. Gases caught in the near vacuum behind the shell glowed, then winked out.

For Cherrid, it seemed the world had shaken itself. He breathed in on something hot and noxious, and coughed to clear his lungs, then half jumped, half pulled himself up till he was beside the artillery commander.

Seconds passed. The captain scribbled a note on a small pad of paper, then gave it to the gunner, who nodded briefly and ran away. Cherrid saw that dirt had covered over the captain's feet as he waited.

He waited, half wondering if he had been noticed; then the captain pointed with an outstretched hand. Between the dotted lines across the valley that were volleys of musket fire, a star twinkled, then vanished. Red sparks settled about it, then were hidden by a dark curtain. The curtain fell. Dirt settled, hiding whatever harm the shell had done.

In that instant, Cherrid knew, finger-sized pieces of glass would have struck a man or several men, tearing away limbs or crushing chests or punching holes through jaws and skulls and genital organs. Exploded dirt and pebbles would have broken arms and legs and smashed out eyes. At this moment, concussion was filling men's lungs with blood. Explosion-tossed soldiers were stumbling into those fires, screaming as their burning skin crinkled and their melted fat bubbled in the flames. Watching from a point of safety, he understood why artillery men were never taken alive as prisoners.

Someday, instead of experience and training, men would have lenses that turned darkness into daylight. Someday, distant objects would be made to seem near and normal men would send orders as instantaneously as Teeps to men far away. Who would need generals then, where anyone could become a general? Who would dare wage war?

No, there would be wars in the rich gadget-glittering world promised by the Plates. He was sure of that. Men were what they were. Like lungs and hearts, generals would still be needed.

The artillery officer raised his head. Cherrid sensed he was breathing deeply and guessed that he was half-mad. Isolation, exposure, unquenched exaltation—some men had that reaction to combat. Angrily, he slapped at the crossed swords on his collar, making sure the man knew who he was, and swept his hands through the air, asking for an account.

The captain was a regular, not a militia man. He sobered quickly, swallowing, then obliged with a sketch. Three companies had attacked on the left, his drawing showed Cherrid—four hundred men, presumably the battalion from Midpassage. The right-hand force would be the two North Valley companies.

A platoon from each made up the reserve. As a shell passed overhead, the captain's finger suggested its position, farther down the hillside, almost on the verge of Killguide Rill. From shapes, Cherrid decided cavalry men and their mounts lingered there also; he could not guess the numbers.

A file of troopers, the artillery captain agreed. To catch escaping Algherans—his face twisted into a soundless laugh. The rest of the cavalry, about forty men and horses, were to have passed around the right, to hold the road at the far side of the battlefield. He snapped his fingers when Cherrid's gestures asked if the blocking force had reached its destination.

Timmithlan lan Haarper had entered the battle area immediately after both his battalions had engaged. The artillery officer had received no subsequent orders from him.

Cherrid swallowed, finding the air thick and moist. It was

obvious from here that Ironwearer Ian Haarper had attacked a force larger than his own.

Deliberately. Without need. Without authorization.

The trees and road flashed redly once again. Gale wind pushed down on him. Cherrid stared at the hillside opposite, seeing it swell as if he were falling toward it, and knew he would have to enter the battle to find Ian Haarper.

He wanted to howl with rage.

"Too late, Algie," a man called out, then laughed and fired at a dark shape gibbering in tree limbs above. A body fell through black night; a shadow writhed mindlessly on the wet ground. The Lopritian shoved a knife into the downed man's neck, then cut open the pack on his back.

The pack was empty. The soldier snapped his fingers philosophically, and wiped his blade on the Algheran's uniform.

I've just seen an atrocity, Tim Harper thought numbly, *and what am I going to do? Nothing.*

This is "mopping up," isn't it? The necessary murder the front-line troops escape. My responsibility, in the end. If it makes me sick, it's my own damned fault for hanging back where I can see this kind of thing.

It was not time yet for mercy. Defeat was still possible.

The battle could still be lost. A world could still be lost.

I'll wear a Teepblind forever. I'll never let Kylene know everything I've seen.

He rode forward in darkness, his stomach sour, the horse awkward as it stepped between debris and bodies.

Far to the rear, Grahan brought one of Timmithial Ian Haarper's detachment of cavalry troopers into the Strength-through-Loyalty Brigade's command wagon. The rider carried a message which he took from the pocket of his shirttail and handed, after some confusion, to Gertynne ris Vandeign.

Algheran unit larger than one regiment found at Killguide Pass. Am attacking at night to gain surprise. Would appreciate follow-up support.

A scrawled signature beneath Ian Haarper's neatly drawn ideograms showed that Cherrid ris Clendannan had read the note. *Send nothing*, he had added, but there was no more information. Gertynne read the paper silently and passed it to one of ris Clendannan's battalion commanders who was acting as the Ironwearer's deputy, who gave it in turn to Rahmmend Wolf-Twin.

Tiredly, Gertynne lowered his head and rubbed his palm across his forehead. How would he tell his brother? he wondered. "Why couldn't he wait?"

Silence was the only answer.

"He couldn't tell what the Algherans would do, if he waited," Wolf-Twin suggested at last. "He probably thought we were in supporting range."

"Not at night." The executive officer continued rubbing his head. "He knew he was alone. He sent this message—Trooper, when did you start?"

"Half a watch ago, sir." The cavalryman swallowed. "It was when the artillery was just started shooting, sir."

"When did you find the Algherans?"

"Night, sir. It was after night. Ironwearer Ian Haarper put us scouts out when the rain stopped, and the Algies was just a few thousand man-heights in front. They didn't have out guards or anything, and we was like standing on their scrape stones."

"Did they see you? Did the Algherans know Ian Haarper's unit was near?"

"No, sir." The cavalryman nodded emphatically. "They was all sleeping. The Ironwearer brought the men up, rested them for a half watch, then sent them to their places, and the Algies never noticed till our cannon started in on them. Never seen anything like it, sir. It was just beautiful. I wish I'd have stayed to be seeing it."

Beautiful. Ris Vandeign grimaced and brought his hands together loudly. "He waited," he said slowly. "He waited till we couldn't tell him not to attack. That bastard! Wolf-Twin, Ironwearer or not, I'm going to tell the Hand to remove—"

"No." Surprisingly, ris Clendannan's orderly, standing in a

corner by the map table, spoke up. "The boy is in command of his regiment. He's supposed to fight the enemy as he sees best. He's— Trooper! Get out of here."

"Sir?" The soldier swallowed again, and looked from face to face. "Is there a message for me to take back?"

"Not yet." Wolf-Twin gestured dismissal. "Don't go far."

The wagon door closed reluctantly.

Ris Clendannan's deputy sighed to end the silence. "Let's see how badly things turn out, Gertynne. Eh? The boy does things his own way—we knew that already, we've let him operate that way. This isn't new. Lan Haarper may require better control in the future, but he isn't all to blame for this, is he, eh? We let him take the point. We didn't tell him to rejoin us. We should have been in supporting distance of him, after all. We should have reached ris Cornoval."

"If he destroys that regiment—" Gertynne nodded angrily. "That's a third of our force, Perrid."

Perrid ris Salynnt snapped his fingers. "Only a quarter in terms of men, and all militia, y'know? None of us ever thought they'd be good for much but shock troops, did we, eh? Let them take casualties rather than the regulars, Gertynne."

Ris Vandeign considered that. From one viewpoint, the young officer was correct: lan Haarper's men would suffer regardless of who commanded them. From another— "He's got Midpassage men with him," he said. "My family is responsible for those people."

"The damage is already done," ris Salynnt said diplomatically. "Ironwearer lan Haarper's career depends on what he does tonight to the Algherans, not on what you do to him. We don't know yet he's caught in a disaster."

"He might even be successful," Wolf-Twin said. The squat Ironwearer leaned back in his chair so he could see through the window, then gestured again as if to wave the cavalryman further from the wagon. "If he really surprised them, the Algherans won't believe he's attacking with a smaller force."

"I don't believe it, either," ris Vandeign said. "And I know he is."

"Gertynne," one of Terrens ris Daimgewln's aides said carefully, pointing at papers under his stylus. "Right now, I would also like to break the boy's neck, but we have other business."

"Well." Mollified, the executive officer smiled faintly. "All right."

"Fine," ris Salynnt agreed, gesturing at Wolf-Twin. "Rahm, now, you were telling us about our requirement for fodder. If we send half the horses back to West Bend, how does that affect the supply problem, eh? Does it help enough to be noticed?"

Time passed. Stars crept timidly from cloud to cloud.

"Drive 'em, boys!" Harper shouted hoarsely, standing in the stirrups so the men could see him against the night sky. "Push 'em. Fight 'em. Hit 'em! Keep pushing!" Overhead, he waved a long rifle. Behind him a campfire blazed, canvas flapped over a fallen tent. More flames showed above a small hillock. Perhaps, between other shouts and screams, between the crackling fires and gunshots, his voice was heard.

"Keep pushing!" he shouted again, pointing with the rifle, and his horse shivered. It was one of the cavalry remounts, trained for battle on level fields under sunlight with a small rider, not for a hillside clearing, and the officer was a tall, very heavy man. He sneezed as gunpowder wafted past, then daubed smoke-filled eyes on his sleeves. "Make 'em run, boys. Push 'em. Shoot 'em—kill 'em—kill 'em!"

Obediently, a handful of brown-uniformed men trudged forward a dozen paces, bent low as they had been trained, then knelt to fire. As they reloaded their muskets, other men pressed past and repeated their actions. Beside them, an officer stepped sideways, arm extended, calling out names and encouragements. A sergeant kicked at bodies, then at men moving too slowly.

Not enough men, Harper thought, worrying even as he saw reinforcements scurrying forward from the riverbank. The two platoons held in reserve, moving without orders.

Too few, too late. He knew now they should have been committed from the start. He was glad to see them, but they would not be enough. If they died here, it would be his fault. His mistake, his wrong judgment, his inexperienced folly requiring others to set matters right . . .

The arm he had raised to halt them dropped as the men rushed past. They were fresh. Their intervention might give a breather to the others. He had no choice but to use them. He shouted instead, pointing, his voice hoarse.

Answering shots flickered from across the clearing and men began to fall. The onrushing columns wavered. For a moment, time seemed suspended. Harper felt as if all the world were present and watching with held breath.

Then a fallen man struggled to his knees and onto his feet.

Time flowed once more. Beside him, a man stiffened, then fell to his left. Soldiers ran past, following the reinforcements. Men shouted and pointed toward the sky.

Harper stared, then swallowed mechanically, forcing down his gorge. For an instant, he thought his heart would stop. Thirty man-heights above, flames spurted from the road bridging the valley. Men were up there, at its sides, kneeling and leaning over the edge, firing at men below.

A handful of men, he guessed when the panic left him, a dozen at most. A squad would deal with them, and he stood in his stirrups to call for volunteers, until a misfire showed the newcomers wore blue uniforms.

Lopritian regulars had entered the battle.

His men had understood before Harper had. It was not fear which made them scream as they ran. They knew that help had arrived. Their voices rang with triumph.

He swallowed again, and rubbed his arm over his eyes to hold back tears. On the ground beside him, a body in a green uniform stirred. Almost unnoticing, Harper leaned and struck at the Algheran's head with the barrel of his rifle, then nudged his horse toward the battle line with a knee. The mare stepped sideways mincingly, avoiding bodies.

Across the valley, a small group of men came to the edge of

Killguide Rill, and waded toward him. One went ahead, reaching the near bank before the others. He vanished for a moment, then clambered over the bank. A soldier accosted him, then pointed. Harper turned toward him, then hesitated and waited for him to approach.

The man shouted meaninglessly as he approached, then stopped, then stepped around several bodies. Behind him, Harper noticed men huddled together on the ground like a football pileup. He smiled briefly at the newcomer's fastidiousness, then dismounted and walked toward him stiffly, seeing at last the lace embroidery of a staff officer on his sleeves.

How many reinforcements had come? he wondered, remembering the often poor relations between regulars and militia forces. Would they take his orders or would he have to share the command? Compromising with his uncertainty, he shouted at his own troops again, his voice louder to him than other screams, before registering slowly that the gunfire had stopped.

Wherever he looked there were men with raised arms. Surrendering.

The battle was over. The killing was done.

Only the wounded could have fears now.

History had been changed.

How will I describe this for Kylene? he wondered. *Lord, it will take me years and years!*

Before him, the regular officer waved a salute. "Ironwearer Timmithial lan Haarper? Ironwearer ris Clendannan wishes to speak to you."

Chapter 2

"*G*iddup."

It was a Lopritian—one of several Lopritians. A man in a plain brown uniform who poked at Lerlt with a primitive long gun. Shapes moved behind him, shadows passing by flames, men leaning over bodies.

He swallowed painfully, his throat sore with weeping, and dabbed at his eyes. "Let me—a minute—"

A soldier knelt by him, turned away without interest, and pawed at Hals's body. Crowing with satisfaction, he tugged the Teepblind from the dead man's head, and shook it in the air. Bits of flesh struck Lerlt's face. The soldier murmured happily and put the metal mesh in his pack, then tugged at Hals's feet.

"Please." Lerlt tried to push him away.

The soldier snarled and waved the knife he had taken from Hals's boots. Sickly, Lerlt pulled himself back.

The first Lopritian prodded his belly with the gun. "Obey you, Algie. Hurry, get up. Keep up arms, you." It was probably every word of Algheran Speech that was in his vocabulary.

Lerlt obeyed awkwardly, fearing that the man would pull the trigger and kill him. He had to stay alive.

Hands patted at him insultingly, pulled free the grace knife from his own boots, pushed at him. He breathed shallowly, panting, trying not to feel the indignity as the Lopritians searched him, closing his eyes while they discussed him and kicked desultorily at Hals's body. He had to stay alive.

To save Mlart tra'Nornst and Alghera and—

It would be so horribly *unfair* to die here!

"I haven't hurt anybody," he pleaded, staring earnestly at the men. "I didn't even shoot at anybody. Look at my gun—smell it—you can tell it hasn't been fired. I wouldn't—"

Then he gasped as a gun barrel poked at his belly once more.

"Shut mouth, you," a soldier said. "Keep quiet. Move."

He tripped, stepping backward into a hole, then caught his balance.

"Go straight." The soldier's gun prodded at Lerlt's kidneys, then pointed toward the river. "That way. Arms up. You not make trouble, Algie."

Lerlt's cheek throbbed. He swallowed. "I won't make trouble," he agreed.

"A great victory, Ironwearer," Cherrid said. "I congratulate you." A scream punctuated the words; he repeated them carefully, begrudgingly, finding conversation difficult.

Timmithial lan Haarper scraped his boots on the ground, kicked mud toward a hissing fire, sighed softly, then nodded, evidently unable to find words. He turned slowly, awkwardly, his left arm hanging like a weight he could not lift, and Cherrid saw rents in the side of his brown uniform but no blood. Shadows danced across his broad face, and Cherrid noticed once more the jagged scar on his temple. The redhead's expression could not be read.

Nearby, lan Haarper's orderly, miraculously returned from whatever bolt hole he had found in the fighting, stirred food in a stolen cooking pot. Men milled about on all sides, reluctant to move away despite the prodding of several officers. In the

background, Cherrid heard orders shouted in accented Algheran Speech. Prisoners were being marched out.

"It is also a great surprise," the older man said, and lan
Haarper raised his eyes to focus on him.

"I was under Nicole's cloak," the big man said, his voice
dull. "We all were. Thank you for appearing when you did,
Ironwearer. That pulled things around."

Did he really think that? Cherrid wondered. "Just chance,"
he said, knowing any battle was too complex for men to identify a single turning point. "People usually find an attack from
an unexpected direction upsetting."

Lan Haarper waited wordlessly.

"What do you plan to do next?"

The redhead sighed. "Talk to Pitar and Dalsyn, find out
what shape their units are in." His hands fluttered without
purpose. "Keep moving out prisoners, collect weapons, bury
the bodies, set up some sort of defense, get some scouts out
front. I'll have to see how many men I have for other tasks."

"Feed and rest your troops."

"Well, that, too." Lan Haarper gestured again. "When can
we expect more reinforcements? Is that whole brigade coming
up?"

Cherrid was suddenly weary. "I will have to look at things
first, Timmial."

The younger man frowned. "I sent a messenger a watch
ago, asking for reinforcements, Ironwearer. You must have
met him."

"Let me look at things," Cherrid repeated.

"Cherrid, isn't anyone coming up?"

"No, Timmial." Cherrid hesitated briefly, letting the words
sink in. "I think your regiment should fall back."

"For *chrissakes*!" lan Haarper shouted. "Fall back! We've
fought a battle, Cherrid. We've won! We can beat Mlart! We've
got momentum! We have to keep going!"

His lips tightened. "No one moves forward till I say so,
Timmial."

"Cherrid, we gave you a victory! Don't throw it away."

One day, Cherrid told himself, half pleading. *Let me have one day, one choice. Gods, guide me! Let me get my balance, let me get into the right stance, give me one bit of freedom before the duel with Mlart starts . . .*

Just one day. "Let me look at things, Timmial."

"For God's sake, man!" Ian Haarper shouted. "Bring up the brigade!"

"Be quiet!" Cherrid snapped back. "*You* do not give *me* orders."

A long moment passed. Then Ian Haarper sagged. "Yes, sir."

You've won a battle, Timmial, Cherrid thought bleakly. *But that is not a campaign, and I must think of campaigns.* Retreat now, maneuver, an exhausted back-and-forth struggle between weary antagonists . . . He could already see an inexorable flood of events, preordained now by Ian Haarper's actions. Ris Cornoval's defeat had not shaped the future; this victory had.

"Sit down, Timmial. Collect yourself," he said gently, and pointed at the ground. When he was obeyed, he asked, "When did you eat last, Timmial? And when did you sleep last?"

"Long ago," the redhead said. He laughed shortly, then began coughing. The coughing turned to wheezing, which finally stopped. "Long ago and longer." He coughed again, stilling it with a hand over his mouth.

"Sit and catch your breath, Timmial." Cherrid turned away and approached the officers on the other side of the fire. Most were his own men, but a pair were in the militia's homespun brown. "Who are you?"

"Pitar Ian Styllin," the younger said, and pointed to men holding back curious soldiers. Cherrid saw blood and caked dirt on his blouse, a finger-length gouge along his jaw. "Those are my company commanders. Do you want—"

"No." He turned curtly to a darker, older, hatchet-faced man in a cleaner uniform. "Dalsyn Ian Plenytk," the man said, and after a moment, "Force Leader, North Valley Battalion."

Lan Haarper's subordinates, competent at first appearance but additional mysteries to him. Cherrid shook his head thoughtfully. "Lan Plenytk, do you have two big men who came through this thing in reasonable shape?"

"Yes, sir." The man's eyebrows rose to ask questions.

"Get them here, and some horses," Cherrid ordered. "I want them to escort Ironwearer lan Haarper about the battlefield, so the men can see him and get back to duty. He's tired and he may be wounded. I want them to keep him from falling over."

"Ironwearer," lan Styllin started, and lan Plenytk silenced him with a gesture. "Let him give us orders first and then get his rest, Ironwearer. He's been up two nights straight now. We can get our own men back to work."

"I outrank you, Force Leader," Cherrid said calmly, "and I outrank him. Do it my way."

Lan Plenytk made a fist and Cherrid raised an eyebrow, wondering if he faced an argument. Was lack of discipline another problem he must settle?

"Obey him, fellows," lan Haarper said, his voice strained. "He's taken over the regiment, haven't you, Cherrid? I've been relieved."

"Just temporarily, Ironwearer." Cherrid did not look at the man he addressed. He feared he was lying.

From Killguide Pass, the captives were taken north, to wade through the waist-deep river and to climb a crude trail which finally met the road. Soldiers prodded at laggards with gun butts. Lerlt was hit on one leg himself, but the blow was weak, and shortly after that an officer's shout stopped the abuse.

Atop the road, the Algherans were placed in groups of five and escorted by a single Lopritian. Their hands were bound behind them loosely, but there was no other molestation. Lerlt, miserable in his dripping pants and water-filled boots, was faintly relieved to find his Teepblind had escaped notice.

It was not yet dawn when they were brought into a small clearing atop the hill beyond the river. Red glowing lanterns hung from tree limbs. Under the weak light, soldiers dressed differently from their captors checked their bonds once more. The prisoners were given time to pour water from their boots and to knead cramps from their legs. This second set of soldiers became their escorts then: Lerlt could see small groups of men ahead of him on the great road as far as the lantern glow could reach.

A handful of guns—two long brass cannons and several smaller ones—were at the roadside. Gouges in the earth showed where they had rested when fired; tree trunks gleamed redly, blazed and scorched by the cables used to train the guns. Hawsers and tackle were being stowed in wooden boxes as Lerlt's group of prisoners passed. Fallen bark and small empty sacks littered the ground. Beside the road, a group of men on horses waited patiently; a gray-haired man's eyes flickered over Lerlt and beyond.

Slowly, a horrid suspicion rose in the time traveler's mind. At the edge of the clearing, beside an empty wagon, he stopped and turned to the guard. "Where are the rest of your guns?"

"This is it." The Lopritian used Speech with a clipped South Alghera accent, and Lerlt had a moment to wonder where it had been learned, while he waved his musket gently, then brought it back to point at Lerlt's midsection. "A regiment doesn't usually get much more."

"Regiment?" The Algheran paled.

"Steadfast-to-Victory Regiment," the guard said calmly. "Militia, out of the Northern Valley, except for us gunners."

A regiment. Lerlt wanted to faint. "We thought . . . Another division, at least—or two—"

Now he understood the haste with which prisoners were being taken from the battlefield. The guard did also. "Don't get any ideas, Algie. There's a brigade of regulars just up the road; there'll be enough guns to impress you."

Lan Plenytk's escorts returned finally, as the horizon dipped below the pink-and-orange border of the morning sky. Cherrid's staff had remained about him as bodyguards and aides; it took a gesture from him to let the militiamen approach. In the background, silhouetted men bent over shovels; lines of soldiers carried boxes from tents to waiting wagons.

The looting was over. Cherrid had resolutely contemplated his notes while the surviving militia men stripped the bodies of the dead and dying.

"Where is Ironwearer lan Haarper?" he asked, seeing the men were alone. A notepad was in his lap; unlike lan Plenytk and lan Styllin, he did not rise.

"With the doctors," one said casually, then strode over to lan Plenytk, whose face showed he welcomed an interruption. "Do you need us anymore, sir?"

"Is he ill?" Cherrid asked loudly.

The soldier turned back, his face showing surprise. "He told us to leave him there. Sir. He's all right, though."

"He's watching the surgeons, Ironwearer," the second soldier said. "He's talking to the men before they get cut. They want to see him, too, and—some of them are in a bad way, sir."

"Get him out of there," Cherrid said.

"Well, sir." The second soldier swallowed. "The truth is, lan Haarper, he might not come."

A staff officer stepped toward the soldier, then stopped at Cherrid's gesture. His face was livid, and Cherrid wondered briefly what minor threats he thought would intimidate a man who had been through battle.

Cherrid looked at faces, then stood. "I had better go talk to him. We need him here." He turned to lan Haarper's battalion commanders. "You gentlemen know what I want now. You can begin doing it."

"Under protest," the younger man said. "If Timmial says—"

"Do it," Cherrid snarled. "Or I will replace both you and lan Haarper! You make your protest to the Hand, back at the brigade, child, if any of us live so long, not here. You do not give orders to me, and you do not disobey orders I give you, not now, not ever, no matter how much fighting you have been through. Is that clear!"

"It is." Lan Plenytk laid a hand on Ian Styllin's shoulder. "Come on, Pitar. Lan Haarper told us to take his orders."

"Peasants," a blond aide muttered as the militia officers left. "One generation up from serfdom and they—"

Cherrid, holding back his own annoyance, put up a hand. "Forget it, Derrauld. They did their duty very well this night. Let's remember that first."

"Yes, sir." The blond man lowered his eyes.

"Come along. Let's find those doctors." Cherrid did not know where the surgeons were working, but he stepped confidently, backtracking the path of the soldiers who had been with Ian Haarper. His staff moved with him; he knew he could count on them to guide him unobtrusively.

As the morning sky grew paler and the ground more distinct, he saw that the battleground was not on a mountainside proper, but on a plain which abutted a steep rise. The field sloped downward to the banks of Killguide Rill, which was a chocolate-colored stream about two man-heights wide inside a channel of twice that width. The slope was gentle, its existence obscured by a succession of hillocks and rising and falling ground. Bushes and clumps of weeds were scattered over the ground, as were a few stunted trees. Between them, the bare soil was gray and laden with pebbles.

The ground stank. The sinus-piercing reek of gunpowder was everywhere, as were the fetor of urine and suddenly released bowels. Sweat and blood-stained metal left other scents in the air. The cloying sweet stench of decaying bodies was already present. Overriding all this were the gentler aromas of torn vegetation and clay. Cherrid's nose wrinkled; he blamed the smells he noticed on the sluggish river, then forgot about them.

On the hillside, a diagonal swath of glistening earth ran from the edge of the road down to the plain. Dirt and rocks lay beneath the path, allowing Cherrid to recreate in his mind the scramble of Algheran troops released from marching to build their camp. High above, in the defile which held the road, sunlight glinted from cannons. The Algherans had left their artillery on the road then, unattended, but in place for the next day's advance.

So. Another mystery about the wayward Algheran defense was solved.

"How many men did we lose up there last night?" he asked, pointing at the elevated road with his chin.

"None, sir," an aide said.

"None? Not even wounded?"

"It was a surprise, I guess . . ." The aide's voice trailed off.

Or Ian Haarper had his battle already won, Cherrid finished mentally. Had the young Ironwearer's scouts told him the Swordtroop force was not defended by artillery, or had he reasoned it from the position it occupied? Or had he been only lucky? Did it matter now? "I must have been out of my mind, trying that stunt. Even if it worked."

"It did work, sir," the aide insisted.

In daylight, that seemed unimportant. "Aide," he snapped, not caring which officer responded. "Check out those guns. If horses are available, tow them back to the brigade. Otherwise, heave the bigger ones into the river.

"Aide! I'm due a report from the cavalry commander. Get him to me.

"Aide! There should be wagons behind those guns. I want a count. I want to know what is in them. I want them moving north. I want to know what else is there.

"Aide! Start a collection point for rifles and ammunition. Destroy all the muskets we took from the Algherans.

"Aide! Start a collection point for blankets and tents.

"Aide! Tell Major Ian Plenytk that if he isn't already, he is to guard the captured food."

Men ran to obey.

The sun had cleared the eastern hills when Lerlt's group emerged from the forest; the sky was already blue with a gray haze on the western horizon. A sea of brown grass, matted down here and there by yesterday's storms, surrounded the black-surfaced road. Birds fluttered into the air suddenly, then sank back to the ground on a nearby hillock. Their cry was indistinct.

"You can take five minutes to rest," the guard announced, stepping back from the prisoners and placing his musket on his shoulder. "Sit over there."

Awkwardly, like cattle, the Algherans turned about as he gestured at them and lowered themselves to the pavement with the sun on their backs. Water trickled in a small channel at the side of the foundation; under their feet, bugs and pieces of straw swept past. Lerlt, breathing hard, rubbed sweat from his forehead onto a sleeve and contemplated the waterlogged ground.

Another prisoner nudged him. "What unit you been with?" His voice was high-pitched and unpleasant.

"Huh? Dicovys division," Lerlt said, then in case that was not enough, "Second regiment . . . Uhh, first brigade." He shook his head wearily, then closed his eyes, hoping to be left alone.

"That Ironwearer Wilthir's unit?"

He didn't know. Dumbly, Lerlt snapped his fingers.

"Thought that's been Wilthir's," the man said plaintively.

"I just got there," Lerlt lied. "I was a replacement. I didn't have time to learn the officers."

"Oh. You from the city?"

"No," Lerlt said, sighing inwardly. "South Alghera, from one of the Minursil settlements." A pair of half-truths—Minursil had ceded the settlement to Hujsuon when the new Sept was organized, and in the diminished Realm of Lerlt's day, the southern portion of Alghera was only the central part of the land Mlart governed.

"You sound Northern," he was told. "Why you been with us Dicovys?"

Because Dicovys and Nornst provide Mlart's bodyguard and Nornst is too small a Sept to hide in. I was going to be a good soldier and get rewarded and get promotions and be in that bodyguard and . . . Me and Hals and . . .

Suddenly the whole idea was much less sensible than it had once been. Lerlt began to wonder if it would ever have worked. Now Hals was dead and he was a prisoner and Mlart was still in danger and the rewards the time travelers would bestow upon themselves were very far away and very tawdry. He was very small, he realized, compared with the entire world, very insignificant, and very weak. He wanted to cry.

An elbow poked him again. "Why you with Dicovys, you being Minursil?"

Hujsuon, he thought bitterly. *Cimon take it, Hujsuon! I'm Hujsuon and my Sept is as good as anyone else's, but I can't say it because we won't be legal until four centuries from now. They'd laugh at me if I told the truth.* "I was contract labor in the north," he lied. "Dicovys owned my papers."

"Happens, doesn't it?" The man beside him leaned away at last, then cracked his knuckles comfortably. "That been some storm yesterday. Like enough, you think it'll do the ground good for next year's crops?"

"Like enough," Lerlt agreed dully.

"Yeah. Hey, he got killed, you know? Ironwearer Wilthir!" The intruding, plaintive voice was suddenly cheerful. "Trying to form a lineup I been in, and he had his arm up in the air with a sword, and then—bang! You could see blood just jump out the back of his neck! There been this Loprit officer close, too, real big officer on a horse, I thought I might shoot at him, but we been falling back, you know? Running is more like it— didn't want I should shoot at him and be by myself and I figured, he been a big enough target I could leave him for someone else."

"Please," Lerlt said. "I don't want to hear any more."

"Been't no more to say." The plaintive tone came back. "Like enough, it'd've made no difference. Payback for Wilthir. Hard to think that, him being dead, Wilthir. Mounted up on Cimon's scales he is, and then going one place or the other, even as we're here remembering him."

"Please?" Lerlt said again.

The hateful voice turned practical. "Wonder if He puts 'em

in a line, old Cimon, or does He take 'em as they come to Him?
Bet Wilthir would line the men up for Him, and go first to set
an example. Knowing he wouldn't have much to risk, you
know?

"You and me now, we still got time to do good in, thank the
Lady! Time to do some more bad in, too." The Algheran
cackled hideously, and dug Lerlt in the side again. "Time to do
some more bad in!"

"Hush up, Algies!" A gun barrel slapped against Lerlt's
collar. "You got air to talk, you got air to walk. Let's go!"

Oh, Hals! Never had Lerlt felt so lonely, and as he rose he
stared longingly at the wet plain, half wondering if he could
escape before he was shot down, half hoping death would not
be painful.

But he was not yet willing to risk dying. Escape must still be
possible, he told himself. The other men with him might go
into prison camps, but they had nothing better to do. His knowledge was greater than theirs, his will stronger, his education
much deeper, his cause more praiseworthy. The Lopritians
only thought he was a prisoner. At a better time, in a better
place, he would escape.

He did not realize most prisoners shared those feelings.
When he noticed, infrequently, that his steps were shuffling
and that his eyes saw only the feet of the men before him on the
road, he blamed these facts on exhaustion. He thought it was
hunger which stilled his imagination, and lack of sleep which
robbed detail from the world he beheld.

Thus subdued, he was brought quietly into captivity.

By sunrise, the initial orders had been distributed. There
were many more than three sleepy officers then, though to
Rahmmend Wolf-Twin's relief it had not been necessary to
rouse the men, except for his own often abused quartermas-
ters.

The squat Ironwearer, standing outside the command wagon
to be revived by the dawn air, watching soldiers swallow break-

fast under the trees and teamsters loading wagons and artillery caissons on the elevated road, felt moderate surprise at how normal the brigade's camp looked in the morning. There were differences a specialist might note: fewer riders than were normal could be seen since the cavalry picket had been pushed out to a great distance, and the officers overseeing the wagon loading looked often to the north—yesterday, they had looked only south, in the direction of the advance.

To his eye, the men were unruffled, though he was sure that many of them had heard the gunfire during the night. They would be discussing the significance, even as their officers did, but they were waiting for a decision, rather than acting as if one had already been made. A good sign, he thought.

Several scouts who had gone with ris Clendannan had returned, bearing confused accounts of fighting. Ironwearer Ian Haarper had not yet been overwhelmed—that was their only common thread. They brought no reports from the man himself—evidently he and a cavalry escort had actually gone onto the battlefield to direct matters—but a scribbled note from the regiment's artillery officer described the initial attack. Ironwearer ris Clendannan had put his signature on that also, which was comforting in a fashion.

We will not have Algherans for breakfast. Wolf-Twin eyed the surrounding landscape with relief.

The campsite ran along a hill perpendicular to the road. It was defensible, according to the specialists, because there was a clear field of fire before it, and no nearby higher ground. Gertynne ris Vandeign, aided by—at least accompanied by— his engineer brother, was on the crest already, placing colored stakes to guide troops to fighting positions. Artillery officers were up the road, pacing off distances. The Hand of the Queen had breakfasted, dressed, and was now closeted with his chaplain.

In short, the brigade had prepared as well as it could for an uncertain future and was waiting on events. It was for that reason that there was no rush into forward or backward motion, though he did not expect the men to understand the fact—did not expect most of the brigade's officers to understand, either.

Nearby, a woman in a white dress leaned over a fire, stirring the contents of a large pot with a twig. Smoke billowed about her. She was dark, though not so dark as Wolf-Twin, heavy-bottomed, and of indefinite age. Turning, she coughed to one side, then noticed his gaze and nodded familiarly but said nothing, for which he was grateful. Awkwardly, he nodded back, wondering if he should recognize her, wondering which rumors she had heard this morning, and which she had chosen to believe.

An army unit inevitably pulled civilians in its wake, most of them women. Some camp followers were only whores, but for most it was a form of employment; for small amounts of money and food they washed clothes, fixed meals, and nursed the sick. In a real sense, they were part of the brigade's strength, but it could not spare men to defend them during a retreat, and it could not afford to let them flee before it did.

Wolf-Twin grimaced. With great luck, three soldiers out of each four would return to Northfaring fit for duty at the end of the war, but only one camp follower in three was apt to last that long. Of course, the women were easy to replace, and he knew that most of those who would be lost would simply fall away from the brigade without being killed by the Algherans, but the responsibility was still partially his.

His stomach growled.

"Sir?" Two young officers came around the corner of the wagon and approached at a brisk pace, then saluted. They were his subordinates, and this formality seemed ominous, but Wolf-Twin kept the thought from his face as he nodded at them. "Gentlemen? What's the problem?"

Yesterday, a dozen wagons loaded with hay and oats had arrived from the farming settlement at West Bend. It was not enough fodder to sustain the horses until the brigade reached Barlynnt's Tower, so Wolf-Twin had ordered the wagons emptied and sent back for another load. Had something gone wrong?

"Sir, I don't know if I should tell you this, but—" The older of the two spoke first, a dark-haired man who was handsome in a rather plain fashion, though an unsophisticated use of cosmetics marred his good looks. A circular scar marked the center of his forehead, and captain's insignia showed on his sleeves. "It's something I—uhh—saw." He stopped and waited expectantly.

I hate this nonsense, Wolf-Twin reflected. Why couldn't the Cimon-taken Teeps simply say they read thoughts, and why couldn't they make up their own minds about what was permissible to say to Normals?

"It's not a Second Compact matter," the younger, thinner, and taller man said to the Teep. By repute, Dighton ris Maanhaldur was the illegitimate son of the Hand, and thus a cousin of the Queen. He was not normally this decisive. "You told me, Dieytl. He's going to find out shortly, anyhow."

Wolf-Twin snapped his fingers impatiently. "Tell me, Ian Callares."

The telepath swallowed. "The wagons, sir. I don't think we should send them away yet. Lan Haarper has casualties and he's taken prisoners."

He had twelve wagons . . . Packed, pulled by doubled teams of horses, they would hold two hundred prisoners, forty guards and their drivers. But prisoners would be sent back to Northfaring or F'a Loprit, rather than the much closer West Bend.

The brigade might not see those wagons again until the end of the campaign, Wolf-Twin realized. "I'd rather see our men ride than prisoners," he said, smiling smoothly as he made the refusal. "The Algherans wanted to march into our capital, and we can let them do just that."

"I meant our men, but some of the prisoners are also hurt too badly to march," the Teep said evenly, and beside him Dighton shook his head gravely.

Unconsciously, Wolf-Twin began sucking at his lower lip. How many wounded men did Ian Haarper have?

"About half his regiment," Ian Callares said before the

question was asked. "Maybe half of them seriously. About the same dead and missing."

Five hundred wounded. Two hundred fifty dead, and that many more likely to die. Just counting Lopritians. Wolf-Twin swallowed nervously.

The Teep swallowed again. "And there's thousands of prisoners, with too many hurt to count."

"Thousands," Wolf-Twin said hollowly.

"Yes, sir," the Teep said. "A lot more than this brigade."

Dighton ris Maanhaldur put the common thought into words. "It's a complete disaster!"

Two large tents had somehow survived the fighting. Behind them, men were clumped around ambulances and cross-shaped tables sitting on sawhorses. Cherrid watched from a distance, his nostrils distended, then quelled his stomach and went to inspect the tents. Injured men were in both, as was the damp reek of blood and sweat and sickness in too small a space.

Lan Haarper was in the second tent. When Cherrid entered, he was pouring out liquor into glasses which passed from man to man across the floor. "Must be from the tra'Dicovys' own stock," he was telling the men. "Shame to think this was wasted on the Algies. Hey, you guys!" He raised a bottle to his lips. Fluid gurgled, though when he lowered it, the level seemed unchanged. "Good stuff! You gonna let me have it all, or you want some, too? Who wants a refill? Pass this back!"

It was not clear to Cherrid that the men were listening to the young Ironwearer, and when his eyes adjusted to the gloom, he saw that half the wounded men wore green Algheran uniforms. They had small glasses of liquor, too, and they drank with the same silent concentration as the Lopritians, their eyes and minds focused on the same bleak vistas.

"Who comes next?" someone said, and Cherrid saw that four burly men had entered. One carried a canvas stretcher; another held back the tent fly.

"Bensie over there's in good shape. He's got an arm injury and a tourniquet that ought to come off." It was the voice of a different Ian Haarper, someone more subdued than Cherrid knew. He had to strain to hear it.

Bensie, when he appeared, was a small man in green pants. His shirt was missing, and a band had been fastened about his right biceps. Blood had caked on his arm and hand. When he was carried into the light, Cherrid saw bones and red filaments of flesh protruding from what had been an elbow.

To his surprise, the man was conscious, and Ian Haarper tried to force another drink on him. "Doctors want to take a look at you, Bensie," he said lightly, using Algheran Speech as fluently as a native. "You want to spit in their eyes, swallow a little something to spit."

"Don't let 'em cut me," the man whispered. He sniffed loudly, and Cherrid realized he was weeping. "I gotta have both arms to work at my job, Ironwearer. Don't let them cut me."

"Hey there." Lan Haarper patted the little man's good shoulder. "They're going to look at it, that's all. They won't cut you if they don't have to. Doctors are lazy people just like you and me, fellow. Don't worry."

"Promise, you won't let 'em cut!"

Cherrid saw Ian Haarper's face twist. "They won't cut you unless they really have to. Is that good enough?"

"Go with me," the man whispered. "Don't let 'em cut me, Ironwearer."

Lan Haarper swallowed. "Bensie, I have to stay here," he whispered back. "Lot of people here who need looking after."

"Go with him, Ironwearer," Cherrid ordered, and wondered why his voice sounded so metallic. His mouth was sour.

Lan Haarper blinked, then swung his arm upward into a half-finished salute. "Cherrid? I didn't see you."

"Take him out," Cherrid told the stretcher bearers, and glared at the young redhead until Ian Haarper's eyes dropped. "Come with me."

"I thought you were going to tour the battle area, Timmial?'' he asked when they were in cleaner air. The operating tables were before him; lan Haarper stood where he could ignore their existence.

"I did." The man grimaced. "But everywhere I went, the people who came with you were giving orders to the troops."

"I told them to."

"I figured that, Cherrid. I didn't say they were bad orders. I didn't make an issue of it. I just— I saw I wasn't needed there. So I came here."

"You are not needed here." Cherrid snapped his fingers. "There are surgeons to treat these men, Timmial. You are wasting your time."

"I know some medicine," lan Haarper said weakly.

"That's not what I saw. I saw a sulking boy hiding from responsibility, Timmial, and it was not very pleasant."

Lan Haarper froze, then swallowed. "You think what you want, Cherrid. Now let me get back to those men. You can bawl me out later."

"No," Cherrid said. "That's an order, Timmial. If officers need to see them, their captains are sufficient. You can find something else to do."

"Sleep?" The younger man curled his lip.

"An excellent idea." Cherrid hesitated. Lack of sleep was surely one contributor to the boy's near hysteria. He wished he could order lan Haarper to go to bed, but the young Ironwearer seemed certain to disobey, so he compromised with another truth. "We are going to be very busy for the next year tenth, Timmial. You will be sorry for every minute of sleep you lose."

"What about the men?" Lan Haarper pointed with his head. "Don't they have a right to see someone watching out for them?"

"Demons seize the men!" Cherrid snarled. "They are out of the fighting now. They will never see combat again the rest of their lives. They do not need watching."

Lan Haarper showed shock. "Some are going to *die*, Cherrid!"

"All—men—die!" Cherrid snapped, and somewhere near

a man screamed. "Timmial, the men did not see someone caring for them! They saw someone holding back his puke, and that is all! You were doing nothing for them! Get those stupid ideas out of your head! If you really had wanted to help them, Ironwearer, you would never have gotten them *butchered*!"

"I didn't 'butcher' anyone, Cherrid."

"Turn around, Timmial," Cherrid said, growling. "You look at your handiwork and you tell me that is not butchery. Look!"

The surgeon had finished his examination of Bensie's injury. "Sit down," he might have said to the little man, and the litter carriers had lowered the Algheran to a seat on the wooden operating table. "Let me get another look at that," he might have added, and then, "Umm-huh!"

If there had been more of a signal, Cherrid had not seen it.

The procedure was mercifully quick. The attendants seized the little man and laid him facedown on the table, then fell upon him. One sat on his knees, to keep his legs immobile; one pressed down on the healthy shoulder, and the other two held firmly to the arm requiring surgery.

As Bensie screamed, the surgeon was already pouring alcohol on the wounded elbow. Within seconds, he stabbed at the arm with a scalpel, slicing three times to encircle the arm and to draw an incision across the circle. Like a shirt cuff, he rolled the skin back to reveal Bensie's arm muscles. As Cherrid watched, blood vessels bulged along the gray-tinted flesh; crimson spurted over the surgeon's hands.

Without a pause, the surgeon dropped the bloody scalpel into a bucket at his feet and took a short-handled axe from a hiding place beneath the trestle. Haste did not seem necessary now—Bensie had ceased screaming and his heels were no longer kicking at the rear attendant—but with one continuous motion, the surgeon raised the axe over his shoulder and brought it down with his full strength. The sound of snapping bone and the *th-chunk* of the axe striking wood came simultaneously.

Still moving quickly, the doctor dropped the axe headfirst into his bucket, poured more alcohol over the bleeding stump, brushed molten black pitch over the cut arteries and veins, then folded the cut skin back into place, and sealed the entire end of the arm with more pitch.

Bensie was no longer moving. The surgeon put an ear to his back for a moment, then gestured. The attendants moved the little man gently onto the litter and carried him around an ambulance and out of sight. The surgeon went the same direction with the severed arm—it seemed too small to belong to any adult now—then returned with a mug in one hand.

Brandy, Cherrid reckoned, watching the surgeon sipping his drink. *Brandy and amputations for as long as daylight lasts . . . Why, in those thousands of pages of records the Fourth Era left us, are there so many methods for killing men and so few to make them well?*

There could never be an answer to that.

With his resolution stiffened by the surgeon's example, he could speak to Ian Haarper once more. "Is this what you wanted, Timmial? Is there enough glory here for you?"

"It wasn't glory," the big man said brokenly, and Cherrid saw that glistening trails of tears streaked his cheeks. "I wanted to beat Mlart. I've got to beat Mlart, Cherrid. I don't have a choice. But—God, Cherrid! I knew people would get hurt, I knew this had to happen, but not so many! Not anything like this!" Suddenly, the tears were quicker and hotter, and all that Cherrid could hear was the sound of Ian Haarper weeping.

"All right, Timmial. I believe you." As gently as he would have touched a child, Cherrid patted the redhead on the shoulder, and said the words forced upon him. "I relieve you of your command. Relax now, Timmial. Let me look after your regiment.

"And I will use your victory."

Chapter 3

"*A h-hh-hhm,*" *Ironwearer Rahmmend Wolf-Twin said,* awkwardly leaning forward to keep his balance on a grass-covered hill slope and engaged in an unaccustomed professional task. Casting about for additional words, he dragged his foot back and forth through the long grass, stumbling slightly as his toe uncovered an anthill, and frowned at the scurrying insects. At his side, he sensed without looking, Dieytl lan Callares was frowning at him.

It would have been very satisfying to have that foot on Timmithial lan Haarper's neck.

"Transfer at full rank," he said, repeating his last words. "You'd receive regular Lopritian salary and perquisites for Blankshields, with the same chances of promotion, or better, and in peacetime—"

Someone snickered. He looked up, staring at the seven mercenary officers sitting on the hillside above him, uneasily bearing the weight of their fourteen beady Algheran-hired eyes.

"No speak you language," an artillery lieutenant said cheerfully. "You speak us our language in, hokay?"

A lie—Dieytl had nodded gently. Wolf-Twin frowned again.
In the background, discreetly arrayed behind some shrubs, a
squad of Lopritian soldiers frowned.

"We will teach you our language," Wolf-Twin said carefully, "if you gentlemen are as intelligent and capable as Lopritian children."

"Won't be here long enough," a colonel said, looking about
with more satisfaction than any Lopritian that morning. "Mlart
will get us out. Just be patient, men; let Chubby give us his
little spiel, then sit tight and wait for the next fight." Insultingly, he did not use Algheran Speech.

Wolf-Twin dropped pretense. He looked directly at the Teep
and was not surprised to see him nod. No again. None of the
Algheran mercenaries was willing to change sides.

"You are not going to be here," he snapped at the officers. "Mlart will not save your butts. You are prisoners of
war and you are going to a prisoner-of-war camp in Fohima
Loprit and you are going to walk there on your own two feet
and you will rot there for the rest of this war unless Mlart
tra'Nornst is so desperate or so dumb that he decides to exchange for you and because you got beat at eight-to-one odds
there is no chance in a Gawargian Hell that he will ever have
any of you back in the Swordtroop ever again, even for digging latrines, and frankly I'm just as pleased to know none of
you fuckups are ever going to give orders to good Lopritian
soldiers! *Is that clear?*"

It was not his first set of prisoners this day.

"Okay, mister," the guard said. "You water that tree." The
barrel of his musket waggled. Uneasily, Lerlt edged past wilted
grass and soggy leaves till he faced a contorted tree trunk, then
unlaced his pants and tried to forget the gun aimed at his back.

Time passed.

"Hurry up, mister," the guard said.

Behind him on the hillsides were five thousand watching
men.

Lerlt jerked convulsively but unproductively. Nothing happened. Nothing. He stared desperately at the urine-blackened tree and prayed for deliverance.

"Get to it, mister. People are waiting on you."

Please! "I'm trying," he said sadly. "Really. Could you— could you—" He sniffed. "Can you point the gun away?"

"No way," the guard answered. "I'm going to shoot you, mister. I put a hole in your back which comes out where your pecker is and then you'll piss. Anyone asks, I'll say you started to run and—"

Lerlt gasped with fear and his bladder suddenly released, almost causing him fatal embarrassment. Red-faced, he stood before the tree trunk, hosing it from side to side with faked nonchalance, listening to drops splatter upon the ground, while the guard laughed until he wheezed.

"It always works," the guard said at the end, still cackling while Lerlt pulled his pants shut and wished the Lopritian dead—dying—wanting to die—screaming for death . . .

The guard jerked his musket toward the hillside. "Now get back to your place."

Where was that? A portion of the hillside was covered with sitting men, arranged in a square. When Lerlt had left his position, he had expected to return to it without difficulty, but he had not counted the lines of men he had passed, and now it was obvious that the captives were not as evenly arrayed as he had thought. He could not find the space he had left and felt additional dismay at this new loss.

"Somewhere up there," the guard said, reading his hesitation. "Get moving, mister, so the next man can come down. Don't piss your buddies off."

Which frightened Lerlt again, knowing the threat in the words. At midday, when food had been distributed to the prisoners, there had been fights, and the Lopritians had watched but not interfered until the violence ended. A man had been carried out then, dead it was said. No one had been punished.

A company of guardsmen and a squadron of cavalry surrounded the captured Algherans, but they would not protect him.

Even in battles, he had never felt so alone, so defenseless.

Then, in the third rank, he saw a tall blond man with broad shoulders and a disdainful expression.

Herrilmin ha'Hujsuon? Here? Could it be?

No. That was too much to hope for. Impossible.

But if it was . . .

Lerlt began to hope again.

When he woke, it was late afternoon. A handful of puffy white clouds sat on the horizon. Wagons were crossing over the river on the road high above—he could hear the creaking carriages and the hoofbeats on the dark pavement. A work gang, deployed in a slanting line along the nearby hillside, passed wrapped parcels from man to man. Sergeants shouted.

Tim Harper rose onto an elbow, then turned and winced. The grave diggers, with unsentimental efficiency, had gathered bodies beneath an overhanging bluff, then covered them by starting a small landslide. Hands and feet still protruded in places; as he watched, one determined man pushed down an outstretched arm, then piled rocks over it to hold it. Stones clinked against stones; dirt slithered through the interstices; dust rose.

I should have supervised this, he thought. *I was in charge.*

It was an unemotional thought, as if the scene he watched were behind a glass which kept meaning and involvement at bay. Dutifully, however, completing a ritual, he added, *I'd have seen that the bodies got—*

Reason penetrated. *Got what, chum? What kind of "proper burial" could you give them? Six feet of earth, with metal caskets, Christian chaplains? Rifle volleys and folded flags? How about medevac helicopters for the wounded and six weeks in Thailand for R and R? How about veteran's pensions and a GI Bill, too? Be serious, fellow!*

It's a damn poor world. They're as nice as they can afford to be and I should accept what they accept.

The thoughts did not make the sight more pleasant. Warily, fearing additional surprise, he let his gaze move past the gravediggers, then turned to the other elbow to see the rest.

The battlefield appeared smaller under daylight. The fallen cook tent was visible from where he lay. He recognized individual trees and shrubs which he had passed during the fighting. Things which had seemed far apart last night were now only dozens of yards from each other.

There were fewer people.

Cherrid's threatened retreat. His jaw tightened reflexively, but it was a mechanical gesture. He was too numbed to feel anger, too detached. He was only an observer now.

Pebbles moved. A footstep sounded behind him and he recognized it without turning. He waited for the too shrill voice.

"Good afternoon, sir."

"Good afternoon, Quillyn. What's happening?"

"I've been burying," his orderly said. "Bodies."

"Good," Harper said.

Seconds passed. Quillyn coughed. "Ironwearer ris Clendannan wondered if you would return with him. He's going back to the brigade shortly, in a wagon, and the rest of us later."

Harper shrugged minutely. "What was the butcher's bill, Quillyn?"

"Sir?"

He stopped and swallowed, then stared earnestly at Harper. "Sir, are you hungry? There's still some time, if I fix you a meal? And everything will seem better."

Harper sighed.

"I'm not really hungry, Quillyn."

I screwed up, he admitted to himself. *I didn't have to do it this way. Killing Mlart was the only essential thing and I could have done that myself, by hiding in Midpassage and shooting him as he rode through town. I could have used Kylene to identify him and killed him and bailed out, back to the Project, and that would have been it. I didn't have to get fancy.*

I thought I could be a general, and I wasn't good enough.

I wasn't good enough, as a general or a person.
I killed men for nothing.

In the end, the young Ironwearer rode back to the brigade
with Cherrid ris Clendannan in one of the Algheran supply
wagons. Cherrid took the reins; his silver mare and lan Haarper's bay were hitched to the rear.

Riding with them were twenty man-weights of gunpowder in
small barrels. It was a safe load in Cherrid's estimation, especially when so firmly lashed in place, but the drivers of the
vehicles before them and after left more space for him quickly,
so there seemed to be two groups of wagons on the road with
one unwanted interloper between. Privately, he was amused.

Timmithial was silent and motionless, staring ahead with his
hands between his knees, as if traveling to his execution, and
Cherrid found nothing to say until they had passed the spot
where the artillery had been placed the previous night.

Some ruts and fallen branches alongside the road, some rope
burns on the trees . . . A work detail was already salvaging the
discarded casings. In a decade nothing would be left to remind
an unobservant traveler of the battle.

"Beautiful country," he said then, for want of more sensible
things, wanting lan Haarper to understand he was not dis-
graced.

"Fair, for woods," the boy said slowly. "I've been through
here in the past, prospecting. Nothing valuable unless you like
to look at trees."

Cherrid smiled. "I grew up by the marshes, Timmial, on
land no one should have ever farmed. Until I left home, I never
saw trees, nor anything but gray flat fields smelling of kelp and
seawater and which reached for as far as gulls could view. The
little children strained stones out of the mud with their fingers;
the bigger ones carried endless buckets of water to wash out the
salt; adults built dikes and dredged canals . . .

"I remember being on patrol once. With Grahan, in some
lost-as-Cimon section in the west of the Mother Continent.

Green as grass—I doubt I was as old as my horse then. It had been raining and Grahan and I came through some small town where there were children, and three of them were out in the streets playing. They were digging channels for the rainwater to run in and making little dams out of mud and floating wood chips like boats and pushing them with their fingers. All the sorts of things we had done as children but in miniature. And they were having fun! That was so strange that I just wanted to stay there and watch them. Completely forgot I was supposed to be looking for the enemy. Grahan had to bully me into moving on—he's always been the practical one of us.

"Anyhow, it is very pleasant to see ground no one is trying to improve."

"Where was your homeland?" the boy asked politely.

"An island, the other side of the world. You will not have heard of it. It was not special."

"Do you miss it?"

"Not enough to go back." Cherrid flicked a rein lightly. "Grahan and I came here as mercenaries, three centuries ago, before the Kingdom was formed. There was a need for fighters then—and sometimes a need for men who could negotiate instead of fight. We have done well here." *Poor Grahan*. "He might go back someday."

"So you were founding fathers," Ian Haarper commented. "Not many people get to claim that."

"Grahan more than I," Cherrid said candidly. "I was an ordinary soldier a long while before I learned to be anything better. Grahan . . . He saw that just fighting people was not enough long before I did. Practical, like I said. I used to think he had Teep blood."

"Does he?" Ian Haarper asked, looking straight ahead.

Cherrid waved a hand to dismiss the idea. "No no. He's a normal man. Nothing extraordinary. Better than average as a soldier . . . For as far as he went." *Poor Grahan*.

"He was never good on independent duty, for some reason.'' Cherrid sighed, feeling he had said enough, but to assuage lan Haarper's curiosity he added, ''It was politics that hurt his career.''

''Molminda's coup,'' the boy guessed and he felt annoyance.

''Queen Molminda, if you will, please. She's your sovereign while you serve her, Timmial, and she has done nothing to merit your disrespect.''

''Sorry,'' the boy said, and Cherrid remembered he was a Vandeign dependent and wondered what sort of nonsensical tales Merryn ris Vandeign had told him.

''The Andervylls got us out of a very bad situation,'' he said gruffly. ''The previous King was—permitted—a great deal of corruption, and there was need for him to go. It was before your time, Timmial, so take my word for it. Anyhow, that is not what made Grahan choose retirement.''

''Okay.''

It was a very paltry concession, one which made Cherrid grit his teeth, so he continued, ''It was principle, in a way. Grahan felt the Kingdom was too 'ordinary,' for want of a better word. He began to wonder if independence really mattered to the common people, and eventually decided it did not. And from that—well, I guess that was Grahan's business.''

''If independence doesn't matter, why defend it?'' the boy mused. ''I can sort of understand that, although it's an awful long-range view. People ought to be spared disruption and violence in their lives. It's worthwhile defending them against that—I suppose you told him that.''

''Yes. He said change was worthwhile, too.'' Cherrid frowned.

''A *liberal*!'' Lan Haarper chuckled. ''I thought the breed was extinct. I'd like to talk to him sometime.''

''Well,'' Cherrid said again. Uncomfortably, he saw he was troubled by the notion of Grahan and lan Haarper exchanging ideas while the boy was in his present mood. Too often he had watched men push chance thoughts through their minds for centuries, following ideas down winding channels into uncharted wild lands from which they never returned with complete sanity.

"Grahan is with the brigade," he pointed out. "He has not abandoned any responsibilities. He just is not ambitious now."

"Sure." Lan Haarper nodded curtly.

"Move!" someone whispered behind him. "Trade places."

Lerlt hesitated, wondering if the voice was aimed at him, but the words were not repeated. He heard slithering at his side. When he turned, a newcomer was seated at his right; the man who had been there was farther away.

Brown hair, smooth, center-parted. A man of medium height, medium build, an expectant look. *Another Agent. Of course.*

He looked familiar. *Jhern? Jerd?* Lerlt struggled for a name, to express his relief properly.

"Don't shout," the man said sharply and his name came suddenly to Lerlt.

Gherst. Faltin Gheherist ha'Hujsuon. Ha'Minursil originally, but he had married into Hujsuon. The woman was a third cousin, on his mother's side, and related to . . .

She was still at the Present, in the lost Alghera.

A Septling. That mattered more than a precise genealogy.

The newcomer looked around him carefully. "You're Lerlt? Where's your partner? Couldn't you stay together?"

"He's dead." Lerlt suddenly felt miserable again. "It happened during the fighting. A cannon shot hit him. It blew his head apart!"

"Tough. So the Lopritians got the body? Was there anything on it to give away what he was? Did they get anything off you?"

"No. No. I don't think so. We were careful." Lerlt choked back tears. "I thought I was all alone."

"You're not. There are two others, and maybe more. My partner is here, and Herrilmin. You know we got Herrilmin?"

Herrilmin ha'Hujsuon! Here! It was true! Lerlt suddenly felt his fears ebb. "I thought I saw him, but I didn't think Nicole's cloak was that big. I thought I was just guessing."

"Why didn't you go look?" the other asked. "He saw you."

Because the Lopritians had told the captives not to move, Lerlt thought grumpily. He hadn't figured out a way to move across the hillside without being noticed, and he was being blamed unfairly for his caution. "I thought I was wrong," he said. "I thought he was going to go into one of the northern divisions. That's what he said when we were still in the Station and I never saw him all the time I was here."

"Well, he changed his mind or something. He's here now."

"Thank the Lady," Lerlt said with feeling.

Then reason conquered other emotions. Herrilmin was both strong and rash. He was only one man and the Algheran Agents were surrounded by thousands of captors. "What's he going to do?" he whispered.

Gherst ha'Hujsuon leaned closer. "Get us out of here."

Lerlt thought his heart had stopped. "How?"

"Never mind," the brown-haired man said, and Lerlt understood he did not know what Herrilmin planned, but was simply willing to trust the big man.

He had the same confidence. Herrilmin was close to the Sept Master himself. He could perform miracles, if any Hujsuon could.

"What do I have to do?" he whispered.

"Move over where he is," he was told. Gherst pointed with his chin, then indicated the sentries with a head shake. "Over in that corner. Take your time, so *they* won't suspect anything. But before nightfall."

"All right." Resolution flooded Lerlt.

"You're not an officer," the other said suddenly, and Lerlt saw captain's insignia on his shoulder. "The rest of us are officers."

Was there disdain in his voice? Lerlt thought he heard it. *I would have been,* he told himself. *There wasn't time. Hals and I didn't have chances to distinguish ourselves, that was all.*

We didn't tell lies about our qualifications.

"We didn't want to draw any attention," he said carefully. "Hals thought privates had more freedom to move around, and since I was with him . . ."

"Well, it is a problem," Gherst said in a low voice. "We've been told they're going to separate the officers from the rest of the men tomorrow and send us north by ourselves. I don't know how we'll keep you with us. Can you get back to the Project by yourself?"

"No!" Lerlt stared at him with open dismay. "My time machine is back in F'a Alghera. I can't get to it till the end of the war."

"Same here," the other admitted. "Do you have your locator?"

"Not with me." Lerlt nodded unhappily. The tiny radio receiver for detecting the presence of time machines was fragile, and he had feared that he would misplace it during the campaign. He had buried it for safekeeping in the park by the river before leaving F'a Alghera. "I didn't want to risk losing it. It's in Alghera, too. I didn't think—"

He waved an arm to encompass the unfair world. "Who would have expected any of this?"

"No one." The brown-haired Agent bit his lip. "Herrilmin says he's got some ideas about what happened. Anyhow, he kept his locator. He says he knows of a time machine north of here. If we can get to it. But I don't know about you. If—"

A time machine in the middle of Loprit? Why? Lerlt blinked, thinking of the strangeness of that, but peril made the mystery unimportant. He did not want to be left behind.

"Let Herrilmin decide," he said quickly. "He can figure out a way for us to stay together."

"Well," Gherst said slowly, and Lerlt realized how fearful he was of making decisions.

It was as if he had been given a key. "Let's leave it up to

Herrilmin,'' he said, barely concealing his contempt. "We can
do what he decides.''

You would have left me rot, he thought, watching the other
Agent scuttle away after agreeing hastily. *Whether I'm your
Septling or not, because I wasn't pretending to be an officer.
I'll piss in your face for that.*

He was going to piss in everyone's face.

Tim Harper, after an inconsequential interview with the
Hand of the Queen, wandered aimlessly about the camp.

He spoke to no one. Cherrid ris Clendannan had no need of
him and his own duties to perform. The handful of acquaintances he could claim within the brigade were likewise busy.

In any event, he did not feel like talking to anyone. When
the leading companies from the Steadfast-to-Victory regiment
appeared, after marching from Killguide Rill, and began to
encamp on the hillside, he stayed away from them and confined
his peregrinations within a boundary of strangers.

Teamsters patching harnesses, an elderly woman washing
shirts in a bucket, soldiers joking as they inspected their muskets, a solitary officer in the distance with surveying tools,
women sitting side by side on a log chatting to themselves as
they waited to be noticed by amorous customers, a limping
man with plates in both hands serving artillery officers, a
youngster with a farmboy's face atop his blue uniform putting
an arm on a horse's neck in a small corral: strangers all.

People he had fought for, he realized, and with, and in the
end they were still strangers, as untouched by his actions as
they were now by his watching. Were he to die that instant, he
would be no more to them than an inconvenience for gravediggers. If he vanished into air, he would be forgotten within
days.

By nighttime, Harper's mind had led him into a bog of
"honest thought" which he did not understand was close to
depression.

Alghera had taken him in, he recalled. The Warder of the

Realm himself had presided when the Dicovys Sept adopted him. He had Algheran friends. He was on first-name terms with several Sept Masters, and the Algheran had trusted him as an Agent. He had loved an Algheran girl.

Sometimes he had thought she would eventually love him. Friends. Family.

As sentries changed at the start of the fifth watch, Harper was still awake. Unclothed, in a pair of clammy blankets, he blindly swept bits of grass from beneath his body, thinking about that. Those were very real ties, to be weighed carefully against his afternoon realizations.

The end of the war. He grunted. The end of the war—the real war—was not close.

He'd done nothing to make it closer.

Ris Clendannan was right, he understood now. He had caused men to be butchered for no good reason. He had fought his battle very poorly.

His artillery fire had been too concentrated. He should have plastered the entire Algheran encampment.

He had not scouted well. He had not known that the Algherans had left their guns unattended at night. That had been an undeserved piece of luck.

He had not made use of his cavalry detachment. He had been wrong to keep a company in reserve when every man was needed on the firing line.

He had not coordinated the attack of his two battalions. It had worked out all right, but Dalsyn Ian Plenytk deserved the credit for that.

He had not had the wit to seize the bridge over the ravine—Cherrid had seen its importance in two minutes and he had not in weeks of thought.

Five sins for five fingers. He ticked them off, repeating them, then made a fist as if to clench the largest sin of all.

Pride. He had wanted to win his battle alone. He'd asked men to do too much, without anticipating the consequences. He could have waited another day so the full brigade met the Algherans. He could have stung the Algherans just enough to advance without preparation and meet the brigade. He could have tried to wheedle another battalion from the Hand, or at least more cavalry or more artillery. He could have waited till morning for reinforcements.

He had never seriously considered those possibilities.

Blindness. No wonder ris Clendannan had relieved him.

I tried to please too many people.

That was an even bigger sin, the error not even Cherrid ris Clendannan could see or punish. It had been enough to kill Mlart tra'Nornst. That would reestablish history in proper channels.

An assassin's bullet. Nothing else had been necessary.

But the Algherans of the Project wanted their legendary Warder to remain alive, even as they craved the results of his death. Harper had had enough respect for the man's accomplishments to share their feeling, and he had wanted to spare Kylene from involvement in political murder.

Stupidly, it seemed now, he had abandoned his real task for an invented one, hoping military defeat for the Algherans of this era would have the same effect as killing their leader. Ten thousand deaths instead of one . . .

The oldest human psychological trap, and he, the time traveler who knew so much, had fallen into it as thoroughly as any French farmboy who enlisted in Napoleon's legions for *la gloire* and as blindly as any English peasant who ever drank to a recruiter's health and woke with the Queen's shilling in his palm. The glamour of war—the honor of war!

What a monstrous fool he had been! To see no other solution to his difficulties. To seek no other solution!

Cut and run, he told himself bleakly. Leave the army, return to Midpassage, assassinate Mlart as he had originally planned, return to the Project.

Cut and run. Do what was necessary. Nothing else was honorable.

Never forget what he had done.

Never forgive.

Chapter 4

Lerlt felt his heart beat, and heard his ears ring.

"Get that captain over here," Herrilmin ha'Hujsuon whispered hoarsely; and Fesch ha'Hujsuon crept away on hands and knees. Fesch was large and clumsy-seeming, and Lerlt held his breath, expecting the younger Agent to wander into some sleeping man at any moment and ruin Herrilmin's plans. Beside him, Gherst ha'Hujsuon breathed raggedly. To Lerlt, the sound was as loud as wind gusts in a storm; it seemed impossible that the Lopritian sentries watching the captured men would not come to investigate.

Only reason told him that six thousand men make enough noise during a night, even when most are sleeping, that a few dozen sentries cannot pay attention to every minor disturbance. Fesch was perfectly safe; Herrilmin's plan would work if everyone performed his part.

"Move over." Herrilmin's body was only a silhouette in the darkness, his full size concealed by the night, but his gestures were emphatic. The smaller men obeyed, following instructions the blond man had given them in the afternoon, then waited, keeping silent while Herrilmin irritably drummed his fingertips loudly on his thigh.

Fesch returned eventually. The Algheran he brought with him sat down in the middle of the time travelers, then scooted backward at Herrilmin's touch till he could talk confidentially. Seated beside the big Agent, he seemed a child by a man.

"Are we ready to go, Major?" To Lerlt, even as a whisper, the Algheran's voice was reedy and repellent. He realized he hated the man. That he and the officer were similar in build and appearance did nothing to change the feeling. He waited with something like glee.

"Not yet," Herrilmin said, pointing with an arm over the captain's shoulder. His voice was vibrant and full of confidence. Lerlt realized once more how much he admired the blond man. "We need to wait for those sentries to move a bit further. And I wanted you to see—heaven!"

With the last word, his arm bent. He seized the captain's chin with one hand, a shoulder with the other, and pulled in opposite directions.

Lerlt heard a subdued pop which he knew he would remember all his life as he fell on the dead man's legs. They were still moving; he could sense blood flowing in them even as the Algheran's heart beat for the last time.

"Get his pants off," Herrilmin whispered, his voice gruff and fast. "Yank 'em down."

Suddenly everyone was moving. Gherst tugged ineffectually at the dead man's boots, while Lerlt unbuttoned the sides of his trousers and Fesch lifted up the bottom of his tunic. Herrilmin was still holding the body erect; his hands had moved to cover the corpse's now silent mouth.

"Leave the loincloth," Herrilmin muttered, and Lerlt sensed from the tone he was as tense as the others. The knowledge sharpened his own mind.

He pulled the dead man's pants down to his knees. "You finish getting them off," he whispered to Gherst then, and moved away, so he could remove his own clothing.

Hesitantly, the brown-haired Agent moved up from the boots and worked trousers down the body's legs. Lerlt smelled urine and feces and knew the captain's sphincters had released. Gherst was very close to those stinks, he thought, feeling satisfaction. He hoped the other Agent would get the mess on himself after removing the clean trousers.

"Here." Fesch held out a tunic and took Lerlt's in return. His voice was unemotional. Lerlt wondered what he felt.

For a second, he waited, wearing only his loincloth and boots, feeling air touch his bare skin, almost enjoying the cold dirt and grass under his buttocks. He wanted to shout at the world. He was an undressed man on the verge of great deeds; the Algheran captain, with no more clothing now, was a thing and nude. Smiling, he kicked at the dead thing.

"No bruises!" Herrilmin's fingers stung his cheek.

Lerlt snapped his head back without resentment, knowing the slap was justified, sensing that in the midst of death and despair, it was proper that he receive a small portion of pain. He pulled the tunic on quickly and began to button it.

When he was done, Gherst held out the dead man's trousers, mutely, like a trained body servant. Lerlt bent his head to hide his satisfaction.

Fesch was on his knees beside Herrilmin. Awkwardly, he tried to fit the dead captain's arms into the sleeves of Lerlt's discarded tunic.

The blond Agent stopped him. "We'll let Lerlt do it," he said, his voice low and hard. "This is for him, after all."

"He's too heavy for me," Lerlt whispered, knowing he did not want to touch the body. "I won't be able to move him back."

"Fix the clothes then," Herrilmin ordered and Lerlt heard annoyance. "Fesch and Gherst will take care of the rest."

"All right," Lerlt agreed, as the others looked at him. The task was menial, the cooling body as unpleasantly soft and clammy as he had imagined, but he bent to it, telling himself as he manipulated the flabby flesh he would soon be wealthy and important enough that he would not longer perform menial tasks. He hoped the others heard that message in his voice; he hoped they understood he was contemptuous of them; he hoped they realized he was vicious.

Part Two: Calculations

Chapter 5

"What are you thinking, Timmial?" ris Clendannan asked. "You seem so pensive, and yet things are going very well."

He was willing to be expansive in the morning. He had spent a quarter watch already signing some of the orders drafted during the last day and a half—Gertynne ris Vandeign had imposed on Terrault ris Andervyll to sign all the documents, leaving Cherrid to decide which ones to implement—and issuing additional commands to his staff. In the afternoon there would be more paperwork to deal with and more discussions with the Hand of the Queen, but for the moment his office duties were done and he was free to be outside.

It was a lovely clear day, with just a touch of frost in the air, and his scouts had not reported any reaction from Mlart tra'Nornst's remaining two divisions. Breezes, familiarity with the local climate, and several "reliable general impressions" from Rahm Wolf-Twin's Teep suggested that stormy weather might be expected tomorrow, and that was fine also. Cherrid expected the Algherans to be troubled by bad weather more than his force, and the rain would be good for next year's crops.

Thunder and clouds were evident enough on the far side of the ridge, where a battalion of Her Majesty's Own Puissant Guards Regiment drilled with the captured Algheran cannons. He smiled as he listened to some of the juicier oaths shouted by the professional artillerymen attempting to train his infantry, knowing that despairing men do not swear loudly.

Prevailing winds blew the gunsmoke in the direction of the prisoners, who, Cherrid hoped, would be overawed by the weaponry aimed in their direction. None of the Algheran troops were telepaths, he had been told, so the prisoners would not realize the Strength-through-Loyalty Brigade's regular artillery was preparing to retreat to the north in the next quarter watch.

The Lopritian wounded who seemed able to survive the trip had been sent north in the afternoon of the previous day; some of the camp followers had gone with them. Much of the brigade's food stocks had gone with them as well, but Cherrid felt it was a price worth paying to remove encumbrances.

The wounded, Algheran and Lopritian, who could not be moved Cherrid had left at Killguide Pass, to be tended by a physician and volunteers from the teamsters. There were not many; the arithmetic of battle dictated that half of those with severe wounds would die soon from their injuries. Accepting those odds, Cherrid had had any Lopritian with a chance for survival taken north. Those who would die would be free men to the end.

The physician carried a letter to be delivered to the Algheran general offering a temporary halt in hostilities and an exchange of prisoners. It was a pro forma gesture, made because honor demanded it. Cherrid was too much of a realist to think Mlart tra'Nornst would accept it. The Algheran knew his Swordtroop divisions outnumbered the Lopritians; he would understand intuitively that handling the prisoners was beyond the brigade's capability.

Logistics destroyed armies as well as any battle.

Other camp followers tended to the Algheran wounded who could pay them and buried those who had died during the night. The survivors were being fed their own rations, but the food was not cooked for them. Cherrid did not have enough soldiers to use on those tasks if he had wanted to, and the thought had not occurred to him. In fact, the captives were being treated more gently than was normal in this era. It kept them from turning restive, and he had reasons to want them lulled by kindness.

The captured officers who had not yielded to Wolf-Twin's blandishments—two of them, both captains, had finally agreed to change allegiance, and Cherrid, unimpressed by their qual-ifications, was still trying to fob them off on ris Daimgewln—had gone at dawn with a heavy escort.

Ris Andervyll, to Cherrid's amusement, had risen to see the captives off and had even made a short speech, implying their stay in Molminda's capital would soon make them her friends, confidants, and supporters.

"Good riddance" had been Wolf-Twin's only comment as the officers marched off. Cherrid had not asked whether that applied to the captives or to their guards: a company from ris Daimgewln's half-mutinous Defiance-to-Insurrection Regi-ment. The squat Ironwearer's uniform had been more rumpled than ever before in Cherrid's memory, but the man himself had seemed in good spirits, arguing only when he was told to use a labor force drawn from ris Daimgewln's men rather than from the prisoners.

He was asking a lot from Her Majesty's Artful-or-Industrious Requisitionary Corps and the young major, Cher-rid reflected. It was inescapable, yet Wolf-Twin had not reached his first century in age. Life had not fully sea-soned the quartermaster, and he would have to be protected from breaking under strain during the remainder of the cam-paign.

It was convenient that Wolf-Twin had a Teep officer under him to probe Cherrid's mind to clarify ambiguities and situa-

tions for which orders had not been given. Not that either of the
Ironwearers or the Teep would admit that such was happening,
but Cherrid was sure it would. Self-preservation was certain to
make a superb subordinate out of the Teep.

Almost wistfully, he wished it were possible to have a Teep
attached to each major unit of his force.

More sensibly, he wondered if Wolf-Twin's Teep could be
induced to stay with the army after the war ended. What had
the man been before the campaign? A money broker, wasn't
it? An unstable occupation, an unsavory one in some eyes,
but no doubt a profitable one for a patient man who could
read minds. A promotion, a minor peerage . . . No. There
were very real limits to the rewards that could be offered to
Teeps, and besides, the man had not demonstrated inborn
military ability.

Subordinates could be found at any time. Leaders were rarer
and deserved both the honors and more careful handling.

"What are you thinking, Timmial?" he asked again.

"Nothing," Ian Haarper muttered. Numbly, barely moving
his head, he stared at the devastation made of the landscape by
the waiting brigade. Latrines, rifle pits, cook sites, litter, horse
droppings, rows of stacked wooden boxes and barrels under
guard, scraps of color on the hillsides from flowers not yet
trampled by soldiers or camp followers in the distance . . .
Cherrid wondered what else the boy was seeing.

Late last night, he had wakened on his couch with a
cramped leg. To stretch the muscles, he had walked to the
window of the command wagon, and there he had watched as
Timmial sat by a fire, staring into its depths with the same
painful intensity.

The boy had been nude. As the flames flickered beside him,
Cherrid had seen crimson lines and spots gleaming across his
reddened back. Old scars. It had seemed impossible that a
living man could survive so many wounds.

A man so very young. And so very strange.

As he retreated to the couch, Cherrid had realized he would
not share the man's memories, even with his own youth re-

turned as a reward. What distractions saved Timmial from his thoughts?

In the morning, he reflected that several of the women following the brigade were attractive. Crude and avaricious, as was also be to be expected, but he had known titled aristocrats with the same flaws. Cherrid had been celibate since his wife's death, and he had watched these ladies with an experienced but detached eye. He would not have taken it amiss today if an unmarried lan Haarper retired to a darkened tent with a woman for a spot of active companionship.

However, the youngster was married and an Ironwearer. His marital fidelity could be taken for granted. Cherrid would have to find some other method to restore his spirits.

Something had to be done shortly. Fighting lay ahead, and Cherrid wanted the big redhead back with his regiment when it happened, but he would not give men who had fought so well a disheartened commander.

Temporarily, he had given the Steadfast-to-Victory to young Derrauld ris Fryddich, to preserve equality between lan Haarper's two battalion commanders, but that was a stop-gap solution; ris Fryddich had not admitted it yet, but the blond man was beyond his capabilities with more than a company. Besides, Cherrid had a vague memory of some dispute between the young noble and lan Haarper in the recent past; the Midpassagers had no doubt told the story to the North Valley men by now, and it would not do to suggest favoritism to them.

"He-et up!" a driver at his left called out, and flicked a rein so it slapped against a horse's rump. It was a mechanical gesture, without emotion; the heavily loaded wagon moved no faster. Still, the plunder was moving north, away from Mlart, and that gave Cherrid satisfaction.

"He should make about ten thousand man-heights today," Cherrid said comfortably, turning beside lan Haarper to rest an arm on the boxes behind them. "More for the next day, but I want the prisoners to stay well ahead of us."

Lan Haarper stared at the wagons before them on the road

and said nothing. He leaned forward and scratched at his shin.

"What do you think, Timmial?"

"Nothing." The redhead straightened up. His eyes turned
to the spot where the shrunken remnant of his regiment was
camped and swiftly moved away. "Do what you want, Ironwearer."

"Hmmm." The older man looked the same way, noticing
Merryn ris Vandeign moving among the men, and frowned.
Officially, the militia regiment was Lord Vandeign's command
and Ian Haarper—now ris Fryddich—only functioned as an
aide, but the elderly noble was a pacifist without the military
skills of his brother and possibly pro-Algheran as well. Until
now, he had remained apart from his men except at ceremonial
occasions, and Cherrid had assumed that was his natural incli-
nation.

But the militia had just shown its fighting ability, and the
Vandeigns were inveterate intriguers. Of course, Merryn might
simply be acting out his self-appointed role as a priest of the
Cimon and Nicole cult, but that might be considered meddling
as well. Certainly, the Hand of the Queen would insist on
restoring the distance between the Midpassage noble and his
men, and Cherrid agreed completely.

Lan Haarper regarded Merryn ris Vandeign as a friend,
Cherrid knew. He probably thought he owed his appointment
as de facto commander of the regiment to the man, but it had
really been Lord Vandeign's unwillingness to use him that
had caused the Hand to give Timmial his position. War and
politics were often intertwined that way, Cherrid had
noticed—Grahan had once written a small uncirculated
monograph insisting that they should be—and the fact no
longer shocked him, but he thought it just as well to leave
young Ironwearers with their illusions.

Still, this was one more reason to put Ian Haarper back in his
place.

"Have you finished sulking?" He pretended it was an idle
question.

"*I'm not* sulking." For a second, Ian Haarper clenched his

jaw manfully. Then the tension left his face, and he was again a resentful, troubled boy.

Cherrid sighed. "What do you call what you are doing?"

"Nothing. Not sulking." Lan Haarper shook his head abruptly. Cherrid had the impression he had reached a conclusion of some sort. One which troubled more than it reassured.

"Lord Clendannan, I'm sorry. I wanted to do something valuable. Things didn't turn out as I expected, and I still have that thing to do. So I'm thinking about that."

Really? Cherrid wondered. "Do you want your command back?"

The redhead hesitated. "Maybe it's just as well that you relieved me. I did what I could there, and now I have to try something else. I can leave the brigade with a clear conscience when we get back to Midpassage, can't I?"

Cherrid felt dismay. "I do not want you to leave, Timmial. The brigade needs you. I need you. Your men need you."

"I—" Lan Haarper tossed his head again. "I've got other things to do, Cherrid. The men don't need me."

"Other things?" Cherrid raise an eyebrow. "More important than remaining with us? You can have your command back."

"More important than that." Lan Haarper's face was frozen.

"Don't you want to be back with your men?"

The young man sighed, and emotions flowed over his face too quickly for the elderly Ironwearer to read. "I do, Cherrid," he said. "In some ways, I enjoyed . . . being with them . . . more than anything else I ever did."

"Leading them," Cherrid said quietly.

"Leading them," Timmial said, his face showing he regretted using the words but could not deny them. "I always knew what I wanted them to do, and how it should be done, and they always came through for me, as if it were the most natural thing in the world. And it was wonderful."

He swallowed. "Even in the fighting, when I didn't know

how it would end . . . to have men coming to me for orders and knowing what to tell them and having them do what I ordered . . . I was scared and I was worried and it still felt—I felt like that was what I made for, Cherrid! As if that were the only thing in my life I'd ever really been good at—the only thing I ever did that used every strength and ability I had and none of my weaknesses. And it was something that mattered, that I wanted to be good at, that I'd never ever dreamed I really would do well . . . I could have died there and I would still have been—happy.''

He whispered the final words. ''Men shouldn't feel that way, Cherrid.''

''Some men do,'' Cherrid said. ''They are hard to find and Loprit needs every one it can get. All of your strengths, you said, Timmial, and none of your weaknesses. How else should it be? Should men die for commanders who give them anything else? Timmial, I promise you—what you felt during your battle, you can feel again, in your next battle and your next and your next, whether you command a regiment or a brigade or, if your ability takes you so high, to all the armies of the Kingdom.''

Lan Haarper looked at him sickly. ''Cherrid—it's not good to enjoy battle. Men shouldn't have leaders who like killing.''

''Did you like killing, Timmial? Or did you just accept it?''

''I—I accepted it. It's something I had to do as a soldier and it never bothered me. But I was just one man then, killing one man at a time. It's something else with a unit, when you're thinking 'We'll kill half the men in their right flank company, and hit their hinge as they pull back' or 'Second company has thirty effectives left; let me find a spot where they'll take only ten more casualties.' That didn't bother me, either. Until it was over.''

Until you saw that hospital area, Cherrid thought grimly. *I should have thought to keep you away from there.*

But how could I guess you would seek it out?

He kept his features steady. "Soldiers have to be led by men who accept killing. That is a very different thing from liking to kill, Timmial. Men who like killing for its own sake or accept killing without reason make very poor generals—and none of them become Ironwearers."

"I don't feel like much of an Ironwearer," the boy said slowly. "I did stupid things and you were right to criticize me. I'm thinking, maybe I should . . . hang it up? Quit."

"Don't rush into that." Cherrid spoke just as slowly and emphatically. "When you wear those swords on your collar, let the Teeps judge you. Do not do it yourself."

"The Teeps . . ." Lan Haarper's face turned sour, then relaxed. "All right. The Teeps."

So he had made another decision. Cherrid's face softened as he saw his thoughts strike their target. "I suggest you think about that and do nothing rash for a while.

"In the meantime, I have work for an officer to do. We have to contend with all those prisoners. It's your fault that they are here and you ought to sweat some with the rest of us. It is too late to send you out with the deer-hunting parties, and it is below an Ironwearer's dignity to ask the troops about their feet—besides, Wolf-Twin's Teep is already doing that. Can I assign you to fix the soup?"

"Soup?" Lan Haarper's eyebrows raised.

"Soup," Cherrid said firmly, and when he had explained, the young Ironwearer laughed for the first time in days.

"What will they do with the other prisoners?" Lerlt wondered aloud, and Herrilmin ha'Hujsuon only grunted, as if he guessed the question was simply intended to pass time or refused to consider himself one with his Septlings.

He did look different from his Septlings, or from anyone else, Lerlt admitted. Twenty days of marching and fighting had worn every other soldier in the Dicovys division down to taut flesh and tauter nerves, but Herrilmin was still fresh-looking, fit and rested-looking, even slightly pudgy in a way no civilian would notice. His uniform was clean and unrumpled also—that was enough by itself to make him unique among the captives.

Marching would reduce Herrilmin to humanity again, Lerlt thought contentedly. The day had been cool at its beginning but it was too warm now for exertion to be comfortable. Dust clouds hung in the air about the men marching at the end of the column of prisoners. The roadbed was reserved for wagons, and the Algheran officers were being herded along its side, through grass and weeds where the marching was not easy. Now and then Lerlt stared upward at the road; he envied the riders in the wagons, who were above the dust and who sometimes felt breezes.

The prisoners were only a few hundred men, arranged in ranks of four, but they were guarded by a company of Lopritian infantry and a troop of cavalry. Together they cut a wide swath through the vegetation. Lerlt noticed that whenever he passed a bush it had already been stripped of any berries it might have and trampled upon by men displaying their ill temper. It seemed ironic that a handful of prisoners would inflict more destruction on the countryside than an entire brigade had a few days before.

On the other side of Lerlt a man coughed harshly. Lerlt fought the urge to do the same, then repeated what he asked, aiming it at the rank a man-height ahead, and after a moment Fesch ha'Hujsuon turned his head.

"Trade them, I suppose." His broad face showed surprise that Lerlt thought the matter worth raising. Lerlt noticed idly that the dust was already caking on his forehead. "We traded prisoners with the—you know who—almost up to the end of the real—the other war." Conspiratorially, he lowered his voice in places and supplemented the words with nervous gestures. Lerlt wondered if he thought the soldiers behind the column paid any attention to what the prisoners might say.

Fesch's green uniform was muddy and bore a lieutenant's stripes on the sleeves. The simulated rank was the lowest among the surviving Agents, and to Lerlt's amusement, Fesch even behaved like the junior officer. He wondered if that was a natural characteristic of the man or simply part of the role he had assumed. In either event, it was useful to have someone to run errands; he would have to invent some to keep Fesch employed.

"They aren't going to trade." Gherst had turned also to enter the conversation. *Married*, Lerlt remembered, looking at him. Part of the Sept in a way none of the other Agents were. It seemed unfair.

And the brown-haired Agent showed more intelligence than his partner; he was not sure yet if that meant Gherst thought faster or simply waited to speak until he had thought.

"It's simple arithmetic," Gherst said. "Say it takes one soldier to control two prisoners. Then Mlart needs one division to control South Loprit and his prisoners; he's lost one division; that leaves him with one division. That Lopritian brigade has a division of prisoners; tending them leaves no one left to fight. So Mlart has one division, and he's due reinforcements, and the Lopritians have nothing. Good odds, no?

"Now if he trades, one division for one division, he has . . . call it two and half divisions to use against one and a half divisions. The same superiority in numbers, but the odds are not as good. So he won't trade."

Without a trade of prisoners, the Agents would not be released. They would have to win their own freedom, which meant relying on the success of Herrilmin's plans. So far, the big man had disclosed none of his scheme, even when pressed. But Lerlt had noticed that when he thought he was unobserved, Herrilmin tapped meditatively on his thighs, a nervous gesture which was new to him. He worried that the blond Agent had made promises he did not know how to fulfill; on a deeper level, he worried that Herrilmin was prepared to sacrifice the other Agents to gain his own freedom, but he suppressed the doubts loyally.

"I don't understand," he grumbled. "If it's just that simple, the Lopritians must be able to do the same figuring. They wouldn't have attacked us, and they wouldn't have beaten us. I mean, did you look at them? They were sloppy—*poor*! They didn't all have uniforms even and their guns were all different types. The ones who captured me had muskets, for Cimon's sake, and everybody in the Swordtroop had rifles. It isn't just numbers, Gherst; you get your head under the Lady's dress like they did, you can laugh at numbers.''

Gherst frowned, either at the argument or the impiety, but said nothing.

''I don't know, but—'' Fesch began, then stopped as if he expected an objection. ''I know a bit of Lopritian. I overheard some of the things the soldiers were saying. Did any of you get the impression I did, that they didn't expect that battle? That was my impression.''

Surprisingly, Herrilmin spoke. ''They had better information than us. They knew how we were spread out, and that our artillery wasn't available. Maybe they even knew who our officers were—have you noticed none of the people here are Ironwearers? Plenty of Blankshields who signed on for easy work and weren't worth bull pucky during the fighting—those who weren't hiding somewhere—but every Ironwearer in the division was killed or hit too badly to keep fighting. Every one, and there must have been a dozen or more. Think about it.''

Fesch broke the silence first, after swallowing. ''Well, they're like that, ain't they? I mean, Lerlt talked about how the Lopritians weren't like the Swordtroop. I met some of the Ironwearers here—had to report to them, that is—and they weren't like the ones at home, either. I mean, I said something to one once—I didn't think his order made sense, and it was just about sentry duty, after all—and he stared at me like I was a bug and told me I was in the army to die and he was in the army to die and he would do the thinking about where and how dying made the most difference.''

He swallowed again. ''I've known Teeps who were more human.''

It was a long speech for Fesch. Lerlt raised his eyebrows in admiration.

Herrilmin, however, was scornful. "They weren't dumb enough to commit suicide, not all of them. You know who can shoot at a target at night and not miss, as long as it's living? You know who can tell the difference at night between an Ironwearer and an ordinary officer? You and I can't, but you know who can, and I'll give you a hint—it isn't the average Lopritian, either."

Lerlt swallowed involuntarily, as did Gherst and Fesch.

"They wouldn't use Teeps, would they?" Fesch asked almost in a whisper. "They know we don't. They're not—" He gestured minutely toward the infantry platoon marching on the heels of the prisoners. "I didn't see any of them marked. Nobody said anything about having Teep riflemen."

"Do you expect them to tell you?" Herrilmin snapped. " 'Oh, by the way, prisoners, that man there and that man and that man are Teeps we haven't branded so they'll look like Normals and be able to read your mind without you knowing it. Please try to escape now.' Or 'Oh, Warder Mlart, General, sir, we have three battalions of Teeps who can make mincemeat out of the Cimon-taken Forest Guard, and we know where you're going to invade, and they're going to be waiting for you, just in case you're curious, so please do invade South Loprit where you're hundreds of thousands of man-heights distant from any part of our country that is worth beans.' Get serious, Fesch. This isn't a game."

Gherst shook his head thoughtfully. "He's right, Fesch. They wouldn't think it's wrong. Most of these people are pagans. They've got the Plates, but they haven't accepted the full message yet."

"And that's not the only thing I can tell you," Herrilmin confided. "But no—you're not ready yet. Think about what Gherst just said, though. It'll give you some idea of what we're up against. And we can all thank the Lady we managed to hold on to our you-know-whats."

With the last words, he tapped his hair significantly, and

Lerlt held back a smile, amused to see that even the big bold blond man could be reduced to silly gestures rather than open Speech in the proper setting.

He wondered also how much real fact there was in Herrilmin's words and how much guesswork. Mlart tra'Nornst employed Teeps in the Swordtroop, Lerlt knew, most of them in noncombatant roles long held by tradition to be compatible with the Compacts, but some of them on his personal staff. The notion of Teeps with arms was an intimidating one, to be sure, but the telepaths were just too rare to waste as infantry.

Herrilmin ha'Hujsuon might be beyond his depth. Lerlt considered the thought for the first time and wondered what it might mean. He remembered that Gherst had turned away at the end of Herrilmin's words, his face carefully blank. Lerlt wondered if he shared the same kind of thoughts now. He wondered if Gherst and Herrilmin would come into conflict.

He wondered what other "surprises" Herrilmin had to relate.

"Looks like you are doing very well, Timmial," Cherrid said, inspecting the narrow pit Ian Haarper had ordered dug after lunch. "When do you think this will be ready?"

He had to raise his voice. Nearby, soldiers were dressing slaughtered deer with swords taken from the captured officers. The amateur butchers were more enthusiastic than skillful, and quite noisy. Sullen barefoot prisoners loaded barrels with meat and brine and placed them on wagons. Cherrid wondered how much of what they saw they understood.

"Hold on, Cherrid." Timmial raised a hand to his ear to show deafness, then went to the further lip of the trough to supervise the pouring of another barrel of dirty water. His own voice carried well. "Easy, men. Don't splash it. Right there. Good. Good. Good . . . Don't get any of it on you. Take the barrel back and brew up another batch and for the Lady's love, don't use that barrel for anything else, ever."

Meanwhile, Cherrid knelt on one knee and poked a finger in

the mixture. "This is very warm," he said when lan Haarper came back to him.

"Of course it's warm. You want—Cherrid, you Cimon-taken fool! You went and stuck your finger in, you idiot. What sort of example are you setting? Here!" Lan Haarper bustled about to produce a bucket of hot clean water and a sliver of soap. "No, you don't stick your finger in again, you scrub and I'll pour the water. If this gets contaminated, I'll have to boil another Cimon-taken bucket and I'm trying to get by on one. No, I don't have a towel, dry it in the air, that's the best thing anyhow. Did you get anything on your boots?"

"Just being curious," Cherrid said, shamefacedly. "It wasn't that risky, is it?"

"It ought to be. You specified killer soup, that's what you're getting." Lan Haarper pointed at his trough. "Canvas and clay lining to keep the water from running into the ground. We've dumped in bread crusts and spoiled meat and anything else the cooks are throwing out to make a broth, and the water is as close to body temperature as we can get it. I think we'll put in some hot rocks tonight to keep it brewing."

"It seems—" Cherrid looked for a word. "Elaborate? When the Garwagers did this to my outfit, they just took buckets with dirty foot coverings in them and made us wash our feet."

He shook his head reminiscently. "Talk about frightening! Our old-timers thought they would cut off our big toes, so we wouldn't be able to walk for a year. Which is what we would have done to them! Still, that would have been better than getting a spear up the butt, which is what I expected.

"Ah-hh! No one would have ever thought I would see as much of old age as I have, Timmial."

Lan Haarper smiled briefly. "And some of you got off from your foot bath without trouble, I'll bet. Well, you were dealing with barbarians and we know a lot more. You see, what you're looking for, what does the damage, is something like a very, very small plant that likes moisture. We want it to be happy and fruitful and to multiply and to subdue the Earth, so we feed it and keep it warm and wet and it obliges."

The big redhead nodded abruptly. "Another day and drinking this stuff might be enough to kill you. If you can give us that much time, we'll take your prisoners tomorrow morning."

"That would be fine. Mlart has not moved yet."

"Doesn't he know we're here?" Timmial raised an eyebrow.

"Oh, yes." Cherrid smiled wryly. "He has his own—very trusted sources, let's say, since as everyone knows all Algherans are much too devout to use Teeps in ignoble ways. But he will not have all the details and he has some problems of his own. Ris Cornoval seems to have held on to the citadel at Barlynnt's Tower with some of his men, so that has to be masked. Most of the tra'Ruijac's division is scouring the countryside for more prisoners and its own stragglers. And Mlart needs to reorganize his supply line and distribute the food taken from the conquered towns—that involves civilians who will not be happy, so it is political and will actually take up some of Mlart's own time.

"It is hard work being an occupier, Timmial. You should feel a little professional sympathy for General tra'Norst."

"Not much." The redhead grimaced briefly.

"Well . . . I doubt he wanted this war any more than any of us. Some of the idiots in Molminda's court just thought—oh, well!" Cherrid sighed.

"Anyhow, it takes time for orders to move down the line and to get troops ready to fight. Particularly when the troops are not expecting another fight. I think Mlart originally planned to gobble us up with ris Cornoval, and never dreamed Terrault would make us move too slowly to link up."

He smiled cynically. "History is going to say that our slugabed Hand of the Queen was a military genius, Timmial."

Chapter 6

It was not quite as much fun as slinging poisonous snakes and smoke grenades down the ventilation shaft of a Viet Cong strongpoint, Harper reflected the next morning, but he would have an interesting war story of his own to tell if he ever met Rangers again. He said as much, suitably translated, to Dieytl lan Callares as they stood near his "soup pit."

"It hasn't been the war I anticipated, either," the telepath admitted. "Nor for them." His head shake indicated the mob of Algheran soldiers who were being herded barefoot through the shallow trough of dirty water.

Harper himself wore First Era combat boots with two pairs of socks, both in need of washing, a militia man's khaki shirt and pants that had been—would be—part of his camouflage uniform centuries later in the Forest Guard. The tunic was modified with extra pockets in front to carry a pair of flat-hilted knives. It, too, was in need of a wash, or incineration.

Harper also needed a wash, and a haircut and a comb.

Over his motley uniform, for the morning was cold, he wore a fleece-lined leather jacket with unfastened seams. The tops of his miniature sword hilts showed above the collar of the jacket. He wore no other insignia.

In comparison, even standing in mud a hundred thousand man-heights from any major city, Ian Callares managed to dress fastidiously. He had procured a pair of regular army uniforms with the proper rank patches from some source— Harper could accept that, but the blue uniforms actually fit the man as if tailored, and the lace on them was still white. His hair was combed. His body was clean. Carefully applied cosmetics made the brand on his forehead seem perfectly round so it looked like decoration more than scar. Completing his outfit was a set of suspiciously clean and unscuffed boots.

If Fifth Era men had shaved, Dieytl would have reeked of aftershave. But human facial hair had been genetically engineered out of existence; Ian Callares's smell instead was a faint echo of Ironwearer Wolf-Twin's cinnamon-and-spice body greases. Harper recalled that Gertynne ris Vandeign also managed to dress well during the campaign, but the executive officer was a high-ranking noble. Lan Callares was a conscripted commoner from a small town with a temporary commission; it was nearly impossible to imagine this parade-ground dandy reporting daily to the notoriously un-natty Rahmmend Wolf-Twin.

"Those poor slobs," Dieytl said lightly, watching the Algherans. "I had a touch of this once and it seemed to last forever. Is there a reliable cure for it, by the way?"

"There are powders you can put on your feet," Harper said, wondering if that was true in this era. "The best thing probably is soap and water to get your feet clean; then keep the feet dry and exposed to plenty of warm sunlight and open air. That would clear it up in a ten-day period."

He glanced upward, noticing storm clouds gathering on the western horizon, and shrugged philosophically. Fall was wet in this world, and winter was definitely moving in. It would be half a year before anyone in either Alghera or Loprit could bare their toes in "warm sunlight."

"Used to have something called 'trench foot,' where I came

from. Makes this seem like a *picnic*—a feast—in comparison. Can't give them that, thank the Lady.''

''Hmm.'' Lan Callares had his own thoughts to muse over.

The prisoners were not in formation, but moved between lines of guards armed only with sticks. Watching soldiers made them remove their boots but not their footwrappings as they approached the water; mounds of different-sized boots grew in the background, and from to time Lopritian soldiers picked through them.

Another of Cherrid's ideas, relying on the assumption that the well-advertised Algheran reputation for quality manufacturing would extend to soldiers' boots as well, but most of the Lopritians who approached the piles went away empty-handed. Harper, remembering that despite his current circumstances he was himself an Algheran, felt something very like chagrin.

Close at hand, the prisoners were encouraged to roll up their pant legs before stepping into the ''soup pit'' and watched as they trudged around in the water. The Algherans took the experience lightly: they laughed as they moved through the muck; some of them kicked the dirty water at each other and at men who had not yet entered the pit. Now and then, under-officers tried to keep groups of men in formation, but the attempts failed uniformly; the prisoners were not accepting discipline today.

As they emerged from the water, the prisoners were escorted to the road by grinning Lopritians. They were led back—slowly, for the sake of their unprotected feet—to the far side of the hill and left under light guard. Camp followers fed them for the last time with captured rations.

Though overhead clouds promised rain for the afternoon, human beings were immune to colds in this era. The prisoners were not given cloth for shelters nor material for fires, and they did not expect them.

They had less than one more day of captivity to bear.

They had not been told that Mlart had refused to exchange his own prisoners for them, but many of them could guess

that. Cherrid's announcement, read that morning by a sten-
torian Lopritian sergeant, had simply admitted that the brigade could not continue to feed so many captives and that,
after appropriate hygienic treatment, they would be left to be
reunited with the Swordtroop. A vague last paragraph suggested the whole matter was proof of Loprit's moral superiority and military prowess, but none of the prisoners—
however nontelepathic—nor their guards had taken that
seriously.

The announcement had sparked a handful of would-be de-
sertions; some prisoners had even volunteered for service with
the brigade rather than return to the Swordtroop. Cherrid,
weighing matters, had decided after a brief consultation with
Ian Callares and several other officers not to allow this; except
for mercenaries, he preferred to leave the disaffected men with
Mlart.

"It beats getting a spear up the butt," Harper said, recalling
ris Clendannan's comment from the day before. He turned to
Dieytl and pulled the telepath back a bit so the prisoners would
not hear his words. "Do any of them realize what's happening?"

"No." Dieytl was confident. "Some of them have guessed,
but they aren't sure. The guards don't know, either, most of
them. They've been told, and allowed to tell the prisoners, that
this will remove calluses from their feet—we had problems
after that keeping some of the guards out of the water—and we
took their boots away, so they can all guess we don't want
them to march well and that this is part of it."

He looked away from the frolicking Algherans to stare at
Harper. "You probably could have told them the truth without
trouble. Was it genuinely honorable for all you Ironwearers to
tell them lies?"

"It never came up for discussion," the big redhead admitted, wishing for a moment that contemporary languages had
the wealth of names for graduated degrees of truth that had
enriched First Era tongues. "We knew we couldn't handle the
prisoners and that Mlart refused to exchange for them; this

gives them freedom without hurting us—and without helping him. The idea was just so good that, uh, omitting a few trifling details didn't bother us.

"Besides, it wasn't intended to deceive the prisoners so much, as it was as a surprise for Mlart. We hope he takes these men back with open arms and tries to march them after us. Let him put boots on them again, let him feed them, and the further they get away from the southern cities, the better. When they can't march and he has to send them back . . . They'll be like prisoners that he's stuck with, but because they're his own men, he'll have to take better care of them. The more trouble he has, the better off we'll be.

"Blame Mlart, if anyone, Dieytl. We offered to trade men and he turned us down. It's just the Lady's cloak over him that we didn't—"

Harper shut his mouth suddenly, realizing that massacres of prisoners had been commonplace only in the teeming-with-humanity First Era world. Long lifespans and a small population—and maybe the example of Ironwearers—had done for human character what no religion or movement for moral reform could accomplish in his day: even in wartime, human life was now valuable.

"We could have been nastier, "he said, covering his confusion. "We could have thought of something. Cut their toes off, for example."

Dieytl accepted that with a murmur and pointed with his head at a sight Harper could not see. "Speaking of nastiness, I wish you could look into ris Clendannan's mind with me. He has two horrible tasks to perform, which he can't delegate, and he's putting both off to the last minute." He grinned.

"What?"

"He has to tell the Hand that we need to leave behind his—what would you call it?—his traveling combination palace and bordello? Cherrid wants the horses for pulling cannons, and he has to explain gently that the brigade can't spare them for pulling the royal—"

"White elephant?" Harper suggested. Then he had to explain: "Once upon a time, there was a kingdom called Siam where white elephants—you know what an elephant is? Okay—were held to be sacred and thus property of the king. And when the king was annoyed with any of his subjects or felt they were becoming too rich or powerful, he would pretend they were greatly in his favor. As proof of the royal favor, he would give them one of the sacred elephants to tend. They couldn't let the beast wander off or kill it and they couldn't refuse to accept a gift from the king. But feeding an elephant bankrupted them."

Amusing. For all the differences in cultures, there was a precise Fifth Era synonym for "bankrupt."

The telepath chuckled appreciatively. "Ris Clendannan must have a million stories to tell. I hope he writes them down someday before—well, he has to persuade this bit of royalty to let one of his white elephants go. That'll be the easy part."

"Are the girls the hard part? Are they leaving, too?" Harper guessed, wondering how morose Lord Terrault ris Andervyll would be with nothing but male companionship.

"They'll stay." Lan Callares smiled again. "No, ris Clendannan has to persuade Ironwearer Wolf-Twin that we should leave the command wagon behind as well. It's just as big as the Hand's and just as much an elephant."

"White elephant," Harper corrected.

Lan Callares ignored him. "He can just order it, of course, but he's working Rahm hard, he wants him happy. But Rahm just loves that little office in the back. There's a desk for him and shelves and all those pigeonholes—he's had so much fun figuring different ways to categorize his papers and sticking up little labels for those of us who can't read his mind. He's never had anything like it on any other campaign, and he thinks it's the greatest contribution to organized carnage man will ever see in this era. It's one idea of the Hand's Wolf-Twin really appreciates." He snickered wickedly.

"Uh-hh," Harper said stupidly. It was not right for lan Callares to criticize his superior officer, and he had been about to say so, but he realized at the last moment it was simply a confidence shared between two men from the same town. As much as anyone in this world could be, Dieytl was an old friend. It was a sign of his increasing alienation from events that he had forgotten that.

"How is Kylene?" he asked now.

"Lonely and bored?" The telepath snapped his fingers. "I really can't tell you, Timmial. I don't have the power to reach that far. She could touch my mind all the way here from Midpassage, if she wanted, but that's her. I've never even heard of another Teep with that much range."

He hesitated slightly. "She's very special, you know. We hope she'll have three or even four children someday."

How much did he know? Harper wondered. Yes, Kylene was special—she had been one of the world's very first telepaths, from the time before the dawn of the Second Era. Had she remained there her children would have been called the Skyborne; they might have ruled the world.

Fear touched him. Seventy millennia after their fall, the Skyborne were still remembered and hated by nontelepaths. For her own safety, Kylene's heritage had to be kept secret. "Who's 'we'?"

"Other Teeps. I'm not the only one who noticed her range. All through Loprit, we're eager to keep her bloodline alive."

A chill ran up Harper's back and did not leave despite the knowledge that a Teepblind hid his thoughts. "Still trying to breed a master race, Dieytl?" he demanded. "What has Kylene told you about her background?"

The angrier-sounding question was the rhetorical one and Dieytl showed he knew that. "Kylene has come from a long way off and she developed her power in isolation, not knowing of other Teeps. You've asked her to pose as a Normal, for reasons of your own—I don't sense either of you understood how dangerous that is. That's all I've seen, Ian Haarper. She's kept other details hidden. She *knows* she has secrets she can't share with us, and we know that, too. So we don't look."

"How do I know that?" Harper asked, knowing he would never receive a satisfactory answer.

Once, years ago, he remembered, he had promised two frightened old men who were Algheran Sept Masters that he would kill instantly any telepath who betrayed the secrets of the time travelers. He had not guessed he would become friends with the partner he had requested; he had not guessed the partner would be Kylene Waterfall.

It had been a foolish promise, another of his hasty decisions made without understanding. He had realized that from his first sight of the small angry girl crossing the hangar floor to his levcraft, even before hearing her irate demands to be taken back to her vanished homeland.

Nausea touched him, then receded as he realized he would not harm Kylene. Had she seen that memory within him? Surely she had, when tending him when he was helpless. She had fled, after all, then returned anyhow.

He realized now that deep within him he had always carried that resolution. Had that been part of her reason for returning?

"You'd have to be another Teep." Dieytl's face showed patience and Harper guessed he had said that twice. "We do allow each other privacy, Ian Haarper. If we couldn't do that . . . I think we really wouldn't be human then."

"Must be stressful," Harper said, trying to lighten the conversation. "Curiosity is also a human trait."

"We aren't Teeps till puberty, as you know. We have time to learn to live with mysteries. As for the 'master race,' Ian Haarper, we Teeps simply want to be better at what we do already. Does that need more explanation?"

"I guess not." Harper's words were grudging.

"There aren't enough of us to run a world now. And whenever our numbers get high enough to frighten you 'Normals' "—bitterness put quotation marks about the last word, but Ian Callares's face was strangely unmoved—"you cut us back to where we can be tolerated, don't you? Yes, it was our world once. How can we Teeps forget when you people will not let anyone forget? How can we not wonder what it was like to be a master? Or not wonder what went wrong? Or not wonder whether, in some far different era, Teeps will rule again? Is it wrong to wonder, Ironwearer? Is it so un-usual?''

"No, it's very human," Harper said gently, realizing this was not a conversation he would repeat, even to Kylene, for there were men who would kill telepaths who spoke this way, hearing such words as a violation of the Compacts. He would keep Dieytl's dangerous words a secret; now he truly under-stood that telepaths could do the same.

He forced a grin. "I've always thought people with red hair should run the world. Kylene tells me it would be disastrous. Actually, 'intimidating' is the word she uses, but that's a joke which doesn't translate."

"You should—ahh—treat her more as a wife." The telepath coughed, and Harper reflected that mind readers must find tact a strain. Idly, he wondered if it was his or Kylene's feelings which were being treated so delicately. The thought was sub-merged by annoyance; not for the first time, he regretted that he and Kylene had posed as husband and wife in Midpassage.

"Think of the children," he said sourly. "Those three or four rug rats."

"Well?" Dieytl watched expectantly.

"There wouldn't be any. I've got a problem of sorts, I'm not going to have kids by anyone. Kylene can be a real wife to someone else."

"There's more to life." Dieytl made a gesture, which he assumed to be reassuring. "Someone could stand in for you, if—"

"No." Harper was about to say more, to insist that any woman he married would bear his children or none, but good sense stopped him. Even if it were genetically possible, no one gave a damn for any children he might father.

This was not his world. It never would be.

"Kylene's kids," he forced himself to say, scowling with unfocused hatred at the idea of Kylene enjoying the touch of any other man. "You discuss it with her."

The telepath read his face. "It was only an idea. It doesn't matter, as long as you love each other."

"We don't." Harper spoke harshly. "She's a good kid. I like her and maybe she likes me, but that isn't love. She's my partner now, but we'll break up when this campaign is over. We won't work together again. I may never even meet her again and that's fine by me. The sooner the better, in fact,"

Cut and run. Cut and run. Cut and run.

Oh, Kylene!

Dieytl eyed him skeptically and Harper was forced to keep speaking despite his nausea. "If there was a button in the air right there that I could push that would make me love Kylene. I wouldn't do it. You understand? I wouldn't push it. Not for any reason at all!

"Now, let's drop this. You've had your say, and I'm sure Kylene would be pleased, but I've had enough. Let's go over and look at those boots; something has got me puzzled about them."

He left the spot immediately, detouring around the last of the prisoners as they stepped into the "soup pit."

Lan Callares came afterward, his face troubled, his mind engaged in what he himself could not decide was conversation or merely worried thoughts.

"These aren't Algheran!" An irate Harper was pitching worn-out boots in all direction as Dieytl approached. "This stuff is all Lopritian! You know what this means? Cherrid gave orders that the prisoners weren't to be bullied, and yet our men must have already forced the Algherans to change boots with them. No wonder those bastards were laughing! Aw, shit! How am I going to explain this to Cherrid?"

Dieytl had the grace to blush.

Cherrid's day would not have been complete without unnecessary meetings. The most important one, because his plans could still be challenged there, was at midday in the soon to be abandoned command wagon.

"Ten hundred ninety-two effectives, one hundred nineteen sick, fifty-four under arrest, total twelve hundred sixty-five for

the Defiance-to-Insurrection,'' ris Daimgewln reported, looking up from a small piece of paper. ''Not counting the company escorting the prisoners.'' He leaned to the side and rested
an arm on the table. ''Eighty-two more, counting them.''

''Thirteen twenty-two effectives, seventeen sick, two under
arrest, total about thirteen fifty,'' Cherrid said, and wondered
if anyone in his regiment really was under arrest. He had
made the numbers up as he said them; they were approxi-
mately correct, and if a more accurate count was needed one
of his staff, sitting in the chairs at the side of the room, could
supply it.

''Three hundred seventy effectives, two hundred twenty sick
and recovering wounded, no one under arrest. Six hundred
total.'' That was Dalsyn lan Plenytk's contribution to the meeting, his first words since the initial introductions.

Taciturn, Cherrid wondered, or naturally cautious? The man
had rubbed his fingers irritably on the tabletop during his pre-
sentation but raised no objections. He had not seemed awed by
meeting the Hand or the other nobles. He had chuckled appreciatively as Rahm Wolf-Twin deftly steered him from the chair
he had originally chosen to one with intact legs.

Of course, the man was walking blindfolded in a dark room.
At his own request, Derrauld ris Fryddich had been removed
that morning from command of the Steadfast-to-Victory Regiment; he now commanded one of its shrunken companies. Lan
Plenytk was present as the regiment's senior officer; perhaps he
expected promotion to commander, but neither Merryn ris Vandeign nor the Hand had said anything to him about that. In fact,
both nobles were waiting for Cherrid to nominate a commander, and he had reasons for remaining silent.

''Two hundred sixty effectives, three sick, no arrests,'' a
morose captain reported. He was the acting commander for the
brigade's artillery; lan Haarper's victory and the acquisition of
the Algheran guns had tripled his responsibility but apparently
not his capability. ''I need a lot more men,'' he said glumly
and obviously, thus confirming Cherrid's opinion.

Wolf-Twin looked up from the notes he had been making in his writing block. "I've twenty-seven men, all with cardiac arrest."

There were chuckles around the room, but Cherrid appreciated the truth of the remark. The squat quartermaster had not been pleased to hear that the command wagon—his office in it, rather—was to be abandoned, and many of his men were busy now boxing the mass of papers that had accumulated in it. During the meeting, as he listened to feet shuffling behind the partition that divided the wagon, Cherrid had privately reflected that Her Majesty's Artful-or-Industrious Requisitionary Corps had selected the wrong option in dealing with its paperwork, but he could not tell Wolf-Twin how to perform his job.

Cherrid's own methods for preserving essential records were simpler: he had told his staff to keep only the papers likely to survive if the Algherans destroyed the brigade in battle.

"Thirty-five hundred men," the Hand of the Queen said pensively, his finger pointing at calculations on his writing block. Scars from a youthful duel showed across the knuckles. "To face—" He rummaged through his notes.

"Twenty-two thousand," Cherrid said. "Minus whatever ris Cornoval can keep about him, minus six thousand we are giving back, minus whatever Mlart needs to keep the south subdued. He will come with . . . Eight to ten thousand is the likely range, unless he is even more a gambler than I expect."

Or unless ris Cornoval surrendered quickly. It was not necessary to say that aloud; he paused, knowing everyone would have that thought.

The Hand sighed. "I'd prefer to retreat as long as we can without any battles. There must be a few more men we could get out of Midpassage. If we fall back to Northfaring, there's what's left of the garrison there and the local militia and whatever additional conscripts ris Ellich can scrape up. Ris Mockstyn may be able to spare us one of his corps. It wouldn't be the sort of poverty-reaching gamble you're asking for."

Cherrid nodded swiftly. "We cannot rely on ris Mockstyn. We do not know what kind of pressure he is under now, and he has to defend the capital. For all we know, when he hears Mlart is in the south, he may decide to strike at F'a Alghera—I would, in his place—and it will be our duty to send him reinforcements.

"We have to fight. The longer we wait to fight, the worse the odds against us will be. Even with help from ris Mockstyn, we cannot possibly get reinforcements as fast as Mlart will. He has had years to build up garrisons in the Torn Coast area, and I do not care what Molly's Beloved Counselors have told her, it was not because he had to suppress pro-Lopritian demonstrations by her still loyal but former subjects."

"She gets better advice," ris Andervyll said defensively, his glance showing he wished the commoners would leave the room.

"That is very well, Terrault, but it does not change the fact that Mlart is ahead of us in men and material. We should have had stockpiles up and down this road and real garrisons in port Junction and Barlynnt's Tower, but we do not—it all went into chasing half-naked savages through the Necklace Lakes, did it not?—and we have to fight him now, with what we have now."

"I advised against it," the Hand muttered. But he had profited from that war in land and slaves . . . it was well known. "If that's germane, Cherrid."

"It's an old matter, not worth airing again," Gertynne ris Vandeign agreed, looking icily at the commoners in the wagon. Cherrid was intrigued to see him lock eyes with Ian Plenytk.

"I was in that business, too," ris Daimgewln commented. "Quite a lot of us were, Cherrid, including some others I can name in this room."

Cherrid stilled a sigh. "I apologize if anyone feels I have muddied his fur. I was simply trying to amplify my point."

"You made your point earlier," Gertynne said. "You haven't answered or even raised one issue that I think many—" His eyes moved around the room again. "—most of us would wonder about. What happens if we lose a major battle? You said casualties will be light, but what if they're severe? What if the Algherans kill or capture all of us, the way young Ian Haarper has?''

"Well, I think . . ." Cherrid mimed indecision. "Young Ian Haarper is on our side, after all."

The remark brought a few laughs, while Cherrid wondered what Gertynne was up to. Judgment should have brought the man to only one opinion, but it was impossible yet to see which side of the argument Gertynne was taking. Mentally, he cursed ris Vandeign's deviousness, even as he was speaking.

"Ironwearer Ian Haarper, that is. The worst that can happen is that the Algherans kill or capture all of us. In that case, the result is what it would be if we were in the bag with ris Cornoval—there will be two to three divisions of the Swordtroop running unopposed through the Shield Valley toward Northfaring and F'a Loprit as fast as they can, with more behind them. Which is exactly what will happen if we simply retreat without resisting them."

Gertynne began to say something, then stopped and looked at the Hand, as if seeking permission. Evidently he found it. Cherrid suppressed a scowl; he wondered at the wisdom of the gods in giving Teeps to a world where subservience was so treasured that fraudulent respect was treated as genuine.

"Still, thirty-five hundred men is a sizable force," Gertynne said. "If added to other forces. If we just threw it away . . . I don't know what the effect would be on the country."

Silently, Cherrid thanked whichever God it was—even including the Algheran Lady Nicole—who had ensured that Grahan had considered that objection and found a counter for him. "If we just throw away the Shield Valley, without a fight, Gertynne, what effect would that have on the country? Especially, coming two days after a major victory.

"And, gentlemen, what about that victory? What Ironwearer Ian Haarper did was absolutely stunning, wasn't it? And I have heard nothing but complaints about it from the people in this room. But that victory—the same victory we were laughing about a few minutes ago—is the only thing that has given us the opportunities we have now. We still have problems, you say? We will always have problems. We ought to stop moaning about them and think of the good side of things—like having the entire staff of officers of a Swordtroop division and an Algheran Sept Master in our prisoner bag—like having a division's complement of wagons and artillery to add to ours— like turning six thousand of the enemy's good soldiers into sore-footed miserable souls who *know* Lopritians can outfight them.

"I tell you: maybe we do not appreciate all those things. But I tell you who will: the people of Loprit, the people of Alghera, Mlart, anyone else in the one world who can read. We have got Leiman and Scee correspondents with this brigade, you know; the Algherans had them with their division; they are telling the world what we did. Not just Ian Haarper—there is credit enough for all of us. We will look like geniuses."

The Hand only looked embarrassed, Wolf-Twin and ris Daimgewln puzzled. Gertynne ris Vandeign sourly retorted that he preferred sleeping with truth to war correspondents. Dalsyn Ian Plenytk, Cherrid was pleased to see, seemed genuinely unmoved or even amused by his words; perhaps one of the correspondents had explained to him how quickly news and fame evaporated.

"You asked what people will think, Gertynne, and I have tried to tell you," he said. "They will think something is terribly wrong if warriors such as we just retreat, and I have told you what that something will be."

"It's such a gamble," Gertynne complained. "You *think* this will work, Cherrid, you say it will, but are you *sure* it will? Nicole's cloak has always been over you, I know—let me take that back, please—you're good, Cherrid, you're very good, but Mlart tra'Nornst is also good, very good, maybe the best general in the one world! I won't say he is, it might just be Nicole's cloak over him, too, but the Algherans say he is. Other people say he is. They may be right. *He's never been defeated!* Not once, Cherrid! So how can you be sure your plan will work?"

To his dismay, Cherrid saw Gertynne was not alone in his

objections. He was echoing the Hand's opinions; it was rare for Andervylls and Vandeigns to agree on any issue, and most of the men in the room understood instinctively what the safest side to take in this argument would be. He knew suddenly that his campaign was about to be lost, betrayed by men who knew better but who could not rise above factional politics.

As a result, he foolishly lost his temper.

"Nothing is certain in war," he snapped. "I told you two days ago, we could lose South Loprit in an afternoon, and we still can if ris Cornoval doesn't hold out. Ris Mockstyn can lose the whole country in half a watch. The Queen's Beloved Counselors may all go insane and sue for peace. Mlart may die laughing at us. Anything can happen, Gertynne."

Gertynne sighed and rubbed his cheek with a palm. "It's not enough to sway me, Cherrid. I understand about ris Cornoval and ris Mockstyn and the advisers, but it's this campaign here I'm worried about. This brigade. Convince me about it."

"What do you want from me?" Cherrid shouted. "A guarantee?"

"Can you give me that?" ris Vandeign asked softly. "Say you're certain we can win this campaign and you'll have my vote."

Too late, Cherrid saw the deadfall he had triggered. His prestige and thus his value as a supporter of the ruling family were at stake now, and he was forced to gamble with them to win ris Vandeign's support—support the saturnine executive officer surely knew he deserved. He had no choice now and Gertynne recognized it.

Blind old fool! And young Timmial thought he made mistakes!

Thank the gods Grahan is not here to see this. And my Brindylla!

He paused, looking at all the eyes that stared back at him. Gertynne raised an eyebrow, waiting on his answer.

"Steadfast-to-Victory goes with the Ironwearer," Dalsyn lan Plenytk said quickly. "We've already proved nothing's certain in war; we don't ask for guarantees."

It was too late, but Cherrid appreciated the gesture. He rose from his chair and stood to make his own.

"We will defeat the Warder of the Realm, Mlart tra'Nornst, and the Swordtroop of the Algheran Realm in the Shield Valley," Ironwearer Cherrid ris Clendannan said firmly. "Loprit will win this war. You have my promise."

After that, the vote was unanimous.

Chapter 7

Following the Meeting, inevitably, came meetings.

Naturally, the first was with the Hand. As ris Andervyll leaned across the table toward him, Cherrid had time to reflect he had made a mistake in underestimating the man's native caution. He should have explained his plans privately before the meeting, he realized, and he prepared himself for a warning or even a rebuke.

But ris Andervyll did not show anger. "I understand your sentiment but you were wrong in thinking your young Ironwearer has not been thanked," the Hand said instead, in an undertone. "I spoke to him last night and mentioned a peerage, and he turned it down—otherwise it would have been announced to the brigade today. He told me he came from a country which had never had royalty nor aristocracy and he was pleased to remain as he was."

Cherrid was stunned. "I apologize for him, Terrault."

The Hand waved that aside. "Not necessary. He was quite polite."

"But—" The old Ironwearer's vocabulary did not include

the phrase "Quixotic fool"; he muttered an equivalent under his breath, an adage from his homeland about strangers who wished to dance—it was a euphemism—with the local residents. "Do you want me to talk to him?"

"No. I'm writing to Molly. There's to be a winter's honors list—frankly I'd move it forward if it didn't suggest a need to buy support—and your young man will be on it. It'll be our secret till then, but by springtime, he'll be the Baron of Something or more likely the Earl of Somewhere—Molly will make up a title for him, if he's still reticent. I imagine his lands will be in the west, bordering the Necklace Lakes you dislike so much; that is where the Crown has land to bestow, after all."

Titles and lands were not empty honors, Cherrid well knew. Most aristocrats were distinguished from commoners only by the form of their names. No doubt, as Grahan would point out, lan Haarper's—ris Haarper's—rewards were the by-products of politics; they were, nonetheless, munificent.

Your Ironwearer, the Hand had said. *Your young man.*

Cherrid understood then that the accolades soon to be extended to Timmial were the Hand's gesture of confidence in him. He swallowed, and only centuries of discipline kept tears from his eyes. "Terrault, this is truly regal. I can't possibly tell you how deeply moved I am."

Ris Andervyll smiled. "Well, we want to tie that youngster down—we can't have him stay a Blankshield and hare off to the other side the next time Loprit gets in a war just because the pay looks better, can we? Besides, people need to see that Loprit remembers its defenders."

He pushed himself away from the table with that remark and shook his head. "Lord and Lady help us if this kingdom ever follows any other rule. Good day, Cherrid; I'll let you get back to your job."

Gertynne ris Vandeign came up as ris Andervyll turned. His hand was extended. "No hard feelings, Lord Clendannan, I hope. Personally, I agreed with you all along, but you know how it is."

Cherrid hesitated, then noticed bystanders watching with fascination. Purposely, he avoided recognizing faces, then reluctantly took the empty hand and pretended clasping wrists had meaning. "I am a simple man, Gertynne," he said politely. "Why don't you explain how it is?"

The executive officer hesitated in turn. His hand was still in Cherrid's grasp; he removed it slowly, then leaned over the table so his head was close. "I couldn't help but see a lot of doubt in the room, to be honest."

"So did I." Cherrid's face was impassive.

Gertynne leaned further, lowering his voice. "I thought it was better for an ally to express the doubts, so they would be in a form you could rebut, and that's what you did. You handled the situation magnificently, Lord Clendannan. A lesser man would have let us make a terrible mistake."

Cherrid's lips tightened a long moment. Then he stood and extended his hand so Gertynne was forced to take it again. "Thank you for your confidence," he said, and his voice filled the room so every other conversation was stopped. "Defeating the Algherans is merely my duty as a loyal servant of the Queen—"

"Our duty," Gertynne said hastily.

"—and I rely, as ever, on your own great abilities, Gertynne, and the knowledge that I have your full-hearted support. Our good Queen Molminda can expect no less than our best effort now from either of us, can she?"

"Of course." Gertynne's eyes moved, observing the bystanders even as he faced toward Cherrid, but he managed to smile despite the reactions he saw. That was a skill learned in Court circles, Cherrid supposed; he wondered if it had any practical benefits.

Enough was enough. He dropped Gertynne's hand and wiped his palm on his trousers. "I have enjoyed our little conversation, ris Vandeign, as I'm sure you have," he said, "but I know you are eager to do serious work. I will let you get back to your job."

* * *

"What was that all about?" Dalsyn lan Plenytk wondered. "Those sparring matches?" He was alone with Cherrid in the command wagon, after the Ironwearer had waved aside other conversations and dismissed his staff. The glass of water Wolf-Twin had poured for him was still in his hand; he sipped from it minutely after asking his question.

"Politics," Cherrid said curtly. But there was no good reason but prejudice to leave the commoner ignorant of what the nobility knew; perhaps he would need the knowledge in days ahead.

"Gertynne's grandfather was one of the men who made this kingdom centuries ago," he explained. "Perhaps he could have become king, but he did not try to win the crown and for that, his family has never forgiven him. In the last century, after the old man died, Gertynne's father was executed for plotting against the king, and Gertynne and his brother were required to watch. Their father was betrayed by an Andervyll—at least an Andervyll carried the tale. Now that the Andervylls have taken power—after a coup of their own—the Vandeigns feel they have lost what should have been theirs. They are jealous; they hinder the Andervylls as much as they can and still keep their ears over their necks. It is all . . . pathetic. Very petty."

The surveyor raised an eyebrow. "Does Gertynne hope—no, that's silly."

"What Gertynne hopes is between him and the Teeps," Cherrid said dryly. "He is still alive, so he is certainly not a fool. He is not overtly disloyal and he is able enough that the Hand puts up with his troublemaking. He has been at the Court for many years also, he is well known. I suppose you could say, he is a pest because he's been allowed to be a pest—not that I want it said I called a Lopritian nobleman anything of the sort!"

Lan Plenytk murmured softly, "He's advertising himself. He won't be disloyal, but if enough people want the Andervylls to go, and Loprit needs a new king, clever, able, hardworking, high-ranked Gertynne will just have to be available, won't he?''

A tradesman's analysis, Cherrid thought. Royalty and would-be royalty operated on loftier planes. They bargained, yes; they sought to keep old supporters and win new ones; they orchestrated alliances . . . But to treat loyalty as a commodity was to cheapen it. People were more than cattle who would be content with the best cud and the best resting place, or the best deal. He was sorry to see Ian Plenytk's limitations so quickly; he hoped the man would transcend them someday and recognize human dignity.

The man was young, of course, as so many junior officers were. Startlingly young, in fact, even younger than Timmial Ian Haarper in appearance, though Cherrid was sure that was not so. Younger than Wolf-Twin, certainly.

Where are the older men in these militias? he wondered. The solid middle-aged men of one to three centuries whose resolution and skill kept an army together—where were they among the Midpassage men and the companies of the Northern Valley?

In the ranks, of course. As they were in his own regiment. He knew the answer before he asked the question, and only elderly inertia made him keep asking. Spears, bows, muskets, rifles now, the odd projectile-less weaponry promised for the future in the Plates—new weapons and experience continually dictated new tactics. Soldiering changed too quickly for any but professional soldiers to master. Old men could not cope with such wildness. It was young men, coming new to war, who saw it as static and simple; inevitably, they brought further change.

Dismaying as it was to the *very* old men who remained on top.

Self-consciously, Cherrid shook off his wayward thoughts and brought himself back to the matters at hand. He nodded slowly. ''Making a king of Gertynne? I cannot imagine it ever happening.''

Lan Plenytk grimaced. "What was the grandfather like? What kind of king would he have been?"

"A bad one. He was a terribly hard man," Cherrid said, willing to have the topic changed. "Also named Dalsyn, by the way—that might amuse you. He was old-fashioned in many ways, even then. He hated cities, for example. He never learned to write, though he could read, slowly. He would have kept Loprit a group of small towns if he could, and it would never have worked.

"He would have hated what Loprit has become. He hated what he was doing, knowing what the result must be, but he did it anyway." *We all did.* "It was one of the things that made him hard. But he knew he had no choice.

"We could all see that. Fohima Alghera was growing every day and its country was growing with it. We had to build our own cities to oppose it, or the Algherans would have swallowed us eventually, without even noticing they had done it. We would have been just like the Necklace Lakes people are now."

Lan Plenytk raised his eyebrows. "*They're* barbarians."

"So were we," Cherrid said honestly. "Just about, most of us. Oh, our manners were better than the Lake folk, I recall. We did not let our old people starve to death quite as often and never admitted it when it happened. Our marriage ceremonies lasted longer. We did not plant our dead in cornfields to fertilize the lands. We did not make men slaves—then. We thought that was enough to make us civilized and them savages, but the dumbest and coarsest men in your battalion today probably have better manners than we did and can read and write, too.

"We copied what we could from those demon-seized Algherans, that is the truth. We and Innings both, even if it is not polite to say so these days. And if you were old enough, you would see that the Necklace Lake people have copied from us the last few centuries. There is nothing new in this world."

The words made his mind return to thoughts he had already chosen to ignore. He coughed and went to the map table and beckoned the other to join him. "I believe we will face Mlart about here," he said, pointing. "We need to discuss our dispositions, because they will determine our marching order."

For the first time that day, the talk became comfortingly technical.

When Ian Plenytk was gone, Cherrid looked about the command wagon, realizing this was the last he would he see of it. It had always been unnecessary, more hindrance than luxury in his estimation, but he was strangely reluctant to leave it.

Knowing he was foolish, he patted the worn leather of the couch he had so often slept on. He had never found sleeping on the ground a hardship, and his aides would see that he had more than a saddle for a pillow, he was sure. His nights would still be more comfortable than those of the ordinary soldiers. But he would be forced into relying more on those aides now; he would have to reckon how long it took them to erect a tent before he sought his bed at night; he would need their intervention to preserve privacy when he spoke to others.

Outside the wagon men marched past in unison—less than a platoon, he reckoned from the sound. A sergeant barked march commands; muted voices indicated men were talking in the ranks. A work detail, then, soldiers headed for combat with some part of the brigade's tedious and never-ending housekeeping chores, not guessing an officer overheard.

He had always enjoyed listening to the enlisted men when officers were not about, Cherrid admitted. A sane man must do more than give orders and promise obedience; it was liberating to hear a conversation which did not include references to rank and duties and in which the requirements of military protocol were ignored. Besides, good soldiers did their jobs without needing officers; it was immensely comforting to feel as one with thousands of competent men.

Visible to the men, he would lose that pleasure. He hesitated, while he could afford the delay, before he left.

Someone knocked on the door of the wagon, then came through without inquiry; a painfully thin, tall young man with captain's insignia and Requisitionary Corps badges on his uniform.

The Teep Ian Callares would have told him he could enter. Cherrid nodded recognition. "Good afternoon, ris Maanhaldur. What can I do for you?"

"I have a request from Ironwearer Wolf-Twin, sir. He wishes to set fire to the command wagon when we withdraw."

"Personally?" Cherrid raised an eyebrow. "It has been my experience, Dighton, that the enemy will take care of that. The Algies will likely burn everything we leave but the latrines."

"Er, yes, sir." Dighton fidgeted, as Cherrid continued to look at him.

A fine boy, the old Ironwearer thought, appraising the young noble. He would never amount to much as a soldier, but the campaign was seasoning him; at the end of the war Dighton ris Maanhaldur might stand on his own two feet.

Despite his name, the boy's true lineage showed on his face: he had the hooked nose Cherrid had seen on many of the Andervylls in past centuries. The family trait had skipped Terrault and Molminda for some reason; Cherrid had never heard a satisfactory explanation of this.

"The Ironwearer fears the enemy will make use of the command wagon and that we should deprive him of its facilities. Sir." Dighton managed to say that with a straight face.

I wish he would, Cherrid thought, privately enjoying an image of Mlart tra'Nornst discovering, as he had, each of the protruding springs in the wagon's couch. "That is very nicely put, Dighton. What did the Ironwearer really say?"

"He said he'd never given anything up to an enemy before and that he'd rise up to Cimon before the Algies got anything from him this time except a drinking jug with piss in it. Minus the adjectives, sir." The boy's face was deadpan; his eyes twinkled.

Cherrid grimaced. "That's a Teep's report, Dighton. There is a narrow line between honesty and rudeness. You must learn to be candid while staying on the civilized side."

"Yes, sir." Ris Maanhaldur stiffened.

"You may tell Ironwearer Wolf-Twin that his request is granted. I wish you also to tell him that over the years I have given up great quantities of matériel to people I fought against and survived with my character intact."

"Yes, sir."

"Very well. You may leave now." He looked around the wagon once more, imagining flames leaping over the map table and devouring the dark-paneled walls and furniture, remembering the confrontations it had seen, the low-voiced discussions with Grahan, and the long nights he had spent alone with his thoughts, crafting plan after ephemeral plan as he stared into darkness.

Mlart. Undefeated Mlart tra'Nornst. The best general in the one world.

He inhaled deeply and let the air out slowly.

Nothing here but wood and old leather, he reminded himself, and rapped the couch with his fist to prove the point. It was all replaceable, all forgettable.

How childish of Wolf-Twin to take his little loss with such pique!

The prisoners were given a break for lunch on the second day—small portions of cooked grain ladled out from a southbound cook wagon—and when Lerlt looked around he could not see Herrilmin or Gherst, though they had not been far from him when the column halted.

Lopritian soldiers had mixed with the captives and were eating the same rations, with the same lack of enthusiasm. Lerlt expected to be stopped at any moment, but he was not, so he wandered about the area, eating out of his hand. By the expedient of looking at whatever the guards looked at, he saw the other two Agents finally, side by side in front of a stunted tree.

"An officer," Herrilmin was saying, loudly enough for Lerlt to detect annoyance. "Surrounded by . . . No way . . . Walk up to . . . Shoot him." Gherst said something in a lower voice and after that Lerlt could hear nothing clearly.

Curious, he was wondering if he could approach them without being noticed when the Lopritian officer in command blew on a whistle. To Lerlt's disgust, the guards began to shout at their captives then and drove them back into a compact herd in which sensible conversation was impossible.

"Where were you?" Fesch asked as the march resumed. "I looked all over."

"Just standing around," Lerlt said. "I don't see how you missed me."

Fesch's chagrin provided a tiny lift for his spirits.

Before third watch, in late afternoon, the last elements of the brigade were in retreat, or as Cherrid's staff preferred to call it when in his hearing, "movement."

The Steadfast-to-Victory Regiment led the way, in payment for the fighting the militia had already seen. Ris Daimgewln's garrison troops were next, and the Guards Regiment took the rear, because Cherrid had the most trust in his own troops. That was the approximate order of march; in fact, things were not organized so smoothly.

Inevitably, orders were lost or worded confusingly. Small detachments managed to lose themselves, or were separated from their parent units by fate or assignment. Camp followers and teamsters answering to no authority wandered up the road as whim struck, becoming interspersed with the soldiers and blocking other traffic. Artillery crews halted here and there to replace broken wheels under their guns, confidently asserting their priority when they began moving again, at the expense of other vehicles. Boxes shifted in the overloaded supply wagons and had to be restacked by passing infantry units. Men on horseback drifted in all directions, while the cavalry officers anxiously pressed the Hand and Gertynne and Cherrid for orders which, when received, they would never obey.

"Gods help us in any real retreat" was Cherrid's comment to his staff, but he took the confusion in stride. Ironwearer Ian Haarper had once described moving troops as like shoving locusts across a heated plate; Cherrid appreciated the whimsy but he had too much experience to find the insight novel. Much of war was a contest in managing—or tolerating—disorder.

Fortunately, there would be few decisions to be made today. The Hand of the Queen and his two mistresses rode in a wagon just ahead of the Midpassage battalion, at Cherrid's suggestion, less to avoid danger than the loss of dignity to be found in the jostling for position in the middle of the column. Gertynne ris Vandeign and his brother, and Wolf-Twin and ris Daimgewln, kept close to ris Andervyll.

Timmial Ian Haarper trudged on foot behind the militia regiment he had once commanded, leading a pair of horses. Wolf-Twin's Teep stayed beside him when he was not engaged in work; Cherrid did not get close to see whether they spoke or simply provided company for each other.

Cherrid himself and his staff, after riding the length of the brigade, halted for a brief lunch and settled into a place between his regiment's second and third battalions. Nominally, this was the rear-guard position, but the equivalent of another battalion of laggards and strays wandered even farther behind them. Cherrid was untroubled, knowing the stragglers would catch up with their units as soon as Mlart began pressing.

By fourth watch, when there was barely enough light to fix supper and the brigade came to rest, the van had moved seven thousand man-heights. It was less than Cherrid had hoped for, more than he had feared.

The sky was clear. He asked Grahan to wake him early, then retired contentedly to his own blankets in one of the ambulances.

He had no dreams.

                        *   *   *

The prisoners also camped beside the road that night. They were given rations and blankets from wagons which had kept pace with them; they were allowed to build grass fires to heat their food and themselves.

The four time travelers united around one small fire. It did not give the heat of the fires larger groups had built, but it required less effort to keep going; the crackling of the burning grass was low enough to permit conversation, loud enough to discourage eavesdroppers.

It had been a long march by Lerlt's standards, longer than yesterday's, longer than any he had endured while with the Swordtroop, and marching without musket and knapsack had done little to shorten it. When the fire was built and his food eaten, he wrapped himself in his blanket and his thoughts.

When he was the old and famous Master of Sept Hujsuon, he would set aside forests where no hunters but the God Cimon were allowed. There would be springs built at each Hujsuon settlement from which no human would drink because they were to ease Lady Nicole's thirst. Extremely old, a Warder revered through Alghera and much of the nearby world, he would die and rise to Cimon. Rejuvenated, waiting judgment, he would hear the Gods praise his piety; then Cimon would show his judging scales already decreed his verdict after weighing Lerlt's soul: all his sins were light ones compared to the great deed of destroying Chelmmys. Modestly, he would explain he had simply been under Nicole's cloak; opportunity had placed him where he could do what any mature, deliberative, pious person would do. Cimon, unfooled, would give his seat of judgment to Lerlt for a spell; he would be allowed to decide the fates of men's souls. Later, Nicole would . . .

No, the guardian of the hearth and hearthsharers was unlikely to permit liberties to any former being from the one world. There would be a niece then, or a daughter, unmentioned in the Chronicles, bored with heavenly perfection, beautiful, with the Goddess's own powers and capacities, seeking excitement, never allowed to meet one-time mortals before this—

A breeze blew billows of aromatic white smoke over him. Harshness filled his lungs. Incautiously, he coughed; the switch with which Herrilmin had been stirring the fire swatted at his side. "If it's not offensive to your dignity, you might spell Fesch at picking up fuel for the fire."

"Fesch is the junior officer," he protested. "It should be his job."

"I believe that Fesch came into the Project before you did," Herrilmin said, his voice admitting no doubt. "You're the junior, considering that."

Herrilmin had entered the Project long after any of the other Hujsuons, but neither man regarded that as significant.

"Fesch volunteered to get grass," Lerlt said. "If he had wanted more help, he could have asked for it."

"Go help your Septling," Herrilmin growled. His thumb pointed a direction. Reflexively, Lerlt's head turned, and in the corner of his eye he saw that Gherst was behind him with grass in his arms and listening.

"I was going, in just a minute." Lerlt was furious but unable to argue under Gherst's eyes. He pushed himself out of his blanket and moved to obey.

Mercifully, Fesch ha'Hujsuon had been out of hearing range. He was in a small depression when Lerlt reached him, snapping twigs from a dead bush and adding them to a pile at his feet. He nodded respectfully when Lerlt came near. "Am I done now?"

"Herrilmin wants enough grass to last awhile," Lerlt told him. "He said we should both keep at it."

"Okay." Fesch took the decision philosophically.

"I don't see him doing any work," Lerlt grumbled.

"He's been sick," Fesch said, surprising Lerlt. "I heard him talking to Gherst. The tra'Hujsuon sent him on some errand to give him time to recuperate. He was bringing cargo back from the Present and stopped to see what was happening here. Then, he got trapped—like us.''

It did not quite ring true, and Lerlt nearly said as much. Provisioning the Station was uninspiring work; it was usually assigned to men whose competence was not trusted or who had in some fashion annoyed a Sept Master.

But that was not the important point. "He's got his time machine here?''

"Not here. It's south of us, and there are two armies between, so it's closer, but it's no easier to get to than the ones we left in F'a Alghera.''

Lerlt cursed.

Fesch snapped fingers in agreement. "Anyway, he's with us now, and he seems pretty definite about finding another time machine to the north. I guess we have to trust him.''

It was not a conclusion Lerlt would have reached. "Herrilmin was fine when I saw him last,'' he said. "Wasn't he with us when we left the Station?''

"Sure, but—'' Fesch waved a hand to dismiss the problem. "Things happen. He may leave and come back at the same time we do and still get two seasons older, if he— Do *you* go straight to the Project at the end of a mission?''

"No. Sometimes, but not always. Like everyone else. Why?''

Fesch's voice dropped. "Did you ever do a private mission, for Vrect tra'Hujsuon? Just for the Sept? Buy some land for Hujsuon, for example, that we passed up originally?''

Lerlt had not, and he was not sure that other Agents had acted for their Septs that way, but he had heard the same mixed rumors and conjectures.

"No, but so what?'' he said. "If all the Septs are doing it, it doesn't matter, does it? No one is going to get hurt by it except the unSepted and some Associations.''

"Well.'' Fesch tossed his head uncertainly. "I think that's what Herrilmin was doing. Something private, for Vrect, that we aren't supposed to know about. But he makes hints. Gherst is bothered.''

It made sense, Lerlt thought. "You aren't sure of that?"

"No, I'm not." Fesch sighed and gestured with his head. "Anyway, back to real things. We can go where we want to pick grass, as long as it isn't past them."

Guards. Darknesses against darkness. By the fire it had been possible to ignore their existence.

Back to real things, indeed. Lerlt went to his knees and tugged at clumps of grass, while he thought about Fesch's revelations. Herrilmin and a time machine not far away, and two armies in between . . . Two and a half armies, from a prisoner's standpoint. Was escape really possible? He stared at the Lopritians, waiting for time to make their outlines clear. Only a pair of enemy soldiers could be seen and they were far apart. Yes, he could imagine possibilities . . .

He plucked grass desultorily till Fesch had moved out of sight, then let his feet carry him toward the nearer soldier. One at a time, he thought. He could throw grass at the soldier, seize his musket while he was confused, club him quickly with the barrel, shoot the second soldier . . . The other Algherans would rally and overpower the Lopritians, attacking the surprised soldiers in their camp while he used the captured musket to kill the Lopritian leaders . . . His heroism would be praised when he returned to the Project, but he would be modest and explain any Agent could have done the same.

And he would speak to Vrect tra'Hujsuon about private missions for the Sept. Like Herrilmin, doing whatever it was that Herrilmin had done.

"Back off, Algie." The Lopritian raised his musket when he was man-heights away and followed Lerlt with the barrel. Behind him, Lerlt saw another line of campfires, but no foragers. For themselves, the Lopritians had wood, he realized enviously.

"Just getting grass." Lerlt smiled politely, and wondered if his expression could be seen.

"Lot's left where you are." The Lopritian used his own language, speaking slowly and loudly, as if to a retarded child. Lerlt thought about acting as if he misunderstood, but the soldier's gestures with his musket were unmistakable.

"It's taller over there." He pretended reasonability.

"Wild animals out there. You wander too far, Algie, and nobody'll ever find your bones. Stay where you're protected."

Protected. Lerlt grimaced at the word, but before he could respond, a second soldier appeared behind the first.

"Got a problem here?"

"No problem, unless it's itchy feet." The guard's head leaned toward Lerlt. "Algie here wants to wander a bit, sir."

The second soldier snapped his fingers loudly. "He gives you trouble, shoot him. Stay alert!"

"Yessir," the guard said quickly. "You hear that, you? Stay on your side." His voice was eager, but the officer he was trying to impress had wandered away as suddenly as he had appeared. Lerlt sneered, using the protection of darkness.

It was pointless to tempt fate now. As the Lopritian juggled his musket, Lerlt ducked his head in pretended submission and retreated. He had tried to escape, he reminded himself. The other captives had not; he was more heroic than them, even more than the other Agents. Cowards, cowards, cowards— viciously he slammed his handfuls of grass into the ground after he pulled them, knocking dirt off the roots, striking off heads.

Eventually, tugging up grass became tedious. Without conscious intent, he meandered past one of the larger campfires, coming closer when he noticed he was not challenged. No one asked him for his armful of grass; he left it on the ground and mingled with the captives gathered around the fire.

"—bastard lied to the Muster about his preparations," someone was saying. "We weren't ready for this one by any means."

"Nornst and Ruijac," someone else said, sticking his hands

toward the crackling grass. "Playing to the unSepted as usual. *They're* always ready for a war. It isn't the Cimon-taken mob that has to pay taxes for these things."

A man spat into the fire. "It's the mob that takes the killing, though. You'd think the rabble would learn someday, but the Monster keeps them fastened to him like a new bride."

"It's his promises," a voice called from across the fire. "They're going to be just like the Septed, without working for it—of course they love him. They never loved us, after all. And those Blankshields he's been hiring—some of them are commoners who quit Alghera a long time ago—you want to guess what kind of message that sends?"

"Not just promises," another voice responded. "Even the mob would learn if he never gave them anything but talk, but I've seen plans, with my own eyes, for two settlements Dicovys wanted to build in the last decade which had to be canceled because he let squatters keep the land. Let him fight these stupid wars is the way I see it—better to bleed Loprit and Innings than the Septs. He'll get in trouble someday; we'll outlast the fucker."

"Does that mean you're going back to the Swordtroop after you're ransomed?" someone asked, and there was general laughter.

It dawned on Lerlt—finally—that they were discussing the Warder of the Realm, Mlart tra'Nornst. He stepped backward and twisted sideways, so his face would be obscured, and leaned confidentially toward another prisoner. "Is anyone planning to escape?" he asked quietly.

"What's the point?" the man asked him, and snapped his fingers. "We're small fry, most of us. A couple of Blankshields will have trouble raising their ransom money, but Dicovys looks after its people. We'll be all right, we'll be home before a year tenth passes, without risk. What's your worry?"

Lerlt's cheek twitched, and he raised a hand to press it into stillness. "Don't like to take things for granted," he mumbled, hoping his voice would not be recognized at a later date. "There's such a lot of us."

He couldn't think of anything else to say. He stood, waiting till he was sure he was being ignored, then sidestepped away from the man and away from the fire. He couldn't stand the company of other Algherans, he realized. When the figures around the fire were indistinct, he bent over and picked an armload of grass as quickly as possible, then returned to his companions.

"Thought you'd fallen in quicksand," Herrilmin said when he got there. As a greeting, it lacked warmth. Lerlt had the feeling Herrilmin would have enjoyed watching someone sink into quicksand. Gherst and Fesch nodded more politely but said nothing. They were all wrapped in blankets. Fesch pointed to a small pile of grass drying near the fire, and Lerlt dumped his armload on top, hoping no one would notice how little he changed its height.

"Just checking around," he explained, and waited for someone to ask what he had found.

Herrilmin obliged at last, sounding bored. His eyes were fixed on something small in his hand.

"These Dicovys," Lerlt said, shaking his head, then sitting before the small fire. "They're real bastards. None of them are trying to escape. They aren't even trying to cause trouble for the Lopritians. They think they're going to be exchanged as soon as we get to F'a Loprit." That was enough of an indictment of the other Sept to express, in his mind. Dimly, he suspected the disrespect shown for Mlart the Great might not bother his companions as much as it had him; that was another discovery he did not wish to make.

Herrilmin sat up and stared at him with disbelief, the expression turning swiftly to anger. "Did you tell them anything? Lerlt, I'll kill you if—"

"No. No," he promised quickly. "I just listened. I didn't say a word."

"All right." Herrilmin sank back on his elbow and put his hand into a pocket. "Just be careful, Lerlt. There's more going on than you know. Just be patient."

The last was muttered at the fire rather than him. Lerlt sought his own blanket, breathing easier, but still uncertain what the big man planned.

What was it that Herrilmin had done for Vrect?

The ground was rough and the air turned cold. He slept uncomfortably.

Chapter 8

*A*t midday, *Cherrid made a decision he hoped he would not* regret, and split the brigade in half. The problem was a shortage of water. Small streams were plentiful during this season, but none were large enough to satisfy three thousand men and their camp followers. Consequently, the Steadfast-to-Victory and Defiance-to-Insurrection regiments went on ahead after lunch with one battalion from Her Majesty's Own Puissant Guards Regiment. The other two battalions stayed in place for another day tenth.

"Babying your men, aren't you?" Gertynne ris Vandeign had asked blandly when he proposed the division to the Hand, but it was not a serious remark. "I will be happy to put the Guards first, or last, just as long as they do not have to drink mud," Cherrid commented, and the executive officer nodded quickly, as did all the others.

Mlart was not in range of the brigade yet; only Ironwearer Ian Haarper, who had joined the discussion after Cherrid gestured for him, mentioned the real difficulty: rear units, for reasons no one understood, were especially prone to marching sickness.

"Boil your drinking water," the boy suggested. "That stops *dysentery* as well as anything. It's in the Plates somewhere."

"It's not," Merryn ris Vandeign said flatly, in one of his few contributions to any discussion, and the youngster jerked his shoulders in response.

"Try it anyhow. I've seen it work."

"We do not have time for that, Timmial," Cherrid said. "We can give the water a chance to settle and flow and we will take our chances."

Lan Haarper grimaced but made no protest.

One by-product of dividing the brigade was that more of the stragglers caught up. Cherrid had enough free wagons to ferry most to their proper units. They were primarily from the leading regiments, it seemed—or else his aides were kind enough to spare him contrary knowledge.

Another was that the workload for his scouts and aides increased, because they had larger distances to ride. Cherrid put his supernumeraries who could ride well to use as couriers.

Timmial lan Haarper was too large to be a proper cavalryman and only adequate as a rider, but he was available. Cherrid allowed him to protest his inexperience for several minutes, then sent him forward as a scout.

His instructions were, "Find me a battlefield."

The prisoners marched farther on the third day than they had on the first two. There was no pause for a midday meal; instead in late morning they were given mugs of water with dried grain in the bottom.

Lerlt was about to drink the water and dump the grain, as Fesch did, but Nicole's cloak covered him at that moment. He glanced around and saw that the older prisoners sipped just enough water to keep it from splashing out of their cups and let the rest stay with the grain. It was awkward, marching with a cup wedged between his side and his belt, but he trusted the experienced soldiers knew what they were doing. By afternoon, some of the grain had swollen enough to be chewed without losing teeth, and Lerlt was as pleased with his discovery as if he had reasoned it out himself.

Fesch had fallen behind. Gherst, like Lerlt, had watched the other soldiers and was able to share some of his grain with the younger man when he caught up.

Some of the prisoners were allowed to ride in the supply wagons this day. They were older men, as a rule, who had difficulty continuing to march.

Lerlt toyed with the idea of pretending he was lame until a man just ahead of him settled to the ground and refused to move. He stayed to watch, claiming he wished to help when the guards approached, but they pushed him away. A surgeon came to look at the man, along with an officer and more soldiers. Lerlt could not see the Algheran after that through the screen of onlookers; he saw the muskets rise and fall over and over. Later he saw the man, bandaged and unconscious, on one of the passing wagons, but by then he had convinced himself he could continue to march.

"Just a moment," Dieytl lan Callares said, not bothering to turn as a rider came up behind him.

He sat cross-legged—lean, olive-skinned, frowning, gray-uniformed—on the bed of a poorly sprung wagon, surrounded by wooden boxes. A flintlock pistol in a cloth holster rested against a hip, a paybook in a pocket over his heart. A thumbprint-size scar was at the center of his forehead.

The pistol's two barrels were empty, and the paybook was still blank.

Nearby, a musket and someone's discarded clothing lay between two of the boxes. As the vehicle wobbled, his body swayed, but he kept the writing box on his knee steady with one hand and continued copying orders with the other, pressing the stylus down firmly.

Even an army in retreat has its paperwork.

"Ironwearer Wolf-Twin—" a reedy voice began behind him.

"—wishes to see me and give me new orders. Consider it said, Dighton." Dieytl finished his writing, looked for mistakes to correct, then peeled sheets of paper apart and waved the topmost in the air to dry. In front of him, a stolid teamster flicked reins, encouraging the horses which pulled the wagon. He had not turned about, either.

Near the horizon and beyond there were other wagons on the road, many of them wide and cloth-topped, like moving loaves of bread. Each of those had four teams of horses and two drivers, with orders to pass on without rest: the ambulances carrying a lucky few to the hospitals at Northfaring.

Swelling bodies of the unlucky occasionally lay at the side of the road. By now, Dieytl had learned to see them without noticing their existence.

The road was wide and straight, black-surfaced, smooth and shiny in appearance. Like obsidian, Timmial lan Haarper had said once before he became or re-became an Ironwearer; molten rock frozen like glass after being thrown from a volcano. There were live volcanoes on the western edge of the continent, he had once told Dieytl; a man could walk gasping for air from the height yet be on the lip of a crater and stare all the way down through the skin of the Earth to the raw flesh of the one world itself. A man could—

He *tchk*ed his teeth silently, and wrote numbers on the corners of the documents. A copy for the recipient, the elderly Ironwearer ris Clendannan; a copy for the Hand of the Queen; a copy for Ironwearer Wolf-Twin, whose various duties included keeping duplicate records; yet another copy for the Royal archives . . . The boxes around him contained reams of military correspondence, all of it seemingly valuable as pure iron to judge by its treatment, and all of it likely, if he were any judge of future events, to wind up as tinder for Algharan bonfires.

Like the matériel the brigade had already left behind. Was the Algheran general—Mlart tra'Nornst himself, according to Algheran thoughts—sleeping now in one of the great wagons the Hand had insisted on taking on the campaign? Was he, like the Hand, enjoying the favors of two women on an oversize bed, to celebrate his triumphs?

Mysteries. The man was beyond the reach of Dieytl's mind. Even telepaths sometimes had to live with unanswered questions.

"The Ironwearer—" the reedy voice said.

"Yes, Dighton," he said mechanically. Inside the writing box was a cover for his pen and a narrow-necked ink bottle. He fastened both in place, then stored carbon paper and several of his copies, then latched the box's cover securely. Overhead the sky was more gray than blue; straw-colored grass and bushes lay on both sides of the road. A single tree with bare limbs stood sullenly on a hillside. One of the horses sidestepped, flicking its tail out as a poor counterbalance; the wagon bobbed, and Dieytl rocked with it, keeping his eyes on the horizon.

In the far west, Timmial had said, there were mountains which made the Rims of the Shield seem hills, and great deserts where the air shimmered over flat surfaces like this road; travelers saw distant cities, bodies of water, scenes of worlds which never were . . . He had found his wife there.

Far away, Dieytl thought wistfully. A farm hamlet a few day's march away and Midpassage two days beyond that— those were great distances with the Algherans riding the brigade's heels; those were his long-away horizons.

Home. Midpassage was home and longing for it almost brought tears to his eyes. *Home.* All his life, it had simply been a place where he lived.

He turned finally, looking over his shoulder at men far enough behind to be faceless, nondescript bodies trudging along the sides of the road. Their home also, for many of them. Did those weary anonymous men remember . . . ?

He had no wish to know. He exhaled heavily, then turned the opposite way and handed a document to the scowling scarecrow of a man riding beside the wagon. "I'm done. I can see the Ironwearer now, Dighton. And you can take this back to ris Clendannan; he's expecting it."

*   *   *

Rahmmend Wolf-Twin was a thousand man-heights ahead, in a wagon between lan Haarper's Steadfast-to-Victory Regiment of militia and ris Daimgewln's Defiance-to-Insurrection Regiment. Lan Haarper was sitting by him when Dieytl saw them, the big red-haired man gesturing with both hands as he spoke to the squat dark-skinned quartermaster. Wolf-Twin listened patiently, alternately nodding and shaking his head.

Hitched behind the wagon were their horses, a roan for lan Haarper, a white and black spotted mare for the other Ironwearer. Both seemed to sag under the weight of their saddles, though neither animal was small.

Empty paybooks, Dietyl thought snidely. His career as a money broker would have ended quickly if he ran it on army lines.

Men passed his view slowly, wearing the brown and gray of the militia. Here and there were brighter colors, pieces of the blue-and-red uniforms the Northfaring garrison had worn. An emerald jacket on one man had once belonged to an Algheran cavalry trooper. On each back was a long musket and ammunition pouch. Rolled-up blankets were wrapped over their shoulders, replacing the packs which had disintegrated in the rains. Their motions were economical, steady, without superfluous movement.

He heard no conversations.

But at the rear of the column, ris Clendannan's men still gestured and spoke with some animation. He turned, staring for a moment at a trio of wagons surrounded by milling cavalrymen. The Hand of the Queen was there, easily visible at the front of an ambulance, silent and motionless as a wounded soldier. About him were other nobles, speaking in too loud voices to each other, or quietly to the troopers: Terrens ris Daimgewln, Gertynne ris Vandeign, his brother Merryn, youngsters seeking recognition and promotion . . . All very natural, but for once Dietyl saw his rulers as fallible and very ordinary beings. Was it possible that the Algherans with their almost classless Septs and elected leaders had constructed a better society than what men would naturally build?

What would Timmial say? he wondered. Something unsettling, perhaps? In peacetime, they had often met at the tavern in Midpassage for beer and conversations. Even then, it seemed, the man had had secrets to keep behind his strangely shielded mind.

Like his marriage. Like his disturbingly quiet Teep wife, Kylene. Years had passed while he knew Timmial, and until she was there, he had never heard of her existence.

Before the war. Before all secrets and all weaknesses were exposed.

Far behind, out of sight now, were ris Clendannan and his men. The rear guard. Mercifully, everything was peaceful at the moment. Dieytl watched from the side of the road, then slipped past the end of a file of infantry and waited to be noticed as he approached the wagon.

It was lan Haarper who nodded at him, then took his arm as he stepped up on the axle and pulled him over the side. Wincing as he squatted on the dusty bed of the wagon, Dieytl brushed as much dirt as he could from the rest of his uniform. Luxury, he reflected wistfully, was really nothing more than regular bathing and clean clothing.

"How's Kylene?" lan Haarper asked.

"Fine," he said automatically, giving a mechanical answer to a mechanical question. Lan Haarper's wife was too distant for him to probe, and he had tired of explaining that to the Normal.

"Good. You want to go north?" the Ironwearer asked, his smile suggesting that Dieytl was content just where he was.

To Midpassage? Yes, and for good, Dieytl thought. But Wolf-Twin was looking at him, his eyes solemn, the pudgy lips on his dark face moving in and out like a pouting child's, and Dieytl realized he needed a more serious answer.

But what was the question? They expected him to know, didn't they?

He froze for an instant, unfocusing his awareness from his body. On one side of him was a void, an emptiness reflecting a man's shape but no consciousness; on the other the alien shadows of animals. Then, in a dizzying fashion he could never hope to explain, he was suddenly in two minds, seeing through two sets of eyes and listening with two sets of ears.

Almost obediently, Wolf-Twin thought out what he would have spoken if Dieytl had been a Normal: Timmial was to seek possible sites for delaying actions along the road to Midpassage. He was willing to take Dieytl along if he wanted.

Behind those thoughts were others: clarifications, reasons, expectations. The ideas that might have been said aloud, Dieytl examined. That much was scrupulous and should not cause resentment.

The most prominent thought was that Wolf-Twin wished him to leave the brigade for some while to keep from answering ris Clendannan's questions about the following Algherans. The Hand was opposed to using Teeps that way; Wolf-Twin himself thought it unlikely the help he gave was reliable and feared that ris Clendannan, provided with too much knowledge of Mlart's movements, would become reckless.

He was sure enough of his own judgments not to ask Dieytl for opinions which would differ.

Deeper than that, Wolf-Twin ruminated on the current state of the army and its supplies, evaluated factions in Queen Molminda's governing councils and the army command, computed the resources that could be husbanded for sieges or future battles. Self-confidence, ambition, and impatience blazed beneath the squat Ironwearer's stolid composure, but Teeps learned not to probe motives without good cause. Dieytl pulled back, in a sense forgetting Wolf-Twin's opinions as he exited the man's mind.

A battle within days? That was enough of a discovery. Exhaustion and disbelief kept Dieytl's stomach from turning, but something of what he felt must have showed on his face. Lan Haarper said nothing, but he raised an eyebrow quizzically as he waited for Dieytl to speak.

Ironwearers. How alien they were!

"I can't do it, but thanks," Dieytl said ruefully. "I've got too much work to do here, as it is. Good luck, Timmial."

At nightfall, Mlart tra'Nornst had reached the brigade's old camp and collected the enlisted men from the Dicovys division. He had one other full division with him and part of a second. Lopritian resistance continued in Barlynnt's Tower; parts of the city were still besieged.

Cherrid had that information from Dieytl lan Callares's mindreading of the cavalry scouts preceding the main body of the Swordtroop. The Algheran general himself was too distant to probe, Dieytl reported; he agreed wryly with Cherrid's comment that Teeps could not work miracles.

Weighing Dieytl's report and guesses from his own cavalry, Cherrid felt the main body of the Algherans was roughly thirty thousand man-heights behind him. It was too great a distance, it seemed to him. The brigade had to be closer to the Algherans to be an effective lure. All was lost if Mlart chose to destroy ris Cornoval first and only moved north with his force united.

The pace the brigade had set was of his own making, but he snapped at his staff that night and even at Grahan. It was not till the end of the fourth watch, when only he and sentries were denied sleep, that he decided Mlart would have suspected a trap in a slow retreat. The Algheran had larger numbers and a reputation to uphold; he would pursue the Strength-through-Loyalty Brigade relentlessly.

Evening strength reports told him the brigade now had 3,093 effectives, 315 sick and wounded, and 21 men under arrest. About fifty men had died; a surgeon wanted another fifteen sent away to the north.

"Do this," he endorsed, and stared at the numbers before him until they could not be read in the dying firelight.

Then Cherrid was able to sleep.

Near dawn, three men on horseback with their remounts cantered past the sleeping Algheran prisoners. They carried extra rations, simple surveying tools, and writing boxes for making sketches. They spoke very little. The leader was tall and red-haired, with a scarred temple.

If Lerlt's tired muscles had permitted him wakefulness, he would have thought them of no importance.

Rations were reduced for the Strength-through-Loyalty Brigade on the third day of their retreat to the minimum needed for the soldiers. Cherrid, mixing intuition and judgment, halted the march after slightly more than fifteen thousand man-heights had been covered.

There were more camp followers than before resting at the side of the road on the fourth day as the brigade moved on, and some were clearly too exhausted to continue. Marching sickness had infected them as well; the sour smell of diarrhea filled the air above the great road. Some of the forms lying on the ground might be dead already, Cherrid knew; they certainly would be by the next day, and their numbers would increase steadily. Grimly, with a sour taste on his tongue caused by more than the stench, he pretended he did not see them. When an aide persisted in drawing his attention to them, he snapped that only men with guns deserved to be fed, then invented a task that would keep the young officer out of sight for the remainder of the day.

The brigade halted well before evening this time, less to draw Mlart onward than to give the troops extra time for cooking meals, tending their sick, drying their wet clothes, and digging latrines. The deer meat that had been harvested a few days before was almost gone by now; his supper rested like a stone, heavy and indigestible, in Cherrid's stomach that night.

Strength reports gave him 3,064 effectives that evening, 290 sick, and 8 men under arrest. He received no surgeon's report, which might be either a good or bad omen.

Throughout the fourth watch, he heard men shuffling to the latrines and back, and wondered if they did so in normal numbers. He was terrified of being incapacitated by marching sickness, he realized with an old man's clarity; when morning came, he would send Grahan to the Hand to solicit some bottles of wine or even ask that his drinking water be boiled as Ian Haarper advised.

In his dreams, he hovered unseen over Mlart's army while wagon after wagon of supplies and reinforcements poured into the Algheran camp.

Tim Harper dreamed also that night, with his head resting on a saddle and only a blanket between the stars and his body. Onnul Nyjuc was in his arms; the war against the Alliance was over and she loved him, but her features were indistinct. As his lips moved toward her, she became smaller; her hair turned from blond to raven black; her face became narrower and freckle-specked; her eyes became almond-shaped with green irises.

Ejaculation brought him awake. Shamefaced, moving stealthily so he would not disturb the two engineers, he wiped himself clean with his underwear, then set it aside for discard in the morning. Over his head, alien stars glittered; though he tried, he could not force them into constellations of either the First or Fifth Era.

He lay without sleeping the rest of the night and let the engineers believe it was responsibility which caused him to wake them at dawn.

Looking backward, Cherrid saw tiny men and horses on a ridge the brigade had crossed the day before, and knew they were not his own cavalry. This was unsurprising, but an annoyance nonetheless, a feeling which lasted even after the enemy troopers were lost to sight behind another ridge.

His aides showed discomfort more openly than he himself allowed, one going so far as to leave the road for a while and discreetly, out of Cherrid's sight but not hearing, retch up the breakfast he had taken.

In the early afternoon, cavalrymen congregated at the rear of the column and rode south, out of sight. A day tenth later, most of them returned, at a faster pace than they had left, excitedly speaking of a great clash. After putting together the stories, Cherrid's staff reported to him that two Lopritians had received wounds from enemy muskets and that two Algherans had been killed in return and several more wounded. Cherrid suspected that the honors and the wounds had been equal, but he was unwilling to sacrifice enthusiasm on the altar of fact; he let his aides send the report to the Hand.

Pragmatically, at the same time, he sent another aide to locate Dieytl lan Callares. The aide returned after a quarter watch with the information that Rahm Wolf-Twin had protested his officers had other duties to perform and would not release the Teep. Cherrid found this amusing rather than bothersome; despite the aide's insistence on Wolf-Twin's sincerity, he was sure the squat Ironwearer, who had remained in the front of the column with other high-ranking officers, was deferring to the Hand's religious prejudices rather than his own feelings.

He was about to send the aide off again, with a firmly worded note, when lan Callares arrived. Satisfied, he snapped his fingers and made paper tearing gestures at the young officer; the aide complied, sulkily it seemed to Cherrid, then looked for other tasks. Cherrid waited side by side with the Teep while his third battalion marched past, then gestured toward the enemy cavalry, which, undeterred by catastrophic defeat, had reappeared and continued to move toward the Lopritians.

Lan Callares turned his head slightly, as if looking for individuals, though his eyes were closed. He frowned, then smiled ruefully. When he spoke, he answered Cherrid's irrelevant curiosity first: "Just a habit, Lord Clendannan. People are more comfortable with Teeps when it looks as if they have to work to see into minds."

He smiled again at Cherrid's murmur. "The main body is about ten thousand man-heights behind us. Mlart and his staff are further behind, still out of range—that's probably intentional. Ris Cornoval is still holding out, as far as the cavalrymen know."

Ten thousand man-heights was less than a day's march. A night's march? Cherrid shuffled plans inside his head.

"No one I can reach knows of secret plans," the Teep commented. "They all expect to rest at dusk and catch us in another couple of days. No, they wouldn't disobey orders to keep going, but they've got problems with stragglers and food themselves."

Cherrid had no reason to hide his thoughts. "If I were Mlart, I would tell them to catch us tonight, attack while we sleep, and plunder our food."

"You're a nasty old bastard," Dieytl said evenly, and Cherrid chuckled without taking offense.

"Those stragglers—?"

"Not much of our doing," the Teep admitted. "What it seems like is that Mlart took the men who weren't from Dicovys out of that division and used them as reinforcements. The rest are still sitting close to where we left them. I don't know if he knew they'd been infected, or wants them to have Dicovys's officers, or what."

"Algheran politics," Cherrid said, half-confidently. He did not understand Mlart's reasoning, either, but he had often observed that governing men who lacked a king and strong nobles was three times as complex as it might be.

"Hmmm," the Teep murmured. "Anyhow, it doesn't seem that Mlart is being seriously troubled by the men we infected. I'd guess he's learned about it—someone must have understood what happened, but I can't see it.

"I'm sorry, Lord Clendannan, but there are ten thousand minds there, and I can't see them and I don't know any of those Algherans. I'm not good enough to be selective about which minds I see into; I can only check here and there and hope I'm not missing anything important."

Can't I get him away from Wolf-Twin? Cherrid wondered. Would that make a difference? Inhaling deeply, he waited and considered possibilities. "Well, Teep? Dieytl?"

The telepath swallowed. "I'm better as a quartermaster, sir.

Wolf-Twin does have work that has to be done, and I can't force people to think about the things I'd like them to think; I could spend all my time at this, and still not have anything more to tell you."

He swallowed again. "I don't want to be close to the fighting, sir. I'm sorry."

Cherrid sighed, but he had given the man the freedom to turn him down, and was not really surprised. "A little knowledge is better than none, Dieytl. I appreciate the help you have given me, Captain, particularly since it was volunteered, in the face of . . . Sometimes, you know, I understand just why people in the past were so afraid of giving power to Teeps."

"What Teeps can do makes everything else so complicated. They ought to be—controlled—or normal people will lose direction of their own lives." Lan Callares spoke without looking toward him, his voice without feeling.

Those were his thoughts. Cherrid shook his head gravely.

" 'Use turns to reliance, reliance to dependence, dependence to slavery,' " the telepath continued, still showing no emotion. "A little aphoristic, to my tastes. Timmial said that one night, when we were drinking."

Fifty million Normals cannot be governed by a million Teeps, Cherrid thought. *A commoner can aspire to nobility and sometimes achieve it. Non-telepaths cannot hope to become mind readers.*

He let the thought hang between them for a moment, then coughed. "Let's take care of the Algherans first, young man. Some conflicts our sons can handle."

"I don't have children." The Teep's words were a peace offering.

"Nor do I," Cherrid admitted. "Well, I have work to do, I can see. Tell the Hand I told you whatever you see in my mind."

Chapter 9

Cherrid's "work" was, of course, the writing of more orders. In consequence, the fifth day of the march ended late; the sixth began early.

Mlart's cavalry ranged no closer—perhaps there had been substance to the tale of that clash—but the main body of the Swordtroop surely receded, a fact confirmed near midday by Dieytl lan Callares. Cherrid breathed easier.

Not all remained so well. What was left of the hastily butchered deer was inedible; Cherrid had the stripped carcasses dumped into the streams the brigade passed, with less hope of tainting the water than of annoying the Algherans. This had been the last of the meat; the brigade was forced now to subsist on corn and parched grain.

In midafternoon, a cavalry troop caught a vagrant and unwary rabbit, an old bachelor buck weighing twice as much as a man, which provided full plates that evening for the cavalry and a sliver of meat for everyone else. One trooper was injured in the struggle by a kick to the stomach; throughout the brigade that night he was toasted as an honorable casualty of war, and ris Daimgewln semi-seriously proposed to Terrault ris Andervyll that the Hand add an honorific "lan" to the man's name.

Attempts at humor did not end there, unfortunately—gossip among his staff told Cherrid that the Midpassage men at the head of the column, exposed daily to the sight and stares of the Hand's two plump mistresses in the wagon just behind them, were joking about roasting and consuming the women; one had approached them with a stick, explaining he needed measurements to construct an oven; others within their hearing debated the proper use of spices and the composition of stuffing mixtures.

Ris Andervyll, recognizing the difference between jest and plot, pretended to misunderstand the conversations that reached his wagon. The women were not so tolerant, though Dieytl lan Callares had assured them they faced only verbal fricassees: they complained with equal volume and shouted threats and insults back at the soldiers, doubling the Midpassagers' jocularity and annoying the Hand.

Neither Gertynne nor Merryn ris Vandeign, who should have handled the matter, had interceded with the men. Cherrid took the task upon himself and went to speak with Dalsyn lan Plenytk.

"It's a dumb gag," Dalsyn admitted. "It got started and enough of them think it funny that it keeps going. They want to show how rough and tough they are, that's all." His hand waved toward the men marching by, many of them wearing green garments taken from the Swordtroop captives. "Let them have their game, Ironwearer. It's not hurting anyone and they've earned it. They'll get tired of it eventually."

"I would like it stopped now," Cherrid said. "It is a distraction and we do not need it."

"The Hand hasn't bitched about it."

Cherrid frowned. "The Hand is a gentleman, *lan* Plenytk."

Dalsyn paused for an instant. "It's really the women's fault, in a way; if they walked some of the time like anyone else or fixed rations, the men would think better of them, but they stay in that wagon acting like queens and getting full rations cooked for them without lifting a finger . . . Tell them to act like common people and everything will be all right.''

"I am not going to do that," Cherrid said, letting anger show at last. "I am telling you to tell your men to shut up. If they have so much energy and cheerfulness, it can be put to better use. They can dig all the latrines and cooking pits for this brigade, for example. Is my meaning clear?"

Dalsyn stiffened. "Yes, Lord Clendannan."

"That's good." But Cherrid was still annoyed, and he had another barb to insert before he left. "I cannot believe I would have required this discussion with Timmial lan Haarper."

The younger man's eyes flickered. "Probably not. He didn't run things with threats."

"I am talking about discipline, not threats," Cherrid said. But it had taken half a minute to formulate that rejoinder; he knew it was not an effective answer. He threw his hands up and sighed. "Just do it, lan Plenytk. I am trying to treat your men reasonably. Is it too much for them to act with normal human civility?"

"No." Dalsyn nodded slowly. "It would help, you know, if they had Timmial back. They'll obey me, but—they'd be happier."

So would I. Cherrid shook his head silently.

That evening he had 2,883 effectives, 456 sick, and 11 men under arrest. "No more arrests," Cherrid told his officers. "Keep the men in the ranks or kill them if they deserve it."

It was cloudy the next morning and drizzle began to fall on the rolling countryside in early afternoon. Staff officers hastily raised tarps over a pair of wagons to cover the Hand and his party and themselves. In the rear ranks of the Midpassage Battalion, men turned about and marched backward, uselessly holding hands over their heads to keep the rain at bay, and

screamed in unconvincing falsetto voices that their makeup
was simply being ruined and that their delicate complexions
would absolutely never recover.

The Hand turned to Gertynne ris Vandeign for a discussion
of the weather's effect on the coming year's crops. It was not
a subject either man knew very well, but they made the talk
last. The Hand's mistresses sat in a separate wagon. They had
actually accepted the rain stoically, and now, observing they
were being neither defended nor supervised, they responded to
the soldiers with gestures they had certainly not learned at
Court.

To one side, Dieytl lan Callares smiled cynically, reflecting
that everyone but him had found a distraction to make the rain
bearable. Imperceptibly, he reined in his horse, then shook his
head as Dighton ris Maanhaldur rode up. "Thought I'd drop
back some and see how the wagons are holding up."

Dighton made a well-practiced gesture of resignation.

"Tell Wolf-Twin if he notices. I won't be long." Dieytl
smiled at the younger man's disbelieving grimace, then turned
his horse about and left the road. Wagons rumbled by over his
head as he rode south; he paid them no heed.

As the last of the infantry passed, he rode his horse back up
to the road. The rain had increased. He passed several camp
followers who sat with cupped hands collecting water to drink;
one nursed a child. Behind masks of fatigue and rain, they
seemed sexless and infinitely ancient. He could do nothing to
help them; Dieytl found his own relief sensing that their minds
retained an individuality their bodies did not show.

He came to a halt midway between the retreating column and
the stationary cavalry rear guard. His eyes closed and he moved
from one world into another with a reality and beauty which
Normals could never appreciate. In that instant, beyond the
clear bubble which was his own consciousness, the multicol-
ored spheres of other minds moved in stately harmony, each
radiating its own distinctive hue through a revolving nimbus of
emotion.

As his perceptions transported those spheres into the orb

which was Dieytl, they swelled, revealed unimaginable detail and coloration. Above the world that was a mind, he gazed into continents of thought and plumbed seas of memory. His own identity was shunted aside until he chose to resume it. Until then, he heard with others' ears, saw with others' eyes, felt with others' hearts.

Harness jingled. A horse neighed. He heard hooves clopping on the pavement. Dieytl opened his eyes on the Normal world, but for an instant two views of reality coincided in his mind. He touched heels to his own horse to catch up with the cavalrymen who had just ridden past him.

"Enemy cavalry on the back side of that hill," he reported to the tall young lieutenant leading the troop.

"So I heard," the man said. "Can you say how many, Captain?"

Dieytl pointed. "About twenty. They're aware of the squadron that's there already."

"Ahh-h." The lieutenant wiped rain from his face and black hair with a sleeve. "So if I go up the road, sir, and split my force evenly, we'll outnumber the enemy on one side of the road?"

Dieytl was hesitant, especially after viewing the images in the cavalryman's mind. "Those are good-sized hills," he warned. "I don't think you'll surprise them."

"Maybe we'll frighten them some," the lieutenant said wryly, his mind showing likelier but far more mundane pictures of misfiring rifles and distant fleeing horsemen. "This isn't weather fit for fighting, after all. Want to come along, sir?"

Dieytl pictured an angry Wolf-Twin waiting for his return and reflected that "sir" was not a word he had often heard in his brief army career, despite his temporary rank. "Sure."

"Okay, stick by me, sir. Remember I'm commanding." The cavalry officer made gestures with his hands to direct his men, then leaned confidentially toward the telepath. "Thought you might like to see some real action, sir, instead of hanging around the headquarters with the other Requisitionary Corps farts. I've watched you staring after us, and talking to Lord Clendannan, too. Were you asking for a transfer?''

"Something like that," Dieytl said diplomatically, recalling ambiguous thoughts in Cherrid's mind which made his remark a bit less than a total lie.

In fact, he had speculated that the bad weather might have brought Mlart tra'Nornst and his staff closer to the body of the Swordtroop. Riding with the cavalry would place him another one or two thousand man-heights closer yet and provide an escort. This was not weather in which a fight was likely, and this was his best chance to find really valuable information for Cherrid ris Clendannan. He was very grateful to this ignorant lieutenant.

"Of course, the final decision isn't Lord Clendannan's."

"Well, our officers listen very carefully to ris Clendannan. My major swears by that old man," the cavalry officer said. "Couldn't love him more if ris Clendannan owed him a debt of honor and was getting sticky about the payments, though I don't suppose you've been there."

Dieytl smiled, professionally mute.

"You keep asking him for your transfer and someday you'll get it."

"I'll remember that," Dieytl promised. *I want to go home, Cherrid. I want to go home, I want to go home.*

He was struck from the front on the left side of his jaw, as he turned to answer another comment from the lieutenant. The impact was just below his lip, and it came from a bullet of about the shape and weight of the first joint of an adult man's index finger. The bullet was bronze with a hollow center, its velocity nearly 150 man-heights per second; fired by a sharpshooter from a camouflaged pit near the summit of the hill, its trajectory was slightly downward.

Air resistance affected the path but not the shape of the bullet. It began to flatten at the instant it touched skin, and continued to bloom into a mushroom-shape metal wad as it passed through muscle and bone. With this blunt contour, the bullet slowed rapidly. Virtually all the original kinetic energy and momentum of the projectile was transmitted to a thumbprint-size cross section of the man's face.

Much of the bone of his left lower jaw and lower palate was shattered and pushed to the rear, along with quantities of flesh and blood. Skin was ripped from his cheek from as high up as his eye socket. For an instant, at the back of the jaw, a grapefruit-size bulge formed below the ear, then burst under the pressure. Shock waves within the tissues of his mouth ripped his tongue halfway from its root and split it lengthwise like an overcooked sausage. Teeth exploded from his jaw like enameled popcorn and added to the lacerations of the tongue and oral cavity; some penetrated the nasal cavities.

He had not yet begun to feel pain. His conscious mind was still forming his remark to the lieutenant, and his senses had not even analyzed the sound of the gunshot, though that had reached him even before the bullet did.

The body is resilient. Arrested at this point and properly treated, the injury would have been disfiguring but not necessarily fatal. But to ask that would be to ask the impossible.

The bullet had struck his face off-center while his body was moving. Its force whipped his head back and turned it simultaneously at awkward angles, crushing vertebrae, distending and rupturing the top portion of his spinal column. After that, his limbs would never respond to his will.

The head's momentum pulled his body backward from the horse as well and spun him in midair. He struck the road on the damaged side of his face; its unyielding surface rammed the bony prominence above his eye into his left temporal lobe and cracked his skull. Bone splinters punctured his left eye. Brain tissue was forced through the optic-nerve channel into the cavity this formed; more spewed into his sinuses and between his cranium and the skin that covered it. Blood poured from his mouth.

He understood none of this. He was filled instead— suddenly, by his senses' sluggish and misleading report—with body- and mind-searing pain which erased all other sensation.

It was pain so intense that he had no chance to realize he also felt loneliness and surprise and grief, nor opportunity to examine his certain knowledge that this agony would never—
End.

The Lopritian officer's horse had bolted along with the others when the enemy cavalry force fled from the ambush, but the officer still lay where he had fallen on the black pavement. The two Algheran troopers who claimed to have fired the fatal shot both dismounted to search the body.

The blood that had pooled beneath the body was washed away in pink rivulets when they turned it. The falling rain cleansed the face of gore; the more perceptive Algherans reflected that the man had once been handsome, even with a branded forehead.

It was a Teep's body, but an officer's, and it had not cooled much before they reached it. Semi-superstitiously, as if fearing it would return to life, the two troopers treated the corpse with more respect than it deserved. They did not recognize the patterns of lace on the blue sleeves, so they cut off an arm of the uniform for their superiors to analyze. The boots were too large for either of them, but of good material; they took them as well.

The body carried no papers of interest and nothing identifiable as money. When they were through with the search, the two men lifted it and left it at the side of the road as the troop leader ordered. It was an officer's body; Teep or not, enemy or not, it might receive proper burial at some time.

Meanwhile the Lopritian flight went on. The enemy cavalry had retreated to the next hill. The Algherans remounted and continued their reconnaissance.

Lerlt welcomed the rain, at first, thinking it would soon bring the prisoners' march to a halt, but that did not happen. The initial sprinkling stopped in early afternoon, but the sky was still covered. Only ragged golden borders showed that a sun remained behind the gray clouds and darkness on the horizon showed where rain continued to fall.

On the roadbed, drivers lashed at their horses. Lopritian officers conferred to one side of the prisoners; they dispersed, and soon the ordinary soldiers began pressing near the Algherans, telling them to hurry.

Soon the rain began again, in earnest, cold and hard. Lerlt's clothing, already damp, became wet through and through. Water covered his face and ran over his eyes and pooled in his boots. It became difficult to see further than the rank just ahead, and moisture filled his nose. He became separated from Fesch. Men stumbled on all sides.

When Lerlt stopped, someone pushed at him and shouted; a thunderclap hid the language. The Algheran was bent over with his hands on his knees. He pushed back, trying to win time to breathe, and a musket butt thumped his ribs. More surprised than hurt, and off-balance, he fell onto the muddy ground, crushing bedraggled wildflowers. Blurrily, he looked up, seeing a soldier behind a curtain of rain posed with his musket to strike again. He put his arms up to protect his face, but the soldier settled for prodding him with a foot. Lerlt scurried away on hands and knees and got to his feet when he was beyond the man's reach.

After that he kept moving for endless day tenths, though his pace was not always rapid. He kept himself surrounded by other Algherans, and trudged onward with his face down, waiting for the agony to stop. Daylight ended but the march continued.

Finally there were Lopritians on both sides of him in the darkness, shouting incomprehensible words and waving their muskets. Lerlt moved in either direction but could not avoid them.

Suddenly the sky was even darker. Then the shouts about him were in Algheran Speech. The men ahead of him ceased to move. The muddy ground was turned to plank floor and the rain was stopped, though he was so wet this took time to notice.

He was inside a building.

A barn, he realized at last. Protection. For a moment he let himself enjoy the discomfort of the Lopritians who remained outside in the rain.

Then his own discomforts returned to mind. The barn was crowded with Algherans, noisy men still half-blind with rain, bellowing foolishly at each other and stepping onto each other's feet as they bumbled about the interior. His clothing was soaked and getting no drier in the cold dank air. The mortar that coated the baked-dirt walls was crumbling when he pressed against it and left streaks of gritty material on his clothing. Instead of proper windows to admit light, there were only openings crudely covered with frames holding translucent cloth. The rough plank floor was dirty to begin with and was now liberally mud-bedabbled—no proper place to sit, and surely a degrading and hard bedstead in the evening. It was dangerous to sit down, with so many men milling about, and only some stalls along the wall provided convenient places to lean and regain strength—unfairly, but not to his surprise, bigger men than Lerlt had already bullied their way to the few comfortable spots in the barn.

Outside, rain continued to pummel the one Earth. Jagged bolts of lightning rent the dark sky. Thunderbolts crashed. Lerlt, seeking to move away from the gaping entrance to the barn, stumbled on a floorboard. An elbow caught his chest, then his face. "Watch it, mate! Well—"

He tumbled from wood onto concrete, then scrambled to his feet, but not before warm liquid splashed from the wall onto his face and hands. An older man stood before him, his hands buttoning up his fly.

"Careless twit! Watch where you're going, will you?"

Lerlt breathed heavily, wanting to wipe his hands across the other man's face. "Bastard! I can kill you for that."

"Bastard, eh?" the man growled. He raised a hand head-high and snapped his fingers. "We can see about that. Who are you?"

Lerlt did not have enough light to read the man's rank patches, but he suddenly noticed they were larger than his own and more ornate. "Why should I tell you?" he demanded.

"Why indeed," the older man said, looking upward as if the roof were leaking on him. "Keep your name."

"Magister?" a basso voice asked from behind Lerlt.

"This fellow walked into my piss and blamed me," the man said. "Doesn't think much of my ancestors. He's gotten dirty, like his mind. He needs another bath."

The man had friends, Lerlt realized.

"It's all right." He stepped backward—

—onto air. He kicked uselessly as hands gripped his elbows and upper arms and lifted him above the ground. There were two sets of hands, from two men. Both were the size of Herrilmin or even larger. They wore black-and-scarlet uniforms rather than the green of the Swordtroop; they lacked rank badges but crossed metal swords gleamed on their collars. Housetroops, acting as bodyguards—Lerlt suddenly realized whom he had confronted, and was too terrified to continue struggling.

"Do you want him back, sir?" the taller Ironwearer asked.

"I'm sorry, tra'Dicovys," Lerlt said quickly, but no one listened.

"No," the Dicovys Sept Master nodded curtly. "He didn't recognize me till now. I don't need to know him."

"You can let me down," Lerlt said. "Look, I apologize. It—it was a mistake. I'm really sorry."

"One bath coming up," the taller Ironwearer said, and the two of them walked out of the barn, still supporting Lerlt by the arms. Insultingly, they continued to hold him in the air even in the rain, without breathing hard, and stood without blinking as the water splashed onto their faces.

Ironwearers and Ironwearers. Lerlt suddenly recalled the only Ironwearer he knew by name—a red-haired Agent he had sometimes seen at the Station. Another giant and another Dicovys. A morose man with strange interests, as Lerlt recalled, but for all that a human being—the implacability and lack of

emotion of these men was something he could not understand.
He felt as if he were in the hands of trained but still dangerous
wild animals.

Even animals tire of their fun at last. After the third thunderclap smote his ears, the Ironwearers finally released Lerlt.
"Be careful, punk," the taller one said, leaning over to speak
in Lerlt's ear. "If you can't be polite, at least make sure you
know who you're rude to." He managed to make it sound like
an uncle's advice.

Lerlt staggered back into the barn. He didn't know if it was
rain or tears which dripped down his face.

"Here he is." A hand reached out to accompany the voice
and grabbed Lerlt's arm as he drifted by the stalls. It was
Gherst ha'Hujsuon's voice.

Lerlt turned, to see the other three Agents. Herrilmin was
leaning against the wall of the stall, his hat in his hand, picking
at the lining as if that mattered more than anything else. Fesch
was beside him, sitting on the stoop of an unlit doorway in the
interior wall of the barn. Lerlt glimpsed additional stalls behind
his back. Gherst was at the edge of the stall; it was his arm
which had caught the smaller man.

"We missed you, Septling." Gherst sounded sincere but
Lerlt waited before he spoke, expecting one or the other of the
Agents to comment on his encounter with tra'Dicovys and his
thugs.

But nothing was said. His demeaning mistreatment had not
been witnessed. The blush faded from his cheeks, unnoticed in
the barn's gloom. "Just looking around," he said weakly.
"Where are we?"

"West Bend," Gherst said. "Where'd you think?"

He nodded dumbly. The name was meaningless.

Fesch opened his mouth, saying something without sound,
and raised his head as if to show confidence. Lerlt stared, then
went closer, and Fesch moved his mouth as if to shout again.

"Tonight." It was a whisper.

Tonight. Lerlt had a mad vision of the four time travelers

running down the great road as the rain poured upon them and soldiers shouted. Tonight? In this impossible weather? He wanted to scream in protest.

But the effort was too great. Emotion drained from him: feelings and fears and sanity alike splashed soddenly on the muddy planks in a great but brief torrent. Tonight, of course. Maximum risk coupled with maximum discomfort— why had he ever thought Herrilmin's plans contained any other ingredients? Tonight, of course, when failure was guaranteed.

We won't mind the rain when we're dead, he told himself. It was funny. He smiled at his joke, then laughed at it, and laughed louder when he realized the other men would not enjoy it. When they stared, he laughed even louder.

Herrilmin slapped him suddenly, dispassionately, then leaned back against his wall and watched Lerlt quietly. Gherst and Fesch also watched, without moving.

Lerlt felt drops of water dripping about him. He turned, awkwardly, but the dripping continued. The eyes watching him continued to stare.

Would they leave him behind? He couldn't permit that to happen. "This is great weather for it," he said hoarsely, hoping to be understood. "Real great weather."

Herrilmin snapped his fingers, and Lerlt could breathe again. He had won a reprieve.

Rain continued through supper. The meal, when it came, was no more than the grain and water they had been fed on other days, but bins of cracked meal sat against one wall of the barn. The prisoners were able to supplement their rations with the tasteless stuff; the more ambitious secreted additional meal in the pockets of their clothing.

Gherst had been born in an agricultural settlement. From his incautious remarks, Lerlt learned the meal was food for cattle. Where were the animals themselves? Outside, Gherst guessed, in pens beyond the prisoners' reach, guarded against the hunger of both the captives and the Lopritian soldiers.

Who would be the guards? Gherst shook his head to show ignorance, but a smile touched his lips. Lerlt was sure he lied but could not understand why.

Though meat was unobtainable, fire was not, despite the rain. Outside the barn doors, Lopritian soldiers huddled in collective misery around their sizzling campfires; inside, the prisoners used straw from the lofts as kindling and tore up floor planks for fuel. A dozen fires were banked against the barn's pastel walls of earth; the interior space soon became bright and warm, almost friendly in semblance, though in the middle of the floor smoke settled, adding a grainy scintillating gleam to what vision showed.

Herrilmin brooded darkly all through the meal without speaking, though when Fesch mentioned securing meal for the future, he was quick to gesture "No." When Gherst clumsily dropped his mug and broke the handle, the big man swore at him and threw it at the wall where it broke into even more pieces.

The blond man's nerves were troubling him, Lerlt guessed. In some ways that was a welcome development, but his silence was contagious. Three times Lerlt started to say something to breach a lull in conversation and discovered none of the others had words to contribute. Fortunately, the other Algherans were making enough noise with their own conversations that they did not notice the behavior of the Agents.

After the meal, the Lopritians pushed a wagon filled with blankets into the barn. There was a great deal of smoke in the air then; the Lopritians did not stay and only partly closed the big door when they left. Lerlt could not tell if that helped ventilate the space or not.

The fires were still burning, so there was no immediate rush to the wagon. One by one the time travelers approached and removed a blanket. Lerlt was the last. He turned slowly to record a last glimpse of captivity, then followed his Septlings, passing over what was now a dirt floor to the stalls in the side of the barn.

No one felt like talking. They wrapped themselves in the blankets and pretended to sleep. Perhaps several managed it.

Timmithial lan Haarper returned to the Strength-through-Loyalty Brigade at what would have been sunset on a drier day. He was on foot, leading a horse. The two engineers were not with him.

"Thought you'd want what we had in a hurry," the big man told Cherrid when they were together in one of the ambulances at the back of the column. "So I kept coming. The other fellows are trying to keep their heads above water somewhere back. Hooo, it's wet!" He had been rubbing a towel through his red-brown hair; he shook his head now and water drops flew to every corner of the narrow vehicle.

"No rust?" He eyed the towel suspiciously.

Cherrid was patient. Rain was still drumming noisily on the canvas top and sides of the wagon, and neither moon nor stars were visible through the clouds. Even on the great road, travel was not practical now, so he was stuck to this spot and presumably the Algherans were equally stuck. The race with Mlart tra'Nornst could resume tomorrow, and Cherrid comforted himself with the knowledge that he had ordered all the horses and vehicles up onto the roadbed as soon as the rain became severe; he had other problems to cope with, but at least he would not spend all the next morning pulling wheels out of mud.

Conspicuously but uselessly, lan Haarper wiped his hands on his dark trousers. Behind him, Grahan coughed and extended a second towel. The young Ironwearer smiled sardonically and wiped his hands once more, then reached inside his tunic for sheets of folded paper. "Nothing really matched everything on your wish list, Cherrid, but this one rates a possible. It's about fifteen thousand man-heights this side of West Bend."

The papers were almost invisible in the gloom inside the ambulance. Grahan guessed his need without words and adjusted the fuel mixture in the overhanging lanterns, giving

Cherrid enough light both to see where water had penetrated the back curtain of the vehicle and to examine the papers without squinting. Lan Haarper, at a gesture, seated himself on a stretcher and began to pick mud from his boots.

Cherrid reflected that the man deserved a meal, but such details were Grahan's province.

The man also deserved to be told a friend had died. That was a task he could properly do, but not one Cherrid welcomed, and he admitted to himself he would not raise the subject unless lan Haarper said something which led naturally to it. Perhaps someone had told him already. No doubt someone would, perhaps more tactfully than he.

Perhaps a meal was coming, too. Uncomfortable with himself, he moved beneath a light and concentrated on the papers.

There were three crude maps, which he deciphered slowly. One was a frontal view of a low ridge before some hills, with stands of trees and hollows in the ground indicated roughly; another showed the same ridge from behind, under a wavy line which was evidently one more ridge; the final map showed some of the details between the brigade's position of three days ago and the river at West Bend.

Cherrid translated the sketches to mental images almost reluctantly. A child could have drawn them better, he admitted, and he remembered wistfully the details shown in the *paiynnings* lan Haarper's young wife produced. Kylene's pictures would have shown him the scene as clearly as the big map in the abandoned command wagon. The engineer's drawings were sadly inferior.

On the other hand, Kylene's pictures did not include distance measurements or lines to show possible gun elevations.

The wagon swayed. Cherrid's legs compensated immediately, but the motion was repeated within a second. Bizarrely, it was not accompanied by any increased sound of wind or rain. The Algherans? Someone pushing?

He stopped what he was doing and listened carefully, unsure if he was hearing wind or voices.

Something bumped against the bottom of the wagon, and it rocked once more. He definitely heard a man's voice then—a blasphemous curse, in Lopritian. A woman's voice, answering.

Puzzled, he looked at Grahan. "Did you hear anything?"

"I guess I did," Grahan admitted, but it was Ian Haarper who moved to investigate, by going out past the front curtain flaps. Cherrid winced in sympathy, realizing the man would have to begin drying himself all over again.

"Hey, you two," they heard Ian Haarper bark, his voice clear even through the thick felt. "Knock it off! Get out from there! Find some other place for that! You're bothering the big chief!"

Inside the wagon, the "big chief" realized suddenly he felt much more cheerful. He was smirking at Grahan, who for his part stroked his cheek with a finger, hiding his mouth behind a palm. "All you can do some nights to fight off the cold," Grahan said reminiscently, and Cherrid chuckled with his own recollections.

"*Damnitalltohell*, Wandisha," Ian Haarper shrieked so the whole brigade could hear. "I thought you had more *damned* fucking sense! Don't you know how you're bothering Lord Clendannan?"

Hidden from view by the curtain, Cherrid and Grahan chortled at each other until their knees shook.

When the laughter died, Cherrid was left with 2,790 effectives and 509 sick. The brigade's prisoners had been detailed to tend the sick under the direction of the surgeons.

One surgeon had become ill with marching sickness. Cherrid knew that was the day's second important loss.

Chapter 10

"*G*iddup giddup, c'mon Lerlt," someone whispered, and Lerlt felt himself being shaken. For a moment he tried to ignore the rough treatment, but it was repeated. A hand over his mouth kept him from complaining. He shook in protest and his shoulder pressed wood rather than soft bedding. He was stiff and sore; his eyes were puffy and sleep-crusted. He knew he needed rest.

Slowly, remembering where he was, Lerlt came awake.

"Don't make a sound," Fesch whispered hoarsely, as if his own stupid voice were not a sound. "Still fifth watch. Thought you'd never wake up."

Lerlt grimaced, but kept quiet. He stretched and sat up slowly, with his blanket crumpled in his lap. There was very little light, and it took concentration to make out what was happening. Fesch was beside him; someone was still huddled against the wall; someone else leaned against the wall by the window, his hand pressing against the oilcloth—Gherst, from his size.

The passageway to the main portion of the barn was blocked or filled with darkness. None of the other Algherans could see them. In a vague way, Lerlt was troubled by that, as if it were treachery to escape captivity.

Herrilmin looked up and removed something from his knee, then tossed it to Fesch. It was a blanket. "Give me his."

Lerlt was trying to find his boots in the darkness. He blinked, not understanding, so Fesch leaned and took his blanket and threw it back to Herrilmin. The one he had received he pulled over his head, and Lerlt suddenly realized it had been cut in the middle to function as a kind of crude coat.

Herrilmin's idea, obviously. How clever! "Where did you get a knife?" he wondered aloud.

"Piece of glass." The blond Agent looked up to receive his praise, then returned to poking at Lerlt's blanket. "From Gherst's mug."

"Oh." Lerlt busied himself with fastening his shoes.

"He's gone by," Gherst said in a low voice. Lerlt glanced at him and noticed for the first time that the cloth over the window had been cut. Gherst was peering through the slit.

"We're not ready yet," Herrilmin said. "Next round."

A sentry was out there, Lerlt guessed. He swallowed nervously. "What do you want me to do?" he wondered aloud.

"Follow orders." Herrilmin did not bother to look up. "Fesch can fill you in."

"Yes sir." Fesch was swallowing, too. The instructions he gave Lerlt were filled with stutters and senseless gestures. Lerlt was still digesting them when Gherst held up a hand and commanded silence.

Escape was surprisingly easy.

The rain had slackened, but it remained heavy enough that the guards were not diligent at their jobs. There was only one guard to watch the entire barn, and from Gherst's observations, he simply walked around the building over and over without varying his pattern. That made no sense to Lerlt; it

seemed foolhardy for Herrilmin to have expected such behavior.

No wonder he wouldn't tell us his plans. He shivered, wondering what other pieces of luck it would take to escape.

"Okay, he's around the corner." Gherst exhaled, then
pulled up one corner of the oilcloth to create a triangular opening. "Who's first?"

"Lerlt," Herrilmin said. "If he sinks in that muck, we all
will."

Lerlt did not want to be first, but he felt unable to argue. He
let Fesch push him toward the window, and then, after a bit of
awkward maneuvering, slid feetfirst through the opening.

Meanwhile Gherst was mumbling to himself.

The window was only waist-high, the need for gymnastics
minimal. He caught his breath when he was on the ground and
remembered incredulously that as a child he had done such
things almost daily and without thought.

"Give me my blanket." It was cold outside, and he had
taken the bulky improvised coat off to fit through the window
opening. He did not move from the spot until Fesch had handed
it to him and he was inside it once more.

"Is it muddy?" Fesch's whisper.

"Of course," he whispered back, trying to make it seem like
a shout. "It's been raining, if you forgot."

"Is it too muddy?" Herrilmin's voice.

He stomped back and forth for a few seconds, leaving the
protection of the wall and returning to the window. There
seemed to be sheds nearby, but none of them were lit, and it
was a surprise when he stepped from grass onto the bare earth
at the side of the barn. "Not too bad. We won't sink."

Herrilmin turned away. "Stay on grass if you can," Lerlt
heard him say; then Fesch was clambering through the window.

Gherst was next, then Herrilmin. When the big man was
through, he leaned again over the window, fiddling with the
cloth which covered it.

"Seventy-nine seconds," Gherst said clearly, as his head

emerged from the hole in his blanket. "Eighty seconds. Eight-one seconds."

Herrilmin ignored him, and Gherst punched the man's back lightly. "Eighty-three seconds."

"Let me get this—bastard!" Herrilmin muttered.

"It's not flapping," Gherst said, his voice reassuring. "Eighty-six seconds." While he was counting, he sounded worried.

Herrilmin cursed again and threw something small on the ground, then put his thumb into his mouth. Fesch held out his blanket and Herrilmin struggled into it, then sucked some more on his thumb.

Gherst was already sprinting toward the corner. Lerlt followed.

"Hide here," Gherst ordered when they were on the narrow side of the barn. When Lerlt asked for an explanation, he only shook his head and gestured with a hand.

"Get down," Fesch hissed at him, and acted out his own words, lying down against the foundation of the barn and arranging his blanket to cover his feet and head, so he seemed shapeless and almost invisible.

The others were doing the same. With misgivings, Lerlt copied them. This was another part of Herrilmin's plan that had not been explained to him, and he was furious with Fesch for skipping so many details.

Gherst moved first, while Lerlt was still learning to breathe again. The seconds of almost discovery, as the guard's feet squelched past in the mud, had seemed to last for watches. Lerlt had been paralyzed with fear.

Fesch pulled him up from his knees. "Come on, come on," he muttered. His voice was excited; that had the effect of calming Lerlt. He was preternaturally conscious of his well-being and the sharpness of his senses. He was sure he heard the departing steps of the guard on the far side of the barn and that he saw each fold of Gherst's and Herrilmin's blankets as they ran toward a storage shed about fifty man-heights distant.

"Lerlt! Wake up," Fesch shouted, then turned away and ran after the two other men. Lerlt followed, running effortlessly and tirelessly through the rain, feeling invincible.

At the back of the shed, he stopped, looking for another destination. Herrilmin seized his arm and pulled him sideways, behind the structure. The force seemed excessive, and he was about to protest when he heard the man's hard breathing.

So Herrilmin was nervous also, like Fesch, and like Gherst, bent far over now at the opposite side of the shed, with his compulsive counting. Lerlt shook off the man's hand, and looked for the next spot to run to, realizing the other Agents needed directions from him. Other sheds, a loading platform beside the road, a fenced area which was probably an empty corral . . .

Herrilmin took a small object from his pocket and held it before him, then turned from side to side. A locator, Lerlt realized. It buzzed when he faced to the north, so evidently there was a time machine nearby.

Or a radio. But the savages of this world had not mastered the Plates well enough to manufacture radios.

Herrilmin mumbled to himself and Lerlt wondered how far away the time machine was.

Gherst stepped backward suddenly, then came over to Herrilmin while Lerlt was still looking about. "Right on schedule," he whispered. "He didn't see the window."

"He might next time," the big blond man whispered back. "You see those trees there beside the road? Let's go there next." He turned to Lerlt, his hand squeezed into a fist. "Run this time, will you? Don't cut it short, and hit the ground behind the trees. Start carrying your weight, mister, we can't afford to baby-sit you anymore."

Baby-sit? What on the one Earth was Herrilmin complaining about? He had left Lerlt in the dark, deliberately keeping every detail of his plans to himself. Was Lerlt supposed to be a Teep, to read his mind for everything he should know? Lerlt wanted to scream with indignation, but—

Herrilmin was edgy and he was large and very dangerous.

Lerlt had no doubts that he would not hesitate to kill in any situation that he thought justified it. At the very least, he could attack Lerlt with his bare hands and leave him behind unconscious to be discovered by the Lopritians.

He needed Herrilmin to reach safety. So Herrilmin needed to be mollified. It was as simple as that, he realized angrily.

Only Herrilmin's size mattered, not justice, not logic.

"Sure," he said evenly. "Whatever you say, Herrilmin."

The big man had already turned away. "Let's go." His words were aimed at no one. Then he was running, leading the way to the trees. Lerlt heard mud splatter. Gherst was right behind.

"Let's go." Fesch struck Lerlt on the shoulder, his voice hard, and ran after the others.

Lerlt followed, feeling fear and anger, awkward in the flapping blanket. When he reached the trees, he found a separate trunk to hide behind.

He watched for discovery by the guard. He watched to see what movement the others made. When they ran across the road, he ran after them. When they took refuge behind another shed, he was with them but stood apart.

The shed was an outhouse, he found—a simple wooden structure sitting on a concrete base which failed to pen an obnoxious odor. A narrow dirt lane ran immediately behind the shed; a long slender house three stories high was before it. The house was unlighted. A silhouette showed coal heaped on a covered platform at one side. Beyond the house was the wider street he had glimpsed when running across the great road. Other narrow houses and larger buildings which might be dormitories loomed darkly around the time travelers and Lerlt understood they were in the middle of a small town.

People. Danger. He shivered unconsciously, feeling strain in his back, feeling the weight of countless sly malicious eyes upon his back, sharp stabbing knives thrusting him against the stolid walls of the outhouse. He forced himself to breathe.

Cold water ran like urine down the insides of his pant legs.

As he realized that, at the same time, he felt the weight of his blanket-jacket, soggy with rain, on his shoulders. The cloth was near saturation. He would soon be wet all over. Apathetically, he wondered if that would increase his misery.

A town. Filled with menace and the risk of discovery, but there should be better clothing somewhere within. Clothing which was dry, which did not resemble uniforms. And weapons.

And horses. He considered that notion blankly, dismally admitting his ignorance about horses, but confident despite that that he could ride well enough to outdistance pursuers. There must be a stable in the town. Surely Herrilmin's plans included horses.

Herrilmin waved a fist and ran to another outhouse, then another. Lerlt wondered if he knew where the stable lay or was simply guessing.

But the blond man did not lead them to a building. He moved stealthily to the end of the lane and over a rut-laced cross street, which petered out on one side beyond the gate of an enclosed field. A footpath brought them up a waist-high bank. Herrilmin hesitated on the top, then stepped aside to leave room for the others.

Lerlt saw no stable. He saw black shapes within blackness, which took concentration to interpret. There was a high drop at his feet. Trees were on the horizon, and below them another bank ten man-heights distant. Between the banks was a dark rippling surface which gurgled and laughed at his surprise. A river. He looked for a bridge across, but could not find one.

Cimon seize Herrilmin! How much time had he wasted?

"Let's take that boat." Herrilmin pointed with his chin, then rushed down the bank to the river. Lerlt trailed after the others, balancing himself carefully on the wet grass and mud, feeling both rage at Herrilmin's insane luck and an obscure disappointment.

The boat would be old, he knew, the planks rotted through. It would be useless. He was sure of it.

They would all be captured. They would know the mistake they had made in not explaining their plans to him. They would spend their hours in captivity bemoaning their errors . . .

The three of them. Lerlt would not be there. Guns and voices would boom and while the other Agents froze in indecision and uncomprehending surprise, Lerlt would spring into the icy waters and swim to freedom. Lerlt would move too quickly for the Lopritian sharpshooters to take aim. Lerlt would outrace his ponderous pursuers and alone win freedom. Lerlt would steal a horse and ride to F'a Alghera, skillfully leaping fences and other barriers, as he rode undetected to F'a Alghera and his hidden time machine. Lerlt would return to free the captives, and back at the Station, Lerlt would be modest and gracious as the men he had rescued praised him.

But at the water's edge, the only roaring voice was that of the river. Reluctantly, he moved toward the others.

What Herrilmin had found was a small rowboat, gray in the darkness, lying keel up beside the river, with a blunt stern and seats for two men. When he got to the boat, Herrilmin and Gherst had turned it over so it rested on its side. Fesch kicked repeatedly at the rocks where it had rested. Herrilmin was probing the interior with his left hand; his right arm hung stiffly at his side.

"We have to find oars," Gherst said inconsolably.

Lerlt took heart. The water moved, after all. Surely it was enough that the boat floated. He looking about, seeing no anchor. A thin rope ran instead from an oarlock to a nearby stake. He tugged on it, but the stake was too stolidly rooted, so he looked for a sharp rock and began trying to abrade the rope.

"Let that go." Herrilmin tapped Lerlt on the shoulder and turned away from the river. "The oars have to be nearby. Let's go look. Fesch and Gherst, get that thing ready."

Resigned to the waste of time, Lerlt followed the big man, and a short distance upstream, they came to a cut in the bank. A broad dirt path ran from the river, then joined a street which went on toward the great road.

Lerlt saw fires in the distance, where the soldiers must be camped, and realized suddenly that in the lengthy period of time that had passed since their escape, he and the others had actually gone only a short distance. His steps lagged. He felt his heart pounding.

"Come *on*," Herrilmin snapped. "One of these buildings. No one's going to carry oars very far."

There were buildings large and small before his face, standing by themselves between the cross street and the bank. In the rain Lerlt could barely recognize their outlines, but they seemed ominous. He hesitated, afraid of approaching them.

You go in. I'll watch. He couldn't say the words aloud.

"Come on," Herrilmin said angrily. "Lerlt, move your feet." He grabbed the smaller man, his hand making a fist at the gap where Lerlt's neck protruded from the blanket, and pulled him onward. Lerlt tried to push back but the blanket hampered his arms, and he was too intimidated to strike the other man. Fearfully, he let Harrilmin pull him like a leashed dog.

"We'll look here first." Herrilmin opened a door on a small shed with one hand and thrust Lerlt before him with the other.

It was not an outhouse. He recognized that immediately, and then stumbled. The obstruction was on the floor; bulky, heavy cloth with a tarry feel and a musty odor. A tarpaulin, he guessed. Rotten, useless, kept but left to decay by some peasant unwilling to abandon any material possession. He cursed and pushed it aside with his feet when he rose.

He was in a storage shed with wooden walls and an earth floor. There were no windows, and very little light came past Herrilmin in the door. The rain had washed all smells from the air, but Lerlt's hand touched round shapes in a waist-high box, which might be apples or small gourds. He moved farther, keeping one hand in the bin, and reaching with the other.

Wooden shelves, a candle stub, wooden matches . . .

"There's a candle here," he said, but Herrilmin barked a no at him.

Lerlt kept groping. More shelves, jars, cobwebs . . . He cursed softly and wiped his hand on the damp blanket. Beside him Herrilmin was moving, rummaging in the back corner where he had kicked the tarpaulin. "Here are the oars. You should have found them, Lerlt," he said.

"I found food," Lerlt said, barely keeping his temper. That was equally important.

"We can get—wait! Quiet!" Herrilmin whirled and moved to the side of the door.

"Who's there?" A woman's voice. "Rusty? Is someone there?"

Lerlt felt his throat constrict. His head turned as he looked for a place to hide. There was none.

Herrilmin gripped the door's crosspiece and pulled it inward slowly. The hinges squealed a protest. Lerlt stared, barely breathing, hoping.

To his horror, Herrilmin did not close the door. The blond man waited a second with it near to him, then pushed it out again, then waited and pulled the door back in. Meanwhile, he stared through the gap between the door and its frame.

"Is anyone there? Rusty? Here Rusty."

The woman's voice again, after what seemed like hours. She was very close. Lerlt knew despair and knelt on the floor, hoping to be overlooked. Herrilmin pulled the door closer.

"Rusty?" The latch jingled. Lerlt held his breath, praying the woman would go away. Simultaneously, he wondered how she avoided seeing Herrilmin.

A dog barked near him suddenly. Softly. Mournfully.

The door moved. The shadow that was Herrilmin moved.

"Rus—"

Then Lerlt heard slaps. A thud. Garments slipped against garments. A dark shape fluttered in front of him, then fell heavily onto the ground.

"You found some food?" Herrilmin asked loudly and leaned over the shape.

Lerlt swallowed. "Is she—"

"She's past bothering us. What kind of food?"

"Canned stuff. Apples." Lerlt could not take his eyes from the dark form in the corner, but the fear of being discovered was waning in him. He felt warmth and something like relief now. Only the echo of the tension he had felt remained, and in a strange way he almost enjoyed it.

"There's probably more stuff in her house." He was prepared to be as practical as Herrilmin.

"Good idea. I'll go look there." Herrilmin's voice was calm. "You get the oars and what you can from here."

"How will I carry stuff?"

"Use her clothes for a bag. She doesn't need them."

Herrilmin paused a long moment. "We're going to have to get rid of her, you know. We don't want to leave any sign that we were here. Look for a rope . . . and a sack."

"A rope? To tie her?"

"To hide the body. We'll dump it in the river, weighted down so it doesn't rise. People will think she took the boat, if anyone notices it missing at all. Yeah. We can wrap her in that sail and . . . that should do it." Herrilmin half snorted, half coughed contemptuously, then went out.

Lerlt was alone. Herrilmin was gone and Lerlt let himself feel a touch of joy. He kicked at the dead woman to express relief, then went back to the shelves and lit the candle.

The woman's body was crumpled up in the corner, half sitting and half lying on the discarded tarpaulin. Her head was twisted unnaturally. The flickering light showed Lerlt that she was dressed in a shapeless pullover garment and that her hair was dark and short, her face wide with plain features and a creased forehead. The skin on her face and legs was heavily tanned, with middle-age coarseness. She had been heavyset but not stout. Her hands and soles were callused.

Her jaw dropped and moisture glistened on her lips. Lerlt

bent over her with the candle and saw that drool mixed with drops of blood dripped from her mouth. The sightless eyes stared at him blankly.

He pulled the tarpaulin from beneath the body and spread it on the floor, then seized the woman by her legs and tugged it onto the heavy cloth, while the corpse was still pliable.

Its arms were stretched over its head on the ground when he was done, so the woman's breasts were raised high and because of the pulling her shift rode up about her waist. She had worn no undergarments. Lerlt pushed the shift higher and spread her legs apart, then put her hands between them.

Playing with herself. He grinned, imagining the woman alive and playing with herself. Not for her own pleasure, but for his. She would be terrified of his anger, sick with shame at what she was forced to do, and inevitably her body would respond to those busy fingers and complete her humiliation. She would be filled with rage and fear and self-hatred and he would watch, whip or knife or stick in hand, supervising her performance, encouraging her. A firelight, brands, manacles, privacy . . . just for him.

He breathed heavily, standing over the body, enjoying the fantasy and the sight of her nakedness, filled with power, knowing someday he would be free to indulge that or any other whim.

"Woof, woof," he said softly, amused by his mockery, wishing she were alive to hear and fear him. He understood now Herrilmin had mimicked the dog's voice a short time before. He understood it had been a lure to capture her. "Woof! Woof! Ar-r-r-r-ff!"

Near the apple bin, he found a rusted butcher's knife. He used it to cut through the cloth on the body so he could pull it free. The woman's heavy flesh was till warm. No blood pulsed through the ponderous breasts when he put his hand on them but they were still plastic, still soft to his touch.

Yielding. Unresisting. And they were going to get rid of her, anyway. He glanced toward the shed door, wondering how long Herrilmin would be in the house; then slowly, awkwardly as though he used another person's hands, without concern, he pulled the blanket over his head and began to undress.

"You asleep, Cherrid?" A voice in the darkness.

"Of course, Grahan. Didn't you hear me snore?" He turned awkwardly on the too short stretcher, trying not to dislodge the too narrow blanket, and heard wood creak threateningly beneath him. Rain was still falling on the ambulance. Somewhere near him it was dripping inside the wagon.

Inside my boots, I'm sure. An Algheran secret weapon.

Idly, he wondered what warfare would be like if generals could direct bad weather against each other. He had seen so many marvels come into being in his lifetime; why not this one?

It was a thought for another day, he told himself. That peaceful day at the end of his life when he wrote his memoirs, in retirement, at the long table in the kitchen of his country home, in the morning sun, where he could read passages to the cook and scullery maids and force Grahan and his butler to be literary critics. Really, that sounded so pleasant that maybe he would write his memoirs, despite his past oaths to do no such thing.

How would generals use weather against each other?

"You didn't breathe like you were sleeping."

"All right, I was not sleeping," he admitted. "Trying to, but not getting there. I am not used to sleeping on a stretcher. It is much too firm."

"Maybe some symbolic objection?" Grahan wondered.

"No, just not used to it. That's the simple answer, Grahan, and it is good enough for me. You listen to the Teeps too much—I think all that talk of theirs about 'symbols' and 'the hidden part of the mind' is hokum. Or maybe some joke they like to play on us Normals. There's nothing about it in the Plates, is there?"

"Maybe not."

He heard Grahan moving, sitting up in the darkness on the opposite stretcher, and realized the other's sleeplessness would keep him awake as well as his own.

How could generals use weather against each other, during his own lifetime? In big wars, perhaps, covering whole nations. Advances would be made where weather was good, rest and re-supply would go on where it was bad . . . Weather affected logistics, any fool knew that. Perhaps you could keep track of weather over a whole country, guess how it would develop, and estimate the effect on enemy preparedness? Scientific estimates, supported by calculations instead of crude guesses . . .

Not for a nation. You needed to track weather over an entire continent.

A war that covered an entire continent? Could any human mind, Normal or telepath, keep track of a conflict that large? Could any cause be so great to inspire war on that scale?

More material for the memoirs, he told himself. And post-ponable. Grandiose notions had to wait for grandiose periods of free time.

Seconds passed in the darkness. "I actually miss that stupid old couch," Cherrid muttered.

Grahan chuckled. "Maybe we can arrange an exchange with the Algherans—one couch for one Ironwearer?"

"I can give them Wolf-Twin," Cherrid said instantly, the focus of his thoughts changing to a better target. "Did you hear that idiot berate me this afternoon after lan Callares was killed? He seemed to think I ordered the man to commit suicide."

"Is that what is bothering you, Cherrid?" Grahan asked. "One man's death? He was a soldier."

"One important man," he answered. "Lan Callares was useful."

He sighed and clicked his tongue. "I'm feeling guilty be-cause I did not tell lan Haarper about it. And a little bit ashamed because I thought lan Callares was a cow—was afraid of the enemy, from things he had said, so I never told him to take elementary precautions. Now I wish I had issued the right orders and really taken him from Wolf-Twin."

He sighed again. "That Teep might still be alive now, if I had been willing to annoy Wolf-Twin. I did not want to quarrel with another Ironwearer, and now we have both lost."

"Not the first time. Not the last," Grahan commented.

"Sure." Cherrid moved an arm and propped himself up. He saw one glum compensation. "But at least he had a good death, Grahan. Quick and painless, in a worthy cause. Someday we'll have to sing of it."

Give remembrance, actually, he added in thought. The Lopritians lacked formal ceremonies for the dead. Singing a man into the final darkness was a custom in his homeland, not here.

What would a Teep make of that slip in memory?

Had Ian Callares family or friends to regret his passing and mark it properly? He really had not known the Teep very well. There had been something likable about Dieytl, which he and Ian Haarper both had responded to.

Strange how a man acquired additional significance after his death! Dieytl Ian Callares was not yet three watches dead. An unimportant officer and a Teep, and he was already remembering the man as a possible friend.

I would like Mlart tra'Nornst as a friend, he thought facetiously. *My very best friend, if this is the reward they get.*

I'll bet he'd like me for a friend.

"Do we sing of his death before or after we sing about your friend Wolf-Twin?" Grahan asked cynically. "You'd give him to the Algherans if they wanted a spare Ironwearer. What about your little boy, instead?"

It took time to grasp the reference.

"He is not my little boy," Cherrid said firmly. "Don't call him that, by the way. I'm sure he is through growing."

"What a pity." Grahan chuckled. "I was thinking he'd make a splendid horse when he's full-sized. He's what? Fifty? Sixty?"

"Younger," Cherrid said thoughtfully. "Not even forty."

"He is a boy." Grahan was surprised.

"Uh-huh." Cherrid gave up totally on returning to sleep and swung himself up and into a sitting position. "I have to remember that from time to time myself. He gets moody and uncertain; other times, he goes off without listening and does something stupid. Just like a child."

"Takes after you, it sounds like. So how do you enjoy being a father?"

"I do not," Cherrid said. "I am not. I would like to teach him, I admit—he has potential as a soldier if he would buckle down to it. But, I do not know . . . I keep thinking I should give him back his regiment, but—

"Not changing the subject really, you ever meet his hearthsharer?"

"Haven't had the pleasure," Grahan said politely. "Is she a soldier?"

"Far from it! She is—" He stopped to consider and classify. "She is a commoner, but from the upper rank, if I had to guess. Foreign-born; I can't place her accent. Impatient, impudent, impious, all the other imps. Very full of opinions, interrupts a lot, does not like to sit still—one of those women who are moving around all the time."

"Young," the never-married Grahan said confidently.

"Very young, even more than him. But they act like an old couple. When they are in the same room, he looks at her and she looks at him, and they seem to carry on conversations with each other even when they are talking to other people. They are full of private jokes and secrets, just like they are playing some marvelous game. just the two of them, that the rest of us can watch but never understand."

Cherrid sighed. "Anyhow, my point was, he is relaxed and acts much more maturely when his Kylene is around, but that man turns somersaults to please her! Grahan, if that girl child would just tell him 'Timmial, please win the war for Loprit,' he would kill himself trying and probably do it and you and I could retire."

He smiled ruefully. "I could have time to write my memoirs."

Grahan paused for thought. "Did she tell him to lose?"

"I think she did not tell him anything." Cherrid sighed again, this time glumly. "His heart is not in it, Grahan. It was for a while, till that battle of his, and I relieved him and since then he has only killed time."

"He scouted your battle site," Grahan reminded him. "He routed your—uhh—subterranean foes earlier tonight."

Despite himself, Cherrid laughed. But the moment ended, and the worry remained. "I wonder if you would talk to him?"

"Me? About what?"

"About this and that. Just sound him out, about Teeps and the Vandeigns and anything else that comes to mind. Soldiering. His career. Whatever else comes up. Someone ought to tell him about Ian Callares, and I'd rather it wasn't me. That could be your starting point. Tell him that and see what kind of person he is, to your thinking. I would like to know."

"I don't know, Cherrid." Grahan snapped his fingers. "If you've got doubts, maybe you should talk to a Teep."

Ris Clendannan snarled. "The only Teep I could talk to— and it turns out he was doing so against orders from Wolf-Twin—is dead. Besides, he was a friend of Timmial's. I could not get what I want to know from him. Also besides, he was no general."

"I'm no general," Grahan pointed out.

"You know generals," Cherrid answered. "You could have been one, if you had worked at it sensibly."

"It wasn't worth the effort," Grahan said softly.

Not for Loprit. The unspoken ending hung between them in the air as it had on dozens of occasions. Cherrid stared once more at the chasm that lay between Grahan and himself and wondered how long their friendship would remain as a bridge.

"I take it you're not worried about Ian Haarper's qualifications as an Ironwearer?" Grahan asked, impersonally, distantly.

"No." Cherrid tried to smile. "He is brave, hard fighting,

compassionate, diligent, foolhardy, gullible—all the standard virtues, he's got.''

"Then what am I to look for?"

"I cannot say," the old Ironwearer confessed. "See if he is good for Loprit, if that makes sense. If I give him more responsibility, it has to be good for Loprit.''

Chapter 11

"**W**ell, it wasn't that old man, in the first place," Herrilmin said suddenly, interrupting a conversation Gherst and Fesch had been carrying on softly, so his sleep would not be disturbed. "You can forget that nonsense."

He paused, and in the sound of lapping water Lerlt seemed to hear subdued laughter. He listened rigidly, but Herrilmin was not speaking about him. It was not necessary to react, to say anything in response, to plan a defense.

He had not done anything bad after all.

Things *happened* in wartime, that was all. Soldiers did—things—because of the pressure on them. The dangers. That was all. He had nothing to apologize about to stupid Fesch or Gherst or know-it-all Herrilmin. Who had killed the woman in the first place. Waylaid her. Left her body with Lerlt. Was really to blame if what Lerlt did bothered anyone.

Things happened, he told himself. Things happen.

Was Herrilmin's voice amused as well? No, Lerlt decided emotionlessly, the note that rang in it was gloating, as if Herrilmin held some secret which the others wished to know. But Herrilmin was always like that.

The small boat bobbed slightly. A wavelet hit the bow; water spilled over the side splashed against the bag of apples and bread taken from the dead woman's house. Lerlt leaned forward quickly with a cup to bail, pretending everything was normal, as if Herrilmin's eyes were not boring into his back.

What did Herrilmin really know? Nothing. Less than nothing. He had not come back into the storage shed after leaving Lerlt with the dead woman. He had not mentioned the body, not uncovered it in its tarpaulin shroud, not examined it before he and Lerlt tossed it into the rain-swollen river.

Lerlt had thought he had heard Herrilmin just beyond the door of the shed at one point, but he had not answered to his name. Considerable time had passed before he heard the big man's heavy footsteps, and in the time since, he had said nothing about Lerlt's activity. He had noticed nothing.

Things happen.

The woman was virtually nude. The space was small. No healthy man could have ignored her. Herrilmin could have expected nothing else. Herrilmin—

Herrilmin would have his own palaces when time travelers controlled the one world. Lerlt would have his and do what he pleased. That was all.

Meanwhile, in the present, there was space in the boat for one man to sleep, if he could find sleep with his feet between the rower's legs and his head against the feet of the man on the back seat. Gherst and Herrilmin had monopolized the sleeping spot during the first two watches; Lerlt was no longer surprised that he and Fesch, as the younger men, had been shunted between the uncomfortable stern seat and the even more uncomfortable bow.

"Who was it, then?" Fesch asked innocently. "We weren't talking about the one who told us about all the sights to see in F'a Loprit. The other one—the old one who was also supposed to make a speech and just laughed and waved bye-bye at us. Wasn't he the one in charge of that brigade?''

Gherst grunted and pulled at the oars. It was not hard labor, Lerlt had noticed, though over time hands had left their dark stain on the white ash and metal from the oarlocks had been ground into fat black lines at their midpoint. The river did the work and its current carried the boat fast enough. The rowers were really only necessary to keep the bow pointed ahead. If Gherst was pretending to strain now, with frowning brow and tight lips, it was probably to avoid providing Herrilmin with cue lines. Clearly the big man had lain awake on the floor waiting for the opportunity to make his announcement.

It was not a wild or adventuresome river, and the scenery was monotonous: a few trees, and long grass beginning at the riverbank and stretching as far as a man could see. Lerlt pretended to look for hazards in the dirty water; with the greater part of his awareness, he watched Herrilmin. In flashes, he glimpsed scenes of the palace he would have someday.

Herrilmin pulled himself erect slowly, sliding sternward on the blankets to leave space for Gherst and his oars, and leaned his back against the rear seat. Fesch foolishly maneuvered himself into an awkward position that left his knees hanging over the water so the bigger man would not feel cramped. His face showed how uncomfortable that was and Lerlt suppressed a giggle.

Confident that he had an audience, Herrilmin smiled. "That was—we'd call him a Battle Master, that old man. Ris Glendan, Clennun, something like that. He's one of their planners, yes. But he doesn't matter, I read up on this campaign. There's going to be a battle between that brigade and the Swordtroop in two days more, and that old man is killed.''

"Lamehorse Creek,'' Gherst volunteered, and Herrilmin simply nodded in denial. "Burning Forest? I thought that was north of here?''

"Both were north of here. This was a rearguard action; it didn't even rate a name.''

Gherst murmured apologetically, then pursed his lips and tugged at the oars. Lerlt noticed they barely touched the water.

Gherst and he were too clever and Fesch too dumb to ask the obvious question of the expert. A pause followed, which Herrilmin finally broke. "What do you think the name of the battle was that we were in?" He smiled while waiting for an answer, but Lerlt saw it hid irritation.

"I don't know," Fesch confessed.

"It doesn't have a name," Herrilmin said cheerfully. "And why doesn't it have a name? Because it didn't happen."

Gherst feathered the oars. "So it didn't happen?"

"It didn't happen!" Herrilmin snapped. Then, louder: "*It didn't happen! Nothing like it is in the books!*"

"I've seen things like this before," Gherst said calmly. "I think I've been in the Project longer than any of you others, and sometimes what you see isn't just like history books have it. If I were writing books for Algherans to read, I wouldn't be eager to mention that battle, you know. We really had dirt rubbed in our fur there."

"This is different, Gherst. You know it!"

"Probably." Gherst put his oars back in the water. "But I don't think we ought to talk about it."

Herrilmin tossed his head. "These are Septlings. They're concerned, so they ought to know what's going to happen."

"When it happens. Think a bit, Herrilmin. If Vrect wanted them to know, they'd be told."

"Told what?" Fesch demanded. "Come on, Gherst! What's the big secret? Me and Lerlt can be trusted."

Gherst and Herrilmin exchanged looks and Lerlt realized Fesch had found just the words to make them silent forever. He wanted to kick the imbecile.

Fesch had seen the look also. "All right," he said loudly. "Don't tell me. When we get back, I'll ask Vrect myself."

Gherst spat in the water and refused to look at anyone.

Time passed while Herrilmin visibly collected his thoughts.

"I'll tell you what I can," he said at last. "That battle,

where we got mud in our fur—who do you think rubbed it? I'll tell you who. Let me give you the name: Timmithial lan Haarper, the Lopritians call him, *Ironwearer* Timmithial lan Haarper. That's who. He's a big, tall, red-haired man, who wasn't born in Loprit. What's that sound like, Fesch? You know of any big redhead Ironwearers? With a scar on their head and sort of a square face? That sound familiar?''

Lerlt shook himself nervously. The description was almost familiar, and it troubled him.

"There's Timt ha'Dicovys," Fesch said slowly. "That sounds like him. The real old Agent, with gray in his hair? The one that might be nuts?''

"He isn't nuts." Gherst spoke just as slowly. "I was there when he—arrived, I guess you would say. When we captured him. He really did come from outside the Project, Fesch. I don't know about what he says about the First Era, but he didn't come from Alghera, I'm sure of that.

"But his name . . . Dicovys adopted him. Politics—Cuhyon wanted him, too, for some reason. Anyhow, his name is Harupper Timithallin ha'Dicovys. He started off as Timithallin ha'Rupper. Haruppir, Harppir, something like that.''

Fesch swallowed abruptly. "Timithallin Haruppir. Timmithial lan Haarper. Herrilmin, you aren't serious!''

"I'll die if I'm not," Herrilmin said earnestly. "If you listened, the Lopritians were all talking about it. One of the regiment leaders in that brigade was named Timmithial lan Haarper and he was just like I described. That's Timt ha'Dicovys and it can't be anyone else. It was his regiment that beat us *and he did it without any help at all from the rest of that brigade!* Who could do that to us, except a time traveler? Who could do that except someone who knew exactly where our division was at every moment, and knew exactly when we were most vulnerable? Timt ha'Dicovys.''

Fesch nodded stupidly. "But you said, it was Teeps that beat us.''

"I said I had more to say," Herrilmin told him. "Timt ha'Dicovys is—''

Gherst interrupted whatever vulgarity the blond man was reaching for. "Timt thinks the Alliance is right about handling the Teeps," he said quickly. "That's not a secret either, Fesch. He might be willing to work with Teeps. That's what we think."

"But against his own Sept? That was the Dicovys division," Fesch protested. "It doesn't make sense. We're supposed to protect Mlart, not cripple him."

"Treachery makes sense," Herrilmin said. "He's a Teep-lover, he didn't come from Alghera, he wasn't born in a Sept, he lies about his past. He's working against us. I bet he always has."

Fesch continued to frown. "But if he's not loyal, wouldn't the Project's Teep know it? He's an Ironwearer, Herrilmin."

The big blond snorted. "Why believe the Teeps? The man could be spying on us every waking minute, and I'll bet they wouldn't tell us. They'd say that was just 'political,' so the Second Compact wouldn't let them warn us. It'd be funny to them. You trust those Teeps? There isn't a Teep in the one world that wants Alghera to win the war. Remember—

"*We* found the Plates. *We* translated them. *We* gave them to the world, so everyone would learn to guard against them. *We* are the people who made sure Teeps will never rule Normals again, and no Teep will ever forget it! Am I right?"

No one argued, and Herrilmin snapped his fingers with satisfaction. "Now. I can give you proof that Timt ha'Dicovys is working against us, so what do you think we ought to do?"

"I don't know. We ought to ask him. Why he's doing it, I mean. If you say he's working against us, I'll believe you, but he's an Ironwearer, he must have some reason."

"Sure," Herrilmin said, smiling, and Lerlt wondered what other lies he had just told.

Timmithial lan Haarper took the loss of Dieytl lan Callares very well, Cherrid thought. He listened quietly to the report the cavalry officer had made and asked only a few questions about the telepath's death. Then he left and walked alone at the side of the column speaking to no one.

In the afternoon, he came back to Cherrid and asked for additional duties. There were no real tasks to give him, but Cherrid's staff had been drafting orders for contingencies during coming battles; he gave those to the boy to read.

Check for errors, he said. And for the remainder of the day, the boy rode in one of the wagons, his long legs crossed over boxes of ammunition, leafing through the papers.

Perhaps it was educational. They both had understood there would be no errors to find.

"Is he right?" Fesch wondered. It was later in the day and the Agents were on land for a short while. Fesch stared rigidly at a white birch tree which was immediately before him.

"About what?" Gherst said. He leaned forward and pulled the laces on his pants tight once more, then fastened them as if nothing were more important to him.

Lerlt, at the end of the line, in front of the other white birch—there were only these two trees in sight in any direction; ragged waist-high grass, weeds mostly, covered all the ground out to the horizon—noticed Herrilmin lying on his back ten man-heights away, eating an apple with one hand and shielding his eyes with the other as he watched clouds sailing overhead. What was it that Herrilmin saw in the clouds? Lerlt wondered. The Gods had given him more than an ordinary man's body, and more than an ordinary man's bladder, it had developed. Had They unfairly given Herrilmin imagination as well?

"About Timt ha'Dicovys and the rest," Fesch said. "I didn't hear you say yes or no to him."

"Time will tell us." Gherst stretched an arm out and scraped at bark with a fingernail. "Why think too much about something that's going to be answered in another day or two?"

"Well . . ." Fesch shivered briefly, then bent to refasten his own trousers, but he kept his face pointed at Gherst. "We'd have to do something, wouldn't we? If he's right. Could it be some kind of Dicovys thing, like—you know, something like Herrilmin is doing for Hujsuon—''

''Herrilmin's not doing anything special.'' Gherst's voice was too quick, and then too casual, to be believed. Even Fesch noticed. He looked at Gherst with a curious eye.

''Herrilmin does things for Hujsuon which aren't part of the Project. Why can't Timt ha'Dicovys be doing the same?''

''Perhaps he is. Ask a Teep, Fesch. Not me.''

''But—'' Fesch shook uncertainly, from his head to his arms, and down to his knees. ''What if he is working with the Teeps here, like Herrilmin said? What do we do then?''

''We do whatever we do.'' Gherst's voice had a hard, weary, exasperated note. ''Don't invent trouble, Fesch. Once we get to a time machine, we can change things. Don't you understand? *Nothing matters except getting home!* Whatever happens, we change things until it gets right. So if it's wrong, it doesn't matter, we change it. Nothing matters—keep telling yourself that.''

''Nothing matters,'' Fesch mumbled. When Lerlt stepped past him, his head was turning from one birch tree to the next and back; neither tree seemed to give him the reassurance he sought.

At evening, the time travelers approached another town.

Fesch was at the oars then. Following Herrilmin's orders, he let the current carry the boat through a sweeping turn and under a bridge to another turn. The setting sun was in their eyes, so vision was difficult, but the bridge was made of black material and very wide. As the boat passed into a temporary night of shadow, Lerlt glanced at the smooth curve of the overhead arch and realized they were underneath the great road. There was no sign of aging or deterioration, and no point where different pieces of material seemed joined. The bridge, like the road, was seamless and without flaw.

When they were beyond it, they turned back to look at the bridge once more. Sunlight gleamed redly on the surface and down the length of the road, and Lerlt felt a touch of envy that the builders of the Fourth Era had made such a thing for un-worthy Loprit and not for Alghera.

Gherst watched with his head propped on a hand. "We'll do better someday," he vowed.

"No, we won't," Fesch said. "We've got levcraft, so who needs roads? And rowboats." He pushed down on the oar handles so the blades rose above the brown water, looked at both of them, and grinned. "What could be more modern and delightful, more rapid and more spacious, then this graceful, commodious, elegantly styled conveyance?"

"Good shoes," Gherst suggested.

"Turn to your left," Herrilmin said. "Stop babbling, you two. We want to put in at the wharf."

The wharf was small and dilapidated, just a few short docks sticking out into the river. A wooden ladder on one went low enough to reach the water. Lerlt, at the bow of the boat, fastened a rope around a cleat and then to one of the ladder rungs. He was the first to the top.

From here, the wharf—and the town—seemed even smaller and dingier. The dock was made of graying wood, with planks at uneven heights and spaced far enough apart that he could look down into the water. A wooden rail interrupted by a thin chain was the only handhold; it did not look trustworthy.

Piles of lumber waited at the base of the dock and a few overturned boats smaller than the one he had just been in. There were larger vessels in the river, several with sails; none of them had people aboard. A dirt pathway was between the bottom of the bank and the water. Across the river, at wide intervals, pieces of roofs and painted walls could be seen through trees, but no people. He turned about.

A pair of tall buildings blocked his view of the town. The one on the right was blue, built of masonry; it had rows of dark windows underlined by white ledges. The other had no windows but a pair of wide double doors taller than even Herrilmin could reach; a stub of concrete road led to the dock. To the right was a small lumberyard. Beyond it, he glimpsed an orchard of some kind and part of the great road. On the left, a paddle-wheel contraption turned in the river about a thousand man-heights downstream; a low mountain was on the horizon.

"Everyone set?" Herrilmin asked in a low voice when they were on the shore, and Lerlt self-consciously patted first his Teepblind and then the knife in his belt and wondered if he looked as embarrassed as Fesch.

"Time machine is that way," Herrilmin said, pointing with a finger. He patted the pocket holding his locator and the other Agents shook their heads in agreement.

"Stick together," the blond man continued. "Walk, don't run. Don't use Speech, and follow my example." He pointed again. "That's an inn. I don't know about you but I'm Cimon-taken tired of mush and apples and bread and water. I want a meal before I do anything else."

"What if they ask about our uniforms?" Fesch wondered.

"We're Lopritians. We just took these from Algherans. 'Exchanged' with them. That sound all right?"

The others shook their heads grimly. During captivity they had seen enough Lopritian thievery to describe it accurately.

"What about money?" Fesch was still worried.

"Don't worry about it," Herrilmin said grandly. "The Lady's cloak will cover us."

"Huh?"

"We won't pay," Gherst explained.

"But that's—" Fesch pondered a moment. "I guess it's all right. We're at war. But will it work?"

"This town is deserted," Herrilmin assured him. "Every able man is in the army. We won't have any trouble. Besides, this is a war, and things people don't like to talk about happen during war. Ask Lerlt, for example."

He smiled maliciously. "Lerlt's had adventures."

"Oh? What kind?" Fesch wondered.

"Nothing much," Lerlt said hastily. Gherst had the de-
cency to turn away and inspect the view. Herrilmin was grinning at him, though, from behind Fesch's back; Lerlt wanted
to kill him.

"Nothing much," Herrilmin agreed. He leered once more
and moved away with Gherst.

Fesch stared after them. "What happened?" he asked stupidly.

Lerlt's brain began working again. "You know we killed
that woman last night," he confided. "We didn't have to. We
could have left her sleeping but we had a little fun with her
first. You know. It was Herrilmin's idea—he said there wasn't
time for all of us, but for just the two of us . . . Soldiers should
never pass up target practice, that was the way he put it."

"Target practice? You shot her?"

Lerlt nodded with disbelief at such innocence, but managed
to continue. "Not with bullets, Fesch." He reached and
slapped gently at the boy's groin. "That gun. The one all
soldiers carry. Though—don't tell anyone—you could say
Herrilmin's was loaded with blanks last night. If he ever says
it was just me, you'll know why."

"Oh, I won't." Fesch blushed.

"Good man!" Lerlt smiled genially.

There would be a delay while their meal was prepared, the
innkeeper explained. He was apologetic, a burly, sleek-haired
man with a fawning manner. If he sensed anything unusual
about the Agents' clothing, he kept the knowledge to himself. Lerlt wondered semi-seriously if he understood they
were wearing uniforms at all, let alone Swordtroop uniforms.

"Is that the owner?" he asked, when the man had returned
to his kitchen. He hunched forward on his low stool and sipped
cautiously at his beer, which had been sweetened with spices,
not sure if it was to his taste.

The mug cast a sharp shadow across the table. Lopritian
technology had advanced to electric lights of some sort—small
and bulbless and very bright. It took concentration to realize

the faint hissing in the background came from the same lights.

The innkeeper had poured the beer as well—one man to serve as greeter, bartender, waiter, and cook. It seemed typical of Lopritian inefficiency.

Like this strange building itself with its grotesquely high ceiling and the rows of doors along the walls. Bedrooms for travelers, Gherst had said casually, and Lerlt had wondered privately why he seemed so nonchalant about something so bizarre, for surely it was a fearful thing for any traveler to sleep amid strangers instead of in the almost-home of a Sept lodge.

But there was nothing like a lodge in all of Loprit. Nothing like a Sept. Only individual men and women.

Lopritians even owned businesses as individuals, he had heard. It seemed absurd to him, for individuals died, and Septs did not, and ownership could not transcend death.

"An employee," Gherst had commented. "Client. That's a better word." The Algheran term meant a member of a Sept employed in a household of another Sept; it carried some of the connotations he wanted but not all, and he spent far more time than Lerlt thought necessary establishing the differences.

It took money to create a business, he explained. It took more money to run one, and contacts and experience, which few non-nobles in Loprit would have. The owner of the inn was probably an aristocrat who had picked this commoner to run it from day to day. "The client makes what he can from the business, and pays something—a flat fee or a percentage—to his patron. If he doesn't produce, the patron gets a new client,"

The patron paid something to the appropriate royal licensing commission to be allowed to operate, more if he had a local monopoly. The nobles on the commission paid something to the royal stewards, so the Queen would continue their appointments. "The land is leased from the local lord, so he gets a cut of the profits, either from the patron or the client. Maybe the patron of the stage line gets a cut, for stopping his coaches here; maybe he has to pay to be allowed to stop. And so on. There's a lot of negotiation.''

Gherst paused to sample his beer and smile with contentment. "Very stable situation," he said. "More complicated than our ways of keeping the unSepted in line, but it works just as well for them—and the Lopritians aren't plagued with anything like those Cimon-taken Associations we have to contend with.''

He sighed and lifted his mug again. "I swear—no matter how many riots they had to put down, the Muster should never have relaxed the retail laws last century. Those fishbrained Warders we had then! And Ruijac, of course— Minursil was in on it, too, and the Teep Septs, but Ruijac was the worst. The bastards wanted to get out of retail and into services, like Dicovys was doing, but without letting any other Sept take up what they'd left. I've seen figures— Nicole's boobs! You can't believe how much money a Sept can make just from a chain of clothing stores—but that's when conditions are right. When you're fighting an Association for the same market, or worse, those pirates who don't have an overhead . . . Don't look down on the Lopritians, Lerlt, they've got a good system.''

"Sure.'' It was all Lerlt could do to keep from yawning. Did Gherst make lectures in bed to his wife? Probably, he thought.

There were no real mysteries within Gherst now. *The complete Hujsuon,* Lerlt had thought scornfully, listening to his rant. A half-minded man, the ideal of a Housetrooper, for all his education—a fool without personality who drew no distinction between his own life and that of the Sept. He could just see the man in better days, toddling off with other earnest cranks to the periodic Sept investment group sessions. No doubt Gherst would someday presume to advise the Sept Master.

He would never listen to Gherst, Lerlt thought happily.

"Water pressure," Fesch mumbled, and rose to his feet

awkwardly. His eye indicated a question which neither Herrilmin nor Gherst noticed. Lerlt made an excuse and wandered after him.

The rest room was simply an indoor privy: a boxlike bench with three open seats, a cardboard box holding dried corn shucks on the floor nearby, a shallow sink with a running faucet, a hissing arc light near the ceiling. The inn had no other customers; they had the space to themselves.

Fesch stood before a seat, pretending to use it, as Lerlt entered. Lerlt unlaced his own trousers, mimicking the larger man, and looked sideways with interest.

"Little small, aren't you?" he asked casually,

"I don't know what—" Fesch colored.

"Right here." Lerlt turned slightly, opening his hand so Fesch could see. "Looks like I'm bigger than you in some way."

"Kill yourself, Lerlt." Fesch turned away angrily.

"Don't be mad." Lerlt leaned over the seat and spat, hearing it splash on water below. "Give it some exercise, that's how you make muscles grow."

"Not a muscle."

"Close enough." Lerlt snapped his fingers and readjusted his pants. "You wanted to ask something?"

"Yeah." Fesch wet his hands and looked about for something to dry them on, then settled for shaking them in the air. Lerlt waited patiently, enjoying the man's uncertainty.

"I don't like this. It feels like we're being watched. This whole thing, Lerlt—us wandering around like this—it's scary. My back is crawling."

"Maybe you got bugs on it." Lerlt smiled.

"It isn't funny. You know what I mean."

"Yeah." Lerlt snapped his fingers. "It's just nerves. We've been places before this where there weren't other time travelers around. This is just more of the same."

"Up at the Present, yes. But we were with Algherans, then. We knew how to get away."

"We were in battles," Lerlt reminded him. "People were shooting at us. That isn't happening here."

"Not yet," Fesch said unhappily.

"Not ever," Lerlt insisted. "Don't let your nerves control you, Fesch. We'll get through this. Trust Herrilmin."

"Herrilmin." The other man frowned. "About . . . you know. The thing you and he did."

"Target practice?"

Fesch swallowed. "What you did. Is that . . ."

"Target practice? What about it?"

"Come on, Lerlt! You know. Have you done that before?"

"Whenever I can," Lerlt said, lying smoothly. "Everyone does, Fesch. You mean—" He pretended shock, then moved to the sink and rinsed his hands to show he needed time for thought. "You haven't?"

"No. I—" Fesch made choking sounds.

"It's one of the rewards of the job." Lerlt dried his hands on corn shucks, which he then dropped through a toilet seat. The shucks settled without a splash on the water below and drifted back and forth. Lerlt smiled.

"We don't talk about it back at the Station. People might misunderstand. But they aren't soldiers back there. They don't know what kind of pressure we're under here. We've got to do something to relax now and then, don't we?" Idly, he took additional handfuls of shucks and dropped them in, too, continuing until the box was empty.

Meanwhile, he watched Fesch with one eye. "Remember what Gherst said: everything is going to be changed, so it's like these people never existed. Nothing we do to them really counts. One old woman—hah! You've killed more than one person up at the Present."

"Those were soldiers!"

"But live soldiers." Lerlt snapped his fingers again. "These people aren't even alive, you know? The Present's six hundred years away; no one lives that long. You can't really say you've killed anyone here, can you? *You look at it the right way and you see that nothing matters.*''

He paused, but Fesch only stared at him, his breath hard, his face weak and defenseless.

A child, Lerlt thought. A child passively staring at the adult world, uncomprehending but waiting to be made grown-up.

This was more than an argument. Fesch himself could be shaped by Lerlt's words, he was sure. Moved. Manipulated. Transformed. Made *different* merely by Lerlt's will.

His own creation.

"Look, what are you going to do with yourself? When this is all over? Marry one of the cows in Hujsuon, so you can call yourself a man? Settle down in one of the settlements? Screw her once a year, if she wants to let you? Sneak off to a brothel in between, if the Sept gives you enough allowance money, and if you can find time to go to the big city, so you can spend it all, for what you can get here for free? I'm not going to do that!"

"Lerlt, lower your voice."

"Listen to me, Fesch. Live a little! There's no one here to stop us, so take what you can, enjoy it. Everybody else is."

"Lerlt?" It was a child's plea.

"Everybody's doing it, Fesch," he said, then slapped the man on the shoulder. "Come on, we're friends. I don't want to hurt your feelings. Just no reason to leave you out of things, I don't want to do that. We're entitled to some things, you understand? You think about what I said, will you? Promise me that."

"Sure," Fesch said huskily.

In the hallway, as Lerlt guided him back to the others, he shambled. He would always see Fesch as shambling, Lerlt realized, and see the bigger man's spirit as a tiny candle too small to fully illuminate the dark clay of his body, in no way comparable to the merciless glare that his own soul cast at the one world.

That glare. That power.

But without focus. It was disappointing to realize he could easily push Fesch from one state of mind to another, but could not determine what the final state would be.

Well enough. Perhaps, even for Gods, every victory was incomplete. He had done what a mortal could do. His will had shaped the one world and made it, in some fashion, more Lerlt-like. That was enough.

Chapter 12

"*We ought to settle up with that fellow,*" Gherst said. He pushed the remnants of his food about with a spoon. His face was motionless, as it had been throughout the meal.

Herrilmin mumbled something in agreement, but did not rise. He stared instead at his empty mug, tilting it for inspection.

Embarrassment, Lerlt understood, looking from one Agent to another. For all their sophistication, they had spent their lives in settlements or the Hujsuon lodge in F'a Alghera or the Station, where they had simply taken food when it was provided. Even on this mission, until now, they had received their meals from the Swordtroop or from the Lopritian army.

None of them had ever paid for a meal. None knew how.

Lerlt flicked a hand, dismissing problems. "You handle it, Gherst."

"Someone go with me?" Gherst looked over his shoulder nervously, but the innkeeper was still in his kitchen, the only other person in the inn.

Did he drink back there? Lerlt wondered. Did he clean his

cooking ware, or hone cutlery? The Algheran brushed his hip to check on his own knife. Sharp—his thumb caught stickily on the edge. Such a simple tool, but so marvelous . . .

"We'll all go." Herrilmin bumped himself and his stool backward, then gestured to pull the others to their feet. "Lerlt, don't jump in first."

Lerlt swallowed. *All right, I won't*, he thought rebelliously. *You do it all without my help and see how you like it*.

If Herrilmin noticed that resentment, he did not show it. He shepherded the others across the room to the bar. "Fesch, behind the bar. Gherst, go get him." He put himself at the side of the bar, leaving Lerlt at the front, with little to look at but the empty dining area and a stone fireplace.

Bored, Lerlt stepped to the side wall, and the light to the left of the fireplace. At the center of the glare, it appeared two tiny glowing rods were almost in contact; the rods extended beyond the lamp cavity into small recesses. Lerlt took a stool from the nearest table and climbed on it to play with the rods, pushing them in without increasing the light, then pulling them out until the illumination dimmed and the hissing sound turned to a sputter. He pulled further; the light died, and was not reborn when he pushed the rods back together.

As he dropped back to the floor, the innkeeper entered. Gherst was behind him, smiling at some private secret.

"Time to pay," Herrilmin murmured. He glanced at Gherst.

"Of course, sir. Yes." The innkeeper looked away, toward the lamp Lerlt had extinguished and the stool he had been on. "That went out, sir? I can fix that. Let me get it, please."

As he stepped past Herrilmin, he staggered. His arm flew to the edge of the bar and his fingers scratched frantically until he had caught his balance.

"Tripped." His voice was thick. " 'Cuse, gentlemen."

Blood was already dripping onto the floor.

"Let me help." Herrilmin was there to take the innkeeper by the elbows, as if to support him. He brought the arms toward the man's body, and held them there tightly.

Lerlt saw the moment at which the man understood he was captive plain on his face. Something passed over it like the shade from the blind. The features were the same, but the innkeeper seemed to have become another man. "Please," he said hoarsely, and gasped for breath.

Gherst stepped up to him. A contemptuous smile which touched only his mouth was on his face. A long knife which he must have found in the kitchen was in his hand. Slowly, it seemed to Lerlt, he put the tip above the small of the man's back and pushed it home. Then he stepped aside.

Again, something that could not be described passed over the innkeeper's face. His mouth opened wide but only a small yammering came out. Below Herrilmin's hands, his arms were shaking.

"If you make another sound, I will break your neck," Herrilmin said. His face showed strain, and Lerlt saw he was holding the heavy man erect against his hip. "Fesch."

That was a moment which always stayed alive for Lerlt, for the rest of his life. The pasty-faced innkeeper, his face caught in surprise in the semi-gloom, silent in the face of Herrilmin's greater will. Gherst, blandly waiting to the side, his hands clasped at his chest. Herrilmin, angrily waiting for some response from the Lopritian in his arms, blood glistening blackly on his green uniform. Fesch, open-mouthed with something like terror, pushing himself into a corner of the bar . . .

Time stood still. Then Lerlt felt pressure beneath his feet and knew he was walking toward the others. Sawdust was like grit on the floor. The air was thick as he inhaled. The handle of his own knife filled his fist.

"Fesch," Herrilmin called.

"What?" Fesch had put his arm against the wall. He stared at the point of the knife he held in his hand. It was shaking violently. Lerlt wondered if he remembered raising it.

"Come here," Herrilmin said firmly, and Fesch moved, but not quickly, so that Lerlt reached Gherst before Fesch reached the innkeeper. The Lopritian seemed not to see him as Lerlt walked past. His eyes were fixed on the outside door. His face was trembling, and Lerlt saw moisture on the forehead, as if the flesh of the body were already liquefying.

Herrilmin let the innkeeper fall onto his hands and knees. The Lopritian's fists were clenched. His face was down, as if to inspect the blood dripping from his side. Breath was coming from him in staccato pants. High on his back, a handbreadth from his spinal column, the hilt of Gherst's knife protruded, like a handle to move a toy. His shoulder was dark with blood. It streaked his side and his trousers and pooled beside him on the plank floor.

He was already an animal, Lerlt realized without pity. A dying animal, his mind made tiny and conscious only of his pain. It had only taken two knife strokes to cut away his humanity.

Two knife strokes would do the same to him, he realized. A moment of violence and Lerlt, too, could become a mindless thing. And Gherst. And Fesch. And Herrilmin.

It did not trouble him. It was very satisfying to know that memory and education and other trappings of personality were no more than a skin which any determined man could strip instantly from his victim.

"Put it in," Herrilmin told Fesch, like a man directing a child.

"Where?" Fesch was quivering. Lerlt wondered if he was about to cry.

"It doesn't matter, Fesch," he reminded the other man, raising his own knife encouragingly.

Fesch stared at him blindly, then gasped and went to his knees beside the Lopritian. His arm moved up, then down; then he rolled sideways.

He got to his feet slowly, his eyes focused on the knife he had pushed into the man's back. His blow had not been as direct as Gherst's. The handle sloped toward the Lopritian's head. Blood was already seeping from the wound.

It was his turn now, Lerlt realized, feeling thrilled as the other Agents looked at him.

One blow. It must be meaningful. It must not kill.

Unlike Fesch, he made decisions quickly. "Turn him over," he said, his voice thick with anticipation.

Fesch simply stared at him and Gherst did not move. It was Herrilmin who bent without a word to pull the knives from the innkeeper's sagging back. His own knife was in his belt. The two he took from the Lopritian, he left on the floor, putting them down carefully so they were parallel with edges facing the same direction. It was a housewife's gesture, with some strange element of thrift that Lerlt realized was not foreign to him.

Then the big man grabbed the Lopritian's arm and leg and turned him over. He *splatt*-ed on the floor. Still without words, Herrilmin put his hands near the Lopritian's neck and ripped his shirt collar open. He looked intently at Lerlt, then got to his feet.

Lerlt wanted to laugh, realizing he could still surprise Herrilmin.

He knelt himself. The Lopritian's eyes were closed, but breath still hissed reassuringly through his teeth.

"Get his head up," he ordered. "I want him to see this."

After a long moment, Herrilmin put his foot under the Lopritian's head and lifted the toe. Lerlt turned, looking at the stolid Gherst and the fascinated Fesch, feeling both exaltation and condescension at their stupidity.

For an instant he noticed the knives Herrilmin had put on the floor, wondering if he should use the butcher knife that Gherst had employed. But he was in no hurry and there was something impersonal about a big knife. He wanted to do this with the smallest blade possible.

"Watch me!" he wanted to cry out, but it was unnecessary. Feeling the other Agents' eyes on him, he cut the laces on the Lopritian's pants and pulled the front open.

His nose wrinkled. The Lopritian had soiled his loincloth. But in some fashion, that made this moment more satisfying. Without haste, he put a hand on the man's protruding belly, unsurprised to find it soft and clammy. He pushed the flesh upward, toward the chest, then brought the knife down.

The Lopritian tried to struggle. Moisture streamed from his mouth and he gurgled noisily as Lerlt sawed at him. His hands rose to protect himself, but they were shaking and without strength. Gherst came to pull one arm away and stood on the man's hand as Lerlt withdrew his knife and pushed with both hands beside the perforation he had made.

For long seconds nothing happened.

Then the first red-gray bulge appeared at the opening. It swelled past the cut skin and white and yellow fat like a child's balloon. Blood seeped from between the tissues. Then the bulge pushed out further. It stretched.

It was a sausage shape, kinked, flaccidly round, tubular. Red and blue lines which were veins showed on it. It continued to grow and Lerlt was conscious of his own steady heavy breath and the irregular panting of the man on the floor. Suddenly the tube was springing free, and another bulge of material was pushing upward, so the first loop slithered past it sideways, then drooped toward the floor. It twitched like a decapitated snake.

Lerlt wiped blood from his hands onto the man's pants and stood, his eyes closed, breathing deeply, weak, drained. At his feet, the Lopritian animal shook violently, throwing itself about, twisting from side to side on the floor as its intestines spilled out.

"That it?" Herrilmin asked, raising his voice to be heard, and when Lerlt did not answer, he brought his own knife down again, and slashed the Lopritian's throat from ear to ear.

"What do we do now?" Fesch wondered, with awe that sounded close to panic in his voice. Lerlt smiled wanly, feeling strength pour back into his body, then giggled.

"Put him behind the bar," Herrilmin said. "Or leave him. We won't be here long enough for anyone to notice. Lerlt, you're a mess. Go wash off some of that shit."

Spots. Smears. Blood. Lerlt inspected his clothing.

"It'll rub off." He found a towel behind the bar and demonstrated.

"Wash it off," Herrilmin snapped. "Get your clothes wet.

Get yourself wet. All over. I don't want to smell crap every time you get in eyesight."

He tried to grin. "It's not that bad."

"Lerlt, you are fucking crazy! You stink! Do you want to stay with us? Yes or no? If it's yes, go get clean."

"And if not," Gherst said suddenly, "good fucking riddance."

His voice was so hostile that Lerlt instinctively stepped toward him with the knife extended. Gherst backpedaled quickly.

"Watch your shit-filled tongue," Lerlt snarled at him.

"I'll say what I want." The brown-haired Agent's hand dropped to his waist where his own knife remained and pulled it out to face Lerlt. "Big man, huh? Clever with a knife? What are you like against someone who can fight back, Lerlt?"

"Better than good enough." Lerlt bared his teeth, but as Gherst smiled and gestured invitingly with his knife, he sensed the argument was going too far. Gherst was a Septling, after all, not the enemy, so he held his ground but did not advance. "You try me, you low-caste bastard, you'll find out."

"Knock it off, you two," Herrilmin ordered. "We got to stay together. Lerlt, I told you, go wash."

"Make him apologize." He waggled his knife and was pleased to see Gherst step sideways. The bastard was scared. That was as good as winning.

"*Lerlt!* Move your filthy body! You get to the count of two and then I take you apart with my hands. One! Two!" Herrilmin took a pace toward him, his face angry.

It was shammed anger, he was sure, but there was nothing to be gained by making Herrilmin look silly. He stayed long enough to be sure Gherst remained intimidated, than ran to the rest room as Herrilmin reached the last word.

Once there, though, he was not as pleased with himself as was justified. Gherst was a Septling, Lerlt told himself as he slopped water over himself. He should be a friend. They had common goals. It was unfortunate that the brown-haired man had become so emotional, but that was his problem. Lerlt was the more sensible man; it was *his* responsibility to keep the peace.

Were the others talking about him? He left the rest room and waited in the corridor, hidden, listening, but there were no voices. Water was splashing in the kitchen. The other Agents were there, he guessed. No doubt, Herrilmin was lecturing Gherst on his failures.

Lerlt felt sorry for the brown-haired man. He would be polite, he decided. With everyone. For a while.

But the effort was wasted. Gherst ha'Hujsuon did not draw his knife again, but he was only distantly polite to Lerlt's pleasantries. As the Agents trudged up the road that Herrilmin claimed led to a time machine, he stared unmovingly at the rutted surface and saw nothing of the town. Lerlt saw that he got dirt on his boots just the same.

Lerlt dripped from his washing. He walked to the side of the others so the dust they kicked up would not cake on him. He had wrung his clothes out as well as he could but that was no substitute for dryness, and the handful of clean cloths he had found behind the bar had really only rearranged the water on his face and arms.

Herrilmin, true to form, had snarled at him for time wasting when he was toweling himself off, sorely trying Lerlt's newly won philosophy. That was another reason Lerlt was still wet, though not as wet as he had been when the two Dicovys Iron-wearers held him out in the rain.

Had that only been yesterday? Yes—not quite ten day tenths ago and the memory already seemed centuries old.

Things happen. Things change. Much of his annoyance died as he considered the truism.

Fesch, on the other hand, found change hard to accept. Lerlt noticed that he stared at everything with wide eyes and a wider mouth. His head would not stop swinging.

This was an unusual place to Algheran eyes, Lerlt admitted. It seemed too small for a city, too large and spread-out for a Settlement. There was an open field to the right of the road. In the buildings on the other side, candles or lanterns burned in some windows to oppose the twilight, but they did not cast as much light as the quarter of moon that already floated behind tree trunks. Leaves littered the ground and Lerlt wondered why, if the town was inhabited, they had not been raked into piles.

But the town appeared empty. Insects could be heard nearby and that increased the sensation of emptiness.

Paradoxically, for one raised in a metropolis, what Lerlt noticed about the town were the large buildings—the inn and warehouse at the base of the hill on the river side of the great road, the barns and other structures at the far side of the open field. The town's other buildings—houses, he supposed they were called, though they were too small for anything but a single family—were inconsequential in comparison. Long narrow things, taller than they were wide and garishly colored, they had a strangely fragile appearance.

Cobwebs, Lerlt thought, looking at the spindly houses. The larger structures would remain for centuries, but a few seconds of time travel would turn those dwellings to ruins and rubble.

And the people within, as well. *No Septs in Loprit*. Only individuals lived here, to live and grow old and die in isolation, with no form of continuity or meaning to existence.

How can they stand it? In Alghera, there were Associations. Even the unSepted had something to belong to. It was kindness, Lerlt suddenly understood, which made the Associations tolerated in Alghera.

Kindness. Gherst, for all his education, would always be too parochial to understand how the one world was really governed. Lerlt wondered if the man knew with more than his intellect that in this era the Hujsuons were not yet a Sept, not even yet an Association's dream.

"This way." Herrilmin pointed left at a signpost. "Lerlt, careful, or you'll walk into a beehive."

"Ooops!" He moved sideways quickly, and forwent further inspection of the post. Unfairly, it had shown a rider on a horse, rather than bees.

"What's that stink?" Fesch wondered and Lerlt, with those words, suddenly noticed a stench like spoiled lemons.

"Epuratory," Herrilmin said, waving an arm in no one direction. "Acid tanks to dissolve the skin and seeds in ironberries. The local lord does metal refining and some forging here. Made some of the guns the Lopritians took south with them. It smells like they didn't empty out the vats when they closed things down."

"Making cider," Gherst suggested, but the other Agents ignored him.

"How do you know all that?" Fesch asked, and Herrilmin chuckled.

"Maybe I've paid attention to the town." The big man cocked his head and waved. Lerlt saw a child at the end of the road. "Don't say anything . . . Keep walking. Okay."

For a few seconds they waited; then the child went inside. Lerlt noticed that stars were beginning to appear.

Nighttime. He stepped more quickly.

The Agents came to the top of the hill and turned left with the road. The houses seemed larger here, Lerlt noticed, but they were still too small for Sept use. Perhaps it was an illusion.

"That wasn't it." Fesch might have accepted Herrilmin's words but Gherst would not. "You were following Timt ha'-Dicovys, weren't you? What made you do that?"

"Suspicions," Herrilmin said gravely. "The way he acted when we left on this mission. Vrect tra'Hujsuon asked me to pay attention to what he did."

"But he didn't come." Lerlt finally had something important to say. "I remember, when we left, he was still sitting at the table. Don't you remember, Gherst? He tried to argue against saving Mlart, from the start."

"He's here now." Gherst said that slowly, as if it were not a question.

"He's here now," Herrilmin confirmed. "To kill Mlart."

"But why?"

Herrilmin snapped his fingers, but Lerlt recalled conversations he had overheard only days before. "Something for Dicovys, I bet. The people in that Sept don't like Mlart. Saving him was a Ruijac idea, remember? I bet Borct tra'Dicovys put up with it back at the Station because he didn't have a choice, and told his bullyboy to make sure it didn't work."

"Uhh-hh" was Gherst's reply.

"Wouldn't the Teeps stop that?" Fesch's voice was puzzled.

"No. You can't trust the Teeps." Lerlt spoke quickly, trying to say what was obvious to him before he could be interrupted, and felt relief when Herrilmin did not object. "Maybe they're in on the plot, too. You know there are Teeps around the Institute, even though there shouldn't be, and the Dicovys probably do some business with them and—"

"Dicovys does business with everybody," Gherst interjected.

"So? That makes it easier to hide something, doesn't it? Borct makes a deal with the tra'Nyjuc and the tra'r'Sihuc—he's got them right there, after all—not to expose him and when the war's over, Dicovys pays them off. Land or some business deal or some bill in the Muster—it could be anything and who would know but them?"

"Why do that?" Fesch wondered. "If I were a Teep, you know . . . I'd want the Alliance to win."

The others frowned at him and he blushed. "Well, I would. So why are they covering up for the Dicovys?"

"Because they're cheating," Lerlt explained, suddenly sure. "Us *and* the Dicovys. You're right, they want the Alliance to win, so they want Mlart dead, which is why they're doing this, but also they made this deal, just in case, so they get something big no matter how the war ends. And it's not just 'covering up' for Dicovys; they're helping, too. Maybe the Dicovys needs a Teep for part of it, or the Teeps don't trust Dicovys to deliver on their promises after the war of something, so they sent a Teep out with Timt ha'Dicovys, like Herrilmin said!"

"Right," Gherst said sourly.

"Well, am I?" Lerlt turned to Herrilmin.

"I think it's something like that," the blond man agreed. "I don't have all the details." He stopped at the head of an intersection and pointed toward the cul-de-sac they were about to enter.

"Keep your voices down. We're almost there."

They followed him and came to a small gate at the side of the street. Herrilmin smiled and held his hand outstretched. "Gentlemen."

"This is it?" Fesch asked stupidly.

Lerlt had no doubts. To him, it seemed axiomatic that a man doing unusual things should choose an unusual dwelling.

Even by Lopritian standards, Timt ha'Dicovys or Timmial lan Haarper or whatever name he used had a strange dwelling. It was a single-story building, set back from the street by an expanse of low grass, and possessed both great length and width. It was built of wood rather than the pastel-colored concrete of other houses. The slope of the roof was shallower than that of other houses of the town; the peak appeared flattened.

The front windows were curtained and dark—Lerlt thought he saw shelving on one wall as the Agents approached, but could not make out what was on the shelves—but light glowed on patches at the side of the house.

This was the top of the hill. Lerlt noticed that the lawn continued past the house some distance; then came undistinguished shrubbery and tops of trees he could not recognize. It was a large and impractical yard even for a large house; Lerlt wondered briefly if Timt ha'Dicovys had drilled soldiers in it, then wondered if the speculation were really so amusing.

"Keep your mouths shut in here," Herrilmin muttered as they came to the main door. "Don't give things away, or—just assume I've made some terrifying threat, and that means you, Fesch, and you, too, Lerlt."

He tugged a handle near the door latch; Lerlt heard a muffled bell tinkle inside.

A few moments passed while Lerlt reflected that Herrilmin could do nothing to intimidate him; then the rectangular door swung inward on hinges, disclosing a young man in dark clothing.

"Yes?"

A young woman, but in pants. Lerlt blinked as he caught the sound of her voice and only then noticed that her hair was too long to be a man's and that it was not a man's chest in her baggy pullover shirt.

"You're Timt's friends," he heard her say. "You had better come in." She stepped outside, and her head turned from one side to another almost as quickly as she spoke. Lerlt's eyes were focused on her face. He noticed absently that her trousers were streaked with paint and that she spoke with a soft accent he could not place. "Did anyone see your uniforms?"

Even in semidarkness, she had an exotic look, and Lerlt realized both that he wished to be noticed by her and that his damp clothing embarrassed him. "No one important," he said as he stepped past her quickly and entered a narrow antechamber.

"Not in a good light," Herrilmin commented, taking a long step which made his foot connect with Lerlt's ankle.

Lerlt kept his mouth shut and moved through the antechamber to a much larger room, where there was space to wince and to bend to rub his bruise. He realized suddenly the woman had spoken in Algheran Speech.

An Algheran? No—she had the wrong appearance.

Not a wife. No sensible man would marry outside a Sept.

Another relative, then? Unlikely.

A servant, of course, or a slave.

Fesch crowded past while he was still thinking about that. Lerlt, kneeling, noticed the other's torso turn as he inspected the room. Familiarity made him realize the man was impatient to speak, so he stood quickly to administer a kick if needed.

Gherst entered next. Behind him, Herrilmin mumbled something which Lerlt did not catch. Fesch wandered off silently and unscathed.

"Let me give you something to see with," Lerlt heard the woman say, and he turned so he could watch her breasts move as she stretched for a light. It was not a local accent that she spoke with, he realized. He wondered where Timt ha'Dicovys had found her and how she had been trained. He wished to hear her speak again, and he was bitterly envious of the red-haired Ironwearer.

Meanwhile, the woman seemed totally absorbed by the lighting rods she was adjusting. "Yes, the housekeeper is away," she told Herrilmin when the hissing had sunk to a minimum. "Such an old busybody—she comes when she feels like it, but I told her to stay away until Tim' returned."

Her hair was solid black and straight, reaching halfway down her back, her skin not quite pale in the harsh glare of the light. Freckles, Lerlt understood suddenly. All over her body, perhaps—they were especially plain on her face as she turned toward him.

"What are you staring at?" she asked.

Green eyes, almond-shaped and intelligent. High cheekbones in a narrow face. A straight nose. Arched eyebrows. Thin lips. A lightly built body with a long neck. Small rounded breasts, high on her chest. And, yes, freckles. Lerlt wondered if her breasts were freckled. She was very young.

Behind her, Herrilmin was frozen in place, his face tense with malice which she could not see.

"You. You're beautiful," Lerlt said, not caring what Herrilmin might do.

She smiled quickly and waved a thin hand. "You've been away from the Station too long."

Lerlt smiled back automatically.

"You're wet," she said. "Can I get you something? You won't fit in anything Tim' has but . . . let me look."

It was definitely Tim', Lerlt noticed, an incomplete form of Timt. A nickname, then, or a pet name for use by friends. It was hard to imagine the big surly redhead having friends, let alone a nickname, and he wondered why she used it so freely before strangers. He mumbled something at her and started to step out of her way.

"That's enough," Herrilmin growled. "Gherst, Fesch, get your asses over here!" Before Lerlt could react, he reached to swing the woman about with one hand, then hit her in the stomach with the other. The smack could be heard throughout house.

Lerlt, shocked, reacted as if the blow had been aimed at him. He inhaled sharply, then stood, pale and trembling, as the woman doubled up and fell at his feet. She had bitten her tongue, he thought, staring down as she struggled to her hands and knees. Nothing else would explain the agony on her face when she raised it to him.

He was not able to move. He could not help her.

Seconds passed as the woman struggled hoarsely for breath, huddled in on herself. Then Gherst and Fesch were there.

"You aren't hurt half as much as you can be," Herrilmin said sourly, not looking at her. "Don't try your witch tricks on us, Teep, or I'll teach you what pain is really like."

"Not—Teep," the woman gasped. Lerlt saw tears on her face.

Herrilmin kicked her in the ribs. "Don't lie to me," he said, then pulled her head backward by the hair and jabbed her forehead with a finger. "You had a Teep's plaque there. You removed it. You're intriguing against Normals."

"Not," she said. "No, I'm not."

Fesch moved forward, then was stopped by Gherst's arm.

"Fucking Teep." Herrilmin kicked the woman in the thigh, then held his foot back for another kick. "Don't lie to me," he repeated. "*I watched you, Teep!* I know everything about you! You can't hide any longer."

"Not." She swallowed and flinched, expecting another kick, but this time Herrilmin only snorted.

"Gherst, look at her forehead. What do you see?"

Gherst went to one knee and took the woman's head into his hands. "Might have been a Teep plaque there," he admitted. "There's a pit here, in the right place."

"It's a bee sting," the woman said quickly.

"No bump like a sting," Gherst said curtly. "I'd say Teep, Herrilmin. The skin is different from the rest of her forehead."

He stood abruptly. "You're sure about watching her?"

"Very sure. She had a plaque before."

"Then it's a Second Compact matter. Kill her."

"Get a rope," Herrilmin ordered. "I've got questions for her first."

Lerlt realized he was holding his breath. Then Fesch turned and took a step away.

The woman exploded. Lerlt had a confused impression of violence and motion, of noise and a pain in his ankle.

Suddenly the pandemonium died. Gherst was sitting on the floor with the woman leaning against him. Her head was fast in his elbow. Muffled shouts were coming from behind the hand he held over her mouth.

Fesch was propped against the wall, gingerly manipulating his stomach. And Lerlt's shin was throbbing. He had been kicked again. In the excitement, it seemed unimportant.

The woman's toes pounded uselessly on the floor. She was still trying to run, Lerlt realized, even after Gherst had stopped her.

"That's enough." Herrilmin moved forward and grabbed her knees, lifting so her body was parallel to the floor. She continued to kick even then, and Lerlt was amused to watch his reactions as the big man was tugged back and forth by her struggles. Exasperation showed in his voice. "Fesch, Lerlt, find some rope."

The first room Lerlt came to, just beyond the big living room, was the kitchen. He searched and found nothing but a table and chairs, cabinet and cookware, and a coal-burning stove.

Fesch was luckier. Lerlt heard him shout from nearby and returned to the living room just behind him. In his hand, the man carried a ball of twine, which he told Herrilmin was "cord."

Lerlt looked about aimlessly. There were two couches here

and several large chairs. Rugs had been placed on the wooden floor, but even with them and five people present the room seemed empty. It was unfinished, he saw when he paid attention to the walls—the beams and risers had not been covered, leaving bare red-tinted wood exposed above him and on all sides. He concentrated, catching a weak odor of raw wood.

A fireplace was at the near end of the room; an armful of wood was stacked in it. The fire had not been lit, but electrical lights on either side of the mantel were switched on. At the opposite end of the room, a door led to what would be the summer living area of an Algheran home; snow had not fallen yet, but it was decently closed. The exterior wall of the room held two windows which could be pulled inward. He glimpsed a loose shutter beyond one of them and beyond that, on the grass, a mound of green and brown vegetation. It was quite dark and Lerlt could not see stars through the windows.

Inside again, between the windows was a low table which supported a trough holding some pink-topped plants. The ceiling was high on that side of the room, and even higher on the interior side, perhaps two full man-heights. Long curtains ran along the length of that wall. They were pulled back in one place, exposing an opening onto darkness. There was no breeze to move them.

The woman was facedown on the longer of the couches, with a cushion under her face. Both Herrilmin and Gherst were sitting on her, Herrilmin on her back with her wrists in his fist, Gherst on her lower legs, so she was immobilized. Her shirt had pulled out of her pants, exposing a handbreadth of back and waist. What Lerlt could see of her under the two big men was pathetically small and wriggling, like a grieving child.

Herrilmin took the twine from Fesch without enthusiasm and wrapped the woman's wrists tightly, over and over again, then cut the cord with his knife, and passed the ball to Gherst. The motion seemed surprisingly efficient and practiced; Lerlt wondered if they had done this before.

Herrilmin and Gherst stood up, and the blond man turned the woman over while Gherst kept hold of her ankles. Her hair was bedraggled and her eyes shut. Lerlt saw she was silently weeping. Herrilmin slapped her.

She stopped crying then and opened her eyes to look hard at the four men. She snuffled for a moment, then swallowed, and her trembling ended.

"You can't hurt me," she said clearly. "I'm in r'Sihuc."

The smaller of the two Teep Septs. So she was Algheran and a Teep. Lerlt inhaled dizzily.

Herrilmin held his knife where she could see it, then put the tip inside one of her nostrils. He kept another hand on her belly, pressing down. "Don't be funny or you'll be sorry."

"I'm in r'Sihuc," she said again. Carefully, slowly, looking at the knife cross-eyed.

"Be good," Herrilmin told her.

Meanwhile, Gherst had cut a length of cord. He fitted a loop over her right ankle, then lifted her right leg over her left. "Raise her knees," he said to Fesch, and when the younger man had done that, the two of them pushed until her right foot had gone below her left ankle. While Fesch held her ankles, Gherst wrapped them together with the cord and moved to the foot of the couch, where he held the loose ends in one hand, the toes of her right foot in the other hand. "Let her go," he grunted and Fesch stepped back.

Herrilmin moved, holding her shoulders down. "Show her."

Lerlt had already seen strain on her face. When Gherst pulled minutely on the cord, she gasped. For a moment he thought she had passed out. Something electrifying seemed to sweep through the room then, and Lerlt felt himself heavier and more solid in its wake. When he inhaled, richer air filled his nostrils and he tasted salt within his mouth.

Any sympathy he had felt for the woman was gone.

Herrilmin grinned at the other Agents. "This is how people who can't read minds ask questions."

"I'm in r'Sihuc." Her eyes were closed. The artery at one side of her throat throbbed.

"So? There's no tra'r'Sihuc here to protect you."

"Tim' will. If you hurt me like you're thinking he'll punish you." Her eyes opened, then moved from face to face. "All of you. Let me go."

"Hurt you? How?" Herrilmin asked, and looked at Gherst, then at her. "You're his whore."

Her face twitched. "His partner. Not his whore—"

Gherst pulled the cords again. She stopped and Lerlt thought from her expression that she might say more but she did not.

"He left you alone, didn't he?" was the next question.

"What do you mean?"

"Timt ha'Dicovys. He's not here now, is he?"

"He's close. He watches over me," she said quickly, before Gherst could do anything. Herrilmin released her and lifted a finger, and the brown-haired Agent left the cords slack as she tried to swing herself upright. Awkwardly, she squirmed into a sitting position. "Now let me go."

"He's in the army," Herrilmin said calmly. "He's days away from here."

Seconds passed. "I don't know where he is," she said. "But he's close."

"He's here to kill Mlart tra'Nornst."

A longer time passed. "Ask him," she said at last.

"Where's your time machine?" Herrilmin stiffened his shoulders and Lerlt realized he had—they all had—slipped into a crouch as he questioned the woman. Awkwardly, unwilling to be noticed, he straightened up also.

"I don't know what you mean." Enough time had passed to show she had considered several answers.

Gherst pulled his cords again and Lerlt saw that she had pushed herself against the side of the couch to keep from screaming. He licked his lips.

"You think that's cute." Herrilmin paused and Lerlt heard him breathing through his nose in little snorts. He turned and took something from his pocket. "Go find it."

What he gave to Lerlt was a metal box the size of a pair of

fingers. One end was open. Lerlt pointed that away from him and turned to his right until the box tingled in his hand and hummed.

"It's that way." He pointed at a corner. Gherst had relaxed the pressure and as he looked at the others he saw that the woman was looking at him. Staring at him.

"Go find it," Herrilmin repeated.

"It's outside, Herrilmin. It's dark and—"

"Are you afraid of the dark, Lerlt?"

"I just don't know the ground here. I could stumble and—"

"Stumble till you find it."

"Look, it'll wait till tomorrow." He glared at the woman.

"Not unless you want to show it off to the locals, it won't. Go on, Lerlt, before I'm angry."

"I'll find it," Fesch said and put his hand out.

Lerlt pulled away. He knew the woman was enjoying his discomfort. "I'll do it," he said sourly. "Do I get a turn, too?"

"You do." Herrilmin did not misunderstand.

"All right." Lerlt walked past Gherst and looked at the woman. A vein was throbbing on her forehead. He smiled and reached to tug hard on the cords fastened to the woman's ankles. That would teach her to laugh.

She was still sniveling when he went out of the house.

Outside a minute later, he heard a scream but it was muffled quickly and after that the only sounds that mattered were his feet scuffling through the leaves in the backyard and the buzz from the box in his hand.

Other voices from the house did not carry. Light spilled from a window facing a small building at the back of the house, then was blocked as shutters swung sideways. He had hesitated for a moment in case there was a reaction from elsewhere in the neighborhood, but none happened.

The houses nearby could have been vacant. He could see lighted windows in none of them and his ears caught no other voices. The silence puzzled him until he understood it meant the residents had gone to bed at nightfall. Presumably, they all slept until sunlight awakened them. It seemed a bizarre way to organize a life.

He took another step and another toward the hedge at the back of the yard and was rewarded with another buzz from the locator. He was still approaching the time machine, as Herrilmin had promised.

He had more faith in the locator than in Herrilmin, though he had never understood the explanations that described its functioning. It was a tool. There were books to tell people how to make tools, so neither tools nor toolmaking were genuine mysteries. How tools worked, Lerlt felt, could be left to men with limited minds. Fesch, for example—only a few days before, the man had let slip that at the end of the Project he expected to return as an ordinary student to the Institute for the Study of Land Reclamation Issues, just as if the entire Chelmmysian-Algheran war had never taken place.

Other Agents were just as blind, it seemed. Lerlt remembered a score of pointless conversations in the early days of the Project with half-witted youngsters who had asked his opinion of how time travel worked and how time machines could be improved, as if such matters were more important than the power time travel had given them. One pathetic dolt—not from Hujsuon, thank the Lady!—was still babbling about setting up trading posts in different eras. And some red-faced fool from Ruijac had speculated that all of Fifth Era humanity could be transported far into the future or the past to escape the coming Ice Age; he had yammered like an idiot when Lerlt asked him who that would benefit, and fallen completely incoherent when asked what had made him so sure that glaciers would ever cover the Earth again.

Smiling now as he remembered all that, Lerlt came to the corner of the hedge. The yard ended here. A path of some kind began—he could feel pebbles in a concave depression under his feet, even if he could not see it—and almost immediately plunged downward into a deep gully. A few steps along he reached a ledge, or an even spot in the path, and decided he had gone far enough. The ground was rocky and the descent ahead looked quite steep. If a low tree limb, unseen in the darkness, did not knock his head off, the soil was surely not to be trusted to stay in place when stepped on because of the recent rains.

Herrilmin would be annoyed if he did not report complete success, but he would also be annoyed if Lerit broke his leg and had to be rescued from the bottom of the ravine. Besides, it seemed to him that the direction the locator pointed to had changed, which implied that the hidden time machine was close enough to walk to. Surely it made sense to report that to Herrilmin rather than take unnecessary risk and report nothing.

But not too quickly. Herrilmin was not expecting haste.

He kicked at a stone which refused to move.

Not too quickly.

Chapter 13

C herrid kept the men marching into the nighttime watches. Fortunately, there was a quarter moon overhead and few clouds. There was enough light to keep wagons and men on the surface of the road. The men he had intended to station with torches in the distance to guide the brigade were not needed.

Necessarily, the advance was slow, not from the difficulties of darkness, but from the need to protect the horses pulling the wagons. There were frequent halts for brief periods, gauged long enough to rest the animals, but too short for men to fall asleep.

In a full watch, the brigade moved perhaps an additional five thousand man-heights, about half the distance it would have covered in that time in daylight.

The old Ironwearer grimaced when the estimate was given to him at the fifth-watch rest stop. He was about to draft orders to keep the march up without halts until his stomach growled at him. Men would be marching without supper that night, he admitted to himself; they deserved adequate rest.

Nonetheless, the habit of issuing orders at day's end was too strong to be disobeyed, so he called out for an aide with a writing block. He sent a message to each of the regimental commanders, requiring them to check that the horses were fed at the next stop, then sent other aides to find the chief surgeon, Ironwearer Rahmmend Wolf-Twin, and Dalsyn Ian Plenytk.

Cherrid was normally reluctant to reduce the comforts of the sick, but he knew deaths had left vacant space in some of the ambulance wagons. While the majority of the brigade's soldiers rested, he had the surgeons select men who could be moved and consolidated them, then moved supplies into the empty ambulances. That freed up four larger wagons, which he had Rahm Wolf-Twin send on to West Bend, two days to the north, to gather supplies.

A platoon of Midpassage men rode the wagons as escorts. They were to overawe the villagers. Cherrid knew he would be stealing from the peasants' winter food stocks; he did not want violence to make the situation worse.

Including that detachment, the brigade was down to 2,784 effectives and 482 sick men. No one was under arrest, but two men had been shot during the day in ris Daimgewln's regiment: they had been caught stealing food.

For variety's sake, when Lerlt returned, he came to the door at the back of the house, which opened into the kitchen. It had not been fastened, and the kitchen was still empty of interest. A closed door was at the end of a small hallway, and he thought he heard movement, but did not enter.

The living room was also empty, when he glanced at it. Then he noticed the door to the front room was open and ajar, hanging from only one hinge. The room was lighted; a curtain flapped in front of the open window. He heard movement. He drew nearer and saw Herrilmin.

The blond man had his back to Lerlt. He was squatting with his pants down over a pile of what looked like books. He had defecated, and as Lerlt watched he ripped pages out of the books and wiped his backside and dropped them on the steaming brown pile. Urine glistened on the floorboards.

Lerlt snapped his fingers without sound and stepped side-ways quietly so he would not be noticed. As he did, he caught sight for the first time of large plaques of some kind on the walls between the windows and the fireplace. Footsteps sounded from beyond the interior curtains, and he wandered out to see whether they belonged to Gherst or Fesch.

A garden waited beyond the curtains and a stone pathway. Apart from a trapezoidal lighted area, it was too dark to make out detail, but Lerlt noticed small blooms beside the flagstones, then grass. There was even a tree.

Inside the house? He blinked, then noticed the space was not roofed. There was no floor beneath the stones.

"This is—" Fesch stepped from behind the tree, his hand stretched out as if reaching for a word or a leaf. He found a word. "Clever."

"I don't think so." Lerlt moved to meet him, a hand at his belt. "I brought you your knife. You left it at that tavern. Where's Gherst?"

Though he could guess where Gherst was. Herrilmin first, always. Then Gherst, always taking what they wanted first . . . Greedy thieves. He scowled.

He walked past a concrete table and two benches, then turned to survey the space, and kept the scowl on his face. A glass wall, glass doors, shrubs, dark spaces . . .

This house was strange. Unpleasant.

Cimon take Herrilmin. Why did he get everything first?

"You went back to the inn?" Fesch asked. "I don't think that was a good idea."

Lerlt wasn't sure that Fesch thought anything at all, but he settled for saying that he had not been seen. "We need something for protection," he added, and then, since it seemed necessary to explain even obvious things to the man, "We don't have any other weapons and we're surrounded by Lopri-tians."

"I guess so," Fesch said vaguely. Absentmindedly, he took the knife Lerlt gave him and put it in his belt, then gestured with a hand. "This is big enough, you could land a levcraft here, couldn't you?'' His hand moved again. ''Those are doors to bedrooms, his and hers, I guess. There's another in the back, where Herrilmin took . . . I haven't looked in the other rooms yet.'' His head turned back and forth. ''What do you call this?''

''I don't call it anything,'' Lerlt said sourly, annoyed both with the man and the bizarre building. ''It's just an unfinished part of the house. The builders aren't done, that's all. You saw they hadn't finished the interior walls. I don't know why they quit, maybe it was the start of the war, but there should be three or four more rooms here.''

''You think so?'' Fesch sounded disappointed. His foot scruffed at leaves.

''Sure.'' Lerlt frowned. ''Who lives in a house which lets snow inside?''

''Uh-h-nn-no one.''

''So. You said his bedroom was there? Maybe there's something in it. I want to look.'' Lerlt stepped away quickly.

Fesch moved with him. ''Nothing interesting in it.''

''We'll see.'' A light had been left on in the room. Lerlt glanced quickly at the bed and the small table beside it, then opened a freestanding cabinet. Garments were hanging from hooks: shirts, trousers, a pair of jackets. Idly, he knocked them off, then rummaged through the things on shelves. Shoes, socks, more shirts . . . .

''What's this?'' He held out a small white garment with four openings. ''There's a stack of them.''

''I don't know.'' Fesch rubbed a finger over the windowsill, and rubbed dust off onto a bracket protruding from the wall. ''Turn it over.''

Lerlt did, putting the largest hole at the top.

''Look like little pants,'' Fesch suggested. ''You could fit your legs through the bottom holes.''

Lerlt tried that, pulling the garment up to his waist, but it promptly dropped to his knees when he let go. He cursed, then kicked it free.

"If it's Timt ha'Dicovys's, he's bigger," Fesch reminded him. "It might fit him."

Lerlt kicked the garment under the bed. "What for?"

"I don't know. Something religious? For ceremonies?"

It was as good an answer as any. Lerlt ran his hand over the shelves, knocking down the soft piles of clothing, and went on to the next room.

The woman's—garments like hers were on the floor: blouses, pants of some stiff blue fabric, loincloths. The room smelled something like her, Lerlt noticed, without being precise about what that smell was. Maybe it was only his imagination.

There was even less here than in Timt ha'Dicovys's room, but his eye finally caught something bright in her tangled bedclothes—a rectangular thing with hinged pages, something like a writing block, except that this was bigger than a writing block and all the pages were covered with undecipherable print and weird colored images.

Not Algheran script, not Lopritian. Not Common, either, and that exhausted Lerlt's knowledge of languages. Some barbarian nation's writing then, or simply decoration. Unimportant then.

The paper was shiny and slippery between his fingers and Lerlt was able to tear in half only a few pages at a time. It took him a while to finish; then he knocked down the clothing in her closets and left.

Fesch was next door, making clanking sounds. It was a large room, Lerlt found when he got to it, filled with strange devices that seemed to have no purpose other than to emit clanks.

Fesch was seated on a padded bench that was part of one of the machines, aimlessly swinging sideways a handle that dangled in front of his chest. "We ought to take this stuff with us," he said brightly.

"Why?" wondered Lerlt. He crossed the room to Fesch, and pushed at a handle that was a twin to the one the other man was swinging, but it refused to move inward. When he pulled outward—it took a starling amount of effort—chain rattled in a pulley arrangement at the back of the machine and heavy-looking rectangular plates rose up. "What is this shit?"

"Torture equipment," Fesch said. He squirmed and pulled a strap from under his buttocks. "Tie people in with these. But that's not the thing; Lerlt, you realize this stuff is all metal, even these buckles? It's iron or maybe even steel. There's a couple tons here. We can melt it down and—I mean if it's pure steel, there's enough here to buy a Sept!"

Lerlt hesitated, unwilling to accept that. The scaffolding pieces that held the equipment together were heavy and solid when he pushed at them, but foil-coated ceramics would have felt the same. Iron torture equipment? Might as well believe in windows made from diamond. He said as much.

Fesch disagreed. "We handled steel in one of my lab courses and you don't forget something like that." As if to prove his point, he rapped his knuckles solidly on a shining rod that dangled from a chain on another machine, and set it spinning about. For an instant, pain showed on his face.

"I'll bet that's stainless," he said. "Stainless steel. *Very* expensive—I can show you the recipe in the Plates."

"Anything in the Plates is expensive," Lerlt commented. Idly, he pressed at the frame of another machine, and found it too solidly balanced to push over. It would take more muscle than he possessed to create satisfying crashes in this room, he decided. Perhaps Herrilmin could be persuaded to—

"It's late stuff," Fesch said thoughtfully, interrupting Lerlt's musing. "We can make stainless steel up at the Present, but you can't get it here. So he had to import it."

"Or steal it," Lerlt pointed out. Timt ha'Dicovys had a time machine, after all. Lerlt was a little contemptuous of him for putting it to so trivial a use, but it was inexcusable for Fesch not to see what had happened.

"Either way, it took him a lot of trouble." Fesch finally got up from his machine, but he seemed reluctant to leave it. He kept his hands touching it, as he moved about it and peered at the chains and pulleys it contained. "He must have got this house made special, too, didn't he?"

Lerlt thought about that, looking for traps. "I suppose."

"Then what about her?"

Lerlt had to think again. "What about her? She's some cunt Timt ha'Dicovys picked up, that's all. Teeps are good whores, everyone knows that, what else could she be?"

"I don't know. But it's funny, isn't it? Building a house for a woman. Outfitting it. What if he really likes her?"

"Maybe he does," Lerlt admitted. "It doesn't matter, does it? He's not going to marry out of Dicovys so he has to get rid of her when he goes back to the Station. She's just a little twat on the side. He's not going to shame himself and his Sept by making a big deal about her."

"Yeah . . . He shouldn't. But what if he gets mad anyhow?"

Lerlt snorted. "At us? About what? A piece of Teep ass in a whorehouse is one thing, but anything more than that—Dicovys wouldn't stand for someone in their Sept getting involved with a Teep, and the better class of Teeps wouldn't put up with it, either. Besides, we're going to be gone before he gets here. How's he going to know it was us?"

"Guess you're right." Fesch paused, and rubbed a palm over his chin. "There was one other thing though—what about what she said? You know, about r'Sihuc? If she is, and this gets back to the Project, is there going to be trouble about this?"

"No." Lerlt snapped his fingers with certainty. "That was a lie. She doesn't look Algheran, does she? She probably just saw that name in our minds, or he mentioned it to her. And she wasn't marked—she deserves whatever happens. Right?"

"Yeah." Fesch's mind was distant. "But he's an Ironwearer and they're not reasonable. My battalion leader was one—a guy named Wilthir—he gave us a lecture when we came over the mountains about how we were to treat Lopritian women like our sisters and men like brothers and old people like our parents, you know? Or we'd be sorry. And then one of our guys robbed some liquor from a store in the first town we came to—I guess he was a little rough about it. Someone complained and Wilthir heard about it. And he broke both this guy's arms and both legs in a fight and pulled his uniform off so the ambulance teams wouldn't know he was one of ours and made us leave him on the road. We all had to step over him the next day, and he was dead! I mean, you can't predict—You sure he's going to forget her?''

"Nicole's soft butt, Fesch! So he's an Ironwearer. Anybody can be an Ironwearer. Just say that you're one and, and—that does it! Don't make a big deal of it.'' Lerlt waved his arm frantically. "Does this place make you think being an Ironwearer is so special?''

"Well . . . The Teeps have to agree, don't they? I mean, for any Ironwearer? And he's the only one in the Project and I always heard that if the Teeps say you're not really—''

Was such idiocy possible? "He's *working* for the Teeps, Fesch! That's why he's screwing one. It's probably his reward! They're not going to tell the truth about him! They cover up for him. Maybe making him an Ironwearer was even their idea. That's why there aren't any others. Don't you see!''

"See what, Lerlt?'' Herrilmin had sneaked up behind him and entered the conversation suddenly. "Gherst is finally worn out, Septlings. Which of you wants her next?''

"Fesch,'' Lerlt said immediately. "You go ahead.''

"Uh-h-h . . . All right.'' Fesch had hesitated only briefly. Then he snapped his fingers and scuttled across the floor, bouncing off the doorframe in his haste as Lerlt grimaced behind him.

"I don't know if he'll get it up,'' he told the blond man wryly when Fesch was out of sight. "Way he was talking, he was thinking more about Timt ha'Dicovys than the woman. Course, he's got a dinky little dinky, I don't suppose there's much difference whether he's up or down.'' He chuckled.

"That's what you were talking about?'' Herrilmin demanded. "Timt ha'Dicovys? I thought you were supposed to find his time machine.''

"Yeah. Well, it's out there," Lerlt said. "But it's in a gully. We can't get to it tonight. About Fesch—I was trying to tell Fesch Timt ha'Dicovys wouldn't make trouble for us and—"

"Tomorrow you and Gherst bring it up and put it in the backyard. Leave it hidden from the locals."

"Are we leaving tomorrow?"

"Just do what I said." Herrilmin glowered at the machinery in the room, then left.

Lerlt's own turn with the Teep woman came much later that night and it was not satisfying.

The light was on in the room where she was being kept. In the doorway, as Lerlt began removing his clothes, he could see where bruises were already forming on her flanks and throat. The cord that bound her to the bedframe had left thin red-and-white welts on her wrists.

She was bleeding between her legs and appeared dazed. The sheets beneath her were soaked with sweat and other fluids, and a red- and brown-daubed rag lay at the foot of the bed. Lerlt picked it up and wiped at her fastidiously before mounting.

Fesch had selfishly stayed too long and robbed her of her spirit, he found. She brought her knees together and tried to pull them up to protect herself from him at first, but she did not bite or butt at him, and even that resistance ended after he punched her in the belly.

For the rest of the time she was apathetic while Lerlt was on her, either from exhaustion or lack of sleep. In fact, she seemed to be sleeping during the period while Lerlt came erect for the third time, but it might have been a ruse. In any event, her eyes and mouth both opened when he pushed himself into her body again and she sobbed convincingly while he twisted and bit at her nipples.

When he was done, Gherst was ready for another turn.

Herrilmin had taken Timt ha'Dicovys's bedroom, and Fesch was in the woman's. Lerlt found a blanket and slept on one of the couches.

*   *   *

It was still dark, but enough light had preceded the morning
sun to show outlines when the Strength-through-Loyalty Brigade reached its stopping place. Cherrid, nodding sleepily to
himself on his horse, heard approaching hoofbeats first and
raised his head on weary muscles to greet the rider. In the
background, a man struggled with a recalcitrant horse. Muffled
voices could be heard in the distance. The darker places on the
ground were sleeping soldiers, and for an instant, he thought
wistfully of the rest Grahan was taking in the ambulance behind him.

He could not make out features, but the size of the man who
had ridden up was unmistakable. "Good morning, Timmial."

The redhead gave him a sketch of a salute. "Morning, Lord
Clendannan. The artillery is still getting sorted out. I've had
them park their caissons up the road a bit, and unhitch the
horses, so they can double-team the guns. Some protests—I
think they think some crews will steal powder from the
others—but I told them it was your order. Hope that's all
right, sir."

"That's fine, Timmial. We should have time to unscramble
the wagons tomorrow, I'm sure."

"We're killing horses, even so. Those depressions aren't
exactly soaked, but the ground is pretty soft."

"That cannot be helped. The more horses, the fewer men."
He stopped for thought. "We might lay out some rocks tomorrow to hold up the guns."

"I was thinking we could cut some trees, sir. There are some
on top of the ridge. Not enough to make a corduroy road, but
we can rough saw them into halves—some of the Midpassage
men are carpenters, who can do that—and put them into the
ruts. That would make a sort of trail. Also, I suppose, it takes
some landmarks away from the enemy, which may be worth
doing."

"We can try that first then. How are the men holding up?"

Lan Haarper's shoulders twitched up and down. "So-so.
Pretty tired, a little annoyed that they're still working while the

infantry sleeps, but they appreciate being ahead of the Algherans. I suggested to the gun commanders that they pick one man from each gun and let him sleep now, so he can stand guard while the others are sleeping. I think most of them are doing that.''

"That is very fine," Cherrid told him.

"I also told them to impress any of the camp followers they can find. Not that there are many who stayed up with us.''

This was more than "fine," Cherrid admitted. Most of the officers who felt they could be spared were sleeping in the wagons now, and he was very grateful that young Ian Haarper had stayed up to share his vigil and perform some of the work. This went beyond any normal conception of duty.

As for the camp followers— "They should catch up.''

"Hmmm. You think Mlart will give us that much time?''

"I think so. He would not have expected an all-night march from us.''

Cherrid smiled quickly. "Neither did I till this afternoon, for that matter, till I was goaded into it. Always leave yourself a little opportunity for improvisation, Timmial. Be willing to surprise yourself; a commander who cannot do that is a commander who has stopped thinking. And a commander who has stopped thinking— well, for all his virtues, would you turn a battle over to Ironwearer Wolf-Twin?''

Lan Haarper chuckled. "One Wolf-Twin would be more than enough against an army of clerks. But I see the point.''

Cherrid suddenly realized his mind had reached a decision. Uncovered a decision, more precisely: the only riddle remaining was why he had taken so long to see what was obvious.

"Ironwearer, I am restoring you to command of the Steadfast-to-Victory. The written notice will come out this afternoon, but you can begin giving orders immediately.''

A moment passed. Lan Haarper breathed heavily.

"I can't think of any orders to give the men right now except to sleep, Lord Clendannan.''

"That is enough, Timmial. Your regiment is stationed on the left, and I suggest you get some sleep yourself.''

"Well—"

"Go do it," he said, and lied with clear conscience. "I'm going to bed myself as soon as you let me."

The sky was pink and gray over the hills east of Midpassage when three itinerant farm laborers from the kingdom of Innings entered the inn. They were ambulance drivers now, impressed into army service at the start of the war; outside in their wagons, they had fifteen wounded and dying men to transport to hospitals in F'a Loprit, but it was still their custom to begin the day's work, when possible, with a morning nip.

Here was an inn. The door was unbarred when they pushed at it and, for tens of thousands of man-heights in any direction, there was no officer to interfere.

Only gloom, a bad odor, and the sound of their footsteps met them, even when they called out for the innkeeper. They hesitated only a few moments, then moved to the bar, with the idea of serving themselves. One slipped, stumbled, then cried out as his hand touched the floor—and more.

The youngest, an adolescent boy named Rallt Ymer, was closest to the door. He went back to it and pulled it open to admit more light and the drivers gasped as one.

Red glistened on the gray planks.

Blood. Flesh. The parts of a body.

Part Three: Accountings

Chapter 14

"**W**hat do we do now, Pa?" Rallt asked, and on the other side of the body his father swallowed irresolutely. Outside, Rallt could hear the man who had stumbled over the body retching in the street, and half envied him. The air inside the inn was stagnant and, to Rallt's nose, already touched by the smell of corruption; he wished he, too, had an urgent excuse to leave the site.

He did not ask if the man on the floor was truly dead. This was already his second trip transporting injured soldiers to hospitals; he had seen death often enough to recognize it.

"We give this to the Lopriters," his father said at last, his voice husking. "Thee understands? It be their country, their killing, not ours. If we don't tell—boy, we must tell an officer. Be there one in the wagons?"

"Couple'a them, Pa, I think."

"Thee'll look. We both will," his father said, raising his eyes to the door, and from his voice Rallt guessed he, too, wanted to be someplace far away.

Neither was light-footed, but they left the inn as quietly as possible. Rallt held the door; his father ducked under his arm.

Outside, Rallt blinked, surprised to see how bright the morning was, though in fact gray-white clouds covered the sun and most of the sky. He hesitated for a moment, looking at the man clinging sickly to the hitching post. There was a damp brown splotch on the dust between the plank sidewalk and the dark, black pavement of the road, and Rallt felt his stomach organizing his own upset, but his father cuffed him before he could deliver it.

"Thee'll go to our'n, boy. Me and Sarlso can look at his wagon. And if thee finds not an officer, a sergeant may do."

Darkness like that in the inn and similar smells were in the ambulance. Rallt did not attempt to enter but lifted the canvas screen at the rear of the vehicle for his inspection.

There was no room for another person in the ambulance. It already held twelve men on framed canvas shelves, six in two bunks on each wall, and two more on the floor, wrapped in blankets to keep them from moving and disturbing their wounds. Several held pieces of the loaf of bread each had been given at the start of the trip; Rallt was not surprised to see one man had a loaf in both hands and another under his neck. A bucket at the front of the vehicle contained drinking water, another waited for human waste. One bucket had not been filled since the start of the trip, and the other had not been emptied.

To Rallt, the conditions inside the wagon were unexceptional. They did not bother him and he saw no connection between them and the likelihood that only half these men would survive their journey. Four days had passed since the wagon was loaded and no one was dead yet, but already Rallt could see that the authority his father sought would not be found here.

Saliva dripped from one man's mouth; his eyes stared without blinking, catatonically, fixed on his feet. Another shuddered at invisible terrors and wept. A few men still slept in these morning hours—Rallt heard snores.

One man in an upper berth had officer's insignia on an empty sleeve; blood had crusted on the blanket wrapped about his middle. He was babbling to himself in a language Rallt did not recognize and bumping his head rhythmically against the side of the wagon. He lacked the strength to hurt himself seriously, but did not stop even when the boy stretched to clasp his leg.

How hard should he hit to catch the man's attention? Rallt wondered. Surely no harder than his father would hit to wake him in the morning, but even that might be excessive. Weren't all Lopritian officers noblemen, or most of them, and apt to resent even a peasant's touch?

"Rallt! Rallt! Come here!" His father's voice.

Rallt stepped back and dropped the heavy canvas, cutting off the sights and smells of the ambulance, and swallowed thankfully, relieved that he could avoid a decision. Perhaps his father had found an officer. They would be back on the road shortly, in Coward's Landing on the next day, and Rallt remembered a kitchen maid with a pretty knee in the inn there. He patted his hair into place absently as he went to see.

His father had found an officer, a dark-haired man with a thin face who had the floor of the second wagon to himself.

"Thee'll speak for us."

Rallt dodged a cuff automatically and noticed that the man's head had turned to track him. So he was awake and conscious.

Sun drifted over a cloud, and with the additional light, Rallt could see the man wore a brown uniform rather than the more common blue, but there were officer patches on his shoulders. The man was also very pale but Rallt could see nothing else wrong with him until he was closer. Then it was obvious that only one boot tip held up the blanket wrapped about the officer's legs, and Rallt's first reaction was to feel pity for a man who could not stand to work in the fields and must depend on charity.

"What's this nonsense about, man?" the officer asked, and Rallt guessed that his voice was intended to snap, but it came out as a whisper.

"There were a death," he said, then added "sir," in case the Lopritian was also a noble.

"That I heard." The officer tipped his head back and sighed softly, then jerked it back to look at Rallt. "This man—your father?—if I understand his jabber—he said—a battlefield killing—but the battlefield's far away. Why don't you explain? In proper Lopritian, mind you."

Rallt hesitated, not sure what "proper Lopritian" was. The kingdom of Loprit had been founded by settlers from Innings, after all. The languages were similar, though to him the local dialect was the "jabber": a nasal version of familiar speech, omitting some expected words, adding some unnecessary ones, made more complex by loan words taken from barbarian sources.

But it was poverty that brought farmers from the over-crowded south to the wide fields of Loprit. Rallt nodded politely to show his subservience and did his best to explain the matter in slow, clear speech.

Like his father, he soon faltered to a stop, seeing what he said was not comprehended. It was not his fault: both languages lacked the terms he needed. Rallt had a name for legal executions, another for killings in battle, several words for suicide, and still others for accidental death in brawls or in farm mishaps or while resisting robbery. He had no name for murder.

"Come see," he said finally, pleading because the Lopritian had closed his eyes and did not seem to be listening. "Thee'll know it then, sir."

"I'm bleeding, boy," the officer whispered, and Rallt was close enough to smell sweat and to see that beads of moisture were on his forehead. "Look at my leg and you'll see I have to get to a hospital."

Rallt looked. Yes, blood was seeping through the blanket at the place where a shin should be. When he investigated further, he found blood and grayish pus oozing from pores in the pitch that covered the stump. The leg was warm to the touch, swollen, moist, reddish with white streaks along the lines of the veins.

He winced internally, for even by registered coach, traveling day and night along the great road, the hospitals of F'a Loprit were three to four days distant. Mechanically, wishing he could flee and wash his hands, he rewrapped the leg and stood back. His father moved behind him, and without looking, Rallt knew his thoughts were shared.

"Can you fix that wound?" the officer whispered, and Rallt could only guess how much courage it took to avoid screaming. "Don't waste my time here, man."

"Thee's to die," he said simply, for there was no reason not to be frank. "Thee'll not go so far as Northfaring, sir. Come see this other body, please, and tell us what to do. Do this last one thing for thy King."

"Queen," the officer whispered after he had swallowed twice. His eyes were tightly shut and so much time passed that Rallt had to look at his throat to be sure his pulse was still beating.

"Queen," he said again, as if it were important. "My Queen . . . I can't walk—you'll have to carry me."

They were able to get the officer inside eventually, the two shorter men carrying him in a cradle of their linked arms while Rallt held open the door to the inn. There was no seat to hold him comfortably, but they got him onto one of the stools and put a table at his back. Rallt started to bring up another table to place at his side, but the one he went to had used plates on it; he compromised on another stool.

"Water," the officer demanded, still whispering. And then to Rallt, "I'm cold. Get a blanket to put on my shoulders."

Would he look at the body? Rallt wondered with annoyance, but his father gestured that he should obey the command. He did so, but he also took time to check the ambulance for other officers, who might be less demanding. He found none.

When he returned to the inn, the interior lights were on. His father was moving from one to the other adjusting the electrodes to increase the brightness, and the officer was leaning over the second stool, holding himself on his elbows with a mug in one hand and a hunk of bread in the other. He ate like a man who had not tasted solid food for three days—which was, Rallt realized after doing some mental arithmetic, the truth. Despite himself, a bit of his bad temper departed, and he put the blanket over the man's shoulders gently, like a shawl for an old woman.

The officer's uniform was poor stuff, he noticed, made from coarse fabric no finer than his own clothing. Worse, perhaps—the dye in Rallt's shirt had not run in the rain—and for a moment he felt a puzzled embarrassment.

"Move me closer," the officer said, and Rallt and his father lifted him and his stool and moved him close to the body, so he could sit with his shoulders against the end of the bar and his one remaining foot hanging a handbreadth above the bloody floor. "Thank you."

His voice was still soft but it was more than a whisper now, as if the water and bread had revived him. It *was* water, Rallt noticed when he brought up the second stool. A child's drink in a tavern.

Or an invalid's. Guiltily, as if his had been the maiming shot, he recalled the officer was on the verge of his own death.

"Messy," the officer said and drank from his mug. The word was enough an understatement that Rallt looked to his father for guidance, and the older man nodded at him. So it was all right.

"Why didn't you just tell me someone had cut up the innkeeper like a dead rabbit?" the officer demanded and Rallt could not defend himself.

He simply hadn't dared to look closely at the body. "Be it the innkeeper, sir?"

"Oh, yes. That's his face. Talked to him when I was stationed here. He couldn't understand how soldiers could be brave in battle. Neither can I, now."

Rallt, without a response, though the last words had been without emotion, swallowed and the officer leaned forward.

"You didn't move anything?"

"Sarlso tripped over it," he said. "Mayhap he moved an arm or a leg."

Involuntarily his eyes dropped to the floor, then rose before he could decide whether a trail had been made in the blood.

"The clothes were already off," he added, though perhaps the words were not necessary.

Where was Sarlso? Outside, being sick again?

"Not hard enough a trip to tear it apart, I take it." The officer smiled weakly and Rallt understood he was making jokes. "Get me more water, boy, from the kitchen."

Another errand. Rallt wondered if he could ever be old enough himself to call grown men "boys" and give them orders.

He stopped in the doorway, returning with the water. He wondered if his feet were stepping exactly where the killer's had.

His father had a severed arm in his hands and was holding it so the end was close to the officer's face. His expression was grimly determined and Rallt wanted to turn away and throw up in sympathy for what he was feeling.

"Very neat," the officer said in his soft, little-girl voice. He dabbed a finger lightly against the gleaming bone so close to his face, then stroked the cut flesh that had been part of a human shoulder.

"Very smooth. Stiff. You say the joints won't bend. I wonder . . ." His arm rocked slightly, then he touched the flesh again and brought his finger to his nose and lower, then stopped with his mouth open and his tongue out, sensing the eyes on him.

"Taste is the real test, you understand, like with beef," he explained apologetically, but to Rallt's relief, he wiped the finger on his blanket and did not bring it back to his mouth. "It's been less than a day. There's no smell yet. Are the other limbs cut the same way, smoothly?"

He gestured and Rallt's father was able to put down the arm and look at—but not touch—the other severed arm and the cut-off legs.

"Yes."

"And the other . . ." The officer inhaled deeply several

times, and Rallt suddenly realized he was not so impervious as
he seemed. But he was able to keep emotion from his voice.
"Let me get there for a closer look. I'll need you both to let me
down."

Rallt, though he had to stand close to the corpse, was careful
not to look at its chest. He knew a man's body held a heart,
lungs, stomach, intestines, and other contents. He had seen
those in butchered animals and the sight had never bothered
him, but he had no desire to see human organs.

Was that what had inspired the killer? Had he made that long
ripping cut from sheer curiosity?

"Roll it over," the officer ordered, and when Rallt's father
had done so, "Ah-h-h-h." Rallt did not look down to see what
had caught his attention.

"Put it down again. Get me up," the officer ordered, and
Rallt and his father lifted him back to his seat. For a few
seconds the Lopritian simply sat, eyes closed, breathing heavily
as if he had had the exercise. "Beast-mindedness," he muttered.

"Be it all there?" Rallt's father asked and the officer did not
pretend to misunderstand him.

"Everything. But he went in with a knife to cut out those
family jewels and I guess he used the same thing to slice them
up like mincemeat. Pieces of ball and cock all mixed up—it's
all there unless he ate some of it."

Rallt heard gagging, and realized it had come from his own
mouth.

The soldier turned to him. "Ah-hh, someone's gone mad,
mind like a beast. So anything's possible. I wish we had a
telepath to direct the hunt." His eyes were very tired, and Rallt
saw lines were carved deep into his face, as they were in the
very old.

"The ground's very firm," Timmial lan Haarper commented, gesturing with his chin as he rode beside Cherrid on
the lip of a small gully. "Apparently rain washes gravel out of
the walls and it settles. If I had enough men to maneuver, I

could move them back and forth down there without the enemy noticing. What I thought was, just before action, I could bring up some artillery the same way, to reinforce my line. How's that sound?''

"Terrible," Cherrid said bluntly. "How would you extricate the guns if things go badly? Besides, I assume you meant small guns—you could never pull cannon out of that crack—and they do not have much range. The big guns by the road will shoot just as far and do much more damage.''

Timmial was not convinced. "Having our own guns lets us pick our own targets. Just a couple, I'd put them there.'' He pointed to the small hill five hundred man-heights distant and Cherrid noticed men walking upon it.

"There's a little woods about halfway between the hill and Mlart's position. I'd like to cover that with the guns. If Mlart occupies it, I'd smash the woods to splinters.''

Cherrid grunted. With a three-to-one superiority in manpower, Mlart was not apt to employ subtlety. Dutifully, though, he craned his head to catch a glimpse of the woods, and was not surprised to not see it. Lan Haarper had said it was small and this close to winter, the trees were probably leafless. Both factors made it more unlikely that Mlart would seize the place.

Looking further, his eyes moved over the low ridge to his front to the next ridge, a thousand man-heights to the south, where Mlart's army would appear. The men on the hill were looking that way also.

He smiled. "I think we will see the same targets, Timmial. This is a very small battlefield.''

"Till the bullets fly. Battlefields get very big then and help is always a long way away, Cherrid.''

"I have been in battles, Timmial.''

"Sorry. I'm touchy today,'' lan Haarper admitted. "But I meant it about wanting guns. Small guns are perfect for close support and if I could just have four or six of them . . . It would be like getting four hundred reinforcements for the regiment. It'd help a lot, sir.''

Cherrid nodded. "No guns, Timmial. I do not want to lose any and I do not want to waste time retrieving them. This is not to be a full-scale battle, after all. We just want to punch Mlart's nose and slow him up a bit."

"Well . . . how about the hills in back of the ridge? They're far enough back that—"

Cherrid did not have time to continue an argument. "How are you going to station your men?"

"One company on that hill up there, and then I'll stretch out on the right till I meet ris Daimgewln. Nothing fancy."

"I would rather see two companies on that hill. It will be the left of our line and the firmer it is, the better."

"Hmmm."

The big redhead was mulishly about to ask for guns again, Cherrid realized. "I am making a very strong suggestion to you, Ironwearer," he said, and waited for the implication to set in.

"Yes, sir."

"I also suggest—and I have not seen enough of the ground to be certain—that you post men forward on that hill, and backward on the ridge." He cocked a fist to demonstrate. "Like this, so any attack on your right can be covered by fire from two directions."

"That's going to leave men on the hill awful exposed, Lord Clendannan." Lan Haarper thought for a moment. "That's why you want two companies there, but I'm not sure they would be enough. The flank will be wide open."

"I can send some cavalry, about a squadron."

Lan Haarper winced but controlled himself. "Thank you."

Cherrid understood. "Our cavalry is not very good," he admitted. "But we have to make do."

"No one's cavalry is any good right now," the redhead said. "A horse is too *goddamned* big to protect from a bullet and no one has figured out how to deal with that."

Cherrid raised his eyebrows. "Have you?"

"Use them as mobile infantry. Use their speed to get from one place to another quickly but give them the best weapons possible and train them to fight on the ground. It's been done before.''

Done in his homeland, wherever it was, Cherrid supposed. Or attempted. Lan Haarper's people, from his occasional comments, had fought some very strange wars. The old Ironwearer sometimes wondered why a country so successful in battle as Timmial claimed his to be was too insignificant to appear on any map. He had concluded there had also been some defeats the young man was less willing to describe.

But that was no reason to reject Timmial's ideas without fair thought. Dismounted cavalry might well have uses in the proper circumstances—against the Necklace Lake barbarians, for example, though Cherrid considered they would present no real problem until many years had passed.

''We can talk about that after the campaign,'' he said. ''We ought to have a nice long period to experiment with tactics then and we can try out some of your ideas. Mlart is not a young man, you know; he'll be old and stodgy in another century and easy to surprise.''

He smiled wolfishly, certain of that, untroubled by the knowledge that he would be dead himself when that time came. Timmial would see wonders, he knew, and he hoped the young man would gain patience and learn to use it.

''Rather win now,'' the boy said gruffly, and Cherrid chuckled.

''I have seen enough here,'' he said. ''You know what I want and I need to talk to ris Daimgewln. Poor man! Good enough for garrison duty, Timmial, but between us, Terrens lacks the imagination to have even bad ideas.''

''That why you put him in the middle?'' Timmial wondered. ''You want someone without imagination to take the worst of Mlart's attack?''

Cherrid nodded. ''Just an accident. It was where he was placed in the line of march.''

There was no reason to explain that he did not trust ris Daimgewln's regiment in any other position.

* * *

Inside the inn at Midpassage, Rallt listened wistfully to the rumble and squeals of the moving wagons. All too quickly, the sounds faded in the distance, and he turned a resentful eye to the wounded officer, who was now bending over the table which held dirty dishes.

"Come over here," the Lopritian ordered without looking at him, and though his voice was not appreciably louder, Rallt remembered the far-reaching bellows he had heard officers of the Strength-through-Loyalty Brigade use in their camp. He wondered if he was supposed to obey commands now as quickly as a Lopritian soldier and what would happen if he did not.

"What do you see?" the officer said.

Dirty dishes, of course. Rallt scratched behind an ear.

"Four plates," the officer said, not needing his help. "Four sets of eating tools. Four good-sized meals, too, I judge, and all eaten, so probably four men and no women. One of them our killer. Or all of them."

He turned his eyes back to the body. "Hmmm."

Four killers? Rallt was never sure if he had asked that aloud, but the officer looked at him suddenly and Rallt saw irritation in the blue eyes.

"Four men eating. Who served them the meal? The inn-keeper, of course. There's no sign of other staff. Who should have picked up the plates? The innkeeper again. And why didn't he? Because he was dead. So the men who ate here killed him."

It sounded like a guess to Rallt. Four killers were four times as impossible to believe as one killer.

Except to a sick-minded man who went to soldiering of his own free will and with too much imagination. He couldn't find the words to express that safely, so he stayed silent. Only his manner said things for him.

Lerlt was waking about then. Grudgingly, for it was the morning light rather than the attainment of his rest which brought him back to consciousness. Some time passed before he opened his eyes for good and pulled himself to a seat on the couch, more while he contemplated the ruin of his uniform.

The escape, the woman in the shack, the dead man in the inn, the tied-up woman here—had it all been a dream?

No. Reality. It had all happened in little more than a day. The stains on his clothing proved it. The medley of sounds coming from the back room at this moment proved it.

He grinned.

Chapter 15

The back room stank. The bedclothes had been dumped in a corner. On the bare mattress, the nude woman lay facedown, gagged and with a pillow under her midriff. The cords that had held her earlier had been replaced with thin ropes: one that bound her wrists together, another tied to her right ankle. The ropes had been fastened to the frame of the bed so she was stretched over it diagonally.

Fesch was between her spread legs, thrusting himself into her anus. His arms were locked about her chest, his chin tight against her neck. In the morning light, his buttocks were grotesquely large, pasty as bread dough; flesh rolled along them in waves as his pelvis rocked up and down at inchworm pace. The bodies made little sucking and slapping sounds as they moved together; the man breathed hard in small grunts.

Lerlt turned his head to get a breath from the cleaner hallway air before going further.

"Where are the others?" he asked, and Fesch stopped and panted for a moment as he lay on the woman.

"Went to get the time machine. Shouldn't be long."

His expression brightened. "Want to do it together? You stick it to this thing on one side and I'll take the other."

The thought of being close to the sweat-covered Fesch and his flabby buttocks at that moment was almost nauseating. "No."

"You're missing something." Fesch licked his lips slowly, as if he wished Lerlt to inspect the saliva on his tongue. "Too bad you were sleeping. All three of us were riding this little horse the same time this morning. Choked on Herrilmin's cock and things got really wild for a bit. Shaking so fast there, I thought this old thing was going to die, and I was so far gone myself, it was all I could do to hold on. I popped like a bomb and I think Gherst did, too."

He smiled happily and slapped the woman on the flanks. "Didn't happen though. Good old horse!"

The woman did not react.

"So you had fun?" Lerlt was seeing something new in Fesch.

"Well. Something different." Fesch turned serious. He changed his grip on the woman and shifted to push himself further into her. Lerlt noticed blood on his pubic hair.

The woman gasped. He heard it even through the gag.

"Different?" he repeated.

"Yeah, when this was choking—" Fesch began stroking the woman with something like affection—"probably would have turned blue if Herrilmin hadn't gotten off in time—I suddenly realized this was kind of like our property and what we did with it . . . I mean, you remember getting mad as a kid and how good it felt to throw your toys on the ground, even if it would break them? It was like that then—the old toy falling and I didn't care what happened to it. Just kind of interested, if that makes sense."

He chuckled self-consciously, then sobered and looked away. His pelvis thrust against the woman. Her head rose and Lerlt saw panic in her eyes as she strained for breath against the pressure of the man's arm.

"One little pull and I could break this neck," Fesch said,

wonderingly. "Even just by accident. And having this thing know it, too, that makes it all—better—somehow. I wouldn't, you know, but I could."

Lerlt, tempted to shout and startle Fesch into enjoying his ultimate thrill, wanted to giggle.

"I was talking to Herrilmin." Fesch released the woman's throat and began thrusting at her again. "He said he felt something like it in a duel, if he really outclassed an opponent, knowing he just had to press a bit to cut someone to shreds, knowing they knew it."

He stopped suddenly. "I got a hint—you know Herrilmin killed some people in the city games—they said it was accidents, but—I don't think they were all accidents, Lerlt. Lerlt? Is that—murder?"

"I don't know. Not if someone tried to kill him back." Lerlt snapped his fingers. "Who cares? That was in the old F'a Alghera. It's gone."

"Yeah, but—murder, Lerlt?"

Lerlt exhaled sharply, derisively. Fesch had played a part in a murder the night before, and it was just like him to not understand it.

One of Herrilmin's murders, of course—brutally direct and imposing, in its fashion—rather like Herrilmin. It had taken all Lerlt's ingenuity to imprint something extra, from his own personality, on the innkeeper's killing.

Fesch wasn't ready to understand that, he knew.

"Well, Lerlt?"

"Cut her up some, Fesch," he recommended. "That bitch is just lying there for you. Might as well be dead. You want to make her more active, show her you just aren't talking about what you can do. Get a knife and slice into a nipple, for example. That'll get her attention."

"Cimon, Lerlt!"

"Just a suggestion. Another game to play with your toy. You think about it." He waited till Fesch's expression changed, then turned away. "I want to see what's keeping the others."

*   *   *

Gherst held out an arm. "Don't go so fast. You trip and you'll wind up mixed into a wall."

"It's here?" Lerlt looked about curiously. Fallen trees, rocks, grass, dirt, many leaves . . . Any forest hillside, any-where in the one world, must look like this. Yet Gherst stood here at the bottom of a ravine with Herrilmin's locator in his hand and a worried look on his face.

"It's here and we can't get in." Gherst spat at a yellow-topped weed. "Big-brain Herrilmin, he never thought about that."

"The door is stuck?" Lerlt chuckled halfheartedly. A time machine was just a levcraft with an extra motor, after all. Nothing could go seriously wrong with one.

The other man snorted. "You look at it. Go stand there—that smooth spot of grass."

Lerlt inched forward. Despite his caution, he was surprised as a shiny reflective surface suddenly appeared before him.

It *was* a wall. A mirror the size of a wall floating waist-high in front of him. He could see nothing else.

It vanished as he stepped back. Only the hillside and Gherst remained.

"What?" he gasped, and it was Gherst's turn to chuckle.

"Timt ha'Dicovys's time machine," the brown-haired Agent said. "Being Timt, it had to be a little different. Don't you remember seeing it back at the Station?"

Lerlt paused for thought. He did remember, now that he was reminded, a great silvery shape, reminiscent of an axe head, but hugely large—almost bigger than a house—floating above the concrete landing area in the underground hiding place that housed the Project. He had not realized it was a time machine. He had thought it some piece of apparatus which belonged to the Project as a whole, and had never paid attention to it.

"It's *his*? One man's?"

It simply was not reasonable for an individual to own some-thing larger than any Sept claimed. Lerlt wasn't even sure it was possible.

There must be laws against it.

"All his," Gherst said sourly. "And he's got it fastened up some way so we can't get in. Some kind of gadget."

Lerlt held his breath. A device which protected property during the absence of its owner was even more incomprehensible than a levcraft ten times the size of any normal levcraft.

And he knew Timt ha'Dicovys. A moody ne'er-do-well without mind or ambition or even proper pride-in-Sept. It was inconceivable that such things should belong to a man so mediocre.

"Where did someone like him find all this—" He groped for a word. "Super-science?"

"Fourth Era," Gherst said, as if the words had real meaning.

"Nonsense!" Lerlt snapped. "Nobody's been to the Fourth!"

"Timt has. I heard him say it once."

"Then he lied. They tried to send four people there early in the Project—I remember that—and none of them came back. There's a barrier of some kind, like the one that keeps us from going past the true Present."

"Maybe Timt gets around barriers. He's from the First Era, after all."

Lerlt was incredulous. "I thought you didn't believe that nonsense. It's Dicovys myth, that's all! It lets them claim they got a Sept forty or fifty thousand years old. Nobody but them takes it seriously."

"I am changing some opinions," Gherst said, with a ponderous tone that Lerlt supposed he mistook for dignity. "Timt ha'Dicovys is not ordinary, Lerlt. If he says he's from the First Era, I'm starting to believe it."

His voice held tones Lerlt recognized only after he remembered Herrilmin was not in sight.

"You're *afraid* of him!" he exclaimed.

"I looked around his house, Lerlt. I looked at what he keeps with him. He's different!"

"You're afraid of him!"

"I want to go home without trouble. That's all."

"You're afraid of him. That's what's different. You're just like Fesch used to be till he started riding that Teep. Look, Gherst, even if it is Timt ha'Dicovys's girlfriend and you're scared of him, you go back and you start sliding the old piston through the old cylinder block some more, that'll make you brave again."

"Fesch has breakfast stew for brains," Gherst said sourly. "I wish we had never seen that girl now, I wish we had never touched that girl. Look, Lerlt, we're in real trouble. We're two hundred and fifty thousand man-heights away from any other time machine, we can't use this one, we haven't done anything to save Mlart from being killed, and we have done something that's probably going to make Timt ha'Dicovys hate us forever. Doesn't any of that bother you?"

Lerlt found this more amusing than troublesome. "So what? He's just a Dicovys bullyboy."

"He's the *Project Master's* bullyboy! That's what, Lerlt!"

"So? That's because the tra'Dicovys is the Project Master. Maybe Vrect will be Project Master someday. Are we all supposed to be afraid of Herrilmin, then?"

"Vrect isn't going to be Project Master, Lerlt. You know better than that. Nobody'd elect Vrect dishwasher. He ran for Master of our Sept, it must be seven times, and never got twenty percent of the vote. He's a history teacher, Lerlt, and probably not a very good one. He just happened to be the oldest Hujsuon around the Institute when they were evacuating, that's all."

"He's got Herrilmin," Lerlt pointed out. "And Herrilmin is loyal. What did Herrilmin do for the old Sept Master?"

"He's got Herrilmin," Gherst repeated hysterically. "Dogs have got fleas, Lerlt. Does that make them any better? Herrilmin's—Herrilmin's—you could have three Teeps working on Herrilmin's mind, Lerlt, nonstop, and they wouldn't make sense of what he thinks."

"I thought you were his friend." Lerlt was disdainful of backstabbing.

"I listen to him," Gherst said. "He won't shut up. Somebody has to. But you know what he talks about, Lerlt? Getting even with Timt ha'Dicovys. Fighting Timt ha'Dicovys. Killing Timt ha'Dicovys. Destroying everything that belongs to Timt ha'Dicovys. Making Timt ha'Dicovys's friends into his enemies. Does that sound to you like it has anything to do with the Project, Lerlt? Even anything to do with Hujsuon?"

"Things'll work out," Lerlt assured him and moved back into the field around the time machine. On the silvery wall, Gherst's image flickered.

Rallt repeated his instructions. "I visit to all the farmhouses across the river. I ask them if four men have passed in the last day and—and—"

"Which way they went," the officer whispered hoarsely. His eyes were closed. Rallt noticed his hands were pressed tightly against the table, as if to keep him upright. Even in the poor interior light of the inn, his face seemed paler than it had been in the morning.

"Which way the men went," the boy agreed. "I tell them one—at least one—has gone beast-minded and—"

"Just one," the officer whispered. "Don't make it worse."

"One man beast-minded, and I've to see if there's a man or a boy old enough to give us help. And then I come back."

"Forgot the guns," the officer said, straightening himself slightly. Rallt saw that his arms were trembling. Sweat and other odors hovered over his body, and Rallt wondered again if he should go out on this mission.

Thee's to die.

What would he do if the officer was dead when he returned? What could he do for a dying man if he stayed?

"Get the guns," the officer insisted, and his voice was so low Rallt had to lower his head to hear. "Can't let—beast-minded—man—have a gun."

"I'll bring back guns," he promised, then hesitated, for he had never fired a gun. "I'll be back to thee soon, sir."

*   *   *

Herrilmin was on the far side of the giant levcraft. When Lerlt caught sight of him, he was placing rocks in an unstable-looking pile.

Lerlt stepped around the tall rounded front of the vehicle. *What are you doing?* Herrilmin's face kept that question back. "Can I help?" That should get a softer answer.

"Hold me—no. You get on this pile," Herrilmin ordered. "I'll hold you and you push that plate."

Lerlt looked, seeing the outline of a door floating before him. To its side was a white plaque showing deerlike animals hitched to some kind of bulky vehicle. No driver was in sight, and the deer seemed to be leering at him from out of the placard. *Scent of claws*, the ideographs above the picture read, and there were other symbols which meant nothing to Lerlt.

"That thing?" He stretched to touch the horns of one of the animals, noticing at the same time how the glare of the sun on the vehicle changed as he watched.

"Cimon, Lerlt! The little brown one above it. The one Timt ha'Dicovys presses to open the door."

"You can rea—" Lerlt shut his mouth and let the bigger man hoist him into position, then pushed on the hand-sized plate.

Nothing happened, no matter what he did.

"Pull on it," Herrilmin suggested.

"I tried that already. It doesn't move."

Herrilmin cursed. Several seconds passed before he released Lerlt, enough time for the sun to slip a handbreadth further across the sky, enough time to wonder if Fesch was still with the woman. Or Gherst.

When Rallt returned to the inn, the officer was gone. His place had been taken by a tall thin man with black hair. This man had a blue uniform with red trim; Rallt could tell from a distance his clothing was expensive. In the kitchen, someone much smaller in white clothing was opening cabinets.

"Where be—" Rallt started off, then stopped when he realized he had never learned the officer's name. "Been he dead?"

"Dead as my next promotion," the tall man said, walking around the body on the floor once more. He mumbled to himself. Rallt noticed the innkeeper's clothing had been laid out on the floor; brown stains covered the back of the white shirt and dark trousers.

The tall man turned to him suddenly. "Or did you mean the militia man who was here? You're Rallt, I take it, he said you had long legs. Well, I'm Lieutenant Ryger ris Ellich, Lord Ellich if you want to be polite, which would be a pleasant change right now, someone being polite to me, so you might try it, and the cavalry is here, part of it, if I'm still in the cavalry. He's in an ambulance again, your militia officer, and if he can stay under Nicole's feet long enough he'll make it home, to Coward's Landing, which isn't that far, unless you're in an ambulance, of course. Sugally got some wine and broth into him while we talked, which ought to help. Why didn't you do that? No reason to add starvation to everything else that hit him."

Rallt blinked. The words were still sinking in and he hadn't eaten that day, either.

He had done what he was told to do. "I've this for thee," he said, and laid his burden on one of the tables.

"Cimon's bunions," the tall man commented, and stopped his pacing to lean over the table. "An old front-loader, with balls and powder can. Looks like something grand'ther took off to the wars and tried to lose." He touched it carefully. "Does it still shoot?"

Rallt wasn't sure. "It were for squirrels, Lord Ellich, sir."

"For the squirrels, eh? Used on squirrels, boy, or by them?" Ris Ellich sat on a nearby stool and smiled wryly. "Never mind if you can't answer that. We'll load it up and see what you can hit with it."

"Me? Sir?" Rallt's jaw dropped.

"Well, you don't think I can shoot it, do you?" The cavalry officer held his arms up and Rallt noticed for the first time the knotted sleeve that took the place of a left hand and forearm.

"No, sir." Rallt looked distrustfully past the man at the dirty old gun, heavy with its thick iron barrel and hardwood stock, rust sitting in each groove where the hand-hammered leaves of metal touched, and wondered if anyone could shoot it safely.

Ris Ellich crossed his legs and rested his stump in his lap. "So what did you find out? Did anyone see our friends on that side of the river or think they did? And are we getting reinforcements? I notice you didn't bring anyone back."

No one had seen anything suspicious, Rallt reported. He had stopped at six farmhouses, finding people at five. Some of the people had remembered seeing traffic recently moving along the road—ambulances and supply wagons during the last few days, a pair of mounted messengers before that—but no one had seen a group of four men yesterday or today.

"What did you see today?" Ris Ellich pointed with his stump.

He hesitated. "The people I were asked . . . What would thee wish me to have seen, sir?"

"Fifteen wagons, about three hundred men on foot, and three ambulances passed through this town not one day tenth ago. I know, I was in one of those ambulances. How much of that did you see from across the river?"

Rallt's face answered for him.

"They must be gone, aren't they, sir?" he asked.

"Four sides of the dice say so." Ris Ellich frowned. "My guess of the odds, but let's consider. Four men at evening or late afternoon, who pause here for supper. Where do they go? Do they leave a comfortable inn and travel further along the road, at night, when we might suppose them sleepy? If they are going to stop for rest somewhere, why not here?"

Ambulance drivers and teamsters slept on the road, Rallt reminded him. Rooms in an inn were expensive.

The cavalry man was not swayed by that argument. "Rooms are cheap enough, when not paid for, and these folks didn't pay—there's no money on the dead man and an even sum in his cash drawer. They could have had their supper, their sleep, and their breakfast, and then killed this man, but they didn't do so. So they returned to the road, or they found a place to rest here in town, and if they did that, they may still be here. Four men on the road, one of them a soldier—they'd be conspicuous, don't you think?''

Rallt blinked. ''Thee says, a soldier?''

Ris Ellich grimaced, then snapped fingers on his right hand. ''A guess. Maybe all of them. Five sides of dice, say, and the same odds that killer is the soldier.''

He pointed with a finger. ''That's to scare us, you see, us or the other men with the killer or maybe the innkeeper himself if he was conscious. Or maybe it makes the killer braver, but in either case, it tells us what the killer thinks is scary. So what's the worst of those wounds?''

Rallt looked only at the finger. ''I don't know, sir.''

''The mutilation, of course, the sexual mutilation. Cutting off the organs, chopping them to shreds . . . That's a terrible thing, isn't it, so terrible I think most people would never think of it seriously, but it occurred to our killer, so strongly that he had to do what he did. And who worries normally about being wounded in the balls? Soldiers. Getting wounded there—I tell you, that's the one place to get hit that no soldier laughs at. It's the one wound we're all afraid of. To do what he did deliberately . . . I think our killer had to be a soldier.''

The cavalry man grimaced. ''Not a very brave soldier.''

Rallt swallowed. ''Someone told me, sir—a girl at one of the farms—they made guns here in town, at the big buildings on the hill. Would thee have me look there, too?''

''Cannons, wasn't it?'' Ris Ellich pushed the inside of a cheek around with a tongue. ''Yes, you should go take a look around. Are you hungry?''

He looked at the body again. ''Not now, sir.''

''Talk to Sugally when you are. He's a better cook than you're apt to be. Meanwhile, take him along with you. He needs the exercise.''

* * *

Rallt hesitated, wondering if this building really needed examination. The first building he and ris Ellich's man had searched had held bars of metal and lumber planks, the second wooden stands and tripods and curious forms like incomplete furniture. The third had been an outhouse, and Rallt was beginning to understand that finding weapons for the officer back at the inn was not going to be a simple task. Was it really a necessary task?

"Bad smell." Sugally nudged him. "We go next little house, huh?"

That made his decision for him. "No. We look here, too."

He stepped forward against the door, finding it heavier than he had expected, and reluctant to move. "I need thee, Sugally. I've to push on this side, while thee must pull the other. Please."

"We go soon? Smell like—" Sugally gestured, using words Rallt did not comprehend. "Bad things behind my lakes."

"Soon," Rallt agreed. "Come on."

Eventually they managed to slide the door till there was space to enter, and then further to admit light as well. One edge of the door then stuck out beyond the building. At the other, Rallt, having released his burden, gasped for breath. Breathing was a mistake. His eyes stung in the vapor that lingered in the air and when he coughed, he seemed to feel the stench from the interior tear into his lungs like knives. Long seconds passed while he crouched with hands on his knees and regained his strength.

Sugally crept up. "Bad small not so bad now. Not see guns inside. We go now, huh? Tell master we look difficultly."

"Look hard, thee means." Rallt straightened, still breathing loudly. "If we say we look, thee knows we must look."

"Me not know," Sugally said, smiling.

"Shut up, slave," Rallt snapped. "Let it air some and I've to look. Thee can wait, mayhap it be what thee be good for." He was sorry now he had wasted a "please" on the little man.

He was sorrier for his insult inside the building. It was like nothing he had ever seen before and he would have welcomed company, even from a slave.

It was gloomy inside, but the falling sun cast enough light to show that the building was one great room, its interior mostly taken up by a pair of long sloping pans made from some light-colored ceramic. The pans were tilted to make their tops parallel to the ground; they rested side by side on thick posts, and fitted beneath them were furnaces. Behind an ajar fire door Rallt saw ashes and dead embers; a shovel lay on the dirt floor.

The door he had strained to move was coated on this side with a layer of smoky, translucent glass; the same material covered steps leading to a balcony that took the place of a second story on three sides of the building, and the balcony itself.

Either the coating or the thickness of the wood made the walkway more solid than Rallt expected. As he paced its length only his footsteps thudded beneath him.

From this height he could look into the big pans and see they were filled to within a handlength of the top with dark liquid. Dust made black splotches across the fluid; something like scum had caked on the shallow end of one pan and dripped into irregular piles below the lip.

Over the nearer pan was a wooden hopper hanging from a truck which was just beyond his reach. He could not see how it was moved, nor decide what it had held. At the end of the walkway, long-handled implements hung from the wall, things like strainers and narrow-toothed rakes and buckets fastened to poles, which took two hands for Rallt to lift. In a corner was a dark pile of cloths, which tore as he touched them; something moist stung his fingertips as he stirred them and stayed even after he wiped his hand on his trousers.

Men had worked here, he told himself, laboring under conditions as hard as he had ever met in a field. He did not doubt that they had willingly left this place to be soldiers.

Rallt sighed and rubbed his eyes on his sleeve. There were no guns here and other buildings needed to be examined. Like

Sugally, goggling up at him from the door opening below, he was sure the effort would be wasted.

Grahan appeared just before sunset, while Harper was walking about watching the men dig. Wind was blowing around the hill and the big man kept his hands in his pockets for warmth. In the distance behind him, barley and potatoes simmered in kettles, a deserted shack pointed sod-thick walls and denuded roof beams toward the sky.

In the other direction, two thousand man-heights away, the elevated roadbed was visible only through the shadow it generated. Pink and purple clouds waited to meet the rising horizon.

"Getting ready for a visit?" The older man looked beyond the soldiers to the next ridge, where enemy horsemen were already visible. Below, at the foot of the ridge, a sprinkling of Lopritian cavalry had established a picket line. Even at a distance, the tiny horses and men seemed to move nervously.

"More or less. You're inspecting for Lord Clendannan?" Harper had noticed that the old Ironwearer and his orderly were close, but until Cherrid had spoken of Grahan's past he had simply assumed them master and servant. Now he gestured with a shoulder toward the men laboring in the shallow trenches, attentive to what the elderly man might suggest.

"Tsk, tsk. Shocking thing to see good soldiers hiding from a few bullets." Grahan's expression did not match the words.

"More shocking to see what bullets do to unprotected good soldiers."

"Very true," Grahan commented. "But it's a fiend's task to get men out of trenches and into a frontal attack."

Harper paused for thought. "Bearing in mind that I'm holding as much of the front as any other regiment with half as many men, why don't you take five minutes and describe all the circumstances in which the Steadfast-to-Victory is apt to be asked to advance under fire."

Grahan chuckled. "I'd put more dirt in front of those trenches and fewer rocks, if I were you. Cannon strikes, you know—splinters. And put the sod outside, facing the Algherans. That holds the dirt in place better.''

Harper barked orders.

Grahan shook his head appreciatively. ''Cherrid's with the Hand this evening—at prayers.'' He smiled wickedly.

Harper raised his eyebrows. ''Never struck me that Lord Clendannan was especially religious.''

''Not Cherrid, not for your local gods anyhow.'' Grahan's smile widened. ''But our Hand sees himself as a devout man, and one of his women does, and he's heard that lord of yours—Merryn ris Vandeign—is a priest of Cimon. Funny, isn't it—the royal family can't stand the ris Vandeigns, and the sentiment is returned from the other side, but ris Andervyll is so eager to have a priest right now and ris Vandeign is so eager to be a priest, they just have to cooperate.''

He laughed openly. ''Thus the religion produces one of its first miracles in the land of Loprit! I think Cherrid and ris Daimgewln went to see that as much as because they were invited.''

Harper smiled wanly, gesturing at the soldiers digging. They were Midpassage men; he did not think they would like their lord treated lightly, and he hoped Grahan would watch his tongue before them. ''I'd have gone, too, if I had been invited,'' he said, trying through indirection to be diplomatic.

''Is it your religion?'' Grahan eyed him curiously.

''No. I'm familiar with the Chronicles, though. Merryn has a set of the Plates, you know—or a copy.''

''Not a copy.'' The old man seemed quite certain.

Harper raised an eyebrow. How many sets of the Plates had been found? At most a hundred, he thought, and most of those in the last few centuries of this era. ''I'd have thought a set of Plates would be very expensive.''

''Your friend is very wealthy,'' Grahan said quietly.

Harper thought about it. ''You wanted to make that point, didn't you?''

''Why would I do that?'' Grahan did not seem surprised.

''Cherrid wanted me to know that.''

"Cherrid is at prayers." Grahan leaned forward. "We were talking about religion and nothing more, Ian Haarper."

Harper hesitated, then put his thoughts aside for later consideration. Grahan was waiting expectantly, so he said what occurred to him first. "I have to admit the Cimon and Nicole story and all the rest of it seems a little fantastic—a world run by telepaths, a twelve-thousand-year war, a four-thousand-year war." He shook his head. "I doubt you could scrape up enough telepaths to run a small town today, even if they wanted to."

The elderly man pursed his lips and looked at Harper with his head tilted to one side. "And yet, isn't that road over there the very same one the Chronicles speak of—the great indestructible road from the northern plains that led to the port at Embarkation?"

"I've looked." Harper was curt. "I never found Embarkation or anything that could be it."

He did not mention he had watched armies without end moving along the road, thousands of years ago, and it was not simply to conceal his traveling in time. He did not think it proper for men of this era to know that some parts of the legends were true.

"Yes, you were a prospector." Grahan scratched an ear. "You found a couple of very good deposits, I've heard. Isn't it true that metal is usually found at sites of old cities?"

Harper grimaced slightly. "I wasn't a bad prospector. Yes— people have always used metal, so it collects in cities. When we find them, we plant our bushes and farm it out. But as I say, this road doesn't go to Embarkation. It goes off to the Torn Coast and straight into the sea—I don't think anyone knows how far, and certainly not why. If people lived underwater back then, don't you think the Chronicles would have mentioned it?"

"Another miracle, perhaps?" Grahan suggested. He snapped his fingers. "It is a remarkable fact that everywhere in the world where Teep and Normal coexist, there is distrust of each other, and legends which may be echoes of ancient conflicts."

Harper smiled, concealing his own thoughts. "You seem to have accepted a lot of the Chronicles' story yourself. Maybe you should be at that prayer meeting, Grahan?"

"I'm always looking for new ideas," the old man said vaguely. "I'd like to understand things. What does that make me?"

"A philosopher," Harper suggested, then translated the word as Grahan repeated it thoughtfully. "A word from my homeland—a lover of wisdom." He paused, then added in a murmur, "We had a saying: 'Philosophers seek to understand the world; the problem, however, is how to change it.' "

Grahan repeated that also. "Are you satisfied with the way you have changed the world, Ironwearer?"

Harper laughed and wondered if it sounded forced. "I'm just trying to keep it the way it is, right now. I'm only a little boy here, or so Ironwearer ris Clendannan keeps telling me. I'll leave running the world to you people with experience."

"We don't run it, either." Grahan turned and looked to the opposite hillside, where the smoke from scattered campfires was beginning to appear, gray columns twisting in the wind. "Maybe we know too much to try. What would *you* do with the Teeps?"

"Me? Nothing. They're just people, you know. Why do anything?"

"And I've tried to tell you not many people feel that way. It's this world's biggest problem, you know—controlling the Teeps, or thinking we have to control the Teeps. What do you think about that, youngster?"

"I don't think it should be a problem," Harper said. "Why not just let them alone? Forget this business about 'controlling' them. Set up a government in such a way that no one is able to claim power permanently, and neither side has to worry about the other."

"Elections?" Grahan's face could not be seen in the twilight. "Like the Algherans' Muster? Must we copy everything from the Algherans?"

Why not? Harper wondered. "You've got the Queen's Beloved Counselors already. You people copied the Algherans that much. Would it be so horrible to have honest open elections instead of rigged ones? You keep treating the telepaths as a problem and you'll make them into a problem, you know, because all they're going to hear is that they're your enemies and someday they'll believe it themselves. If you Normals could just forget those *goddamned* Compacts, Grahan, and treat them as people, I think every one of your troubles will be over."

"It wouldn't be simple," Grahan said. "Even if I agreed with you . . . When you're my age, you realize, even for Mlart or Molminda, individuals can do only so much."

"They do together," Harper pointed out.

"Is that much different from pure chance?" Grahan wondered. "It can be very tempting, you know, to believe there's a Lord or Lady up there in the clouds who is willing to take charge of things. Well—I've kept you from your work long enough. Good fortune, Ironwearer."

The sun had long since slipped under the rising earth when Lerlt and Herrilmin returned to the house. Fesch and Gherst were eating in the kitchen.

"Where's that girl?" Herrilmin growled.

Fesch pointed with a finger, then returned it to his stew. "Sleeping."

Herrilmin grimaced, and left the room. A door slammed. Lerlt heard clothes falling to the floor, blows, then moans.

The bed creaked and the blows continued.

"He's pretty mad." Lerlt smiled at the two impassive men. "He was hitting the time machine out there like that and not getting in, either."

"No?" Fesch took his plate across the room for more food.

"We didn't find a way in. Some circular openings about this wide—" He held two fingers together. "—going into the vehicle but you couldn't see anything through them. One side door and a big sort of loading hatch at the back and that's it.

We broke a couple tree limbs trying to get in and didn't leave a scratch. Except on Herrilmin.''

Lerlt laughed, and when he stopped, crying could be heard. Fesch brought his plate back to the table slowly and sat down like an old man.

"Any more stew?" Lerlt asked.

"No," Fesch said. "This is it."

"Well, I'm hungry, and Herrilmin is going to be hungry. Why didn't you fix some more while the men were out there working?"

"Fix your own," Fesch said, and as Lerlt waited for a more polite response Gherst stared at him with bleakness carved into his face.

"We fed her and washed her," the brown-haired man said finally. "That was work."

Lerlt snorted. "I'd like that kind of work."

Gherst rolled up a sleeve to show bruises. "I don't think you would."

Lerlt waited till he heard a slapping sound. "Treat her like Herrilmin is doing. She won't give you trouble."

In the background someone was choking, making great whooping sounds which seemed without end. Lerlt remembered what Fesch had described in the morning and smiled, eager for his own turn. "Like that."

"What is Herrilmin doing?" Fesch asked. "Not just with the girl. Why did he bring us here?"

"The time machine. You know." Lerlt stared back, puzzled by the senseless questions.

Gherst blew out air, tiredly. "Herrilmin has a time machine not far away. Fesch and I have one in F'a Alghera, and I think you do, too. Why do we need this one?"

"This is Timt ha'Dicovys' machine so Herrilmin wants to take it." Lerlt chuckled halfheartedly. "What's the problem? Herrilmin was doing an errand for Vrect, and the Dicovys crew got in the way, so they're paying for it."

"Is that little girl Dicovys?"

"Who cares? I wish she were." Lerlt chuckled again and

tried to meet Fesch's eyes, till the other man's gaze dropped to the floor. "Right now, I wouldn't care if that were Borct tra'Dicovys himself."

"I suppose you wouldn't," Gherst said tonelessly. "Did Herrilmin tell you what he told me his errand was?"

"I don't know." Lerlt had been pleased to hear as much as he had from Herrilmin. He had not wanted to anger the big man with questions. "What did he tell you?"

"He's got a bomb, he told me. A bomb from uptime big enough to blow up a city, Lerlt. That's what Vrect wanted to bring back and that's what Timt was trying to stop."

Lerlt laughed. There was no such thing, and Fesch still refused to look at him, which made his enjoyment better.

"Herrilmin is unhinged or he has a bomb big enough to blow up a city, just for us Hujsuons to use. Take your choice, Lerlt. If we're going to be like you, I suppose we'll use it." Gherst pushed his plate away and stood. "I feel like a walk in fresh air, Fesch. Do you want to come?"

"Yes." It was barely more than whisper.

A bomb to destroy cities. Cities, with thousands of waiting, fearful, defenseless inhabitants. Lerlt, sitting in the empty kitchen until Herrilmin tired and gave up the woman to him, filled his waiting with imagination.

"He's very young," Grahan told Cherrid that night as the old Ironwearer prepared for bed in his ambulance. "Polite enough to us old-timers, unless he's goaded, but I think he thinks he has answers for everything."

"I did, at that age," Cherrid admitted. "Youth has to have some compensations."

"He doesn't seem personally ambitious. I don't know if that is patience, or genuine lack of interest. He is foreign. You really should have a Teep question him, Cherrid."

"Which demon-seized Teep and about what?" ris Clendannan said hotly. "Even if I had a Teep, I do not know what I am looking for. I want the boy to stay out of trouble while I am

around. I do not want him to be trouble for Loprit after I am
gone. I want him to make a success of his life. What kind of
questions do I ask? You tell me that."

"I can't, Cherrid," Grahan admitted, feeling old and tired
himself. Couldn't Loprit be trusted to look out for itself? Naturally, he did not say that. "Only time will tell."

Ris Clendannan kicked at the side of the wagon. "I hate that
kind of answer. Oh, it is not your fault, and maybe it will not
matter after tomorrow's battle. Maybe we will all be dead then,
or at least, thoroughly beaten. Is that what bothers me, that
uncertainty, or am I getting senile?"

"You're not senile yet, Cherrid." Grahan smiled. "Just
impatient. It's one of the problems with you youngsters."

After a while, the old men laughed together.

Chapter 16

*A*mid the gasping sobs and moans and his own excitement, he did not notice the pounding on the door. A foot hit his shoulder, jarring him, pushing him back, and he barely felt it. He dropped the knife and leaned forward from his seat on the woman's knee to fall with his chest across her swinging leg and held it captive with his elbow against her red glistening thigh as his fingers scrabbled under her sweat-cold calf for the knife and his arm pressed deep into the soft yielding mattress and salt-sweet liquid dripped from his river-running tongue and all the while her breath, her heart, her fear pounded at him as his breath and heart and determination pounded back at her in an endless, bright-filled, touch-filled, taste-filled moment that made them both alive as they had never been before . . .

Endless magical moment! To cut, to tear, to pierce, to slice while a writhing sacrifice quivered and moaned beneath him . . . To feel his warm flesh tight against a body, thrashing, fighting, rich with sweat and blood and oozing pale secretions, with every nerve and sinew taut as cables, to be plucked and strummed, demanding it be taught to sing . . .

Oh, wonderful!

Emotion pulled Lerlt to high dark peaks, suspended him over unfathomed depths, tossed his fearing frightful soul between the hands of gods, while he himself gasped, jerked, closed his eyes against the intruding world and spurted, warmly, stickily, givingly, sharing himself between her legs.

"Lerlt! What's going on? Open up! Stop that noise!"

Voices in the aftermath of annihilation. Motion pushing through vacuum.

"Open up!" "What's he doing?"

Herrilmin. Fesch.

Pounding against the door he had blocked with the bed. Spittle-filled breathing from the unconscious thing beneath him. Footsteps rushing.

Light and the cool night air dressing his skin. Bruises and fatigue. Liquids drying crustily. Dizziness without a sensation of motion.

Strangenesses.

A knife in his hand, blade bathing in trickling blood, trapped between white thigh and body. As the bed rocked against the swaying door, he stared at it dully, wonderingly. Moved it back and forth, mechanically, with his red streaked hand, waiting for the dimly remembered marvel to begin again.

Pounding behind his back. A breaking sound. Crashes. Crystal splashes. Then steps and meaningless shouting. He pushed himself back on his heels, looking for the proper place to reinsert the knife. Brought it down—

—as something outside of him smashed at his jaw, clubbed his back, swept him downward to the unyielding floor.

Feeling was reborn in him. Sensation.

He lay on the floor, accepting all that happened, slowly recomprehending his surroundings as Gherst bent over the woman, as Fesch pulled himself through broken window shutters and glass, as the two men tugged the bed backward from the door, as Herrilmin pushed into the room.

"Is she dy—"

"Yes."

Lerlt drew himself up in a corner, smiling at the inconsequential words and looks of the other men, wiggling the knife in his hand happily. Nothing mattered anymore.

"Cimon and Nicole." As he watched, Herrilmin kicked at the bed and stared down intently at what he had created. "Take this thing out, you two. Get rid of it."

"Bury her?" Fesch wondered.

"Just dump it."

"What about Lerlt?" Gherst.

"I'll—talk to Lerlt. Get rid of this. *Do it! NOW!*"

"Why, Lerlt, why?" Herrilmin asked when Fesch and Gherst had carried away their burden in the discarded bedding. His voice was weary, pleading.

Lerlt was puzzled. "You said yourself we were going to get rid of her."

"I said we might. When the time came. I didn't say tonight, did I? We might have used her as a hostage, you know."

This was the only night for it, Lerlt thought. Didn't Herrilmin see how Gherst and Fesch were working against him?

But it seemed dangerous to say too much now.

"Cimon, Lerlt! People must have heard her shrieking all over town. Didn't you even think about that?"

He hadn't. Did one think of a butterfly's shrieks as its wings shriveled in a fire? He stared back blankly.

"Get out of my sight," Herrilmin growled at last. "Go take a bath."

Noise, he understood, finally, standing in the bathtub as the cold white water gurgled over his head and splashed pinkly around his feet.

Noise. That was the mistake he had made, permitting the woman to make noise. He must not err that way again.

"Sir." A hand pushed at his shoulder. "Sir."

Harper reacted instantly, sweeping his right arm outward while his left hand tugged at a knife pocketed in the front of his jacket. Then his fist hit cloth; he came fully awake.

Coughs and wheezes from sleeping men were all about him.

The air was thick and moist, saturated with the smell of burned grass. The hard surface beneath was lumber, the lumps behind his head boots.

Not in 'Nam. No danger.

The battles of his dreams were nine hundred centuries behind him. He was in Loprit. In an army facing Mlart tra'-Nornst. And an officer, rather than a sergeant.

"Anything happening?' he asked softly.

"Not yet, but dawn's close," the man who had woken him said, and Harper recognized the voice of a farm laborer who had become a squad leader.

One of the calm ones, thank God. I don't want to deal with excitable people today.

What he wanted was three hot cups of coffee.

Fat chance, chum. "Dandy. Let me get my shoes on."

Wincing as sore muscles complained, he tugged the boots on and dropped to the dirt floor by the squad leader. The handle of a grace knife pressed at his left calf; he pushed it back into its boot-top recess, then, reminded by that act, checked his other knives and the insignia on his collars.

Ready for inspection. Good thing I don't have to shave anymore.

A full world of people who have never heard of Schick or Gillette. Who'd have thunk it?

By this time, he could make out silhouettes and a lighter rectangle which must be an open door. Men lay everywhere on the floor. A distant sparkle showed at an upper corner of the doorway—a star or a planet. It was still nighttime and outside it would be cold. He took his blanket from the bed ledge and draped over his shoulders. "*Lay on, MacDuff.*"

"Sir?"

Harper shook his head, then led the way outside circuitously, stepping carefully into the small gaps between the sleeping men. They were chiefly couriers and aides, he noticed, not his officers. High-ranking messenger boys, most of them transferred to him from ris Daimgewln's staff—in an hour he would have them woken brutally with a clear conscience.

And soon after that, of course, they would begin dying.

Another story not to tell Kylene, when he saw her again. If he saw her again.

Outside, it was scarcely lighter than inside, though more stars were visible. Harper hit with a fist into a water barrel, breaking enough ice to make space for both hands, and lifted a drink to his mouth, then dried his freezing palms on his pants. The day would be clear, he decided, with few clouds and no rain. Good; the men would be comfortable while they fought.

Or would Mlart keep his distance if it rained?

Unlikely. He probably knows he'd make mincemeat of us in a hand-to-hand and he doesn't have time to waste.

Just how far north now were those damned prisoners?

"Are the cooks up, Sergeant?" he asked. "I could use some morning stew."

"We got rid of her," Gherst said, entering the living room from the kitchen. "Laid her out in the gully below Timt ha'-Dicovys's time machine." He frowned, looking at Lerlt as the smaller man finished dressing. "Not like burial but it'll be a long time before anyone finds . . . what's left of her."

"Is she *dead*?" Herrilmin was insistent.

"Of course she is." Gherst spread his arms wide as if still carrying the body. Splotches of blood, both large and small, covered his clothing and most of his exposed skin. He moved unsteadily. He was breathing heavily and his face was red.

"Or close enough it doesn't matter. Nicole's boobs, Herrilmin! How can anyone have lived through what—that thing! What Lerlt did?" He waved his arms foolishly even when he had finished speaking and Lerlt could hear him panting from across the room.

Frost had formed on the windowpanes, Lerlt noticed, and he went to scrape at the icy lace while Herrilmin spoke.

"No way, I guess. Thanks."

"What do we do now?" Gherst asked, and without looking Lerlt could tell he had calmed down, though his voice was still small and worried.

"Get into that time machine. And stick together. You know it's us against Timt ha'Dicovys now."

Gherst shook that answer off. "We can't go back to the Project and pretend this didn't happen."

"We can," Herrilmin said, his voice brittle. "We killed a Teep masquerading as a Normal, that's all. Lerlt got carried away; he made it an object lesson. If Timt gets in our way— he'll have an accident. If Vrect tra'Hujsuon is running the Council when we get back, that's all we'll have to say. Is that right, Lerlt?"

"Sure." Lerlt, unconcerned, stared into darkness, then down as he adjusted his knife's position, admiring the way it hung at his hip.

"Cimon, Herrilmin! When's that going to be?"

"Sooner than you think. I can guarantee you, a time is coming when no one argues with Vrect." Herrilmin smiled. It was too large a smile, and lasted too long. Lerlt wondered briefly if the big blond man was wholly sane, then touched his knife again and wondered if it mattered.

"Soon enough to help us?" Gherst's eyes flickered between Lerlt and Herrilmin. He was tense and poised to run, it seemed to Lerlt, though the empty fireplace was at his back, rather than the doorway he needed.

Gherst was afraid of him! The realization was sudden and pleasurable. Lerlt felt his genitals begin to stir again, and twisted slightly to conceal his erection from the other men.

". . . Got to be more," Gherst was saying. ". . . He does this again . . ."

Gherst was the weakest of the four Agents, Lerlt understood now. All along, his image of confidence had only been a mask behind which this frightened schoolboy hid. He had screamed once in the last few minutes; he was close to hysteria which would betray them all.

Something would have to be done very quickly. Gherst must be kept quiet and, possibly, immobilized—captured before he escaped. Herrilmin and he, acting together—Lerlt moved around the couch and turned to the blond man, expecting a look that would signal action.

But Herrilmin stood in the same place, no closer to Gherst, his eyes showing no emotion that could be read as he watched Lerlt. "I agree," he said tonelessly. "This will be the last time Lerlt plays—that kind of game. Isn't it, Lerlt?"

A moment passed. "Isn't it, Lerlt?"

Lerlt moved closer, waiting for a signal which did not come, although he noticed Herrilmin winking at him. In the corner of his eye, he saw Gherst moving away, keeping out of reach.

"Answer me!" Herrilmin snarled, and his fist suddenly reached out to smash at Lerlt's shoulder. "Lerlt, say something, Cimon take you!"

The blow rocked him. He took time to recover, and realized he had been surprised but not hurt. Herrilmin's anger was only simulated, part of his strategy for controlling Gherst. He would play along.

"I heard you," he said. He snapped his fingers nonchalantly, wondering what answer would please the big man most.

"You aren't going to do this again," Herrilmin said coldly.

"Do what?" Lerlt smiled awkwardly.

"You know what I mean."

Lerlt hesitated, wishing he could pretend he did not comprehend the ambiguous words. "Herrilmin, we're in a war. No one can say what we might have to do."

It took effort he had not expected to say that much. He waited for a response and listened to his breath.

Gherst cursed softly, his face white. "He's giggling, Herrilmin. We got to do something to stop him."

"What?" Herrilmin snapped, angry as Lerlt was at the exaggeration, his voice showing contempt Gherst was too stupid to understand. "He's still up in the air on what he did. What do you want me to do?"

"Make him promise to us, formally. I don't know."

"All the—" Herrilmin stopped to curse, then spun about suddenly. Before Lerlt could react, the blond man slapped him, then embraced him with one arm while holding a fist in his face. "Lerlt, you hear me? You're going to promise all of us, you won't cut anyone like that again. Promise or we get rid of you."

This was still Herrilmin's ruse to fool Gherst, Lerlt realized. The blow had hurt, but Herrilmin's eyes, only a handspan from his own, were blinking furiously, and the big man's body was shaking with silent laughter.

"Sure," he said quickly, amused by his own role in this entertainment. "I promise, Herrilmin. Anything you want!"

"All of us," Herrilmin growled, pretending to tighten his hold. "Gherst, get Fesch in here. Look for him—he should be here by now—"

"He's out there puking."

"Well, get him in here. We'll listen to Lerlt together."

But Fesch ha'Hujsuon could not be found.

"Here, now, level it out," a sergeant ordered, swinging a foot at uneven mounds of black dirt. "Make those Algies guess where you're lying. No reason you have to give them a target."

Harper, drawing near on his horse, had to smile at the incongruity—the sergeant, with his back to the enemy and standing erect on the very top of the narrow ridge, probably presented one of the best targets the Algherans could see.

Although he was out of rifle range. Probably.

At the noncom's feet, resigned men with dirty faces laboriously brought up handfuls of earth and dropped them between the mounds.

"Morning, sir." The sergeant, busy kicking the piles into shape as Harper stopped to watch, was too preoccupied or still too much a civilian to salute. "Major Ian Plenytk's up at the Neck." His head pointed to the shallow gap between the hills at the end of the line.

"The Head," that top hill was generally called now. This narrow ridge had been dubbed "the Arm" where his men occupied it, "the Trunk" and "the Front Leg" where ris

Daimgewln's and ris Clendannan's regiments were stationed. "Back Leg" was the artillery location, on the extension of the ridge on the far side of the road, and "Knee" was the depot where horses and wagons waited.

"Fine. Looks like good work, Sergeant. Carry on," Harper said and prodded his horse back into movement.

Always pay compliments. Cherrid's advice. Harper glanced eastward at the sun sitting two hands over the horizon and wondered how many of the men had had breakfast that day. Compliments were a poor substitute for food.

Dalsyn lan Plenytk was supervising men at the bent-back, "refused" end of his line, on the very end of the ridge. Beyond him, in the Neck, men were driving stakes into the ground at a slant. Further, on the far side of the Head, a small group of horses and dismounted men could be seen.

Harper dropped off his mare. "How's it going?"

"Making progress," the battalion commander commented. "We getting some guns to back up the Neck?"

"Probably not. I asked again this morning, and my messenger hasn't come back yet, but I'm not hopeful. Cherrid still thinks the big guns will get rid of any serious cavalry attack."

Dalsyn cursed, and Harper, who shared his views on defending the gap, decided to switch topics.

"Looks like a bad case of *moles*," he commented, picking the most obvious subject. He used an English word out of ignorance of the Lopritian counterpart, and Dalsyn raised an eyebrow.

Did Dalsyn resent falling from command of a regiment back to his small battalion? If he did, would it affect his performance today? The North Valley man had behaved as a diligent subordinate since the moment he had learned of Cherrid's decision, but the situation was awkward. Telepaths could have talked such a thing out; Normals could only rely on military etiquette.

"Busy little animal, always digging, almost blind," Harper said lamely.

Like an engineering student, he added in his thoughts, remembering that Ian Plenytk, in his normal career as a surveyor, was as close to being an engineer as anyone in this world. What had he been told once? That a beaver was the perfect emblem for an engineering school, because in danger it gnawed off its testicles and left them as an offering to pursuers. *Helluva thing to remember now, fellow.*

Mlart would want more than Lopritian balls.

He could die today, he realized. *No more gab sessions with Kylene.*

"Moles," Dalsyn said, smiling briefly. "Yes, it looks like moles. But they're happier about digging than the men."

"Because good little moles hope to meet lady moles," Harper suggested. "Tell the men they can look forward to that. Or would they really rather hear me shouting at them to keep marching?"

"Probably." Dalsyn spat. "We really need those guns, Ian Haarper."

"I can't work miracles, Dalsyn. Keep the men digging."

"Another thing. That's frozen ground—we don't have tools for all this digging, Ian Haarper. And the men don't take it seriously; they don't see ris Daimgewln's men and ris Clendannan's men busting their butts this way."

"I know it," Harper admitted. "And it's going to kill a lot of them."

A moment passed. The surveyor dropped his eyes. "Hope you're wrong."

Harper shrugged. "Try to see that everybody has a knife or a piece of board, or even a stick with them. Something. When the time comes, I estimate they'll be motivated to excavate."

"Sure." Dalsyn seemed skeptical.

"You might have people fighting to get into a hole."

"What you wanted, isn't it?" Dalsyn turned away, facing the smoke billowing from hidden campfires on the opposite hill.

"Not quite." Harper hesitated. "Someone not in his own hole . . . You tell your officers to shoot them and let the men know. In fact, maybe you should see who has the shallowest spot of trench this morning, and shoot him first, before the Algies get here. As an example, to encourage the others.''

"That's a nasty idea, Ironwearer," Dalsyn said sharply.

"Yeah. War is nasty, Ian Plenytk."

"It wasn't like this before," Dalsyn said. "You weren't like this. Is it you speaking to me, Ironwearer? Or is it your pal, ris Clendannan?"

It's Giap and Ho and Mao Tse-tung speaking, Harper thought. *It's Lenin and Stalin and Hitler and maybe it's Patton and Grant and Stonewall Jackson.*

Useless words to throw at Dalsyn. He sighed quietly.

"I thought we'd win the war with one blow when we hit that Swordtroop division," he said. "I could be a gentleman then. I was wrong, and now it's going to be very, very grim."

"Killing people for laziness—that grim?" Dalsyn asked.

"Grim as I have to be," Harper said. "We're risking more than one little regiment here, Dalsyn. We have to win this war. Shoot one man and tell them I wanted two, if you like."

"We've lost wars before," the man said bitterly.

This time is different, the redhead thought. *Loprit has to win, and Mlart has to die. If not him, it'll be twenty million more, with a nuclear war at the end for the survivors.* And that could not be said, either. "Let's try harder this time, Dalsyn."

He forced a smile on himself. "All right. You don't have to shoot anyone. But by all that's holy, *threaten it*! They aren't civilians anymore."

"Well—"

"What are you doing about food?"

"Diddly," the ex-surveyor admitted. "The men don't have time to cook and those Cimon-lost camp followers are staying so far away, we might as well be the enemy. Maybe they think it's dangerous on the end of the line—couldn't guess why."

Harper chuckled. "I'm going to send a squad of Ian Styllin's men back with one of my staff people to see about getting some of those camp followers. By draft, if necessary. I think we've got a few day tenths before Mlart does anything, so we can give the men one hot meal."

"And if Mlart moves sooner, it won't matter because in a few day tenths there won't be nearly so many of us hungry."

Harper reached for his horse's reins. "That's why you're such a treasure Dalsyn. Positive thinking."

Rallt counted to ten—in Lopritian, to take up time—while the woman at the foot of the garden brandished her hoe and shouted at him. He wished he had Sugally or the gun he had gotten the day before, even the gun unloaded, along for company.

His bare tongue was a poor weapon to wield in self-defense.

And Sugally was burying the body.

"Thee knows, I be most sorry, Patron," he said again, scraping his feet at the corner of the plot, then spread his hands abjectly, since she did not believe him. "The lieutenant did not know thee would wish to can vegetables today and he will only want thee a short while, just to walk over the bridge and back. We be ignorant of much that we should know and we pray for thy help. He's to have thee for a few questions, that were all."

The woman glared at him across the blade of her hoe. Rallt could not decide from her hair or clothing if she was young or old, but clearly she had spent decades practicing that look, and he felt pity for her absent husband. Fortunately, years of exposure to farm owners had taught him to maintain an innocent expression. The woman's eyes slid across his unyielding face and down to defenseless things in the ground. The hoe quivered in her hand. Obviously, she was eager to attack something. "You can just ask your questions here, sonny. I'm busy."

"The question-asking be surely for the lieutenant, Patron. I be no more here to him than—" He groped for a word. "I labor in fields he assigns to me. Thee understands?"

"You send your lieutenant over, sonny. He can ask questions while I boil the jars, if he behaves himself."

It was unthinkable that he would report that to ris Ellich,

unthinkable that he would fail today as he had yesterday, when he and Sugally had found no more guns. "The lieutenant be very weak, Patron. He been hurtfully injured and must not tire himself. The way of it be, thee must go to him. He would be most grateful."

"Well." The hoe's handle touched ground again.

"Please? At some opportunity, convenient to thee?" He smiled. "Someone good and kind as thee to look at, it were good for him."

She hesitated. "Maybe if I have time, tomorrow or so."

"I—we—his friends fear for his life, Patron. Mayhap Lord Ellich can be with us only a short while longer. If thee could meet with him for a meal, or even a few minutes, it would be an act of great kindness—"

"Lord Ellich?" Clearly, Lopritian peasants met socially with aristocrats no more frequently than itinerant laborers.

"The lieutenant, Patron. Did I not say? He be Lord Ryger ris Ellich."

"A lord." The woman patted at her hair.

"Well, yes," Rallt said casually, dragging a foot backward. "But if thee be busy, Patron, Lord Ellich will understand. Mayhap some at another of the farms . . . Here by the bridge, thee must see more of the town than others, but Lord Ellich were most concerned that I return quickly with someone."

She put the hoe down carefully. "I can change out of this old dress in just a minute."

"Well . . ." Ris Ellich probably would prefer clean clothing, Rallt admitted to himself.

He'd thought he could persuade the first woman he talked to.

Later in the morning, the Algheran artillery fired ranging shots. There was no pattern to the firing, and no common target.

Shortly after it began, Cherrid sent the majority of the cavalry forward on the right of the road to see whether all Mlart's guns were in place, but enough Swordtroop horsemen were available to scare off the Lopritian force. About a dozen men were killed or wounded on both sides, and a few horses; then the Lopritians came clattering back, unpursued, on the great road.

Cherrid was not surprised by the repulse. It had never seemed likely that he could wrest control from the Algherans of the ridge they had occupied and defeat their reinforcements as they arrived; he had investigated the possibility as thoroughly as it deserved, and the cavalry's showing was not a bad one in his estimation. He transferred a squadron of the returnees to the left of his line, placing them under Ironwearer Ian Haarper, and waited for additional developments.

Intentionally, no doubt, the enemy guns were firing low. Warmed by use, the same elevation settings and powder loads would give the guns greater range. But at this time, they had little effect. Direct hits from solid shot killed one of ris Daimgewln's sergeants and wounded two men in Cherrid's regiment. A ricochet caused some casualties among the camp followers thronging the road. None of the horses were hurt, and apparently the Lopritian guns had not been spotted.

A subsequent report from his artillery observers informed the old Ironwearer that the enemy had between forty-five and fifty heavy guns, which was about what he had expected. The Strength-through-Loyalty Brigade had thirty-eight heavy guns of its own and a dozen smaller ones; they had been registered before the Algherans arrived on the field.

Strength reports that morning had given him 2,770 men and officers ready for duty; 291 sick and wounded were still waiting on evacuation to the north. Mlart was guessed to have just under 11,000 men.

Chapter 17

The real cannonade began at noon.

It started with a stutter—a single crashing *BOOOM* at the western end of the Algheran line, translated to meaningful sound just as dirt geysered up from the earth rampart that had been built across the great road. As the first stones and sod halted at the apex of their rise, a feather of black smoke lifted over the distant hill, dissipating long before it reached the thin clouds above.

A mistake, Cherrid had time to think. The brief seconds of warning gave men opportunity to seek cover. Perhaps that spared a hundred lives. Or five.

Then other guns joined in, obliterating echoes and men's first howls of pain and dismay.

For what we are about to receive . . .

The sound of the first gun jerked Harper's head upright, and he focused his eyes on the ridge opposite his position just as dozens of parallel flames, thick and straight as burning trees, spouted from the Algheran guns. For a moment, standing erect

293

on the peak of the Head, he looked at the tiny forms of men on the far right of the enemy line as they crept down a trail on the side of his ridge.

Spotters, he thought, watching them turn and wave their ant-antenna arms at invisible men on the crest. Then his eyes rose to the pale blue sky.

Thunder sounded, a rolling ca-*raack*! chased by an equally loud rumble.

Harper swallowed, feeling his stomach churn, and held his breath, determined not to move or show fear until his breath was out. Behind him, horse hooves pounded the ground.

A bludgeon smote the earth. The ground trembled beneath him. Nearby bushes shook in sudden breezes. Shrapnel rattled against soil and rock and metal and wood. Short-lived clouds of white steam boiled from holes punched into wet dirt.

Mercifully, there were no nearby screams.

Harper ran forward, rifle shaking on his back, down the path of matted grass his soldiers had worn, swinging wide about a stand of aspen, across the bottom of a shallow depression, up to its summit, past a pair of granite boulders, along a ledge parallel to the two long trenches below, across the hillside at a slant then back, halfway down the hill until—

On the lip of his section of trench, behind a knee-high earth barrier, a soldier stood, making obscene gestures toward the opposite ridge. Friends shouted with him.

Harper stretched, grabbed the man by the belt, and pulled him onto the seat of his trousers, sprawling across the narrow ditch, then ran on before the man saw who had assaulted him.

In the distance, cannon boomed.

Pitar Ian Styllin also rose foolishly as Harper reached him. The redhead resisted an impulse to give the battalion commander the same treatment and waved him back, then crouched beside him. "How's it look?"

A mechanical question. His attention was in front of him, on the lower line of trench, on the open cove of rock at the bottom of the hill, on the gently sloping grassland before him, on the opposite ridge, on the green-wearing men debouching insect-like from the anthill mouth that was the intersection of the Algheran-occupied ridge and the great road.

The assault force. How large? How well commanded?

He wished desperately for a pair of binoculars, as if they would make all the imponderables visible, even as he admitted they could answer none of those questions. *Why can't I fight with all the comforts of home?*

Cannon continued to fire, erratically, all Algheran.

Lan Styllin snapped his fingers, making no sound Harper could detect, and he wondered if his words had gotten through. Still, he had not noticed any killed or wounded men in the two parallel lines of the Midpassage men. Perhaps things were still all right?

His mind did calculations. Ten thousand feet of front, forty enemy guns, a hill several hundred feet across . . .

Cherrid ris Clendannan had been correct. The two companies on the Head could make this a very tough nut to crack.

Depending on what Mlart did, on how far that centipede-creeping line of enemy stretched out before it moved toward the Lopritians, on the courage of the men waiting for them in these trenches and the reserves on the backside of the hill, on the dispositions Pitar had made and that he had approved . . .

Wasn't it a mistake to let the men of the Swordtroop cover the plain before they were opposed? Shouldn't there be trenches closer to the enemy? Hadn't the men had time to dig communication channels between their lines? Was it too late to camouflage those starkly visible heaps of black earth? Were the men prepared to resist anything but the crudest direct attack?

Pitar nudged him till he bent closer. "What's the matter?"

Boom. *Boom! BOOM-Boom!*

It was too late to make changes. Harper thought of the men he had watched that morning, in the middle of their breakfast, speaking earnestly, quietly, staring at each other's faces as if to store up memories to last for the rest of their lives.

He forced a grin. "I hate being on the defensive."

*   *   *

At Midpassage, the thunderstorm rumble was little heeded.

In the inn, the cavalry lieutenant paused in his questioning of the farm wife Rallt had brought to him. Perhaps Sugally, as he poured wine for the woman, nodded to show his recognition was shared, but Sugally had witnessed battle from far and near. The woman and the boy lacked such experience, and ris Ellich had no reason to give either of them an explanation.

For Lerlt and his companion, on the hillside behind Timt ha'Dicovys's house, a distant battle was the least important development of the day.

Fesch was still gone.

The body of Timt ha'Dicovys's woman was gone.

The time machine was gone.

None of Herrilmin's curses, none of Gherst's muttered excuses, none of Lerlt's patience brought any of them back.

The hardest task of a general is to wait.

For Cherrid, the portion of a day tenth the Algherans took to deploy dragged like night watches. At intervals, when he was sure that under his command progress would have been visible, he mounted the ridge and stood before his own troops—the men widely spaced in columns of divisions at that moment, with a two-company front, each line having two ranks, and the regiment formed in four lines, leaving a four-company reserve stationed farther back along the road—to see what Mlart was doing.

Firing his guns, that was obvious. Not efficiently.

Apparently the Algherans had no clear view of how the Strength-through-Loyalty Brigade was arrayed behind its ridge. As a result, they had not concentrated their fire. They were lofting shells all along the ridge, not aware that the Lopritian line was so thin that individual shots did little damage.

Men were hit, of course. Men died. Cherrid had been within spitting distance of one of Timmithial lan Haarper's staff members that morning when a ricocheting solid shot smashed into the man's head. The officer had been mounting his horse at the time; the headless body had continued the motion, throwing a leg over the saddle even as the frightened horse galloped into a clot of camp followers.

Each casualty was a loss to be regretted, but so far the totals were less than Cherrid had feared, much less than he would have tolerated. He climbed the ridge to take his observations, each time with a clear conscience.

Foolishly, in his opinion, the Algheran general was committing only one of his two divisions to the attack, and was forming it into three fat regimental columns with a fourth regiment at the back for a reserve. In front, and to fill the spaces between the columns, soldiers from half a dozen companies had been dispersed as skirmishers, a tactical innovation which so far had not impressed the old Ironwearer.

Apparently the full Algheran attack would come on the east side of the road. Mlart was not disdainful of maneuvering, so there was a message in his deployment: he was not seeking to win the position. He wanted to destroy the brigade opposing him.

Conservatively, Mlart was forming up the division immediately in front of his ridge, out of range of Lopritian muskets. Another error, Cherrid thought—that would only make longer the distance the Algherans traveled under his cannonfire, and movement on such a narrow stage lengthened his assembly time.

The Algherans were stalling because they were reluctant to face his defenses, the Hand suggested to Cherrid after one of those inspections, but the Ironwearer was too honest to claim that. The simple truth was that time must pass when six thousand men performed any task, whether rising in the morning or forming for attack.

Mlart was probably just as impatient for action as he was. That was another of Cherrid's consolations.

His major cause for cheer was that the Algheran formation provided splendid targets for his batteries. It had been difficult to persuade his artillery officers to hold their fire until the attack was under way, but Cherrid was convinced the results would

justify his decision. In particular, on his last trip to the crest of
the ridge, he had noticed that virtually all the Swordtroop
cavalry was bunched together on the great road—if that continued, Cherrid vowed that despite his disbelief he would offer
a sacrifice to the Algheran gods.

"They're moving!" one of his aides called down.

"Okay. Your cue, Captain." Harper slapped the knee of the
man before him, then the rump of his horse. A cannon sounded
and he waited for the noise to pass. "Go out and cause some
trouble."

"Yes, sir." The officer saluted, raised his reins, and turned
to the sergeant on his other side. "Squadrons prepare to move,
Top."

Somewhere over the Trunk a shell broke open in a puff of
white and red. Shrapnel screamed.

Another *boom*. The sergeant bellowed orders.

I'm in the way. Troopers swung into their seats and Harper
retreated as the horsemen formed, a long column of riders
pulling away four abreast from the confused tangle of their
assembly area into a line behind the captain, like string un-
wound from a ball.

In the middle of the column, a man ducked toward the neck
of his horse as a shell exploded. Dirt splattered. An officer
called out a reprimand.

Half our cavalry. Harper watched stoically as the riders
moved past at a walk. At the end of the hill, the column turned.
The riders picked up the pace, the column lengthened. Its head
vanished from sight.

Two hundred men, with so much to go wrong. He stepped
backward, almost trampling the foot of a private following him
about with a green pennant. Amazingly, the cavalry officer had
saluted, said "sir," not argued with his orders, as if conceding
Harper's right to command his force.

My superior judgment, because I outrank him. Shit!

He knew nothing about the use of cavalry, Harper admitted.
He had ordered the squadrons out only because he hated their

inactivity. Why had that damned captain not argued or suggested something better?

He turned to the private. "I'm going back up the hill."

"Yes, sir." The soldier raised his pennant on its long pole high into the air and swung it about. Another of Cherrid's bright ideas. Presumably the zigzagging meant something to those who had learned its code. Harper had not. He didn't think anyone in his regiment had.

Men rode to meet him as he walked toward the base of the hill. His aides—six of them, doing nothing useful beyond leading around two unridden horses. Harper pointed.

"You two, go across to Ian Plenytk—he's probably at the Armpit. Do what he tells you. Come back to report when he gets into trouble."

"Any message?" one had the sense to ask.

"No. Tell him I said hello."

"How do we get there?" The second officer turned and stared as if hypnotized beyond the hill into the gap between the two battalions.

"Step lively, son. Two men aren't a target worthy of a cannonball."

If they'd just held off this damned war fifty years, I could have had binoculars.

Harper paused near the top of the hill. The soldiers on the back side of the Arm were small from here but still visible as individuals. Beyond them, ris Daimgewln's men on the Trunk were a featureless fuzzy caterpillar line. Cherrid ris Clendannan's regiment could hardly be seen at all, though the mound he had built across the road stood out even from this distance.

Two miles of line. It's too damned much.

But we're dead if we bunch up. If Mlart surrounds us, he'll wipe us out. We have to take up space.

Two hundred, three hundred years, weapons will be better, troops will have to be dispersed, these tactics will make some kind of sense.

Did Cherrid make plans for battles centuries ahead?

"Crazy old man. Four hundred years of being a soldier."

"Sir?" The pennant waver stepped to his side, and Harper realized he had spoken aloud and in Lopritian. The man had understood his words.

"Woolgathering. Just ignore me, soldier."

Was Cherrid envious of the generals of the future who would have binoculars, magazine rifles, radio communications, levcraft, poison gas, all the tools of modern warfare catalogued for men like him in the Plates?

Unanswerable question. Harper could not remember a time when ris Clendannan had expressed dissatisfaction.

Steady. Patient. Confident. We'd fall to pieces without that old man. I think he's an old buzzard at times—and I bet he wouldn't be bothered if he knew that—but in a lot of ways, I'm never going to be his equal.

Except maybe to Kylene. He grimaced.

Kylene's puppy love was a problem to be solved. In retrospect, he wondered if he had joined the army to avoid her. It seemed likely.

He liked Kylene. She was good company and interesting to talk to, even after months of talking—which was more than could be said, he confessed now, for either Sharon or Onnul Nyjuc, his loves of the past. More often than he wanted to admit, he thought about holding Kylene's smooth little freckled body.

But it wasn't going to happen. No matter how hard Kylene tried to entice him. He would go on without her. Steady. Self-sufficient.

Like Cherrid.

Light glinted in the distance. A cannon being moved? Dots which were people crept northward along the shining ebony ribbon of the great road. Camp followers. He hoped they would all escape danger.

"Come on, soldier. We're not earning our pay standing here."

*   *   *

"Great view," Harper commented as he sat down. *Be imperturbable*. He pushed pebbles from beneath his seat.

"I don't need it," Derrauld ris Fryddich said, and beside him soldiers farther down the trench shook heads in agreement.

"What we came for," Harper said. Perhaps he should laugh.

He couldn't. Spread before him and across the low rampart he watched five thousand soldiers advance through the grass of the plain. Behind them, the ground turned color as they trampled it. Straw, becoming mud-dark.

He looked at shadows. Was it one o'clock?

Near the end of the trench, a soldier leaned forward from his knees, urinating onto the rampart, then shamefacedly covered up the trickles with handfuls of dirt.

Earlier, the Swordtroop had poured through the gap on their ridge like that, a muddy river splitting into streams which merged into and lengthened each of the fat columns. Now the Algheran formation was coming on slowly, inexorably, irresistible in appearance as water through floodgates. The couriers and aides trickling behind them were only drops which remained to show where those currents had flowed.

On this side, in opposition, a thin line of Lopritian cavalry stretching out, the tiny toy soldiers jiggling on their model horses.

"Don't worry about the Algies. They're just trying to frighten us." *Make jokes. The men like to hear them.*

Ris Fryddich grunted. "It's working, Ian Haarper." But in defiance of his words, he was looking down his rifle barrel at one of the oncoming skirmishers, leading his weapon smoothly, breathing calmly.

Harper smiled, pulled his rifle off his shoulder, and aimed. *Damned Algherans are probably scared shitless, too.*

Don't think that.

The hill had dead zones, where living men could not be seen from the trenches. An unavoidable evil.

To be avoided. "Try to keep them from reaching the Mouth. If they build up there . . . We don't want that."

"Yes, sir."

One last bit of business. "Remember, you take the battalion if something happens to Ian Styllin. If I buy the farm, Pitar takes over, then Ian Plenytk, then you." Would that happen?

Funny. Circumstances had carried him past his well-earned dislike for ris Fryddich. He would have to work to rebuild animosity. Was it worth it?

"Something to look forward to." Ris Fryddich spat in the dirt before him. "Thanks a bunch, Ironwearer."

"Glad you're happy." Harper patted the blond man on the shoulder and moved back to speak a few words to Pitar.

The Algheran columns had moved barely enough to be noticed. The rock that was the Strength-through-Loyalty Brigade awaited the tide.

Swordtroop soldiers in their sea-green uniforms rushed forward across beach-sand yellow grass, and Cherrid thought of tides lapping toward the shore, with the shell bursts behind like spray over rocks.

The last war with the Algherans had cost Loprit the Torn Coast, he remembered. Would this war regain sea and shores for his countrymen?

"Double-timing it," a voice said at his neck. "I think they started too early." Grahan.

Four minutes had passed. Mlart's men were halfway across the plain, with the rightmost regiment leading. Work was coming to the Queen's Own Puissant Guards Regiment first. Was it accident?

Almost time to change the Guards' deployment.

A grinding *crack* behind him. Air blew past, whistling. He bobbed sideways as metal splashed into earth, threw up hot sparks of dirt. A canister band rolled by his foot, rattled down.

"They don't have far to go," ris Clendannan answered. "Get somewhere safe, you idiot."

"I'm not the lovely target you are, Cherrid."

"Their targets are safe enough." He turned about, looking for Perrid ris Salynnt and his battalion commanders, just below the top of the ridge, and shook his head gratefully as all three men lifted thumbs, Perrid chest-high, the others to their ears, into the air.

No damage. Where had that gesture come from, to spread throughout the brigade in the short period of one campaign?

He turned back to Grahan. ''It's unaimed guns that worry me.''

A bad joke. Not many years had passed since the days when artillery was more often dangerous to friendly troops than to enemies.

Enough time. Even dispersed as they were, straddling shrapnel like a man over a latrine as they just had, his soldiers were being killed and wounded by the Algheran guns—fifteen serious casualties reported so far in the Steadfast-to-Victory, just under a hundred in the Defiance-to-Insurrection, almost as many in his Guards Regiment. He made a face, remembering the ruin left by the solid shot which had smashed through half a file in ris Daimgewln's regiment, killing three, maiming two.

One of the wounded was a farmboy, he had heard, a youngster recruited in Midpassage, who had tried to stop the rolling cannonball with his foot. A lucky man—the surgeons had time now to treat non-life-threatening wounds. The farmboy would probably survive the amputation of his mangled ankle and certainly never hear the laughter of his one-time comrades.

After that . . . Cherrid had no idea how a peasant with one foot would stay alive in a farming community. Did it matter to anyone if that injury was unintentional?

We are going to get better at this. Why couldn't progress lead to a war fought with fists?

Because it took killing to make men admit defeat.

Old question. Old answer.

Enough time. He bent and picked up dust from around a shell-gouged hole. How funny it would have been to delay this signal because an old man's weak fingers could not scrape some crumbs of dirt from the half-frozen ground.

And how pathetic. *I am getting old.*

He swung his arm overhead, throwing out dust.

Other arms swung behind him. Hands jabbed slivers of wood through touch holes into powder bags in thick iron tubes, twisted, pulled forth the dark ant-heap grains, touched them with lengths of sputtering glass-glittery match.

Half a mile away, close enough to be heard, shells were exploding over the advancing troops. As he watched, behind the stakes that guarded the Neck, Harper saw dust billowing up in the midst of the Algheran formations, then holes filled in by running men. While the soldiers moved on, scraps leaked from the rear of their columns. Bodies. Shapes that undulated without mind.

"Show time," Harper muttered.

Without exaltation. The cheers from Lopritians all along the line as the brigade's guns began to kill were not his.

Those were his countrymen out there. Men he had never met, but whom he had to kill, for the sake of their descendants.

Below Cherrid's position by the artillery, Perrid ris Salynnt, as acting commander of his regiment, stood atop the road behind the embankment where both the battalions on line could see him. His arms swept the air.

Double up the ranks. First rank on the firing line.

As Cherrid watched, holding his breath, the men stepped forward, turning eight rows into four. Then forward again, to bring the first row to the top of the ridge.

So thin, the old Ironwearer thought uneasily. There were easily three man-heights separating each man from another. It could not be expected that the men would maintain the unnatural spacing in the middle of combat.

But the orders had been given and he had no improvement to make. Grimly, he remembered the promise of victory he had given Gertynne ris Vandeign.

He was very sorry he couldn't order the executive officer and his useless brother into the firing line.

Meanwhile, ris Salynnt turned to the front, moved a fist in a circle, repeated the gesture. *Fire and cycle.*

Like a machine, the Guards went into action. One by one, without further orders, the ranks stepped forward. Knelt. Aimed. Fired. Stepped backward as the next rank moved up.

The men had already shaken out their musket barrels and were reaching for fresh cartridges even as they reformed in the rear.

Twenty seconds per cycle, including aiming. Five cycles each minute.

Again and again. Like a machine. Cherrid knew of no other regiment in the world that could sustain that rate of fire.

This was practiced. Taught. Tested. Endlessly rehearsed. His veterans dreamed of firing at that pace, and claimed they could do so in their sleep.

Despite screaming. Shouts. Explosions. Muskets firing.

In the last two minutes of the Algheran advance, the Guards Regiment fired over eight thousand bullets at fifteen hundred attackers.

The noise was incredible, thick enough to be felt.

And one bullet in twenty struck a target.

"Oh, God!" Harper was falling off the top of the ridge before he finished the curse and rolled back down to Ian Plenytk rather than crawling, to save time. It seemed already he could hear Algheran footsteps at his back despite the hammering of Lopritian muskets. Algheran commands, Algheran muskets. Bullets thudding into the ground.

"Big problem, Dalsyn," he said quickly. "Don't let your men get out of their trenches. *They aren't stopping!* You hear me? It ain't gonna be a stand-up fight! I just saw the Algies hit Cherrid and they kept on going!"

Big columns cutting through enemy lines. It had been done, hadn't it? Wagram, the Austrian campaign of 1809. By Napoleon.

Christ! Was Mlart the equal of Napoleon? Harper swallowed uneasily, thinking of those thick Algheran columns stuck through the brigade like spears through a boar. What a position! In Mlart's shoes, he would think it was worth all the casualties it had taken to achieve.

Dalsyn stared at him, white-faced, and Harper wondered what his own face was showing.

They're coming right at you, Dalsyn.

You're going to die here, Dalsyn. Sorry, Dalsyn.

"Git!" Ian Plenytk snapped and hit him on the arm. "Cimon have you! Git! Just keep my reinforcements coming."

Harper ran. Shouts and the popping of muskets pursued him.

At the bottom of the ridge, when he looked back, heads were already visible at the top.

Reinforcements! From where? Dalsyn already had his whole battalion on line. Bullets whined past and splashed dirt on his legs. He stared around wildly, close to panic. Too late for Dalsyn. Too late for Cherrid.

Bodies falling down the slope, dressed in green and dressed in brown. Shell bursts, white and red in the sky. *Too late.*

But the shrapnel was only over the Algherans now. The troops were too close together for the Algheran guns to keep firing. That was one advantage for Loprit. He licked his lips.

Cavalrymen were at his sides, crowding closer. Not the ones sent to harass the Algherans, he realized suddenly, but others, with bared swords. A straggler line, sent to hold back men running from battle. They thought he was deserting.

He wanted to laugh hysterically.

"Ironwearer?" It was one of his aides, dismounting. One of the useless half dozen, concerned with him.

Harper sobered, then noticed that enemy bullets were not striking about him now. On this side of the ridge, the men wearing green were lying on the ground or disarmed.

Those were men who had surrendered. Dalsyn was holding.

God, those Algherans looked lost! He pointed to cavalrymen. "Get up there. Collect those prisoners. Toss 'em in the gully, so they'll be safe."

Safe! He wanted to laugh again.

He turned to the aide instead. "Backside of the Head. There's a platoon in reserve. You know the spot?"

"Yes, sir."

"Bring those men as fast as you can. We need them here a lot more."

"Yes, sir."

He waved a hand in dismissal, half gratefully, half angrily.

What he could do for Cherrid?

Nothing yet. Oh, God!

Cherrid cursed weakly. It had been close, much too close.

"Faster with those bodies," a sergeant shouted below him. "Dump 'em, just dump 'em! Over the side! We can sort them out after! Faster!"

Behind him, on the Back Leg, another sergeant, also shouting. The clatter of shell casings falling into a ravine. The guns, still roaring.

On the ridge, the third battalion, his reserve. Stepping forward, firing, stepping back, stepping forward . . .

Over bodies. Over churned red-and-black earth.

Over hands not attached to arms and legs without feet and heads showing exposed brains and unidentifiable things being picked up with shovels by men who feared to touch them.

Between the files of the third battalion, survivors of the first two battalions who had escaped the attention of their sergeants slipped over the ridge, then sneaked back with boots in their hands, packs, handfuls of useless Algheran currency.

He sat down on the ground suddenly and breathed heavily, feeling just as tired as the men who had actually done the fighting. His eyes closed and he could see them again:

Algheran officers at the top of the ridge, walking backward, beckoning with their hands, calling out to their troops. And then countless Swordtroop soldiers in the middle of his regiment, screaming, waving guns in all directions, firing, looking senselessly for the mass of Lopritians they had been told to expect—there had been a very surprised look on the face of one young officer, just before he staggered and fell.

He shook his head.

"You all right, Cherrid?" Grahan, shouting, with a pat on the shoulder to accompany the words.

He thought about it. "My throat is sore." That was certainly the most insignificant hurt on the battlefield. He held his neck to explain his unheard words. *Forgive me*.

In the distance, Perrid was limping at the bottom of the ridge, his back to Cherrid. *Forgive me*.

"I'll get you some water."

"No." He rubbed a hand against his forehead and Grahan brought his ear close to his mouth, so they were head to head.

"Is the Hand all right?"

"Him and all the ladies."

Good. He had feared ris Andervyll would disobey his instructions and stay close to the fighting. A dead royal . . . It was nerve-tingling even now to think of the possibility.

"Wolf-Twin? The Vandeigns?"

"I said 'all the ladies,' Cherrid."

"Are my aides here?" It took too much effort to look.

"You sent them to the Knee with prisoners."

He cursed again, his voice no stronger. "Go tell one of the sergeants—put injured—"

"Cherrid? I never saw fighting like that before. It was magnificent, Cherrid. You did the right things."

He had not, he was sure. *We're getting old, Grahan*.

"Tell the sergeants—put wounded Algherans—on the other side of the road—unless they are close to dying. At the bottom of the ridge—got that? Front side, the bottom of the ridge."

He closed his eyes again. *Fire into the men. Fire into the men!* How many times had he shouted that before the unbelieving gunners understood him and obeyed? How many times had he shouted after that, hating himself each time, but without choice?

Wasn't that what generals were for? To take responsibility for deeds which sickened other men?

I never would have done that earlier in my career.

How had ris Daimgewln and lan Haarper repelled the Algherans in their sectors? What casualties had they taken?

Was someone telling them they were "magnificent" also? Did they want to puke their guts up also, hearing praise?

The brigade as a whole had repelled the Algherans. The view from the artillery location was excellent, and when he stood, he saw the Swordtroop had failed all along the line. All the Algherans who could were running back to their side of the plain, out of range of Lopritian muskets.

He was sure another attack would come.

"Bottom of the ridge," he mumbled. "We have to keep— the Algherans—from getting at the artillery. Now that they know where it is."

But Grahan was not there to hear the explanation.

Harper sent a messenger to Cherrid, then another to Pitar lan Styllin.

When they were gone, he beckoned to his flag bearer, and walked forward slowly, stepping around crawling men until he could collapse by Dalsyn lan Plenytk at the end of the ridge.

Above him, men were stacking bodies—both Lopritian and Algheran—to make the parapet taller. Wearily, he remembered telling lan Plenytk the men would learn the worth of trenches when shooting started. That morning, a million years ago.

Now, men moaned on both sides of the ridge. The lucky were picked up and carried to ambulances which had appeared from out of nowhere. Rahmmend Wolf-Twin's work, he imagined, not envying the way the squat Ironwearer must be filling his time now.

Harper's share of the conflict had been limited to grabbing men and pushing them, it seemed now. And shouting, lots of shouting. Necessary tasks and tiring, but not ones that rated any attention. He knew where praise was really due and had made sure his messengers would repeat it for him.

Wearily, he sat on a rock made dusty by powder. He broke open his rifle, and pushed in a cartridge with black-grimed fingers.

"Very nice work, Dalsyn. You and your men, both."

The surveyor grunted something, glumly. That seemed to fit

the occasion, the redhead admitted. What had Wellington said
after Waterloo?

*Nothing but a battle lost can be half as melancholy as a
battle won.* There was still time for the day to get much worse.

At the base of the ridge, a man waved a tourniqueted arm at
a cavalryman and slipped past, bound for the surgeons. A good
wound, Harper decided. Something big enough to save the
man from labor for a while, maybe enough to keep him out of
the next battle, but not disabling.

We can't all be so lucky. Would he ever see Kylene again?

"How long did that all last?" Ian Plenytk asked, and Harper,
looking at him, saw bullet holes, black-rimmed by powder, on
the sleeves of his uniform.

"Twenty minutes," he guessed. Half an hour as time was
reckoned in the First Era. "I don't think those Algies expected
to find anyone here, Dalsyn."

He paused to consider. "They hit ris Clendannan first, then
us, then ris Daimgewln. I suspect our column was supposed to
go around to the back, or to make ris Daimgewln stretch this
way and thin out so the column aimed at him would have no
opposition."

"That the way you would have done it?"

"No," Harper admitted. "I wasn't clever enough to think of
it till now. And I don't guarantee I'm right, anyhow."

"That the worse you ever saw?"

"No." Harper did not have to elaborate. Lan Plenytk would
not have heard of napalm. *You people have never seen a real
war, Dalsyn. You never saw a man screaming and jerking
while his flesh burns like paper. You never had to shoot a child
who was trying to kill you, never had to dig bodies from graves
in which they were buried while alive, never found a school-
teacher tortured to death to teach the peasants a lesson. You
never pulled a friend from a punji stick smeared with feces.*

*You never lost a war because the folks at home found terror
boring and blamed you for it.*

You just think you know what Bad is, Dalsyn, but you don't.
Lan Plenytk sighed. "When will they start firing again?"

"Soon enough." Harper smiled wryly. "You getting impatient?"

"I'm eager to be disappointed." Dalsyn stood to answer a question from one of his company commanders, then lay down again. A minute passed.

"Take some company?" Pitar lan Styllin stood over them, Harper's messenger in the background.

Dalsyn waved a hand. "Couldn't push it away right now."

"That means yes." Lan Styllin's uniform was relatively clean, though not so clean as to justify fastidiously whisking dirt off some grass with a hand before he sat. Dalsyn shook his head in disbelief.

"How's the looting on your side?" Harper asked blandly.

"Piss poor. I don't think the Algies noticed us. Maybe I should bring my companies over to give them an even chance."

"You should have been here." Dalsyn grimaced. "I saw men leaning over the wall to pull bodies closer in the middle of the fighting."

"Just for clothes?"

"For food. They were eating during the fighting also. Fire, bite, shake musket, bite, pull cartridge, bite." The North Valley man demonstrated.

Pitar chuckled. "We should have eaten the Hand's ladies. Give the men some of what we're fighting for, I say."

Dalsyn grimaced again. "I really would have heard from Ironwearer ris Clendannan in that case."

"Eat him, too." Pitar gestured widely. "After marinating."

"We're sure to see Algies again, you two." Harper didn't fully understand the conversation, and he had already decided he would not try.

"I don't even want to think of it," Pitar said.

"I'd say they start again in ten, fifteen minutes," Harper prophesied. "The guns even sooner, of course."

"I love Ironwearers," Dalsyn commented to no one in particular. "They have such a *wholesome* attitude."

"Fuck you, Dalsyn," the wholesome man said. "Pay attention and you might learn something."

*   *   *

In fact, Harper's facade of expertise was severely damaged during the next quarter watch. The Algheran bombardment was not continued, and the battalions which had retreated milled around aimlessly for considerable time before they started to re-form.

Mlart must be behind the Algheran ridge, the Ironwearer diagnosed, and all decisions were being made by him. Obviously, it had taken time to get the news to him that the Lopritian lines were so thin, and more time to tell the troops they had to make another assault.

Bad management of the battle, he commented to Dalsyn. "Whoever is leading these charges should have made another one as soon as he could."

He and Ian Plenytk leaned over the parapet as they spoke. Neither showed much attention to the men still writhing on the far side of the ridge—nor the odors dying men could not help making—though Harper himself wondered if Dalsyn's stoicism partook so much of willpower as his own.

He beckoned for an aide.

The surveyor seemed startled. "You'd have led a second attack without orders if you were commanding over there?"

Harper spent a moment looking for holes in his reasoning, without finding any. "Yes, I'd have to. Remember, they know about what kind of numbers we have. Just from seeing how long our line is, they should know we're paper thin. So another big attack is the obvious move."

"Obvious to you Ironwearers, maybe, not—"

"Obvious to anyone, Dalsyn."

Dalsyn snorted. "Where do Ironwearers learn what they think they know?"

Being in the wrong spot at the wrong time. Harper wasn't sure that answer was called for. "My country lost a war once," he explained. "And I was in it. Afterward, I got curious and spent some time reading history. I thought I'd find out what we did wrong. That's where I learned what I know."

"What was the main thing you people did wrong?"

Harper chuckled. "Never did find out."

"Oh. So why did you become an Ironwearer?"

"Haven't figured that out, either, Dalsyn."

"Here they come!" a man shouted.

The Algheran guns began to thunder again, and after quick looks at each other, Harper and Ian Plenytk retreated behind the ridge.

Harper had time to dwell upon what he had seen.

Mlart had not added to his assault force, but even with the casualties it had taken in the last attack, it was still twice the size of the Strength-through-Loyalty Brigade. And this time it was coming as one column rather than three, and without a hang-behind reserve that saw none of the fighting.

The time traveler waited with mounting tension and something like curiosity. The big column would manage to cut through the Lopritian line, he was sure, but it was not obvious that it would inflict much damage when it got there. Men deep inside those ranks could not fire their muskets safely.

There was no question of where the Algherans would strike. Ris Daimgewln's Defiance-to-Insurrection Regiment was being plastered. The few rounds of shrapnel which exploded over other positions were either misfires or simply intended to keep other Lopritians in their places.

"The Algies looked very eager," Dalsyn commented between shell bursts. "You got that right."

Harper remembered an earlier remark. "I was willing to be disappointed."

The surveyor laughed curtly.

"Sir?" The aide, overdue, was breathing hard from a short run.

Harper gauged distances, then held his arm up again. "I want you to go to Ian Styllin and tell him *no matter what* he's to keep a platoon in his trenches. I don't want him to move with every man. We have to keep that hill."

"Yes, sir." The aide ran off as another aide appeared.

After the second was dispatched with the same message, Dalsyn turned, resting on an elbow. "What's the rush? Plenty of time. The Algies aren't in musket range yet."

Harper agreed. "But what do I do if one of those fools trips and breaks a leg? Complain to Cimon?"

"Wouldn't have to wait long to do that, would you?"

The redhead outwaited a *thack!* of shrapnel. "I know what I'd say then. But what would you have to say for yourself?"

"I'd just blame my sudden appearance on you."

"My buddy!" In Lopritian, it was as sardonic as in English.

"Better me than Ian Styllin right now."

"Probably." Harper wondered if he should take another look at the Algherans. He longed again for binoculars.

"Why should Mlart go for ris Daimgewln, though? They hit ris Clendannan the hardest last time, and barely dented him."

Go through the middle, encircle the bulk of the defenders, crush them while the remnants of the brigade milled about hopelessly. Was Dalsyn really interested in a discussion of tactics?

"Someone told him our layout," Harper suggested. "Now he knows our center holds the Defiance-to-Insurrection, not the Defiance-to-Invaders."

"Very funny. It still makes sense to me they'd hit old Cherrid again."

"That *is* the Guards Regiment. Ironwearer ris Clendannan must have done something that made the Algies plenty sorry. The bastards backed out fast enough last time, I can believe they don't want to do it again."

He smiled. "That's one mean old man when he wants to be, Dalsyn. If anyone can stop Mlart, he's the one who—" Harper paused, wishing he had bitten his tongue, but forced to finish the thought. "Cherrid can do it."

But Cherrid had not beaten Mlart. The Algheran's armies had overrun Loprit, and only his accidental death during the siege of the capital had held off total defeat.

Cherrid would not beat Mlart. Harper saw that suddenly.

Dalsyn interrupted bleak thoughts. "I heard *you* beat Cherrid."

"In a mudpie fight," Harper said slowly. "Not the same thing, is it?"

The Lopritian snapped his fingers pragmatically. "Let's get to our places. You want the right or the left?"

He could hear the crash when the Algheran column hit ris Daimgewln's line: a volume of shouting and musket fire that must be audible in Midpassage. The collision was visible, as well—one moment the green-uniformed troops were running toward immovable men in blue; the next, green and blue were intermixed, and surging backward together.

But inevitably, the advance slowed. The ranks began to mix as men rushed forward over the fallen; the column began to bulge in front; confusion and disorder swept along its length.

"Let's go!" Harper shouted and jumped over the parapet.

At the end of the line, Dalsyn did the same. Hesitantly, then with greater will, the men began to do the same.

In the distance, as Harper ran, he could see Pitar lan Styllin's men pouring down the front of his hill.

The Algheran formation was dismayingly large. To Harper, it seemed as if he were only an insect attacking some large animal.

But even dogs will scratch at fleas. After the first scattered shots into their midst, as it sank in that men were not falling from missteps at the edge of the column, surprised Algherans were already turning to the new threat. Harper sank to a knee and fired into the mob, then reloaded.

Men screamed even louder, on both sides.

Beside Harper, a man moved forward, crouching, his musket held to his chest in both hands. The Ironwearer lunged to pull him down.

"Shoot!" he shouted. "Don't crowd them! Don't be a fool—get your two shots in and get back!"

That was not the only idiot. Harper, with his gun reloaded,

ignored the Algherans, and stepped sideways, both arms out to keep his men from going too far, occasionally bobbing erratically to keep from being their target.

Meanwhile, he became an Algheran target—fortunately, the one bullet that hit him was in the center of his Kevlar vest. Though it knocked him down, it was not disabling. He was able to get back up and leap in front of the men, capering despite his lack of breath to show them he was unhurt.

Incongruously, while he jumped up and down, his mind let him think only of tall glasses of iced tea.

Dalsyn, at the other side of the irregular line, was luckier, he noticed. Beyond him, an officer or noncom in Ian Styllin's force crumpled at the side of his men; the fallen man was too distant to be recognized.

At last the job was done—this portion of it. The bulk of the Algheran column had reached the top of the ridge. Kicking and screaming men marked the trail it had followed. And behind him, mimicking those actions, were dead and dying Lopritians—the man beside Harper, slowly sinking to his knees, was clutching an arm with red-spurting fingers. Harper shouted at Dalsyn, then tore off the wounded man's sleeve to form a tourniquet as other North Valley men ran back to their trenches.

"Stay here," he shouted. "Someone'll get back to you."

He doubted that was true.

Bodies lay before him as he ran.

Close to sunset, the Algherans withdrew. Gunfire was the cause, rather than the hand-to-hand fighting they had expected. The Lopritians they had attacked had not tried to hold their position, or so it seemed, but other Lopritians on both sides of the ridge had fired volley after volley at them, without risking close combat. Faced with resistance on three sides, the Algheran soldiers, like marbles shaken in a box by musket fire and Lopritian cannons, spilled through the opening in back. Cherrid did not have the means to keep them penned.

Wounded men, baring their injuries for the Lopritians to see, went first, limping or trudging back across the plain. Then men who feared to die and dropped their weapons when muskets pointed at them and went back across the plain shamefacedly, pretending to wounds they had not received—Cherrid's captains on the field had enough wit, or enough fatigue, not to argue with those unsoldierly retreats. Then, with the western horizon tilting toward the sun, in one great rush, the Algherans who were left and who could wheeled about and ran through shadows toward their own lines.

Only Algherans who preferred to be prisoners were left—the despairing brave who sought death found it quickly—and the wounded and the dying.

And the piles of the dead. The lines of the dead. The splotches of the dead. And the falling cloud of powder. And the smell which promised to last a thousand years.

And scurrying men. And rolling weapons. And men stiffly reloading their muskets. And shouts. Screams. Crying.

Through it all, over and over before Cherrid's eyes, the gun crews repeated their rituals and their iron gods spoke for them, spitting flames and death at the heathen onslaught.

With the assault repulsed, Cherrid moved to a seat on a caisson wheel, content for the moment to lean and give no orders. Strangely, after long enough exposure to guns, the noise they made was no longer noticeable as sound but only an ear-filling pressure which never seemed to diminish.

Only part of the battlefield could be seen from here, but he had seen enough, he thought wearily. Soon the runners would come with the casualty figures and he would know what the men had suffered, and how the brigade had shrunk. A view of the field would add nothing.

It seemed to him that he had shrunk as well, along with the brigade, that he had melted at the edges into a smaller, older, more grizzled form, like a child's toy soldier, left neglected outside in bad weather.

Fatigue, he recognized. And imagination, the greatest peril for old soldiers. He smiled wanly.

In front of him was a powder cache, with grime-darkened bags on a wooden platform, surrounded on three sides by piled stones. Through the afternoon, almost without comprehension, Cherrid had watched men approaching the cache from one side carrying small piles of those bags in their hands and men from the other side who arrived with bare hands to take the bags away. Beside the cache was a water bucket. Periodically a sergeant had come by to sprinkle water on the bags and the ground around them.

Now, with evening near, jars with lengths of fuse were being distributed to the gunners. Coiled fuses, black, sticky-coated—Cherrid remembered overseas lands where snakes were eaten, and preserved in such jars, looking like that before being poured, dead but still slithering, onto cutting tables. They had been bland-tasting, the younger Cherrid had found, flavored more by spice and the preserving oil than their nonexistent venom. Did diets change over centuries, he wondered idly, speculating that poverty rather than custom made snake a delicacy, and content now that in his old age his appetites demanded no new varieties of food.

Lighted, the burning match turned red along its skin, contorted inside the jar, and hissed like a captive snake. He smiled, waiting.

A tall gawky soldier stepped past him and put his lighted match on the wall around the cache, then reached hands into the water bucket. A new recruit, Cherrid guessed as he drank, seeing the depot-shelf blue of his uniform, pleased to see some of the new recruits had survived the fighting.

"Watch it there!" a sergeant shouted. "Move that match!"

His voice could not be heard but his excitement showed. The recruit straightened abruptly, his face showing consternation and fear of a reprimand, his long arms swinging out—

—toppling the jar of flaming match. More quickly than anyone could react, it fell at the recruit's feet and shattered on the platform, releasing the burning snake of match to sink glowing fangs into—

—dark bags of powder, suddenly white-rimmed, suddenly dragon-mouthed, swelling monstrously.

That was the last sight Cherrid had of the world.

For watches, it seemed, the guns had been roaring and men had shouted on the ridge beyond his wagon, the back-and-forth screams louder at times than the guns and their muskets alike.

And for watches, wagons had pulled dying and wounded men to the operating tables on the opposite side of the road, been loaded again with the shrunken bodies that had survived that butchery and raced off to the north.

He had been there earlier, to thank the men, to let them know Loprit would remember their sacrifice and reward it when possible, but the effort had been wasted. He had been in the surgeons' way, and the soldiers had been too filled with pain or its anticipation to hear his words. Men he had patted on the shoulder had winced; one had broken into tears.

Terrault ris Andervyll stared at the road now, wooden-faced, not moving except from the tremor of his right hand—his sword hand. At that moment he felt himself the most powerless man in the Kingdom. The loneliest.

The buggy shuddered beneath him and he knew that Gertynne ris Vandeign or his brother had shifted position. But wherever they sat, they were watching him, he knew, waiting for signs of weakness in the Hand of the Queen, in his family and its dynasty.

Outside the wagon, carefully arrayed behind him, aides and other young officers relieved to be out of the fighting pretended to wait for orders and talked among themselves. The farther away the louder, but always cautiously, lest they be called to his attention, so the voices buzzed and droned without meaning like colonies of agitated bees.

Farther back, he was aware, bolder spirits had broken into cases of his wine, not knowing he had noticed, and were passing his vintages back and forth like mugs of tavern swill. Soon their weak discretion would be entirely gone.

The women he had brought from Northfaring were there also.

Was this the way defeat began?

A man came stumbling over the side of the hill, across the road, trying to run but too exhausted.

Toward him, the Hand recognized. Then he recognized the man: Grahan, Cherrid's orderly. What message was he bringing?

I will not flee.

He snapped his fingers for an aide. "Bring a bottle. A restorative for this man."

Not waiting for acknowledgment, he sprang from the wagon.

"Cherrid's hurt!" Then Grahan collapsed in his arms.

Terrault turned, seeing in one frozen moment the gray-and-red sunset sky, the tableau of officers, surgeons, and wounded men, the wagons near and far on the night-surface road, the huddled bands of camp followers, the fearful alarm on Gertynne's face as the news sank in, the foolish incomprehension on his brother's, the unconcerned horses nuzzling the coarse grass. The memory of that scene would be with him for the rest of his life.

"How badly?" The necessary words seemed cruel and inane.

"He's alive." Grahan recovered himself to stand on his own. He swallowed and panted for a moment, and Terrault could see his eyes glistened.

"Alive," Terrault repeated.

"I don't know how long." Grahan cradled his head in shaking hands. "He was near a shell burst—it threw him over—he's not conscious—the battle will be lost—he doesn't hear me—he's dying—he can't command, Lord Andervyll—he doesn't hear me."

"I see," Terrault said softly. *I will not flee.*

Almost against his will, he looked up to the Vandeign brothers, then away, scornful of their cold impassive faces, feeling responsibility flat and heavy on his shoulders like the robes of his investiture.

As ever, that calmed him. "Are we ready to surrender?"

Is it possible? his words meant. Or would Mlart simply overrun the brigade and everything in its path?

I will not flee. I will not surrender myself.

"Don't surrender," Grahan said sharply. "The Algherans aren't pressing now. We can hold till night. Appoint a new commander—that's what we need."

A new commander. Could one be brought from the north in time to do any good? Terrault ground a fist in a palm and walked about, knowing it was not possible, but forced by Grahan's words to consider the thought. In the background, the old man waved off the aide holding a glass of wine.

The brigade had no fit commanders other than Cherrid, Terrault admitted grimly. That was more humiliating to confess than defeat. He turned to Grahan. "Is Perrid ris Salynnt capable of commanding the brigade?"

"No, sir." The man looked regretfully at him.

"Terrens ris Daimgewln? In your view?"

"No, sir."

Terrault looked over his shoulder, to see Gertynne watching expectantly. Beside him, Merryn ris Vandeign, drinking the wine intended for Grahan.

Never in ten million years.

So surrender was still necessary. Surrender or flight.

"Grahan, there isn't anyone fit to replace Cherrid," he said. "I'd do it if I could, but you know leading a company of swordsmen is about my limit."

The old man tried to smile. "Used to do that all right."

"You didn't know enough to judge properly back then." Terrault smiled, knowing this might be his last smile.

"You forgot, Lord Andervyll. There's still Ironwearer Ian Haarper."

"He's—" Terrault gestured helplessly. He had earned honors, but it remained true that Ironwearer Ian Haarper was young, inexperienced, junior to most other officers, and hope-lessly headstrong.

"He won one battle, sir, and a skirmish on our way down."

"Was that skill or being under the Lady's cloak, Grahan?"

"Does it matter now, sir?"

Terrault wished he could weep, as the wounded men did. He shook his head despairingly. "I can't gamble, Grahan. Not with Loprit as the stake."

"Sir—Cherrid thinks well of the boy. If Cherrid could talk to you, I know that's whom he'd recommend."

A very long moment passed, and Terrault was aware again of the guns still booming beyond the hill, and of all the eyes that were turned on him. He tasted sickness in his mouth.

He held up an arm until an aide appeared. "Hand?"

"Find Ironwearer Timmithial lan Haarper. Inform him that by my order and on my responsibility, he is to take full oper-ational command, immediately, of the Strength-through-Loyalty Brigade and to do anything necessary to defend the country. And—and—"

He swallowed, looking at the swallowing Grahan. "Tell the Ironwearer—as I'm sure he knows—he's got all our prayers."

About the Author

Mike Shupp is an aerospace engineer. This is his fourth novel.

MIKE SHUPP

MORNING
OF CREATION

BOOK TWO OF THE DESTINY MAKERS

The epic story of a
war across time

'With Earth's first clay, they did the last man
knead,
And there, of the last harvest sowed the seed.
And the first morning of creation wrote,
What the last dawn of reckoning shall read.'

A WAR IN TIME

He had been Tim Harper, Vietnam vet, Boston
student. But Vietnam and Boston were 90,000
years in the past and now he was Tayem
Minstrel, time traveller, and secret weapon in
the Algheran's desperate fight for freedom.

Kylene was an untrained telepath – from the
barbarian world of *5000 AD*. Harper, the man
from her past, had wrenched her into the
unimaginable future. Now he was to train
her for a mission in time.

But Harper hadn't counted on the disastrous
turn of events which would put his life into
Kylene's hands. And he *had* counted on his
ability to hide his terrible secret from her . . .

MORNING OF CREATION

A selection of bestsellers from Headline

FICTION

A WOMAN ALONE	Malcolm Ross	£4.99 ☐
BRED TO WIN	William Kinsolving	£4.99 ☐
MISTRESS OF GREEN TREE MILL	Elisabeth McNeill	£4.50 ☐
SHADES OF FORTUNE	Stephen Birmingham	£4.99 ☐
RETURN OF THE SWALLOW	Frances Anne Bond	£4.99 ☐
THE SERVANTS OF TWILIGHT	Dean R Koontz	£4.99 ☐
WHITE LIES	Christopher Hyde	£4.99 ☐
PEACEMAKER	Robert & Frank Holt	£4.99 ☐

NON-FICTION

FIRST CONTACT	Ben Bova & Byron Preiss (eds)	£5.99 ☐
NEWTON'S MADNESS	Harold L Klawans	£4.99 ☐

SCIENCE FICTION AND FANTASY

HYPERION	Dan Simmons	£4.99 ☐
SHADOW REALM Wells of Ythan 3	Marc Alexander	£4.99 ☐

All Headline books are available at your local bookshop or newsagent, or can be ordered direct from the publisher. Just tick the titles you want and fill in the form below. Prices and availability subject to change without notice.

Headline Book Publishing PLC, Cash Sales Department, PO Box 11, Falmouth, Cornwall, TR10 9EN, England.

Please enclose a cheque or postal order to the value of the cover price and allow the following for postage and packing:
UK: 80p for the first book and 20p for each additional book ordered up to a maximum charge of £2.00
BFPO: 80p for the first book and 20p for each additional book
OVERSEAS & EIRE: £1.50 for the first book, £1.00 for the second book and 30p for each subsequent book.

Name ....

Address ....

....

....